SOLOMON'S OAK

SOLOMON'S OAK

A Novel

Jo-Ann Mapson

BLOOMSBURY

New York Berlin London Sydney

Published by Bloomsbury USA, New York

All papers used by Bloomsbury USA are natural, recyclable products made
from wood grown in well-managed forests. The manufacturing processes
conform to the environmental regulations of the country of origin.

LIBRARY OF CONGRESS CATALOGING-IN-PUBLICATION DATA

Mapson, Jo-Ann.
Solomon's oak : a novel / Jo-Ann Mapson. —1st U.S. ed.
p.   cm.
ISBN 978-1-60819-330-1
1. Loss (Psychology)—Fiction.   2. Self-actualization (Psychology)—Fiction.
I. Title.
PS3563.A62S65 2010
813'.54—dc22
2010009792

First published by Bloomsbury USA in 2010
This paperback edition published in 2011

Paperback ISBN: 978-1-60819-407-0

1 3 5 7 9 10 8 6 4 2

Typeset by Westchester Book Group
Printed in the United States of America by Quad/Graphics, Fairfield,
Pennsylvania

In memory of Jason Wenger:

*Murdered December 2, 2007, an unforgettable human being
who left behind many broken hearts. To honor Jason's writing
ambitions, a percentage of the proceeds from this book will benefit
the Jason Wenger Award for Excellence in Creative Writing
at the University of Alaska Anchorage MFA Program
in Creative Writing.*

*Jason, I hope heaven is everything you dreamed and more.
You are missed every day.*

And to Earlene Fowler:

For your abiding, generous friendship.

Women's hearts are like old china,
none the worse for a break or two.
—SOMERSET MAUGHAM
Lady Frederick, 1907

PROLOGUE

IN 1898, IN Jolon, California, not far from the Mission San Antonio de Padua, Pennsylvanian Michael Halloran set out to cross the Nacimiento River during spring thaw. Like everyone heading west, he thought California was the land of plenty: the Pacific Ocean full of abalone, citrus groves and artichokes growing year-round, everything necessary to raise a family and prosper.

According to Salinan Indian storytellers, his horses refused to enter the water until Halloran whipped them. On the other side of the river lay his newly purchased land. Everyone begged him to wait until spring runoff was complete. Stay in the hotel for free, the owner said. Halloran refused, believing it was a trick to steal his land. As soon as he entered the river in his horse-drawn wagon, his wife, Alice, and baby daughter, Clara, aboard, he lost control. Michael Halloran was thrown free, but Alice became caught in the reins as the panicked horses tried to free themselves. The wagon flipped over and over in the swift current. Horrified, Michael could only watch from the riverbank while the reins he had used to punish the horses twisted and turned, decapitating his wife. Her body washed ashore days later. Baby Clara was never found.

After Mrs. Halloran's burial, the Salinan shaman predicted her ghost would never rest, because a body without all its parts has trouble finding its way to the spirit world. In the 1950s, Alice appeared to two soldiers on watch at an ammunition bunker on the Fort Hunter Liggett military base. One died of a heart attack; the other never recovered from the trauma. The army denied the reports, but closed the bunker. In addition to the Salinan story "The Headless Lady of Jolon," several Central Valley, California, ghost stories feature a headless horsewoman: "The Lady in Lace," "Guardian Spirit," and "Ghost of a Murdered Wife."

Stories, passed down from generation to generation, can take two forks: factual history, or legend/lore. The word *history* came into English from Latin via Greek and originally meant "finding out," and in some dictionaries "wise man." In modern dictionaries, *history* is defined as "a continuous, typically chronological record of important events." You can *make history*, and that can be a good or bad thing. Sometimes people say *and the rest is history*, which leaves out the most interesting parts. Or you can *be history*, which means you're gone. Disappeared. "Dust in the wind," which is the title of the rock band Kansas's only hit song.

The word *legend* has its roots in Middle English, French, and Latin. *Legenda* translates to "things to be learned." *Lore*, from the German and Dutch *lehre*, translates to "learn."

You would think that between the two we'd get the whole story.

To this day, it is said that on a moonless night in Jolon headless Alice can be seen floating above the Nacimiento River, searching for her lost daughter. She also frequents the old cemetery on the military base. Locals say if you catch sight of Alice, quickly put your ear to the earth and you will hear the baby girl crying for her mother.

Part I

GLORY SOLOMON

A Pirate Handfasting Menu

Roast tom turkey

Apple, date, and onion stuffing

Mashed Yukon Gold potatoes

Peasant bread

Crudités

McIntosh apples

California navel oranges

Mead

Grog

Lemon bumble

Pirate-ship devil's food wedding cake

Chapter 1

ONE YEAR AGO to the day, Glory Solomon had spent hours cooking the traditional Thanksgiving dinner for her husband, Dan: turkey with bread-crumb stuffing, cranberry sauce, mashed potatoes and gravy, and Dan's favorite, the yam casserole with the miniature-marshmallow topping she always managed to scorch. Why he liked it she never understood. Her pumpkin pie was a work of art, with a homemade crust so flaky it rivaled her grandmother's, but for Dan it didn't get any better than blackened yams. Glory had set the table with the china Dan's mother had left them, Franciscan Desert Rose. She ironed and folded linen napkins. She whipped heavy cream to tall peaks. While Dan said grace, she took a slug of wine because religion made her nervous. They feasted and laughed, and when they could move again, they took the horses out for a long ride on their oak-filled property that was ten minutes as the crow flies from the Mission San Antonio de Padua. After that, Glory called her mother in Salinas to wish her a happy holiday, and they both said how much they missed Daddy, gone twenty-two years now. Glory and her sister, Halle, had been teenagers when he died. Next Glory called Halle and interrupted her appletini party because she could never get Halle's schedule right.

This year Glory was roasting three twenty-five-pound turkeys, mashing thirty pounds of potatoes, baking a dozen loaves of baguette bread, and heaping local apples and oranges in bushel baskets borrowed from her friend Lorna, who ran the Butterfly Creek General Store. Not a yam in sight. If Dan were still alive, Glory would gladly have made yams the main course, paid attention to his grace, put her wineglass down, and waited for him to say "Amen."

This Thanksgiving, she made gallons of mead (honey wine), lemon bumble (vodka, heavy on the lemons, to prevent scurvy), and grog, which is basically a bucket of rum with fruit thrown in. These three beverages are what pirates drink, and drink is what pirates do, on any occasion, and who can blame them, the high seas being filled with mortal danger every single second?

The dinner she was cooking was for the Thanksgiving "hand-fasting" ceremony of Captain General Angus McMahan and his wench-to-be, Admiral Karen Brown. Those two and their fifty-eight guests were weekend reenactment pirates who'd been turned away by every church they tried to book for their ceremony. Angus had come to Glory seeking permission to hold the wedding in the chapel Dan had built on their land last September. What would Dan have thought of her holding a wedding there? What was Glory thinking that she could cater and pull off a wedding on a national holiday?

Money.

Angus had spotted the chapel while visiting the tree known as Solomon's Oak. It wasn't in the AAA guidebook, but word gets around when a white oak that isn't supposed to exist in the Central Coast Valley climate grows to be more than a hundred feet tall. The tree had stood there for three generations of the Solomon family, and who knew how long before that?

The oak set the Solomons' property apart from that of the other ranchers, who grew strawberries, grapes, pecan trees, distilled flavored vinegar, raised hens, or ran a few head of cattle, made gourmet goat cheese to sell at the farmers' market—whatever they could do to squeak by and keep hold of their land. Arborists bused field trippers to the tree. Horticulture professors from U.C. Santa Cruz gave lectures beneath its branches. Young men seeking a romantic setting to propose to their girlfriends could not go wrong under the shady oak. In sunny weather, plein air painters descended with field easels. If the moon was full or there was some pagan holiday, say Bridgid or Beltane, a flock of druids would show up, sometimes in clothing, other times without. The Solomons tolerated people on their property because they recognized the tree was special. Most oak trees die before they hit a hundred years of age, but Solomon's Oak had a healthy bole, and from its circumference, the University of California, Santa Cruz, boys estimated its age at approximately 240 years.

"No one else will host our wedding," Captain Angus said as he pleaded his case to Glory a month earlier over the fancy coffee and almond croissants he'd brought to win her over. October, once Glory's favorite month, had been filled with golden leaves and a pile of unpaid bills. "We've tried the Unitarian church, the Transcendentalists, the nondenominational; I've even been turned down by the Masonic Temple, and those guys have a reputation for being somewhat piratical, at least in how they dress for parades."

Glory studied him as he sat across from her at her kitchen table. "How old are you?" she asked.

"Thirty. It's a turning point. How old are you?"

"Thirty-eight."

"How long were you married?"

"Nearly twenty years."

"Wow," Angus said. "That's a long time."

"You'd be surprised how fast it goes by," Glory said, brushing crumbs from her fingers.

"I'm in love, Mrs. Solomon."

"I can see that."

Angus had a red beard and strawberry blond hair that fell to the middle of his back. His eyes reminded her of a kid's, sky blue and hopeful. "And I want our wedding to not just be a legal contract, but wicked, good fun."

Glory hadn't set foot in the chapel since Dan died. As far as she was concerned, the building could fall to rubble. Every time she went out to feed the horses she turned her back on it. Where someone else might have seen beauty in Dan's carpentry and the river rock, all she saw was precious time wasted on faith that failed to save him. Since his death from pneumonia last February she'd been forced to take a part-time job at a chain discount store. Four days a week she drove the freeway to work five-hour shifts for minimum wage. Her supervisor, Larry O., was nineteen and had atrocious grammar. He was authorized to tell her how to stack the merchandise, how to speak to customers, and when she could duck out to the restroom. She was old enough to be his mother.

Dan's life insurance policy, through Horsemen's Practical, a California carrier just about every rancher and farmer in the area subscribed to, paid out $50,000 upon his death, which seemed like a fortune while the Solomons were paying the premiums. But they had no health insurance and hospital bills had gobbled up much of it. By Christmas her savings would be gone.

The pirates wanted to pay Glory $3,000 to use the chapel and to make their reception food. She had chickens, horses, goats, and dogs to feed.

"Okay, Angus. Consider your wedding on."

"Thank you! I can't wait to call the Admiral!" He jumped up from the table and thanked Glory in the nicest way possible—he took out his checkbook.

Over her rickety kitchen table among the crumbs of coffee-house pastry, an unlikely business was born:

SOLOMON'S OAK WEDDING CHAPEL.

PIRATES WELCOME.

The chapel had been Dan's final project. One summer morning over his oatmeal he'd said, "I've got a bug to build myself a chapel. Nothing fancy, just a place to worship out of the rain."

Glory wasn't a believer, but she supported his efforts, bringing him lunch and admiring his carpentry, the work he'd done all his life. He'd finished the chapel just before Labor Day 2002, and darned if they didn't have rain that very weekend. The small building could seat forty on the hewn benches, fifty if you held a child on your lap. It had a pitched, slate roof, exposed beams, and stained-glass designed by an artist with whom Dan traded finish carpentry on her Craftsman-style house in Paso Robles for the windows.

Six months later he would be dead.

Behind the last pew where Glory now stood checking decorations, she'd often brought her husband ham sandwiches and lemonade for lunch. When the summer sun beat down, Dan could drink an entire pitcher of lemonade. He'd take a sip, smack his lips, and say, "I am the luckiest man on the planet."

Glory thought he still was because he saw the good in everyone he met. He just wasn't on the planet anymore.

Just two days before Angus's pirate wedding, Glory stood in her bedroom closet, staring at her husband's shirts. So far as she knew, there was no etiquette/timetable regarding boxing up your late husband's clothes, but the day seemed as good a time as any. In a little over three months, February 28, she would have lived an entire year without Dan. She had folded his blue jeans and flannel shirts into a cardboard box. His neckties, given to him by their foster sons over the years, she kept. Maybe this winter she'd use them to piece a log-cabin quilt. His lined denim jacket would keep someone else warm. His Red Wing boots were practically new. She wrapped them in newspaper and set them on the closet floor. Soon all that remained was his starched white shirt. She pressed it to her mouth, inhaling Irish Spring soap.

"I sure could use your help right now," she whispered. "I have no idea what I'm doing. What if someone loses an eye in the sword fight?"

Once a day she allowed herself ten minutes of closet time. The idea was to restrict her tears to that private place in the house. After she wiped her eyes, she forced herself to recall happy times. The summer evenings they'd ridden the horses to the top of the hill. The dogs racing ahead, flushing birds from the dozens of trees that fringed the property. At the fence line, Dan would reach across his horse to hers, take her hand, and they'd watch the sun go down. Because there were never enough adjectives to flatter a California sunset, he'd say something funny. One time he'd quoted Dylan Thomas in a terrible Welsh accent: " 'Like an orrange.' 'Like a to-mah-to.' 'Like a gowld-fisssh bowl.' "

Glory gathered eggs to sell at the farmers' market, trained her "last chance" dogs, and kept the checkbook balanced. One time she'd forgotten to latch the grain bins, and now generations of mice were convinced they'd reached the promised land. On the desk a stack of dusty condolence cards waited for her to send thank-you notes, but she couldn't abide the pastel card faces or the poems inside. No sentiment could numb such pain. The best she could hope for was the passage of time. Dan had taught her how to build a gate that didn't sag, how to stretch a sack of beans and rice to fill up hungry adolescent boys, and how to love with your heart full throttle.

He hadn't taught her how to live without him.

"Memories you didn't even know we were making will sustain you," she could hear him say, but Glory had her response all ready: "A memory can't put its arms around you."

More than two hundred people came to his memorial service. After the "casserole months" ended, whole days went by when Glory talked only to the dogs as she ran them through their training exercises. She washed her coffee cup and cereal bowl by hand. She could let the laundry go for two or three weeks. All it took was a quick sweep of the wood floors to keep the house clean. Feeding the animals took her a half hour, tops, and after that, the time dragged. Except for Edsel, her house dog, she was alone.

"Glory, you know what they say. 'Widowed early, that's what you'll get for marrying an older man,'" her mother had warned her when Glory was twenty and Dan was thirty-five, and old-fashioned enough to insist on asking her for her youngest daughter's hand in marriage. But their age difference had nothing to do with her becoming a widow. The blame lay on a man too stubborn to take care of himself in California's wettest winter on record.

"It's nothing," Dan insisted as he coughed his way through the farm chores. At night she plied him with vitamin C, zinc lozenges, and NyQuil. "Go to bed until you beat this bug," she told him. It was three days before he gave in, and then his fever spiked to 104. By the time she drove him to the doctor, whatever bacterial infection he had been fighting had entered his bloodstream. They called it a "superbug," antibiotic resistant. Pneumonia raced into both lungs. "Keep a smile on your face for me," Dan asked of her in the hospital. She was too bewildered to cry. How could a fifty-three-year-old man strong enough to lift two sixty-pound saddles die from an organism visible only under a microscope?

Now the wedding day had arrived, and here she was, staring at the shirts she'd unfolded and hung back up. She dabbed at her eyes, exhausted. Her last dime had gone to the food for the pirate menu. She'd been up since dawn, and cooking for days. Two of her former foster sons—hired as servers—were due any minute. She needed to change out of work clothes and powder her cheeks. Get cracking. But she lingered, touching the hangers.

Turned out this wasn't the day to let his things go, either. She pushed the box to the back of the closet, slipped on the blue dress that had been Dan's favorite. She stepped into her dove-gray pumps and picked through her small stash of jewelry in the box on top of her dresser. Pearls today. The single strand of her grandmother's that had yellowed over time. The matching earrings Dan gave her one Christmas when they were flush. All she needed was to gather her silver hair—it had begun turning gray the summer she was fourteen—into a bun and she was ready to open Solomon's Oak Wedding Chapel to its inaugural event. She practiced saying an authentic "Arrgh."

"Kennels," Glory called to the rescue dogs currently in training. Well, *dog* was more accurate, because Dodge was the only one who had a chance at successful placement. Cadillac, a purebred border collie, had been adopted out twice and run home both times. She'd given up trying to place him for the moment and was experimenting with his training to see if he might like something else besides herding her goats. Dodge, a mix of golden retriever and cattle dog, had been scheduled for euthanasia the day she adopted him. Once she could get him to stop jumping up, knocking her over, chasing the mailman, and barking at nothing, Glory was sure she could find him a family. When she'd made a successful placement, she'd visit the shelter and take home another death-row felon. Dog crimes? Growing from adorable puppies to hundred-pound handfuls. Boredom, followed by destruction. Conforming to the nature of their breeds. Mainly dogs needed a job to do. Glory looked to each one to tell her what kind of training he needed: clicker, treat reward, hand commands. She trained them in whatever worked, agility, fly ball, or Frisbee. In turn for manners, the dogs earned long walks, nutritious meals, and gentle affection. When all that was in order, she found them families. She paid home visits before placing them and followed up after. If the owner's circumstances changed, she'd take the dog back, find another family.

Her exception was ten-pound Edsel, an Italian greyhound no bigger than a country mailbox. He had a splash of red on his long white back that resembled an English saddle. Because he moved like a ballet dancer, she suspected he'd come from show-dog stock. To look at him you'd wonder what hard-hearted person could dump such a sweet-natured animal at a kill shelter. Glory quickly learned why. Edsel had a seizure disorder that required medication and a special diet. He lived indoors and had learned to do his business in a litter box. On walks, Glory allowed Dodge and Cadillac to run off-leash, but kept Edsel tethered. Sight hounds could see prey long before humans could. If a rabbit crossed Edsel's path, he'd give chase until one of them dropped. Dodge, the big baby, was terrified of rabbits and tried to climb into Glory's lap when he saw one. Rabbits confused Cadillac. Why did they resist being herded into a pen? When a chicken got loose, Cadillac raced behind it, executing those on-a-dime turns border collies are famous for, and he didn't stop until the escapee was back in the coop. Caddy, with his shocking blue eyes and plume tail, also herded Glory's vacuum cleaner, and when the wind picked up, he went after leaves.

Whenever Dan worked in his shop, though, Cadillac lay down across the doorway all day. If Dan headed to the truck, Cadillac would be in the passenger seat the second Dan opened the door. Glory could feed and train the dog, but Dan was his human. Now that Dan was gone, Cadillac preferred his outdoor kennel to his bed in Glory's bedroom. Nights she heard him howling, she wondered if he was grieving, too. She latched the two dogs in the kennels and gave them each a bully stick to keep them occupied.

She wiped her dusty shoe tops against her stockinged calves and followed the path to the flagstone patio in front of the chapel. She'd covered ten rented tables with white linen. For centerpieces, spray-painted-gold toy treasure chests spilled oversize plastic gems, chocolate coins wrapped in foil, and Mardi Gras bead necklaces. A small pirate flag flew at each table, featuring not one but two skulls and crossbones, one for the bride, one for the groom. Candles in hurricane lanterns awaited lighting. The pirates had omitted flowers to spend their money on food. The reception would begin with live music by the Topgallant

Troubadours and end with a pirate-ship fondant cake that had turned out so beautiful Glory still hadn't come to terms with its being eaten.

November in Jolon, California, could be cold, or just as likely crazy warm, like today, with temps in the eighties. Blame El Niño, global warming, or pollution, all Glory cared about was that today stay balmy enough for a sword fight. When a breeze touched the back of her neck, she looked up and saw ordinary clouds scudding by. Her friend Lorna, who'd turn seventy-five this year, would insist the breeze was an omen of good things to come. Lorna had faith. Dan had faith. Glory had a job to do. She fixed a flag that had gone cockeyed and looked at her watch. In four hours it would be over, and she'd have a check to pay her bills.

The phone rang just as she let the servers into the kitchen. "Make yourselves at home," she called out to Gary and Pete, her two former fosters, and Robynn, a local girl working her way through school, who was sweet on Gary. Glory picked up the cordless. "Solomon's Oak Wedding Chapel. Glory speaking."

"Hey, Glo, it's Caroline. What's all this about a wedding chapel?"

Caroline Proctor, a social worker for the county, had placed each of the foster sons they'd taken in over the years, and she had taken Dan's death hard. Sometimes she called just to talk.

"Hi-C," Glory said, making the old joke about Caroline's name and the fruit drink. "I'm hosting an afternoon wedding here. Just something I'm trying. I've got to get back to it. Can we talk tomorrow?"

"This won't take long. I have a foster girl I want you to take."

"A girl?" Glory walked toward the hallway, straightening the

Ansel Adams print of Half Dome on the wall with her free hand.
Dan could take the hardest kid and turn him into gentleman.
Glory was just the cook. "Not without Dan. You know we never
took girls."

"Hear me out," Caroline said. "This kid is special. She needs a
female-only situation, somebody calm and loving. Take her just
for the night."

"I can't."

"Pretty please. I'm on my knees, begging."

Glory pictured stalwart Caroline Proctor in her khaki stretch
pants and black blazer kneeling on the worn pine floor. Meanwhile, her kitchen had transformed into an efficient assembly
line. The roasted turkeys were golden brown and the skin crisp.
The trays of mashed potatoes were dotted with lakes of butter.
It almost looked like the work of professional caterers. The kids
were dressed in black slacks, white shirts, and burgundy aprons
Glory had picked up at the craft store. Rented steel buffet trays
covered the counters, and the savory aroma of turkey and gravy
filled the room.

"I can't be responsible for anyone else just now, Caroline."

"Look, I know you're grieving. That's why it's you I want her
to stay with, Glory. She's grieving, too."

Suddenly faint, Glory realized she hadn't eaten all day. Years
ago Dan had taken out the wall that separated the tiny kitchen
from the living room, creating one big, open living space. She sat
on the arm of the couch and turned to look at the fireplace. In
the lightning-struck Engelmann-oak mantel, Dan had carved the
words IN THIS HOUSE, HONOR AND WELCOME. After ten minutes
with Dan, no one was a stranger. Glory was getting used to
solitude. Tonight, after the pirates sailed away, she had planned
to light a fire and pour herself a glass of whatever alcoholic brew

remained from the reception. She'd breathe a sigh of relief and put her feet up. But it *was* Thanksgiving, and the image of that lonely foster girl refused to fade. "Okay," she said. "I just hope she doesn't expect much in the way of conversation."

"Glory, you invented multitasking. I've seen you drive a tractor with one hand and beat eggs with the other."

"Only for the one night."

"Absolutely. I'm working on finding her a permanent placement."

That was what Caroline always said, and the Solomons ended up keeping those foster boys until they turned eighteen. "I mean it, Caroline. Tomorrow morning you come back and get her. How old is she?"

"Fourteen."

"What happened to her?"

"Throwaway."

In the world of foster care, that meant abandonment. Throwaways came home from school to discover their parents had moved—without them. They got kicked out of families, locked out of their homes, left in shopping malls—and the thought of it turned Glory's stomach. Sometimes these kids went directly to the police station, but other times they tried to fend for themselves and took to the streets. Drugs and selling their bodies usually followed. When neither parent wanted the child and no relatives stepped forward, foster care was the only option.

"How can she be only fourteen and have no family? Not even a nice old grandma out there somewhere?"

The cell phone connection crackled, cutting into Caroline's words, and Glory strained to hear. "I have to go, Caroline. The wedding party will be here any minute. See you later."

"Bye, hon."

Glory hung up the phone and turned to the servers. "Robynn, Sterno cans on top of the fridge. Gary, butane lighters and backup matches in the drawer to the left of the sink. Pete, can you give that silver ladle a quick polish? You guys okay if I duck out a second?" Gary nodded, so Glory took that as a yes.

She took clean sheets into the second bedroom, recently painted robin's-egg blue on advice from her mother. Feeling down? Clean a toilet. Refinish a dresser. Sew yourself a holiday table runner. Keep busy and before you know it, you'll have forgotten your troubles. The old farmhouse, last remodeled in the sixties, had benefited mightily from Glory's grief. After making the bed, she straightened the bookshelf, screwed a new lightbulb in the rickety reading lamp, and added pen and paper to the desk drawer. Every foster boy who'd slept in that room had made his bed without being asked. Not always the first night, but every night after.

"Mrs. Solomon," Pete called out. "Do you have another extension cord?"

"Of course. I'll get it." In the hall closet, she reached behind Dan's duster raincoat—whenever he wore it, she told him he looked as if he were from the movie *The Man from Snowy River*—found the box of cords, and handed it to the nervous young man.

"Thank goodness," he said.

She patted his arm. "Pete, relax."

"I don't want to let you down."

"Now, when have you ever done that?" She patted his arm. "Nothing goes perfectly, but we'll muddle through. Fortunately, we are dealing with organized pirates. We have a script to follow. Come here, you three." She handed out the copies on which she'd highlighted the events:

5:00 P.M. Ceremony begins

5:05 Mock-duel interruption

5:06 Sword fight commences

5:25 Return to chapel and finish vows

5:30 Broom jumping

5:45 Reception begins, buffet

6:15 Best man's toast

6:25 First dance

6:45 Cake cutting

7:30 Drenching of the scupper

8:30 *Fini!*

Glory had forgotten what *scupper* meant, but there was time to find out. "Don't freak out when the swords come into play. The groom told me they spent months rehearsing. No one will be hurt. At the bottom of the sheet you'll see some pirate lingo. Feel free to use it when the opportunity presents itself."

They looked up at her, blank-faced and worried.

"Smile! Say 'Arrgh!' They're pirates, not college professors. It'll be fun."

"What about the cake?" asked Robynn.

"Leave it in the fridge until just before we set up the buffet. Gary, can you help Robynn carry it to the serving table? It's heavy." He nodded, and they looked at each other shyly. When Gary had come to live with the Solomons, he was an awkward twelve-year-old, showing sheep at the county fair. Four-H had been his lifeline. Now he was twenty-one, and falling in love with a local girl. Sometimes things just fell into place.

"I sure do miss this place," he said.

"You're welcome here anytime," Glory said, and then the doorbell rang.

Robynn pulled aside the kitchen curtain. "Bridal party's here."

Glory hurried to the door. "Welcome, Admiral Brown, Mrs. Brown."

"Please call me Karen," the bride said. "This is my mother, Sheryl."

"Karen it is. Nice to meet you, Sheryl. Come in. I have everything ready for you."

She directed Karen and her mother to the den, which would serve as a dressing room. On Craigslist she'd found a secondhand couch, slipcovered it, and a shabby vanity she'd painted white. With her employee's discount at the chain store, she'd bought a card table and baskets to hold sundries. The styrofoam cooler was filled with bottled water and ice. In the tabletop basket were two curling irons, a half dozen mending kits, pink and clear nail polish, cortisone cream (in case of hives), and packages of panty hose from petite to queen size. "I'll bring you a cheese and fruit tray," Glory said, and turned to go. "Let me know if there's anything else you need."

"How nice!" the bride's mother said. "But, Karen, your dad and I have waited twenty-six years to see you walk down the aisle in Aunt Louise's dress. Are you sure you want to get married in a scarlet corset and a turquoise satin skirt slit up to your hoo-hoo?"

The bride placed her tricorn hat on her upswept hairdo and grinned. "Mother, no matter what we wear, it's still a wedding. You love Angus. So do I. Just for today, try to go with the flow." Karen turned to Glory and whispered, "Do you have any Valium?"

"Sorry." The truth was, Glory had a half dozen Percocet left over from a molar extraction, but she'd been saving them for migraines and really bad nights. "How about a glass of wine? Will that help?"

"Yes. Make it a big one." The bride smiled when the flower girl and ring bearer walked into the room. "Littlest pirates!" she said, bending down to hug them. "Mother, will you look at these two? Aren't they adorable?"

The flower girl's dress was ocean blue and laced up the front like Karen's corset. The boy, dressed in sailor pants, a white shirt with billowy sleeves, and sporting a painted mustache, scowled. They both wore black pirate scarves and plastic, gold, clip-on earrings. On the pillow they'd carry were two candy rings tied with elaborate satin ribbons.

Mother Brown looked at them and said to Karen, "When you have children, I suppose I can look forward to you naming them Hook and Tinker Bell."

"What a terrific idea," the bride said.

When Glory returned with the wine, the mother of the bride was shaking her outfit out of its plastic cover. "It's not too late to elope to Vegas," she said.

Karen touched up her makeup. "You told me if I didn't get married in a church, you wouldn't come to the wedding."

"I did not."

"Yes, you did."

"A chapel isn't a church."

"It's a first cousin."

Glory took a couple of plastic ponies out of a basket of thrift-store toys and offered them to the littlest pirates. "What's your name, sweetie?" she asked the girl.

"Erica."

"And you?"

"Uh, it's Matt. Can I, uh, have the, you know, uh, fire engine?"

"Of course. And here you go, Erica. Tell me which pony is your favorite."

"The black one. She's a girl horse, and she scares stallions for miles around."

"Those are good qualities to have in a mare," Glory said, while the boy rolled the fire engine across the wood floor to its imaginary disaster.

Mrs. Brown twisted to zip her sheath of amber satin dressed up with an attached cape. "Darn this thing."

"Allow me," Glory said, and zipped it for her. "Mrs. Brown, I have to say, you make a lovely mother of the pirate bride."

Karen's mother looked into the door-length mirror and smoothed her dress. "Weddings shouldn't be silly."

"Think what a great story this will make to tell your grandchildren. I'm sure you'd like to check on the chapel to make sure everything's exactly the way you want it. Just past the porch and to the right of the big oak tree."

As Mrs. Brown walked away, Glory thought, bless her heart. Every bride's mother wanted everything perfect for her daughter's wedding because over the years she hadn't forgotten that her own wedding was lacking. Glory had no pictures of her own wedding day. Eighteen years earlier she had thought diamonds and bridesmaids were trivial. Her sister, Halle, stood up for her wearing a dress straight from her closet. Today Glory would have given her big toe for one blurry snapshot. Dan strong and healthy, and she wide-eyed at age twenty behind a bouquet of wildflowers, certain she'd be granted a happy ending.

Ah, well.

Glory walked outside to see how the servers were managing. Cooling afternoon air blew inland from the coastline, carrying with it the faint smell of salt. Surrounded by land the color of wheat, it was hard to believe it was only twenty miles to the most beautiful section of the California coastline, where, depending on the time of year, you might see local otters, migrating whales, or elephant seals. The fastest way there was to drive the recently paved road (G18) across the Santa Lucia Mountains. Of course, arriving safely meant praying for no flat tires or hungry mountain lions or middle-aged guys racing Italian sports cars around the curves and past sheer drop-off cliffs that had no guardrails.

The groom's party arrived dressed in M.C. Hammer pants paired with white shirts and knee-high boots. Angus's shirtfront was an explosion of ruffles. Mike Patrick, the portrait photographer, called Glory over to help with the bounce-flash reflectors. "Look fierce," she reminded everyone. To save the pirates from his hefty per hour fee, she'd agreed to take the candid shots during the reception.

When Glory heard another car approach, she panicked, thinking some guests had decided to arrive an hour early. Then she recognized Caroline's tan Buick Skylark, county-issue. Caroline was the kind of hero Bruce Springsteen wrote songs about. She worked eighty-hour weeks so that for the time they were in the system kids felt safe and well fed. Here it was Thanksgiving and she was on the job as usual. Dodge started his frantic barking, and Cadillac joined in. They knew Caroline's shoulder bag held cookies. Caroline got out of the car, waved to Glory, then walked around to open the passenger-side door. "Come on out, kiddo. Mrs. Solomon won't bite you. Happy turkey day, Glory."

"Same to you, Caroline."

The girl was about five-five, twenty pounds overweight, and her dyed-black hair was pulled back in a ponytail. Metal piercings were in her eyebrow, nose, and lip. Right away Glory spotted a tattoo on her neck, positioned over her jugular vein, of a bluebird.

Glory wondered who would perform such a thing on an under-age child. The girl wore black track pants, an oversize T-shirt, and slip-on tennis shoes. Wardrobe pickings were slim at Social Services.

"Welcome to Solomon's Oak. I'm Mrs. Solomon, but you can call me Glory."

The girl flashed a practiced smile. "Thank you for having me, Mrs. Solomon."

"You're welcome. What's your name?"

"Juniper."

"Nice to meet you, Juniper."

Juniper looked toward the barn because of course the dogs were still barking. They wouldn't shut up until Caroline visited or Glory went back there and told them to knock it off.

"You have a dog?" Juniper asked, while Caroline rummaged through her bag for the mandatory paperwork Glory would need to sign, even to take the girl in for that single night.

"Actually, I have three of them. Do you like dogs?"

"Um," she said, hauling out that polite smile again, "they're all right as long as they're behind a fence."

"They're kenneled. I have a couple of old horses, too. Nothing to write home about, but they're rideable. Do you ride?"

"I'm afraid of horses."

"I only let them in the house at mealtimes," Glory joked, but only Caroline laughed. "If you change your mind, there's a fifty-pound sack of carrots in the barn. Take a few and stand at the fence. They'll come to you." No reaction. What had she got herself into?

"Jeez Louise, where's a pen when you need one?" Caroline said, pawing through her purse. "It's like I'm carrying around my own personal black hole."

Glory couldn't take her eyes off the girl. Juniper. Interesting name. What lay behind that locked-up, blank expression? What did she make of the pirates practicing their sword fight on the sod Glory had laid down especially for the wedding? When she caught Glory looking, Juniper shrugged, as if it would take a lot more than that to impress her. Juniper looked west to the grove of oaks and uncultivated land, and then east. Because the ranch was sunk down in the valley, the hills blocked the city lights. At night, the periodic glimmer of headlights on Highway 101 was all that suggested civilization was in the distance. Glory could tell Juniper was thinking about running away and wondered if she'd try. It would be a long trek to the Chevron station just off the highway, and the first place cops would look for her.

"Caroline, I'm sure I have a pen inside," Glory said, and then Juniper noticed the chapel.

"Is that a church? What is she, a nun?" Juniper wheeled around to face Caroline. "Ms. Proctor, did you bring to me to a convent?"

"Of course not," Caroline said. "Do those even exist anymore?"

"It's a private wedding chapel," Glory said. "Or a layperson's? Shoot, I don't even know what to call it. No nuns." She pointed to the groom's party, who were already drinking and laughing. "Just a wedding."

The girl turned to Caroline, who'd found a pen, but it was out of ink. "You said there wouldn't be any men."

Caroline sighed. "First of all, Mrs. Solomon is standing right here. Talk to her instead of about her, please. And unless she's opened a hotel in the last thirty minutes, I don't think the men are staying."

"They're not," Glory said.

"They better not be," Juniper said, "or you can drive me back to the group home. I don't care if it is Thanksgiving. You promised no men."

Caroline said, "For heaven's sake, Juniper. Mrs. Solomon isn't lying to you. Apologize for your outburst."

"Whatever. Sorry."

By now Dan would have had the girl laughing at his terrible elephant jokes. *Why do elephants wear blue tennis shoes? Because it's so hard to keep the white ones clean. How do you get an elephant in an oak tree? Sit it down on an acorn and wait fifty years.* Despite Juniper's fear of horses, he would have set her on top of bombproof Cricket and let her ride all the way up to the hilltop so she could feel all the open space around her.

"What's with the costumes and the dueling? Did someone forget Halloween was a month ago?" Juniper asked.

"Believe it or not," Glory said, "they're pirates. I'm hosting their wedding. I cooked the food, decorated the cake, and I've hired some kids to serve. You're certainly under no obligation to, but if you're interested in earning a little money, I'm sure the servers would appreciate the help."

The girl stared. "How much money and would I get to keep it?"

"Ten dollars an hour and of course." Glory waited for the smile. It made a brief appearance, then winked out.

"Okay, I'll do it."

"That's generous of you, Glory," Caroline said. "Say thank you, Juniper."

"Thanks," she mumbled.

The three of them walked into the house and stopped at the butcher-block kitchen counter. Glory introduced everyone. "Robynn, can you find Juniper a white shirt and an apron?"

"Sure thing, Mrs. S." Robynn held out a full trash sack.

"Mind taking this bag out to the green cans out back? Make sure you put the lid back on or the javelinas will get into it."

"Javelinas?"

"Wild pigs. They're everywhere around here."

"I *know* what they are," Juniper said. "I didn't think they'd be out in broad daylight. That's all."

Robynn gave her a startled look. "Okay. There're white shirts in the box on the couch. Aprons are underneath the shirts."

Juniper took the trash sack and went out the door. That left Caroline and Glory standing there on the old pine floor that creaked in places and had valleys from decades of traffic flow. Glory walked Caroline back out onto the porch. They looked at each other and Glory said, "Don't you start. Those kinds of tears are catching. I can't afford them or the headache that follows."

"I miss him so much, Glo," Caroline said.

Glory looked across the reception tables to the white oak. She'd turned down two photographers from Germany who asked to photograph it today. Sometimes the tree felt to her like a witness who'd taken the stand but then refuses to talk. She and Dan had picnicked there on nice days. "I'm getting used to it."

Caroline blew into a tissue. "So much bad in this world and a good man dies so young. What the heck's the point in that?"

"Dan would tell you God has his reasons."

Caroline sniffled. "I tell you what. I feel like ripping God a new one. Hey! I finally found a pen with ink in it. You know all this, but I have to say it anyway."

She recited the speech Glory had heard over the years. Not much had changed in the wording, or for the kids it protected. Every time she heard it, Glory felt there ought to be a license required to procreate.

"Sign at the flags. Here's a voucher for you to buy the poor kid some decent clothes and essentials at the nearest Target."

On my next workday, Glory thought. She signed the papers and handed the voucher back. "Do I need this since she won't be here long enough to use it?"

"It'll be easier if you just keep it with all the papers," Caroline said. "If it gets lost, I have to fill out eighty-five forms. If the county cut down on the paperwork, they could hire a dozen case managers."

"I've got a box full of Levi's and T-shirts Juniper's welcome to. So what's her story?"

Caroline's cell phone rang and she held up a finger while she answered it. "What? Come on, it's a national holiday. I haven't even had lunch and it's after four. All right. But you're paying for the speeding ticket." She pocketed the phone. "Sorry. Happy Thanksgiving, right? It is still Thanksgiving?"

"It is. Same to you, Caroline. Guess we're both working today. Do you ever get a vacation?"

Caroline's flinty laugh revealed her past with cigarettes and her present with late-night alcohol. "Let's not even go there."

Glory heard Gary calling her name. "I hate to rush off like this, but I have to get back to the wedding. Could you just give me the basics?"

"You bet. A couple years back, her only sib died. Parents divorced, Mom OD'd, and Dad couldn't handle it so he bailed."

"Jeepers. That's more than anyone deserves in a lifetime."

"Tell me about it."

"What's she got against boys?"

"Her last placement had two wiseacre teenage boys who apparently teased her mercilessly, the little jerks."

"Except for my goat, all the males around here have been cas-trated."

A dark blue truck with a camper shell pulled up and out came the members of the band. They began setting up amplifiers, and Glory worried they'd play that kind of head-banging music and scare the horses off their feed. *Three thousand dollars*, she reminded herself.

Caroline waited for the van's engine to turn off before she continued. "Her issues with men go deeper. After Mom died, Juniper went to live with Dad. He 'relocated' while she was in school. She was on the street for a while, which is apparently where she got the tattoo, and, I suspect, more trauma, but she won't talk about it. Cops picked her up for shoplifting DVDs. That put her into the system. She's a good kid, a little emotional, and she has a short fuse. I promised her I'd find her the best family ever. Hope I can live up to that."

Caroline had heard so many gruesome stories over the years that she could discuss them as offhandedly as she might a shop-ping list. Glory guessed it would be the only way to endure a job like hers. They hadn't even got to the grieving part and already Glory's skin prickled with gooseflesh. Every boy she and Dan had fostered had anger-management issues. Dan had them chopping wood and building birdhouses, but Glory didn't think that would help Juniper. "I'll do my best, Caroline, but without Dan to back me up, I'm not sure that'll be enough."

Caroline shrugged. "One night. Just be normal. That's what she needs."

"Do you have her in therapy?"

The cell phone rang again. Caroline looked at it and sighed. "Sorry. I really have to take this."

"The wedding's about to start," Glory said. "Call me later on tonight. I'll be up late cleaning the joint."

"Thanks, talk to you then." Caroline waved good-bye, speaking into her phone as she left, already on another case.

Glory watched her car back up, turn, and head down the driveway, dust flying up in its wake. The Solomon ranch was isolated, but you could find your way by the trees. The blue oak marked due west toward Highway 1. The fallen Engelmann oak halfway up the hill made a great lookout. Stand up on its stump on a clear day and you could see the tip of the Hacienda Hotel's Moorish dome, designed by architect Julia Morgan. Sit there and share your sandwich with the jays and they'd hop around like avian ninjas. The land was dotted here and there with "promiscuous" oak trees—the scientific term for hybrids—and once or twice, if it weren't for the dogs running along beside her, certain of the way home, Glory might have felt as lost as she suspected Juniper was feeling right now.

Between Jolon and Highway 1 lay wilderness. Left wild, protected by conservation organizations, the tens of thousands of acres featured hiking trails with incredible views. Rivers and creeks wove in and out of the Santa Lucia Mountains, home to mountain lions, javelinas, and the occasional bear. Every year a few hikers got lost or injured, costing the state a bushel of money for search-and-rescue efforts. Heading east between Jolon and King City, coarse golden brush made for a year-round fire hazard, which was why the Solomons grazed goats. The land required irrigation due to the undependable rain cycles. Every rancher Glory knew had an opinion on why he should receive a bigger allotment than his neighbor. But even with all those negatives, Glory cherished each migratory bird that overwintered, the noisy flocks of Canada geese on their way south, and even the javelinas, at a distance.

The nightly howls of coyotes sounded more like an anthem than a warning. Whenever she spotted a California condor, a species once near extinction that had been coaxed back, she felt proud to be a Californian. Sometimes, if humans put heart and mind into it, they could undo their mistakes. She wondered what Juniper McGuire would think if she saw one of those enormous black birds fly overhead. Glory would tell her its Latin name, *Gymnogyps californianus*, the scavenger that could live for half a century, feeding on carrion, picking bones clean to bleach in the sun.

All week Glory had schooled herself on Dan's digital camera so she could take the candid pictures, which in her opinion was the life of any wedding. While Angus and his groomsmen dipped into the wooden barrels she'd bought from a winery up north, Glory pointed and shot and let the camera collect memories. The couple was sailing to Catalina Island in the morning. She wished them a steady breeze like the one blowing through the oak's branches just now. Surely even pirates knew marriage was the mother lode of risks.

"Hey, Juniper," Robynn called, and there she was, the one-night foster, covering the buffet trays with matching lids. "Come give us a hand with the plates?"

Through the viewfinder Glory lined her up and snapped a picture. Then she focused on the oak tree. With its gnarled limbs and lobed leaves, the pirates posed beneath it looked like toy figures. Glory kept a bowl of fallen acorns on the windowsill above the kitchen sink. Before the missionaries arrived, sixty-four documented tribes had lived in this part of California, all of whom used acorn meal as a dietary staple. Three hundred and fifty years later, only a few people remained who could trace blood that far back—such as Lorna Candelaria and her husband, Juan. The cultures were long erased, the stories in fragments. Now acorns were strictly for squirrels. On horseback rides Glory sometimes pictured an Indian mother on her knees grinding the bitter meal for porridge to feed her children. Suppose she'd lost her husband early—a hunting accident, executed by the Spanish, or, like Dan, from plain old pneumonia. How had she managed? Become another man's wife? Deep in La Cueva Pintada, the painted cave, pictographs hinted at those long-lost lives. Glory had studied the stick figures and the drawings of the sun. A California winter was bittersweet, a time for reflection. Then she snorted at herself for thinking such thoughts. The truth was like a mule: on the sunniest day it could kick your heart into pieces.

Guests arrived. Before her, pirates streamed in for the party, dressed in jewel-tone outfits, velvet capes, swords at their sides. When an Anna's hummingbird buzzed by her, claiming a nearby feeder, Glory stood still, hoping the tiny bird would linger, because among the Southwest Indian tribes, a hummingbird was considered good luck on a wedding day.

At the entrance to the chapel, the Topgallant Troubadours performed a Celtic version of Steppenwolf's "Born to Be Wild." The guitar player wore a gray kilt.

"Aren't you in the wrong era?" Glory asked.

He continued playing. "Naw. I'm pretty sure pirates kidnapped Scotsmen, us bein' so entertainin' and all."

Glory did a visual sweep. The aisle cloth was unwrinkled. The minister, in his golden robe and matching miter, had bottled water with the cap already cracked and a folded handkerchief nearby for his brow. Despite the open windows, with so many candles blazing, the chapel was stuffy. The mother of the groom was dressed in a leafy green silk frock that looked Elizabethan, suggesting a lot of leeway in the pirate-costume department. Angus seated her, then escorted the mother of the bride to the front row on the other side. She still wasn't smiling. Glory snapped pictures. She wanted to gently shake Karen's mother by the shoulders and tell her, "Spend your smiles!"

A movement caught her eye, and out the window she saw Juniper standing at the fence feeding the horses the miniature carrots meant for the reception. It was like watching someone burn $10 bills, but Glory couldn't leave the chapel with the ceremony about to begin. The Topgallant Troubadours set down their instruments and lined up in the back of the chapel, singing Stan Rogers's "Forty-five Years" a cappella.

The guitar player in the kilt had a tender voice, and as Glory listened to him extol the rewards of second marriages and marrying late in life, his voice was so piercing she could almost believe he meant it.

Admiral Karen emerged radiant on the arm of her dad. His eye patch was crooked, but he looked leagues happier than his wife. They were just arriving at the podium where the minister and Angus waited when one of the pirate guests stood up and yelled, "I'll be stealin' her from ye!" and quickly grabbed Karen. A bawdy roar broke out from the crowd, and Glory made a mental check by *duel* on her script.

Chapter 2

Angus lifted his sword. "It's a fight you want, is it? When I get through with ye, ye'll be dancin' the hempen jig!"

"Leave us or ye'll taste steel for dinner, you bilge-sucking wharf rat!"

His rival, dressed head to toe in black silk, ran Karen out the chapel doors onto the flagstone patio. He pushed her behind him, drew his sword, and pointed it toward Angus. "All hands hoay!" he shouted, and guests rushed outdoors. Steel met steel in a headache-inducing clash, and while the choreography of the fight was admirable, Glory felt the unmistakable vertigo that accompanied the beginning of a migraine.

Not now, when things were just getting under way.

"Bucko, there be no quarter in which to hide!"

"Fish-feedin', scurvy-ridden—" Angus stopped and wiped sweat from his forehead. "I can't remember my line. Cue, please?"

"Landlubber!" Admiral Karen called out, and the rival turned to her.

"*Landlubber?* Now, that's a word ta crush a man's spirit," the rival said. *"En garde!"*

Behind the ropes, the servers stopped to watch. While the

sword-fight business could have seemed silly, with the costumes and swords it was kind of thrilling and provided a multitude of opportunities for candid photography. Glory pressed the shutter button on Dan's camera and, in the midst of all the hollering, listened for the telltale click of a picture being taken. She pressed the REVIEW button, but there were no new pictures since the wedding began. She checked her settings, switched back to picture-taking mode, and pressed the shutter again. A red light flashed instead of a green one. Dead battery? She'd let it charge all night. There was nothing she could do but run to the house for her old Nikon.

Angus and his opponent parried, leaving divots in the green sod. Glory had to take a step back when they changed direction. She looked up to see Angus reach inside his blue velvet justaucorps coat and pull out a pistol. Admiral Karen's mother screamed so authentically that Glory wondered if she was as surprised as Glory was. Was that a real gun? Of course not. But it was no wonder Angus hadn't found a church to hold his wedding. Most of them frowned on the use of deadly weapons, even as a joke. Mrs. Brown had to be helped to a chair. The photos would have to wait because this whole event needed to be dialed back immediately. Real gun or not, they'd taken the fight too far, got caught up in the play, was all.

"Angus!" she hollered, and held up her hand.

But just then a dark-haired man dressed in street clothing muscled his way from the other direction and reached the duelers. "Drop the gun, now!" he bellowed, and Glory wondered who he was to have a voice like that.

Then she spotted *his* gun. What was he doing? What the heck was *she* doing, thinking a pirate wedding was a good idea?

"I said, drop the gun!" the man roared.

Angus lowered the pistol to his side, but didn't let go. "This isn't a gun," he said, "it's an eighteenth-century flintlock blunderbuss."

"I don't care if it's Howdy freaking Doody dressed in a ball gown, put the thing on the ground *now*!"

The guests loved it.

Now what was she supposed to do? The modern black revolver in the stranger's hand also looked real. It had to be a fake; both of them were fake, right? They only seemed real because these people had practiced the script so well and they'd left out the gun part. Her mind spun. Find Juniper. Make sure the servers were out of the way. Let Cadillac out and cue him to herd the guests if it came to that. Her head began to pound with the unmistakable drumming of a migraine on its way. "Excuse me," she said to every person she bumped into. "Please, may I get by?"

In the excitement guests pushed back and Glory ended up next to the musicians. "Was this planned?" she asked the guy in the kilt.

"Dunno. I'm in charge of tunes, not fighting. Where'd you find that guy?"

"I thought he was a guest."

"Lady, I know every person here. I don't know him." The Scotsman cupped his hands and shouted, "Angus, back away from that dude! He's packing!"

Over the noise of the guests Angus either couldn't hear or didn't understand, so as the person hired to run this wedding successfully start to finish, Glory plowed through the crowd, not stopping until she poked her finger into the chest of the uninvited armed guest and in Angus's as well. "Both of you put the guns away! This is a wedding, not a showdown at the O.K. Corral."

"Mine's fake!" Angus said. "Honest, I bought it on

militaryheritage.com for forty-eight dollars. Look. The barrel isn't even drilled out."

The uninvited guest turned his face to her. His black hair was cut sharply above the ears, close to his skull, almost military-style. She couldn't quite place his ethnicity. Latino? American Indian? Had he been wearing boots and a tricorn hat, he could have passed as a Moorish corsair, but not in a leather jacket and Levi's and holding what she was pretty sure was a nine-millimeter pistol. "Thank God for that," Glory said.

"A sword fight in a wedding?" the man said.

"Yes," Glory said. "The fighting is pretend. We're in the middle of a wedding. A pirate wedding."

"Seriously?" The man slid the gun back into the leather holster under his jacket and stepped aside. The pirates cheered as the duel began again.

"I'm going to shoot blanks now," Angus said. "Just so you know, there are no real bullets, only black powder caps, okay? You might see some sparks, but that's all."

"Sorry about that," the man said. "Ingrained reaction. I used to be a cop."

"So your gun has actual bullets in it?" Glory asked, pulling him away from the dueling pirates.

"That's usually the point of carrying one." The pirates clashed by them. "From over there it looked to me like the real deal."

As soon as he pointed to the oak, Glory realized he'd been taking pictures of the tree without clearing permission from her ahead of time. Having the tree on private property meant she could call the hours people came to see it. Signs posted a hundred yards from the tree in every direction stated so in Spanish, German, Japanese, and Vietnamese. "You're supposed to make an appointment for a reason."

"I can see that now." He turned quickly away.

"Are you *crying*?" she said, but when he looked at her again, he was laughing.

"Sorry," he said. "A wedding inspired by a pirate movie. Who's to blame? Johnny Depp or Walt Disney?"

Glory reached for his camera. "May I use this? It's an emergency."

He pulled it back by the strap. "This is a very expensive camera."

"Mine's got a dead battery and you kind of owe me."

"I don't know you."

"I'm Glory Solomon. I live here and my camera died. Sufficient? Will you at least take pictures of things until I get my Nikon?"

"I photographed crime scenes. I don't do people."

Glory held out her hands. "How hard can it be? Just try not to make anyone look dead. I'll pay you whatever you think is fair. My future is riding on this wedding."

"If they come out terrible, don't say I didn't warn you."

"For crying out loud, just shoot! Pictures!"

He lifted his camera and, hallelujah, began snapping.

She raced into the house for the Nikon. While she fumbled loading obsolete film into a relic, she wondered why this man would be wandering around her little ranch on a national holiday instead of being at home drinking beer and watching some sports event with his kids and family.

By the time she returned, the fight was winding down. Angus was red-faced and winded. The bride pulled her dagger, pointed it at her kidnapper's rear end, and gave him a poke. "Weigh anchor, you ruffian! Unhand me."

"I'll have ye know I'm a picaroon, first-class!"

"And I be the direct descendant of Gracie O'Malley!"

The servers were now cheering on the bad guy, but in the middle of them, Glory saw Juniper standing there quietly, hands at her sides, expressionless. Poor kid. Glory bet she had never envisioned her Thanksgiving holiday to feature guns and swordplay. Glory would call Caroline as soon as the wedding was over; she needed to make sure Caroline was really finding another placement for the girl.

The rival pirate plucked a white handkerchief from his pocket. Angus speared it with his sword. "She's mine again, as she always were," he announced, and the guests began filing back into the chapel for the remainder of the ceremony.

Vows: thirty minutes late, check.

Glory followed the cop photographer into the chapel. When the bride and groom were back in place at the altar, he resumed taking pictures. On the other side of the chapel Glory took her own pictures, keeping in mind she had thirty-six shots, not the unlimited number she would have had on a digital.

"Vows, please," the minister said.

Angus unrolled a lengthy parchment and the guests groaned. "What?" he said. "I learned ta read special for this moment." He cleared his throat. "I, Captain General Angus McMahan, aka Mad Dog, take thee, my fine wench with the stout right hook, as me heart, me soul, and sole reason for plunderin'. I promises to love ye and honor ye; to make ye laugh when yer feelin' out of sorts, love thee through scurvy and fire, in wealth or poverty, and when I speak of treasure, as I am wont to do, everyone within the sound of me voice will know that what I am really speaking about is thee. All of this will I undertake until there are no horizons left to chase and the rum is gone."

Glory looked at Mrs. Brown, who held a tissue to her eyes. The ex-cop or whatever he was quietly made his way to the front of the chapel and took close-ups.

"Oh, Mad Dog," Karen began, reading from her own scroll. "Me salty jack with a crooked smile that matcheth yer business dealings . . ."

In a week Karen would be back at her paralegal job and Angus would return to managing the college bookstore. Glory would have put their check to good use—the mortgage, another payment to the hospital, and having the vet out to see to the goats and horses, who were due for shots. She'd put $1,000 into her savings account and pray that her truck could go a few more months without new tires. There were always sales in January.

The best man untied the white satin ribbons from the pillow and handed the candy rings to the kids. Angus and Karen exchanged wedding bands. Using the ribbon from the pillow, the minister bound the groom's left hand to the bride's right hand. "Whether plundered or purchased retail, a ring is a circle that never ends. Whom God hath joined this day, with the help of Poseidon and many questionable individuals as witnesses, let no one break apart. Now, we have need of a besom, please."

The best man handed the minister an elegant oak branch, the twig end of which was tied with colored satin ribbons. The maid of honor and the best man each held an end down low to the floor. "If you please," the minister said, and Angus and Karen counted to three and timed the leap over the broom perfectly. The moment they landed on the other side, the Topgallant Troubadours switched on the amps and Glory's headache pounded.

At the reception tables, Gary ladled out the grog, and Glory searched the crowd for Juniper. "Why's the drink line so crazy-long, Gary? The pirates are getting agitated."

"Mrs. Solomon, I'm the only server over twenty-one."

How could she have forgotten that? "Hang in there. Let me take a few pictures, and then I'll help you."

She lifted her camera and shot the roasted turkey legs held aloft by the bride and groom before she picked up a second ladle. If she could reduce the line to half, then she could step away from the table to take more pictures. Apparently the ex-cop saw her dilemma because he came up to Glory and uttered the loveliest words she'd ever heard: "If you send me home with a plate of leftovers, I'll take the reception pictures."

"Bless you," she said, filling flagons. "I'll send you home with a week's worth of food."

"Deal."

Before he walked away, Glory called out, "Wait. I don't even know your name."

"It's Joseph."

"Thank you, Joseph." He nodded. She resumed ladling out the mead. As soon as everyone had a glass, she signaled the best man that it was time for the toast.

"Arrgh-hem," the best man said three times before people quieted down. "Marriage between pirates can be a tricky thing. Some days you'll feel like lootin', some days you'll feel like plunderin', but never let a day go by ya don't go to sea and polish your sword!"

A groan traveled through the guests.

"All right, all right," the best man said. "Married pirates, be happy and rob only the rich! May yer sails never falter and may the seas be rocky enough t'keep things interestin'. Now who's up fer gettin' blisterin' drunk and playing full-contact Scrabble?"

Apparently everyone was, considering the response was much hollering and even louder music. Glory wondered if she could sneak a slice of turkey to convince her headache to retreat into its corner.

Juniper walked by, carrying a buffet tray of potatoes to replace the empty one. Under the pins and barbells, she had a pretty face. Someday she'd take the metal out and wonder what she'd been thinking. Glory watched her serve, taking care not to spill anything even though the pirates weren't exactly the neatest diners. Soon everyone had a full plate and a flagon. The Sterno cans stayed lit and the hurricane lamps flickered. Joseph moved through the crowd taking pictures as if he did it every day. There was plenty of turkey and gravy. All during the meal the musicians continued playing, and Glory was on her way to fetch the cake when Gary called her back, panic in his voice. "Mrs. Solomon!"

"What?" she said. "They're married, they've got food and drink, and pictures have been taken. We're in the home stretch."

"Except that we're out of the tankards."

"We can't be. We had three full cases."

"I think the pirates are stealing them. Seriously, they're disappearing and people are asking for more."

Glory sighed. What was she supposed to do? Frisk the guests? "I've got a few more in the house." She nabbed Robynn as she walked by. "How's the cake?"

"I'm on my way to get it." She grinned. "The duel was crazy, wasn't it?"

"It was."

"How come you didn't tell us about the gunman? That was kind of scary."

Glory smiled, pretending it was part of the script. "Oh, just some last-minute silliness. How's Juniper doing?"

Robynn looked back through the crowd. "All right. Kind of keeps to herself, doesn't she?"

"I only met her a few hours ago. Tomorrow she goes to a foster home."

"Oh, that's too bad. I thought she was staying with you. Remember Christopher? I saw him downtown the other day. He said you were the greatest mom ever."

Christopher, one of their recent foster sons, had been in high school the same time as Robynn. He was on his own now, attending college and working. "Thanks," Glory said. "It's easy when you have such a great kid."

They stepped over the threshold into the kitchen. It felt like time travel, going from swords and scarves and buckets of medieval booze to kitchen timers and appliances. When Glory saw her cake, she fell in love with it all over again. A fondant pirate's ship on a buttercream sea. Could anything be more beautiful?

After a week's worth of trial and error, she saw the cake as a turning point in her life. Even if she never booked another wedding, she knew she could make one-of-a-kind cakes to sell. But if today succeeded, there would be other weddings, and that would be twice as good. A way for her to earn a real living. She'd shaped Rice Krispies Treats into a hull shape, then "dirty-iced" it with buttercream, followed by fondant, into which she had pressed hundreds of cuts to resemble planks. Using food coloring made especially for pastry, she painted the hull to look like wood grain. It rode high on waves of sculpted chocolate, crested with giant sugar crystals and luster dust. The wooden skewers for the masts were coated with chocolate, and the sails—oh, my gosh—the sails of fondant were rolled so thin you could almost see through them. The pirate figurines she found at the craft store were anchored by icing to the fo'c'sle, standing one behind the other. That was what marriage was really like, Glory thought, lovers standing one behind the other, facing into a gale-force wind.

Glory and Robynn carried the cake to the cleared buffet table and set it down. "Where did the cop photographer go?" Glory asked Juniper, who'd come over to see the cake. "Can you find him before they cut this?"

"He's right behind you," Juniper said. "Dude? Are you really a cop?"

"Formerly," he said.

"So what do you do now?" she asked.

"This," he said, and took Glory's picture.

There was no time for Glory to tell him she didn't appreciate that. She cleared space at the buffet table for the bride and groom, handed them the knife, and watched her baby be cut into pieces. After the couple had rather messily fed each other, Robynn stepped in to dish up the cake for the guests.

"Can I have a piece?" Juniper asked, hovering.

"If there are leftovers," Glory whispered. "Stand here and help Robynn, okay?"

Besides the fake smile, Juniper was good at pouting. Glory's headache perched over her left eye like a buzzard. Nearby she heard the faint whirring of Joseph's camera. When he looked her way, she mouthed, "Thank you."

A half hour later, the Topgallant Troubadours set down their instruments and stood together to sing another song a cappella. "Barrett's Privateers" was the story of the last survivor recounting the battle that cost them the war. Glory thumbed away the tears in her eyes so the guests wouldn't notice the thirty-eight-year-old widow with the migraine becoming sentimental over a Stan Rogers chantey. She smiled the way Juniper did, fake and polite, and thought, interesting, already she's taught me something.

When the moment came to "scupper the grog," the pirates were busy dancing to a Nirvana song. Glory watched Angus pour a pitcher of drink over his thwarted rival and dreamed of her bottle of Percocet, left over from the dentist. It numbed everything. She sometimes took it on those nights when she couldn't stop crying. Puddles of sticky alcohol, smashed cake bits, and the odd turkey bone were on the flagstone, and instead of fretting about getting it clean, she thought, oh, I'll hose it down tomorrow. The loser/rival accepted his scupper with dignity, squeezed out his long hair, set his tricorn hat back on his head, hugged Angus, and returned to dancing.

This was it. Every planned moment had been pulled off. When things had seemed on the verge of falling apart, Joseph the gun-toting photographer had come to her rescue. Now it was time for her surprise, a gift to the newlyweds. Juniper passed by with a tray of dirty dishes.

"Having fun?" Glory asked.

"Fifty-one percent of marriages end in divorce," Juniper said.

Glory silently wished Caroline luck in finding a place for this one. "You might as well start enjoying yourself because when all this is over, there will be a great deal of cleaning up. Right now I need you to come help me with the butterflies, so let Pete bus those dishes."

"There are going to be bugs? Do I have to touch them? Eww."

"Seriously? I've never met a person who didn't like a butterfly."

"There's a first time for everything." Juniper handed her tray off to Gary, who headed toward the kitchen.

Glory was momentarily speechless.

Inside the greenhouse the air was steamy and thick. In addition to the potted orchids Glory grew year-round, there were maidenhair ferns, crawling vines, and butterfly feeders, flat-sloped dishes suspended from the greenhouse beams. Each dish was filled with nectar and fruit past eating, giving the place a sweetish scent. The butterflies preferred orange slices. Proves they're Californians, Dan once remarked.

"Oh, man," Juniper said. "How can you stand it in here? Even my hair is sweating. Open a window."

"Can't."

"Why not?"

"The greenhouse is temperature-controlled for the butterflies."

"Don't they drown in their own sweat?"

Glory laughed. "Funny you should say that. They'll sometimes land on you if you're sweating, to drink the salt from your skin."

Juniper immediately looked around. "One better not land on me, or it's toast."

"We won't be in here long enough for that to happen."

On the slatted wooden shelf were ten baskets covered with cheesecloth. Glory loaded up Juniper's arms like a waitress so she could carry them to the reception. "I can hear them creeping around in there. They can't get out, can they?"

"Not until we take off the cheesecloth." Glory took the other five, and they started toward the reception tables to hand out the net-topped baskets. "Thank you for your help," Glory said. "Can you place one on each table?"

Juniper looked at her stonily. "I think I can manage that."

As soon as the baskets were delivered, Juniper walked away and Glory found herself wondering where the girl had gone. Back to the horses, to feed more carrots? In the house to pick over the food in the kitchen? Maybe she just needed a quiet moment, and Glory certainly couldn't blame her for that. The migraine headache had moved in, begun decorating, and was about to invite friends over for a party. Were it not for the promise of quiet soon, Glory would have taken off her apron and gone to the fridge for an icepack. "If I can have your attention," she said, clacking a ladle against one of the pitchers. Each clank reverberated inside her head, but the guests quieted down. "Everyone please take a moment to think of your good wishes for Angus and Karen. Then, on the count of three, gently peel back the net on the baskets, and we'll send those wishes up on wings. One, two . . ."

On three, sixty painted-lady butterflies, one per guest, emerged. Some perched tentatively on the underside of the netting; others quickly climbed the rim of the baskets, tasting freedom. Without encouragement, the pirates lifted the baskets high and the butterflies began to use their wings. " 'Happiness,' " Glory read from a card she'd tucked inside her pocket, " 'is as a butterfly which, when pursued, is always beyond our grasp, but which, if you will sit down quietly, may alight upon you.' From Nathaniel Hawthorne, circa 1860. Congratulations, Karen and Angus. Many happy years together. Thank you for the privilege of hosting your special day."

Angus stood up. "Here's to Mrs. Glory Solomon for allowing us to hold our kick-ass wedding here. Solomon's Oak rocks!"

Pirates clapped and cheered, and whether it was the bright orange spots on the fluttering, dusky wings, or too much drink, or the single butterfly that for the longest time perched on the bride's dress, Mrs. Brown began to cry. "I hope those are happy tears," Glory said as she handed her tissues.

Mrs. Brown said, "You were right. It was a beautiful Thanksgiving *and* a beautiful wedding."

Glory squeezed the woman's hand. "I'm glad to hear it."

By nightfall the butterflies would be in the hills in search of pearly everlasting, a summer wildflower that often continued on past the season in California's warm climate. They'd mate and lay pale celadon eggs. A week later, eggs turned to caterpillars. The caterpillar's job was to eat, spin the web, form a chrysalis, then rest inside its papery walls and transform. When it was time, out came another butterfly. Each cycle moved the butterflies farther south. Lorna had once told Glory a story from her childhood, of standing with her great-aunt early in the morning, looking at the Nacimiento River literally covered with butterflies drinking. Sometimes, when Glory couldn't sleep, she called up that image, a body of water covered with orange-and-black wings. She imagined them lifting in unison, as close as anything could get to a flying carpet.

When the painted ladies had flown away, the guests began leaving. Glory looked for the ex-cop photographer to give him his money.

"He already left," Juniper said. "I gave him ten slices of turkey, a container of mashed potatoes and gravy, and six apples. He didn't want the cake, so can I have his piece?"

"Darn it. I didn't get his phone number."

"Don't stress. He left his e-mail address and said he'd send the pictures in a ZIP file. So all you have to do is e-mail him. And it's not like he doesn't know where you live."

"I just wish I'd had the chance to thank him before he left. I don't know anything but his first name, Joseph, right?"

Juniper picked a fondant plank from the edge of the parchment-covered cake plate. "Joseph Vigil. That's a Mexican last name in case you're wondering. He's here visiting from Albuquerque and staying in a cabin on the Oak Shore of Nacimiento Lake. He was married once but he isn't married now. No kids. He has a permit to carry a gun because he was a cop once but isn't anymore."

"Wow, Juniper. You could be a private investigator."

The girl stopped the finger that was about to go into her mouth and flicked the icing away. Her mouth went from relaxed to thin-lipped. The hoop in her upper lip seemed to vibrate. "He said he would send you the pictures."

"Good," Glory said. "If I don't deliver the candids, I'm in breach of contract."

"Yeah, well, tough luck. Cops lie all the time."

Juniper had sharp edges for a fourteen-year-old. Glory wondered if Juniper's father had been a policeman, or if it was her arrest for shoplifting that had left her so bitter. "I have the mother of all headaches, Juniper. Excuse me while I get a pill. Soon as I get back, we'll get started on cleanup, together."

Three hours and several dishwasher cycles later, the servers had been paid and had left, the patio was hosed down, and Juniper and Glory sat alone in the kitchen. When Glory couldn't find her Percocet, she'd taken two Advil but it wasn't working. She held an icepack to the back of her neck, but that wasn't helping either.

"The cake was a big hit," she said.

Juniper didn't respond.

"Do you think I should make two cakes for the next wedding? They do that in the South," she said. "It's called a groom's cake. Usually it's something the groom likes, you know, like a football, or *Star Wars* movies characters. The exact opposite of a frilly wedding cake."

Juniper poked at her turkey stuffing. "This was out for hours. How do I know I won't get food poisoning?"

Glory ignored that, having seen by now it was just Juniper's way to complain. "I'd love to hear your thoughts. If I do start having weddings here—"

Juniper let the fork clatter onto her plate. The noise startled Glory, and she sat up straight, the icepack falling from her grip. She reached down to pick it up and her head throbbed. "What's the matter?"

"Stop making conversation, okay? You don't care what I think. In twelve hours I'll be gone and you can do whatever you want with your stupid cakes and the—weddings."

The pause felt worse than the omitted curse word. "You'll find clean towels in the bathroom," Glory said, standing up, suddenly weary of this girl's hormones or history that made her so prickly. "Will you be all right by yourself for a while? I have to see to the dogs."

Glory let Dodge and Cadillac out for a quick run around the property and hoped the night air would clear her pounding head. The dogs were trained to relieve themselves in a corner of yard nearest the trash cans, and they headed to that patch of dirt first. Glory gave them a few minutes, then followed with the shovel to clean up. The dogs ran down the driveway, past the empty mailbox and the grazing goats behind the fence. On their return circuit, Dodge leaped for attention and hit Glory in the back of the knees so squarely that she almost fell down. "Off," she said, wondering if he had the slightest idea what the command meant. When Dodge barked at Nathan and Nanny, who Glory hoped would soon get pregnant, Cadillac went into gear, nipping at Dodge's heels and herding him away from the fence. Caddy had the poor dog spinning in circles in no time. Since Dan's death, the border collie seemed to live with one eye open, desperate to keep everything in line. It made Glory tired just to think of it. One day off from their usual schedule—training at three, walk at four, dinner at five—and Dodge was jumping up on humans and barking that horrible, supersonic cattle-dog bark of his that had landed him at the animal shelter in the first place.

Glory caught his collar and gave him a quick, reassuring neck rub before letting him go. "You know," she told him, "I prefer the comfort of a schedule, too."

Some of her past rescues had separation anxiety, a difficult behavior to correct. Others, like Dodge, were so desperate for affection they'd dig under fences just to be near you. They destroyed doors and patio furniture. Some took longer to tell you their stories. Cadillac was a mystery sewn inside a silky black-and-white coat that felt wonderful to brush. The collie needed two walks a day. He guarded the horses when they went into the barn looking for dinner. He had his not-so-shining moments, too. He nipped the mailman. When he tried to herd a UPS driver, Glory had to haul him away on leash. On bad days it took an hour of playing Frisbee and the agility-course training obstacles she had set up in the pasture to wear him out. If she shut him in his kennel, he sat on top of his Craftsman-style (Dan did nothing halfway) doghouse, but never actually went inside it.

Cadillac's favorite activity was moving the goats around. He climbed trees like a cat. All gates had to have top and bottom latches because it never took him longer than a day to figure them out. He loved learning new tricks and remembered a new voice command after only hearing it once. Glory had listened to an animal behaviorist on NPR say that you could buy your border collie a squeaky toy or you could buy him a herd of sheep. When Cadillac got that look in his eye that signaled "I'm bored," she understood why he'd been left at the shelter. The minute Glory woke up in the morning until the time she went to bed, part of her mind was on keeping Caddy out of trouble. She wished people who fell for the fluffy, ears-down, masked puppies could see him on a bad day. In the six years he'd lived at Solomon's Oak, Cadillac had chewed the cushions of a secondhand couch in Dan's workshop, spreading stuffing everywhere, scratched the barn door to bits during a thunderstorm, and "antiqued" a 1920s Sioux Star Pendleton blanket. All that was replaceable, if expensive, but when the dog chewed the horn off Dan's Fiesta model Bohlin stock saddle, well, Glory had never seen her husband so angry. The vein in his forehead pulsed and she worried he might have a stroke.

Back at the barn, she gave each dog a quick brushing and threw the fluorescent tennis balls for ten minutes. She scrubbed and filled their food bowls. Dodge practiced his sit-stays and did fairly well, considering the wedding drama had worked him up into a jittery mess. When Glory asked Cadillac to heel off leash and walk by the goats, he minded at first, but sneaked in the tracking posture with his back end higher than his front until Glory snapped her fingers and said, "Quit."

After a final opportunity to eliminate, both dogs settled down in their kennels, ignoring the blankets inside their insulated doghouses, preferring to sit on the roofs until morning. Glory looked up at the house, at the lights shining, and would have rather scooped poop for an hour instead of going indoors to the cranky girl.

But she did go inside, and by the time she did, she'd adjusted her attitude the way she had with each of the foster boys. She smiled at Juniper, who sat on the couch, her hands in her lap. An open Diet Cherry Coke sat directly on the oak end table, though a coaster was right next to it, but Glory said nothing. She walked down the hall and let Edsel out of her bedroom. He raced down the hall, did a lap around the kitchen, and barked at Juniper. "Shh," Glory said, as she fed him the organic diet that helped with his seizures.

Juniper watched silently. "What the heck is that?" she finally asked. "A mutant Chihuahua?"

"He's an Italian greyhound."

"He looks like a starving lab rat."

"I know. But he gets plenty to eat. This is how they're built. Are you still hungry?"

"I could eat some more of that cake."

"I noticed you didn't eat much dinner."

"So put me on restriction."

Glory picked up Edsel and held him out for Juniper to pet, but she shied away.

"Get that skanky rat away from me!"

Edsel wagged his tail. Everyone who met Edsel fell in love with the ten-pound comedian who made Glory laugh at least once a day. The girl's overtired, Glory told herself. She divided the last of the cake into two pieces that each had a scrim of glittery wave frosting. She set the plates down on the coffee table. "Here you go, Juniper."

The girl picked up a plate and began eating. Glory couldn't help staring at the metal in her upper lip. It looked like a fishhook, as if she'd been snagged but tossed back.

Juniper licked the frosting off her fork tines like a five-year-old.

Glory fetched her purse and handed the girl two twenty-dollar bills and a ten.

"Whoo-hoo," Juniper said limply. "I'll try not to spend it all in one place."

Glory sighed. "I'm trying to be nice, Juniper. But you make it hard."

"So? Tomorrow I'll be handed off to some trailer-trash family who need the money Social Services will pay them. I'll be eating mac and Velveeta. They'll be all nice at first. They always are. 'Help yourself to whatever's in the fridge. Make yourself a sandwich whenever you feel like it. Take second helpings.' Then pretty soon they'll say how I'm wasting food and how the money the county pays them doesn't cover how much I eat." She stopped to lick her fork again. "They'll get mad, and it'll be like . . ." She held up her hand as if warding off a blow.

"Please tell me they don't hit you."

Juniper laughed. "People don't have to hit you to make you hurt."

Suddenly the cake looked repulsive to Glory. Thanks to her headache, if she put a bite of the sweetness into her mouth, she knew she'd be sick. She handed Juniper the second plate. "Want mine? I'm not hungry."

Juniper slouched on the couch and took tiny bites, making each one last, scraping the fork tines against the plate to get every bit of frosting. "Ms. Proctor always says my *next* home will be my forever home."

Forever home sounded to Glory like the way she talked about her rescue-dog placements. "I'm sorry this is happening to you."

"Not as sorry as I am."

Dan would have said, "Sit up straight, Juniper," or sent her back to the table. But Glory didn't have the heart to tell her to mind her manners. Since Dan died, Glory ate her meals standing in front of the sink, right out of the pan. Sometimes she stood on the back-porch steps and threw whatever she didn't feel like finishing to the hens. From the freezer she fetched a pint of vanilla-bean ice cream and handed it to Juniper. "Want to go sit by the fire?"

"I'd rather watch television."

"Oops. I don't have a television."

"Whoa. That is beyond retro." Juniper spooned in a mouthful of ice cream and Edsel whined for a taste, but she didn't give it to him.

"Do you have something against dogs?" Glory asked. Juniper took a spoonful of ice cream and Glory heard the telltale click as the spoon met metal—a tongue stud. That was the one piercing she truly couldn't understand. "Did you get bitten by one?"

"My family had a dog once. For a couple of days."

"What happened to it? Did it get hit by a car?"

Juniper set the ice cream down and frowned at her. "Please. You know."

"Would I have asked if I knew?"

Color flooded into Juniper's cheeks. "What is this? Some cheesy psyops thing, you trying to get me to talk about my sister? Did Ms. Proctor tell you to? Did Dr. Lois?" Juniper dropped the spoon and it clattered on the wood floor. Edsel moved in for the kill and dragged it away.

"Sweetie, I don't know what you're talking about."

"Like hell you don't."

Glory got up, walked down the hall to the bedroom, took the spoon from Edsel, and whispered, "Biscuit." He flew by at Mach 1. Dan had often said that if a foster kid didn't take to Edsel, the situation was hopeless. Glory opened the cupboard and got a biscuit, then placed it in Juniper's hand. Juniper threw it across the room, and Edsel, figuring this was a game, went after it.

"That was uncalled for," Glory said.

"*So* sorry."

"No, you're not. I'm pretty straightforward, Juniper. I didn't finish college. I don't know what's in style or out. I lost my husband and I have to make this business run in order to keep on living here."

Juniper continued to look Glory straight in the eyes. "Then maybe you should think about keeping me. The county pays you money, you know."

Glory bit back her words and looked at the clock, dismayed to learn it wasn't yet midnight. This headache was epic; she would have given her right arm for the missing painkillers. Edsel began hoovering his way across the kitchen in search of crumbs. Striking out, he trotted back to Juniper, placing one paw on her knee. This time, though Glory could tell it was killing her, Juniper didn't pull away. Edsel lay down next to her, his head on her feet. The fire Glory had started after the guests left was down to embers. Edsel pawed Juniper's leg and whined. "He's awfully sweet if you give him a chance."

"Only morons give second chances." Juniper got up from the couch and sat down on the hearthrug in front of the fire.

If not Edsel for comfort, what would it take? "So," Glory said, "tell me about your sister's dog."

Juniper gave Glory a searing look. "Did you grow up on another *planet*? Otherwise you're the only person in Monterey County who hasn't heard of my sister, Casey McGuire."

Casey *McGuire*.

Casey, who had disappeared four years ago after taking her new dog for a walk.

The dog, full grown, a new addition to the family, had returned to the home he knew best—Solomon's Oak.

That dog was Glory's border collie, Cadillac. He'd shown up near three A.M. the night Casey had gone missing, his red leash dragging behind him, scratching at the back door, waking Glory from a deep sleep. She'd put him in his old kennel, angry that the McGuires had allowed him to get loose and angry with herself for misjudging the family even after two home visits. She'd waited until noon the next day to call them. She hadn't turned on the radio, she had no television to catch the breaking news, and four years earlier the Internet wasn't so reliable when it came to breaking news.

This was before the Lakeshore neighborhood, made up of old summerhouses and trailers, was razed for development. The McGuires had lived five miles away, across the highway, but even with traffic, Cadillac found his way back to Solomon's Oak. Despite the Amber Alert, numerous search-and-rescue attempts, posters, hotlines, and television coverage, not a trace of Casey was ever found. Officially, the case remained unsolved.

Glory remembered Casey, and her younger sister their mother called June Bug. She had a round face, dark blond hair, and braces. This Juniper had dyed black hair, a snotty voice, and a tattoo of a bluebird on her neck. "I am so sorry, Juniper. I honestly didn't know."

Real tears brimmed at the corners of Juniper's brown eyes. She looked into the fire and not at Glory, and suddenly Glory was so angry with Caroline for not prepping her that she could have slapped her.

Four years had passed since that afternoon in 1999. Everyone presumed Casey was dead, just another innocent girl in the wrong place at the wrong time. Once a year, on the anniversary of her disappearance, the *Herald* ran an abbreviated story. Eternally fourteen years old, Casey, in a smiling school picture, beamed out from the post office bulletin board in the company of kidnappers and criminals wanted for federal offenses. Whenever Glory went to buy stamps, she saw the poster. Lorna kept a dusty basket of BRING CASEY HOME buttons on the counter at the Butterfly Creek General Store. The day after she disappeared, Lorna, Juan, and Dan had ridden horses deep into the wilderness area, searching for her. Helicopters buzzed the area for days. Casey was gone, but here was her fourteen-year-old sister, pierced, angry, and homeless. She had survived the decimation of her family, paying for it with her childhood.

Cadillac would remember her. He understood English, read the subtlest gestures, but one of his uncanny traits was remembering people. So how could Glory tell Juniper her sister's dog was right outside? She wouldn't. In the morning Caroline would pick the girl up and that would be end of things. But then again, it was Glory's fault the scar tissue had torn, so she might as well try to patch things up. For a long while she watched the embers die down.

"Juniper," she said, praying she wasn't making the biggest mistake of her life, "I knew your sister. Nobody in this town has ever stopped looking for her, or hoping for a miracle. Come on, there's an old friend outside who wants to see you."

How far back can animals remember? Behaviorists say it takes a deep sensory cue for a dog to recognize something that happened in the past. The connection relies on voice or scent. Dogs have two hundred million scent receptors in their nasal folds; humans have five million. But scent is only one of the memories the cerebrum contains, and it stands to reason that the limbic system can integrate instinct with learning. Caddy knew every arroyo where he'd once found a rabbit. Dodge peed on the same trees every time they went for a walk. Years ago, when Dan was due back from a job, their old dog Jeep, a mixed breed—"cattle dog and surprise," Dan called him—scratched to get out, then trotted down to the mailbox to wait. He did not lie down to sleep or get distracted by the goats. He did not chase cars, which had been his one fault Glory could not break in their eleven years together. Jeep waited. Nine times out of ten, within a half hour, Dan drove up. Fifteen minutes before Dan showed up, Jeep started wagging his tail. Jeep was the reason Glory started with last-chance dogs in the first place. When he died, she had buried him under the white oak so he'd have a shady spot for all eternity.

Then there were the Solomon horses. As two-year-olds in halter training, they were stabled at the same facility. Over time, they were sold to various people, shown in gymkhanas, had become family horses, spent time on the trail-horse circuit, then were abandoned and neglected, miles apart.

First to come to Solomon's Oak was Cricket, a bone-thin, red-and-white pinto mare pastured alone in a steep and rocky field that Glory and Dan passed every time they drove into town. No matter if it was pouring down rain or a hundred degrees, the horse stood at the fence, looking out onto the county road. Her owner's property featured, among the tires and broken appliances strewn across the yard, two dead trucks and a female pit bull tethered on a chain. A circle of dirt around the dog was as wide as the chain reached. Her water source was a horse trough green with moss the dog had to climb in order to drink. Glory was all for Dan punching the man in the nose, but Dan being Dan said, "Good afternoon," and offered the man $200 for the horse.

A decent person would have given Dan the horse for nothing and been grateful that the animal was off his hands, but this guy took the $200. He refused to help transport the horse to the Solomon ranch, however, so Glory drove home to fetch the horse trailer while Dan stayed with the horse.

She would have ridden Cricket home if her hooves weren't so desperately deformed from neglect. It took the best horseshoer in the Central Valley three visits before he had her hooves properly trimmed to hold a shoe. While Dan drove the truck and pulled the horse trailer, Glory opened the truck's rear window so she could keep Cricket in sight. The pit bull, already named Roadie, rode shotgun. There was no way Glory would leave that dog behind to weather the elements without even a porch for escape. So she slipped the dog's collar off the chain and leashed her, and the dog happily went with her.

Her nipples were so distended that Glory knew she'd been overbred. She had scars on her face, neck, and front legs. Animal neglect made Glory furious, but pit-bull fighting made her killing mad.

"Matthew 20:28," Dan said when the man stood in the doorway and didn't say a word as the Solomons drove away. " 'Even as the Son of man came not to be ministered unto, but to minister, and to give his life a ransom for so many.' "

A year and a half later, Kristen Donohue, the animal-shelter volunteer who called the Solomons whenever a dog was on death row, came in to work one morning to find Piper tied up outside. It was the same morning Glory was picking up a shar-pei/chow scheduled for euthanasia that turned out to be a real sweetheart and now lived on a farm in Castroville. "You looking for a second horse?" Kristen asked Glory, and the minute Glory touched Piper's black-and-white-spotted neck, he began to whinny and lip her

shoulders. After checking him for soundness, Glory had Dan
bring over some tack so she could ride the horse home. The idea
was to tire him out to make the transition to the paddock easier.
Dan's idea was to drive alongside her in case things didn't go
so well.

A mile before they reached the ranch, Piper started whinnying
so hard that shock waves ran up Glory's spine. She patted his
neck. "Calm down, buddy, we're almost there. Fresh hay awaits."

Dan slowed the truck down until they were side by side. "He's
doing great so far. Keep good hold of the reins."

"Dan, I've been riding horses for twenty years. I think I can
get this one home without a wreck."

"I'm just here to provide conversation," Dan had said.

Was there ever a moment he failed to have her back?

They made it up the long driveway, past the white mailbox
that sometimes spooked Cricket, and past the bleating goats. Five
hundred feet or so from the barn, Glory halted the gelding and
dismounted. Holding the reins in her right hand, she reached for
the cinch buckle with her left. That was as far as she got before
Piper yanked the reins out of her hands and jumped the six-foot
fence. There he stood, nose to nose with a squealing Cricket. So
much for Glory's idea of keeping them separate until she could
slowly introduce them. The two old horses whinnied back and
forth like long-lost cousins. Dan opened the gate and eased the
saddle off, then the bridle, replacing it with a breakaway halter
until they were sure of Piper's temperament.

"Looks like we need a taller fence," Dan said as they stood
watching the horses snorting and play biting. Over and over,
Piper lifted his upper lip in flehmen, that peculiar curling ability
ungulates possess and horses use to take in and process scent.
"He's got a lip tattoo," Dan said while the horses reared up and

bucked a few feet just for fun. "Bet we could find out where he came from." Glory didn't care about that. Witnessing this intense conversation reminded her of falling in love with her husband. It was like trying to condense your life story into five minutes so you could move on to the good stuff.

After some digging, Dan verified the riding-school connection, fifteen years prior. From the day Piper arrived, those horses were no more than five feet from each other. Once, when Cricket colicked, Dan put her on pellet feed and confined her separately in a barn stall. When Glory went to check on her, she discovered that Piper, the food hog, had carried half his hay ration to the stall and dropped it into Cricket's paddock.

Glory's last-chance dogs had to be convinced to bond with humans. They could survive in a shelter, bulk up with her, but in a home they would thrive. Glory taught Cadillac hand commands, a variety of whistles, and even played around with the rudimentary basics of search-and-rescue training. Whether she asked him to fetch a Frisbee, round up the goats, or lead the way home, she barely had time to think of the idea before he did it. Tonight she rubbed his ears and asked him to go to Juniper, who stood on the back porch, unwilling to come any further. "Hug," Glory whispered.

Cadillac headed for Juniper, but when he was only a couple feet away from her, without any cue, dropped down and crept on his belly, like a soldier crossing a field, relying on proximity instead of cover. When Cadillac reached Juniper, he sat for a handshake, and when that didn't materialize, he rolled over to show her his belly and batted his paws in the air. He whimpered, sat up on his back legs, and practically wrote her an e-mail; he wanted her to touch him so badly. Glory was proud of him for waiting until the feeling was mutual. Juniper lasted a minute before she came down the porch steps and squatted down to put herself at the dog's level. Cadillac turned over and shook himself, then began to squeal until she allowed him to come into her arms and give her a tongue bath. The moment they touched, his tail began to beat like a thresher. He yipped and licked, and the two of them stayed like that for so long that Glory had to look away. She watched moths circle the yellow porch light. She listened as the wind rushed through the great oak. Eventually, she went to Juniper and placed her hand on the girl's shoulder.

Juniper looked up through her tears and said, "If only dogs could talk."

Chapter 3

NOT SO MANY years back—maybe five—Glory and Dan had driven several hours and paid money to watch one of their former foster sons, Gilbert, give a horse clinic on establishing trust with abused horses. While he lived with the Solomons, Gil spent every waking minute he wasn't in school or doing chores with their horses. When Gil had saved enough money, he and Dan attended an auction, and Gil brought home a four-year-old gelding that Glory took one look at and knew was out of its mind. They came back with a few new dents in the horse trailer, which Dan backed up to the corral, so the horse wouldn't have anywhere to bolt except into the fenced area. It took Gil half an hour to convince the horse to back out of the trailer, and when he finally did, the first thing he did was kick in Gil's direction. He spent the next twelve hours galloping around the corral, flinging himself itself at fences, screaming and rolling his eyes so that the whites showed.

"Guess I'll call him Spooky," Gil said.

Glory and Dan had watched that crazy horse throw that kid five times a day. Glory would have given up that first day, but Gil saw something past the rope burns, the notched ears, and the bucking. "Just one more week," Gil, limping into the house to wash up for dinner, told Dan every night.

When Gil turned eighteen, he found a job with a ranch up north gentling horses, and Spooky was still with him. People called him "the miracle worker" and said his ability to tame whatever a horse had to dish out was something you had to see to believe.

That Hollywood movie about horse whispering was just a story, but Gilbert had a gift. At the clinic he promised that within two hours the bucking and rearing four-year-old mare would not only accept a saddle, but follow him around like her best friend.

"Where's your whip?" someone asked as he shut the corral gate.

"No whips. No hobbles, tie-downs, and no intimidation. This horse has already been abused. I aim to establish a lifelong rapport based on kindness."

"This I gotta see," the cowboy next to Glory muttered.

"A warning," Gil said before he began the demonstration. "Sometimes what I do here brings up emotions. It's my belief that animals can help a human being travel to the wounds of child-hood. The best part is, once you go there, you can fix things. Get on with life."

Dan patted Glory's hand and smiled. Glory had been worried for Gil. You never knew what a horse's mood would be day to day. All it took was a white trash bag flying in the wind to make Piper start stamping and snorting. Glory could tell that some of the ranchers and horse people hearing all this touchy-feely baloney were just waiting for Gil to fail. Maybe their methods to break a horse to saddle weren't as gentle as they could be, but they worked—if you called beating a horse to tell him what you wanted successful communication. "Please let everything go okay," Glory whispered.

"Have a little faith," Dan said.

Glory had watched Gil work with Spooky for a year and a half. Just as she did with her last-chance dogs, Gil had taken his cues from the horse and, one by one, erased his fears. Spooky went from a total nutcase to a mellow, alert cow pony that couldn't wait to load into a horse trailer to go someplace new. He could spot a snake ten feet away and would stop stock-still until the rider on his back saw that, too. Spooky was up at dawn whinnying for Gil, eager to get his day started.

Gil had patiently stood in the center of the ring, taking small bites of a carrot with its green top still attached. The tense filly flattened her ears if Gil so much as looked her way and snapped her teeth when Gil came even a foot closer. In response, Gil walked around the fence, once with his hands by his sides, then on the next circuit he put his right hand, the one holding the carrot, against the fence, allowing it to ping against each metal rail as he passed. The noise caught the mare's attention. After a few of his laps, she followed him, muzzle in the air, sifting through scents. Then the wind came up, blew dirt around, and she spooked. It seemed as if any progress made were lost. But the carrot and the fence had created a new memory, a pleasant one, and eventually she became curious enough to allow him an inch closer on his laps, then to reach out and touch her, first with the carrot, then with his hand. In fifteen minutes, Gil was sacking her out with a saddle blanket. When the mare shrugged off the blanket, Gil picked it up and put it on again and again. When she was good with that, he walked to the center of the ring, a carrot in one hand and the blanket in the other. Twenty minutes went by and nothing happened. Glory was sure Gil would be giving out plenty of refunds.

Instead, the horse came to Gil. She lipped him. He gave her half a carrot. Just for a moment, he placed his arms across the mare's back, then stepped back. They went through this routine for an hour, at the end of which Gil had his full weight across her back and the horse, though nervous, did not rear or shy when he introduced a simple rope hackamore bridle. Gilbert pulled himself up on her back, and she stood there waiting for him to tell her what to do next. Then she whinnied. Glory, who knew the language of horses, recognized the "Let's go" whinny born of longtime relationships. She could hardly swallow for the lump in her throat, and at that moment, the crusty old cowboy standing next to her burst into tears.

"How did you do that?' a woman asked.

Gil turned to the crowd and said, "Patience and gentleness. When I was sixteen years old, I'd been arrested four times, and everyone gave up on me. Best thing that ever happened to me was getting thrown into the foster-care system, because this is the method my foster father used on me. Works on dogs, too, in case you're interested."

Afterward, Dan and Glory drove south, stopping at the Giant Artichoke, a touristy restaurant in Castroville, where they each ordered a bowl of artichoke soup before driving the rest of the way home. She remembered Gil's grin, the mare finally calming down, the smell of the hot soup, and the side order of deep-fried chokes, but she couldn't recall a single word of her conversation with Dan. Forgetting made her panic. Seemed as if for every day that passed since last February 28, she lost another memory of Dan for good. There was no stopping it.

She sat on the back steps wire-brushing dirt off just-gathered eggs while Juniper McGuire slept. The girl had cried herself to sleep, one hand dangling down to reach Cadillac, who stayed by her bedside. However excruciating it was for her to see the dog, Glory knew it made Juniper feel close to her sister. Glory sat on the bed for a long while. Every time Juniper sobbed, the vein in her neck pulsed, causing the bluebird tattoo to flex its wings. Glory wondered what the tat represented to Juniper and thought of Cecil, one of their foster boys, who was a "cutter."

He sliced lines into his left upper arm with razors, knives, whatever was handy. His scars were four ropy, purple lines that reminded Glory of a shipwreck survivor marking time on a tree trunk, IIII days, and poised to carve the fifth slash across the other four. As part of the agreement to keep Cecil, they checked his arms daily. He had hard days and setbacks, but while he was with the Solomons, he never did escalate to five. When he turned eighteen and moved out on his own, Dan gave him a hand-carved wooden cross. "When you feel the urge to cut yourself," Dan said, "look at that cross and think about Jesus. He already sacrificed himself, son. You don't need to do anything but be grateful."

Glory wished she believed in God enough to be able to give Juniper that kind of parting gift, but with all the girl had experienced, she was past religion. Today Caroline would take her to her new home. When school reopened after the long Thanksgiving weekend, Juniper would enroll in a new high school, make friends . . . and Glory would begin working extra hours at Target because Christmas shopping began today. When she wasn't working, she'd send out mass e-mails to wedding planners encouraging them to consider solomons-oak-chapel.com. It had taken Glory forever to create the Web page: Helvetica Bold and five iStock photos. When she posted the pirate photos, maybe things would improve. As of this morning, she had five new visitors on the counter. She'd also noticed the spell-checker had corrected the word *champagne* to read *Champlain,* as in the lake.

As the sun rose, she watched her hens peck at earth, hoping to find an overlooked grain. Her Rhode Island Red, Heather, liked to be scratched on her neck. She was getting on in years and her egg-laying days were nearing their end. Dan had warned Glory not to name feed animals, but too late for Glory to think of Heather as chicken and dumplings. Heather was special, and Glory couldn't imagine life without her.

The phone rang, startling her. She picked up the cordless and looked at the caller ID: her sister, Halle. Apparently this year's appletini party hadn't given her much of a hangover if she was up this early. Glory pressed TALK. "Morning, Halle. How were the appletinis?"

"That was last year. This year we served Sex on Acids. Take a jigger of Jägermeister, add a half ounce each of Midori, black raspberry liqueur, and pineapple juice, and then top it with cranberry juice. They hit you like a tsunami."

"Halle, I'm getting a hangover just listening to the recipe. Doesn't your head hurt?"

"Nah. I'm immune to hangovers."

"Lucky you. I got a migraine yesterday."

"Ouch. Remember how Daddy used to get them? Mom would rub that menthol cream on his temples. The whole house smelled like Vicks VapoRub."

Glory smiled, thinking of her dad, and how that would always remain their common ground. Halle was two years older and loved to tell Glory how to dress, which political opinions she ought to endorse, and to offer solutions to unasked questions, but she adored her sister. "How's my favorite brother-in-law?"

"Bart is on his morning run. The party was so much fun. You have to come next year. How was the wedding?"

"Pretty good. A couple hairy moments, but I pulled it off."

"Don't take this the wrong way, but I'm surprised."

"Excuse me?"

"Oh, it's not you, sweetie. I just know how people can be."

"How people can be *what*?"

"Flaky. Enthusiastic about a nontraditional ceremony and then the closer the date comes, they realize a church wedding is really important."

Halle had six bridesmaids at her wedding dressed in sea-foam green. Glory had Halle. "They were *pirates*, Hal. No church would take them."

"And all the guests showed up? That county road can be so confusing. I worried people might get lost. Plus, your dirt drive-way is rutted. Not everyone has four-wheel drive."

"The road's gravel, not dirt."

"Right. I forgot. I guess that is easier."

Once upon a time, Halle had been Glory's best friend, her confidante, and the person with whom she shared her innermost thoughts. As teenagers, they had laughed about everything, borrowed each other's clothes, and shared a bedroom. Since Dan died, the balance of power had somehow shifted, and too many conversations ended with Glory feeling angry or condescended to. Don't take the bait, she told herself, but a second later she was in defensive mode.

"I got a ton of compliments for the food, and a referral that might lead to another wedding." Okay, the last part was a lie, but it could still happen, she told herself. "Everyone had a lovely time. It's too bad you weren't there for the butterfly release. It was beautiful."

"Yes, the butterflies. That part sounds magical. I hope you got pictures. Who did the photography?"

"Michael Patrick did the formal portraits, and I started to do the candids, until my digital died. Lucky for me, there was a professional photographer here, taking pictures of the oak, and he stepped in." As soon as Glory said the words, she wished she could take them back. She'd just handed Halle a full clip of ammo. "He did a great job," Glory babbled. "They came out fabulous and I'm in the process of putting them on the Web site." Which was another lie, but she would do it as soon as he sent them and she figured out how to download or upload or whatever it was called.

The moment of silence between them was freighted and Glory braced herself for the older-sister lecture. "You know, Glory, it's great it all worked out, but if you plan to create this kind of business, you really ought to take a class. You need a business license, additional liability insurance, and can you afford that? You'll need at least two reliable cameras, video equipment, a health permit, and to move those dogs elsewhere because who wants barking when they're exchanging sacred vows, not to mention the smell?"

"You're absolutely right," Glory said, deflecting Halle's words and steeling herself at the same time. I'm not listening, not listening, blah blah blah, not listening.

"I hope this doesn't sound unkind, but there have been times I've visited you when I could barely hear myself speak over the dogs."

How Glory wished that were the case at the moment! If she mentioned Juniper, a mushroom cloud would rise over Santa Rosa from 22 Marigold Drive. Halle lived a great life, and Glory was happy for her. Bart sold wine internationally and traveled a lot for his job. With no kids or pets, they could lock the door behind them and get on a plane at a moment's notice to places like New Zealand and Hawaii. Their house was three thousand square feet of Spanish style, professionally decorated, and filled with an eclectic blend of contemporary and antique furniture. Halle was a shop-and-lunch kind of wife; Glory was a clearance-sale, beans-and-rice widow. "What are you getting Mom for Christmas?" she asked, changing the subject.

"A red pantsuit from Talbots. How about you?"

"Ten new paperback romances. I made sure to get the ones with the hunky guy on the cover."

Halle sighed. "Why do you encourage her?"

"Mom's sixty-two years old. If she wants to read bodice rippers, it's her business."

"Glory, what about the *Herald*'s 'one-read' novel? *East of Eden*'s a classic. Just a suggestion. It's proven that exercise for the aging brain will keep the mind sharper . . ."

Glory stopped listening. She watched Heather trot over to the empty grain feeder. This was her third visit in a half hour. Could chickens get Alzheimer's? Halle owned a to-die-for pink Chanel suit. She struck up conversations with total strangers, and she kept her gray hair professionally colored and highlighted. Next to Halle, Glory felt like a stumbling frump. The day Dan died, instead of driving two hours north to Halle's house where her sister thought everyone should "gather," Glory drove on home. She unplugged the phone, turned the horses out, and dug their stalls down to the dirt. She shoveled in crushed oyster shell and clean shavings. She scrubbed the algae off the water trough, groomed Cricket, petted the goats, and made a list of every long-term project she and Dan had planned but never got around to. She'd rather have broken her back than sat on the sectional, gray

wool couch and watched her sister greet callers with perfect
manners and heard people she didn't care about say just the right
things. Her mother and Halle knew, as did Lorna and Caroline.
Let the news get around via conversation at the Woodpecker
Café. She didn't want to make bad-news phone calls. She didn't
want to eat catered heirloom-tomato-and-basil canapés, and she
especially did not want to make small talk. She wanted to be
alone in the place where she and her husband had made their
wonderful life together. She wanted to go into his workshop and
touch the tools he'd used to make such beautiful things. She
wanted Cadillac to lie down in the doorway and just for a few
more minutes pretend their world hadn't changed.

Halle held a grudge about Glory's not showing. She was
appalled when Glory told her she'd decided on cremation.

"But there won't be a grave to visit! Where will you bring
flowers? Where will you go when you want to spend time with
him?"

Glory answered, "Dan's favorite flowers were the marguerite
daisies that reseed themselves every year. He'll be in my heart
until the end of time."

Glory knew the only thing that shut her sister up was that she
had no idea what a marguerite daisy was and wanted to go look
it up.

All that chilly February day, Glory had worked until her
clothes were soaked through with sweat. She sat down on an
upturned bucket and told her horses, "I've only been a widow
for twelve hours, and already I'm a failure. Just so you guys know,
I'll do my best, but don't expect too much."

Horses knew the best cure for sorrow was sugar cubes by the
handful. Glory opened a new box and ate a few herself while
she let the horses gorge. Sweetness to cover the bitterness. The

soaring love she felt for her horses pressed against the margins of her heart. The dogs, too. Even when one of them dug under fences or barked nonstop for no apparent reason, they gave her joy. They depended on her now, just as the utilities company expected payment on time. At the end of that first day she told herself, "Sooner or later you have to do something with his workshop. It's criminal to let his lathes and chisels and his work gloves gather dust," but here it was nearing one year later and still she hadn't figured it out.

"Gotta run," Glory said, interrupting whatever Halle was saying. "Love you, Sis, bye." Halle would call back tomorrow. Glory loved her sister even if some days she had to work hard to like her.

She had three dozen eggs to take to the farmers' market. The sunrise was the color of a coral reef. The stillness in the air reminded Glory of how things felt moments before an earthquake. Last night's migraine had left her bleary-eyed. She thought of all the mornings she'd stood at the kitchen sink while the coffee dripped, watching from the kitchen window as Dan finished up his morning chores. He was such a careful man, keeping the brush trimmed away from the house, the fence in good repair, and their animals well looked after. But living rural meant you couldn't ever relax. California had fire season year-round. Would this be the year it came their way? Would it take the farm? Spare the oak? Visitors collected the acorns that fell from its branches. They stood beneath it to make wishes. Dan used to say, "Our tree nudges people closer to the spiritual. They miss God, even if they don't know it."

Glory wished she could believe like that. Have faith in something. She looked at the tree and wondered for the tenth time where the heck her Percocet had gone. Whoever was responsible, she thought, fie on you. May a million migraines come your way.

According to Lorna Candelaria, the closest person Glory had to a grandmother, every tree had a soul, and the white oak's was ancient. Lorna loved telling stories handed down in her family, especially enjoying how they contradicted written history. Under Solomon's Oak was a holy place, the shaman's favorite spot to chant protective songs on behalf of the dwindling Indian tribes. The Spaniards, however, claimed the tree in the name of their queen and Christianity. When indigenous people clung to Old Ways, they were hanged until dead from the oak's branches. As soon as Glory told Lorna about the pirate wedding, Lorna said, "*Buena idea!* The tree will love being a part of weddings!" Lorna, the perfect grandmother, approved of everything Glory did. She smoked, drank beer, had an extensive vocabulary of Spanish swear words, and her shoulder was so wide that Glory often leaned on it.

Glory thought about Juniper, who had no sister, no parents, no Lorna. Could Juniper have taken the Percocet? She didn't seem like a thief, but she'd been caught shoplifting DVDs. Should she suggest Caroline run a drug test? What would be the fallout if Juniper tested positive? She needed a safe place to grow up. Somewhere nurturing. Glory immediately dismissed keeping her because how could she herself be any kind of role model when she spent so much time in her closet crying? Juniper's smart-mouthed crack about keeping her for the county money still stung. Glory's postmigraine aura made everything look as if it had a shadow around it.

She got up and walked quietly through the house to the

shared bathroom with its claw-foot tub and zinc countertop. She opened the medicine cabinet and took everything out of it. Aspirin, antibiotic ointment, Band-Aids, razor cartridges, antacid, bars of soap, nail clippers, a half bottle of cough medicine, Q-tips, but no Percocet. Was she losing it so badly that she'd thrown them away? Maybe yesterday, what with people coming in and out of the house, someone had pocketed it. Not Gary, Pete, or Robynn. They were good kids, never in trouble. One of the pirates? Oh, let it go, she told herself. She took four aspirin, drank a glass of water, and peeked into the guest room. Cadillac looked up at her and thumped his tail on the wooden floor. Always first in line at mealtime, this morning the dog wouldn't leave the girl's side. The sudden devotion squeezed Glory's heart like a vise. She felt that thickening in her throat that wanted to become a sob, but pushed it back. Imagine the mess if you cried every time you felt like it, she thought. That's why you have Closet Time.

Juniper was tucked in as if she already lived here. Next to the mug of water on her bedside table was *Shōgun*, by James Clavell. Between the pages an oak leaf marked her spot. Glory figured Juniper must have woken up in the night and read until she could sleep again. If she finished that book, she'd be compelled to read the sequels. Maybe it was naïve, but Glory believed that there was hope for any kid that read fiction. A willingness to lose one's self in a story was the first step to learning compassion, to appreciating other cultures, to realizing what possibilities the world held for people who kept at life despite the odds. The leaf marking her place reminded Glory of herself at Juniper's age, when she'd carried a book wherever she went.

Enough daydreaming. Having the biggest shopping day of the year off was no minor miracle. She needed to use her time productively, eyes to the future. She considered selling the broken tractor that yesterday's wedding guests had considered a charming artifact and she considered an eyesore. If there were societies of pirate reenactments, were there farmer reenactors? Twice Glory picked up the cordless to call Caroline, and twice she put it down. Glory knew that Dan would already have decided, saying that Juniper had been heaven-sent to them because they were the right people for her. Surely not, unless heaven had it in for Glory. The only certain thing was that when Juniper McGuire woke up, she'd need breakfast.

Glory opened the fridge. Edsel wove between her feet, and she stepped on his toe, causing him to yip as if he'd been branded. She bent down and checked for injury, patting his chest. "You're fine," she told him, giving him a chewy to get him out of her way. He trotted off, settling by the fireplace to work on his treat. When Glory bent down to take out the electric griddle, her head spun with indecision and she felt a hot panic in her chest. Bacon. Fry it. Eggs, just ask her. Scrambled, over easy, or poached?

She decided to make biscuits. The buttery kind Dan loved. Sometimes she made his favorite dishes, hoping the smells and tastes might conjure his presence. After placing the biscuits in the oven to bake, she used flour, milk, and bacon grease to make decadent gravy and wondered how long Cadillac could stand it until hunger won out over guarding Juniper. While the biscuits cooled, she stood back and surveyed the amount of food she'd made. A spread like this could feed a family of ranch hands. She hoped Juniper wasn't the type of teenager who skipped breakfast. She poured herself a cup of coffee and had decided to give her five more minutes when Juniper walked into the kitchen dressed in yesterday's clothes, lugging the duffel. Cadillac was right behind her. Before Juniper sat down at the table, she let

Cadillac out. He headed straight for his breakfast, the stainless steel bowl inside his unlocked kennel. Glory was impressed.

"Good morning," Glory said. "Did Edsel's yelping wake you?"

"I was already awake."

Juniper's hair was soaking wet and her face scrubbed pink. The hardware was missing, and in its place it looked as if she had chosen to ruin selective pores. She looked past Glory to the middle distance outside the window. "Should I wait out front?"

"Of course not. Sit down and eat some breakfast."

"I'm not hungry."

Glory sighed as she set the butter dish down on the table. "What the heck am I going to do with all this food? Call the army? Seriously, Juniper, if you don't eat a little, you'll hurt my feelings."

Juniper pulled out a chair and sat down, dropping the duffel to the floor. She took three slices of bacon and one of the biscuits. "Try the gravy," Glory said. "Why is it that the things that taste the best turn out to be the worst for you?"

"Life just sucks, I guess."

"Would you like the comic section from the paper?"

Juniper poured herself a cup of coffee as if daring Glory to forbid it. "I don't read them."

"Everyone reads the comics."

Juniper looked at Glory. "Some places I stay at don't get the newspaper. Why get invested in Garfield's problems and then not get to find out what happens?"

"That makes sense." Glory sat down at the table. "Juniper, yesterday, at the wedding, did you notice any tankards disappearing?"

She looked up. "I didn't take them. Search my bag if you don't believe me. What am I going to do with a stupid beer mug the size of Texas?"

"Oh, honey. I wasn't accusing you of stealing. All I meant was quite a few disappeared. Gary thinks some of the guests took them home for souvenirs."

"So add the cost to their bill."

"Good idea." Glory watched Juniper put a slice of bacon inside the biscuit, then dip it into a pool of gravy.

"So, what do you think we should do next time? Offer gift bags? Plan for sticky fingers?"

"*We*, as in the royal *we*?"

"No, *we* as in *you* and *me*."

"Does that mean I'm staying?"

"If you'd like to. As soon as you finish eating, put your stuff back in the bedroom. If Cadillac's going to be your dog, you'll have to feed and walk and groom him. I'll show you around the barn later, and you can help me with the horses."

"For how long?"

"Oh, it shouldn't take us more than fifteen or twenty minutes if we work hard at it."

"No, I meant, how long can I stay?"

"Indefinitely, if you'll agree to follow some ground rules."

Juniper's chocolate brown eyes stayed dry. She didn't allow a sliver of emotion into her voice. But Glory had seen her with Cadillac. She knew a soft heart was behind the sarcasm and deliberate aloofness. "Thank you, Mrs. Solomon."

"You're welcome. You should call me Glory." She got up and turned up the griddle. "One egg or two?"

"Two, please."

"Fried?"

"Yes, please. I'll do the dishes every day. You won't even have to remind me."

"I'll take you up on that." Using the spatula, Glory flipped two eggs and transferred them to Juniper's plate without break-ing the golden yolks.

Juniper took a bite of her bacon-and-biscuit sandwich. "The bacon is really good."

"It's maple-cured." Glory brought over more biscuits, dished herself a plate, and reached for the gravy boat. "Breakfast's my favorite meal."

"If you cook like this, how do you manage to stay so skinny?"

Glory laughed. "I'm a far cry from skinny. I only ever cooked like this on Sunday mornings. Pancakes, French toast, blueberry muffins, something special. While I cooked, Dan read the paper. We did the *New York Times* crossword puzzle together."

Juniper wiped her fingers on her napkin. "You have to be really smart to get all the words."

"I'll let you in on a secret. You just have to think like the puz-zle maker. Crosswords are all about puns, double meanings, and odd, three-letter words. Pretty much every crossword has Yoko Ono or Mel Ott for an answer. It's like Scrabble, only harder."

"Mrs. Solomon? I was wondering something."

"Wondering what?"

Juniper set down her biscuit, picked up her napkin, and wiped her fingers. "I don't mean to hurt your feelings, but how come you don't dye your hair?"

"My hair?"

Juniper nodded. "Your face looks like you're thirty, but your hair is totally screamin', 'Bingo grandma.'"

Glory reached up to touch the knot she tied it into every day. She hadn't thought of it in years. "Dan liked it. It started turning gray when I was about your age."

"That's weird."

"Luck of the gene pool. It happened to my sister, too."

"You miss your husband a lot?"

"Truthfully? I hate that I'm getting used to him being gone." Like your sister, Casey, she thought. Juniper could give Glory lessons on missing people. "Hey, do you know anything about making Web sites?"

"I could make one if the computer had a decent program."

"Then I have a paying job for you." When the phone rang, Glory grabbed it. "Solomon's Oak Wedding Chapel. Glory speaking."

"I guess yesterday was a success," Caroline said.

"Other than a few dozen missing tankards, it was."

"What did you expect from pirates? Listen, is it okay if I come get Juniper around two this afternoon? If I can find any place open the day after Thanksgiving to give me a haircut—" Caroline's other line beeped and she swore. "Hold on a sec."

Glory placed her hand over the receiver. "Caroline. I'll tell her the second I can get a word in."

Juniper took a second biscuit and broke it open. "These are good."

"Thanks. Try the strawberry jam. I made it myself."

"Seriously?"

"It's easy. We'll do a batch together. Cherry, apricot, peach, plum, whatever fruit you like."

When Caroline came back on the line, she said, "I'd like to travel back in time and strangle Alexander Graham Bell—"

"Change of plans," Glory said, interrupting. "Juniper and I have decided to give things a go."

"You what?"

Glory looked at Juniper, hoping for another smile, but she was studying the pink rose design on the plate. Glory used the Franciscan Desert Rose china all the time now, thinking, why not? "You heard me."

"This is the best news ever. I knew you two were meant for each other. I'll bring the papers by immediately."

"I thought you wanted a haircut."

"You have shears, don't you? You can trim my split ends and I will give you a twenty-five-cent tip. *Hasta luego*, my friend."

Glory hung up, sat down at the table, and her knees quaked. She'd said so out loud so that meant Juniper was staying. Edsel leaped into her lap and sniffed the tabletop. His peculiar habit of licking at the air when appetizing people food was nearby apparently altered his status from lab rat to adorable puppy dog, though Juniper's laugh sounded rusty.

"He reminds me of the baby velociraptors in *Jurassic Park*," Juniper said.

Glory laughed. "This afternoon we can drive to Target to get you some new clothes. Get you ready for school on Monday."

That stopped the laughter. "You should probably know I don't do so hot at school. They say I'm difficult."

Glory thought about the shrill tone Halle's voice took on when she was fed up with her. "Me, too, Juniper. We can be difficult together."

Caroline sat in the kitchen chair they'd hauled outdoors. Glory stood behind her. Both were drinking coffee and watching Juniper feed treats to the formerly scary horses that were now her best buds. "Is there such a thing as a carrot overdose?" Caroline asked.

"I'll cut her off in a minute," Glory said. She combed through

Caroline's bottle-blond strands that were brittle from too much coloring. Underneath the brassy blond, her hair was turning platinum white. "Ever thought about letting your natural color take over?"

"Never. It's an ageist workforce out there, Glory. We over-fifties have to work hard to fly under the radar. You watch closely as this decade goes by. All us baby boomers will get the shaft, first in the job market, then in Social Security. Soon the world as we know it will be run by twentysomethings and we'll all end up working retail until we drop dead."

"Sounds unpleasant."

"And Medicare? Don't even get me started. I have three friends whose doctors dropped them the minute they turned sixty-two. *Dropped* them." Caroline sipped her coffee. "That should be a mis-demeanor, at least."

"I agree. Listen, Caroline. You're always in a hurry, and I un-derstand that, but yesterday you had time to tell me about Juniper being Casey McGuire's sister. You know how responsible I feel about the dog. Why did you just leave her with me that way? It could have turned out disastrous."

Caroline pointed to the corral. "Look at that horse. He's to-tally pushing the other one out of the way. What a carrot hog."

"Don't change the subject while I have scissors in my hand. I know we're not as close as you and Dan were, but we're friends. Friends tell each other the truth."

Caroline picked at her cuticles. After she'd quit smoking, she'd started in on her nail beds, and it hurt Glory to look at them. "You want some sensible explanation from me and I don't have one. There was time. I just didn't want to go into it while you were so busy with the wedding and all."

"Why does that sound like absolute horse pucky?"

Caroline turned her head and sighed. "Because it is. Please don't hate me. I've been keeping a secret from you."

"Why would you do that?"

"I promised Dan. You're making it impossible for me to keep my word."

Glory's skin flushed hot, then went chilly. She felt dizzy at the sound of Dan's name. "What could you possibly not tell me?"

"The last time I saw him, he made me promise to find the perfect foster kid for you. Someone special to keep you occupied, to make you join the world again."

Glory looked at the scissors in her hand. Even in the sunlight the metal felt cold and heavy. Caroline had come to the hospital a handful of times, odd hours, spelling Glory while she went to the cafeteria or took a catnap. "No way. Dan barely made sense there at the end."

The fine lines above Caroline's upper lip had turned to full-fledged wrinkles where her lipstick bled. "Way. I've never directly lied to you, Glory. It's a sin of omission, I confess. But the last time I saw Dan he made me promise. Every day I rack my brain in this job. A surplus of kids, never enough homes. It gets disheartening to say the least. Until last week I thought I'd made a promise I couldn't keep. Then Juniper came along. Yes, I remembered how you blamed yourself about the dog. I thought it was the perfect opportunity for you to—"

"Make up for letting precious time go by instead of calling the police?"

Caroline reached up and squeezed Glory's arm. "I wish you'd stop beating yourself up over that. As we say in the biz, your past doesn't have to become your future. I find circumstances where kids have the best opportunity to thrive. Look at her. Tell me I made a mistake and I'll take her away."

Glory watched Juniper climb up the arena fence, leap off the highest rung, and run to the tire swing. Her hair was the color of a crow's wing, flashing in the sunlight. Immediately the horses trotted to the other side of the corral in hopes more carrots would appear.

"That right there is a ten-year-old kid who turned forty overnight. Her heart is in smithereens. Her world is ugly. Do we just give up on her? Let her go astray because there's too much wrong to cope with? I knew you'd say no outright if I told you who she was. And then you know what we'd have?"

"What?"

"Two *separate* unhappy people giving up instead of a pair of unhappy people working together toward whatever kind of life there is after so much sorrow. This is the gospel according to Caroline. Amen."

Gospel, Glory thought. A story of good tidings, sometimes true, sometimes metaphoric. It was the perfect word for what Caroline did. She gave up her weekends, her social life, and even salon haircuts to help kids find a home.

Glory slipped the shears into her jacket pocket furious that Dan had used any of his last words on someone else. That he felt he had to arrange life for her after him, that somehow he thought she would fall apart if left to her own devices, made her livid. Smithereens were her way of life, too. "Caroline, I know your job involves client confidentiality, but you should have told me who Juniper was. Last night when I figured things out, I was pretty mad at you. And now? You and Dan talking like that about me? I'm even angrier."

Caroline ran her fingers through her newly cut hair. It looked 100 percent better neck-length versus straggling unevenly over her shoulders. "You have every right to be, Glory. I behaved like a coward. I hope someday you'll forgive me." She started to stand up, but Glory pushed her back down.

"I will if you tell me everything. What else did Dan say?"

"Are you sure you want to hear this?"

"Do you really think I could answer no to that question and go on being your friend?"

"Wow, you are mad. Okay, he said he was afraid to die."

"That can't be true. He was so peaceful at the end. He told me he was looking forward to seeing his brother again, his dad, all his childhood horses. He believed in heaven."

Caroline smiled gently. "He wasn't scared because of what might or might not come next for him, he was scared to leave you."

"Why?"

"Are you serious? You guys were joined at the hip. He was worried you wouldn't have a reason to get up in the morning. That maybe you'd stop living your life. Suicide. He used that word."

They had been joined at the hip, then so roughly wrenched apart it felt like being severed with a machete. Of course Glory wanted to stop living. She wanted to go with Dan. During her first week at Target, she stood at the register plotting ways to join him. She could adopt her animals out; let someone else do the rescuing for a change. Who cared if she sold the ranch? Dan's mom was in assisted living, provided for; Glory could walk into the Pacific Ocean like that writer Virginia Woolf. Or she could move closer to Halle, get a little apartment, take computer classes, and remodel her personality to fit in with the world she'd lived apart from for twenty years. Find an office job. She could go to Halle's parties and be that quirky single woman who made a great listener or could talk about alfalfa crops while everyone else was discussing the political situation in Korea, or haute couture. Start over or stop? She couldn't make up her mind. Her mother had enough Social Security to cover her modest lifestyle. Halle had Bart and bucks out the kazoo. All Lorna had to do was throw a rock and she'd hit a relative. Caroline had her foster kids. Other than providing directions to the white oak, how would Glory be missed? "I'm not sure I can do this," she said.

"What? Take care of Juniper? No one's ever sure of situations like this. You take things one hour at a time. But think of what you're offering this kid. Yesterday she was circling the drain. Today? Rope swings. Carrots. Life on the cutest darn ranch in Monterey County. Call me anytime you need help. I promise I'll come running."

"You're always running off to some kid who needs you. How do you help everybody?"

"Factor in homemade biscuits and it's easy to prioritize."

Juniper swung that tire swing until watching made Glory dizzy. Juniper called out to make sure they'd look at her and waved.

Caroline waved back. "Forty going on fifteen," she said. "For a little while, anyway. Brace yourself for the wonderful world of hormones."

Glory walked through the automatic doors of Target and came face-to-face with red carts. The scent of elderly popcorn assaulted her nose and her gag reflex kicked in. Past the carpeted cart corral, the scuffed linoleum began. The rattle of the automatic doors opening and closing every two seconds slammed against her eardrums. Her hands itched to straighten up the shelves with the dollar-bargain junk, to fold scarves over matching mittens. "I get an employee's discount here," she told Juniper, "so you can spend a little more than the voucher says."

"You work in this place?"

"It's just seasonal help," Glory said, trying to make it sound less embarrassing that someone her age would willingly dress in red polo shirts and khakis.

"Cool," Juniper said. "Maybe we can save up and get a television."

Glory laughed. "How about we watch a video now and then on the computer? Now go find some school clothes while I get a cart." She watched Juniper hustle through the racks, touching the buttoned capes that were supposed to be popular this year, but looked good on nobody and were now marked down 75 percent. Juniper rooted through a pile of black sweaters until she found an extra-extra-large. The sleeves hung down past her hands and it swam on her. Glory knew she wouldn't be able to talk her out of it so she didn't try. An hour later they had jeans, T-shirts, a jacket, socks, underwear, and the giant sweater. "Juniper, everything you've chosen is black. Do you have something against color?" Glory said as they headed to the school-supplies section for a notebook and backpack, also black.

"Black's my favorite color."

"Okay. You'll need gym clothes. Be sure you find out on Monday what kind and where to get them."

"You could look it up on the computer."

"I never thought of that."

"I despise gym."

"I didn't like it either, but you have to take it."

"Can we go to the shoe department next? I could use some shoes if there's enough money left."

Glory frowned. "How about we shop at the mall for shoes? The ones here don't last."

"Better not say that too loud or you'll get fired. Can I get a cell phone?"

Glory tried not to smile. "Let's revisit that when you have someone to call."

"I'll need to call you."

"You can probably do it the old-fashioned way. Let's go to cosmetics. You're welcome to use my stuff, but I imagine you'd like your own things."

Juniper looked at her as if no one had ever said this to her before. "Thank you, Mrs. Solomon."

"It's really all right if you call me Glory."

"I don't think I can yet."

"That's fine, too." Glory reached out and gave Juniper a brief sideways hug. Juniper didn't flinch, and Glory took that as a positive sign.

She had never expected to be standing here watching a "daughter" pick out tampons and shampoo and barrettes. Juniper picked up a name-brand conditioner, then found its generic equivalent. Glory wished she could tell her to get whatever brand she wanted, to pamper herself, to forget about prices. "After we pay for these, let's have a treat at that coffee place. I could live on latte. What's your favorite hot drink? Do you like cocoa or herbal tea?"

"I like mochaccino with a triple shot and extra cream."

"Fine with me, so long as you order decaf."

Juniper walked ahead to the candy section. From the back Glory saw a tall twelve-year-old, studying flavors of Tic Tacs as if they shopped together every day. In her civilian clothes, Glory disappeared, but what a stroke of luck! Larry O. was on the register. She steered the cart in. The employees did this to each other, chose higher-ups to check them out when they were on the other side of the conveyor belt. Partly it was to make them recite the spiel, partly because one of the job's few perks was making someone like Larry O. ring up your economy-size box of tampons.

He grinned at her like a rictus. "Good afternoon, ma'am. Did you find everything you were looking for?"

Glory smiled. "As a matter of fact, Larry, I did."

"Excellent." He had to enter the price code by hand when one of the T-shirts wouldn't register on the scanner. "Is there anything else I can do to make your transaction easier?"

"Not that I can think of."

"Would you care to open a Target account and save ten percent today?"

"No, thank you."

"You'll save ten percent."

"The answer is still no."

"Thank you for shopping at Target and have a pleasant day. Happy holidays, and come back soon."

"You, too, young man."

He handed her the receipt. "Who's your friend?"

Glory tucked the receipt into her wallet. "This is my daughter, Juniper."

He smiled for real this time. "Whoa. Didn't know you had one."

"That's because I keep her locked up. We have to go now. Bye, Larry."

"See you on your next shift, Gloria," he said, watching Juniper all the way to the exit.

"Why do I have to take the bus to school?" Juniper said as they sat down at the café table with their drinks.

"It's too long for me to drive you back and forth every day, and on the days I work, one of us would have to be late."

Juniper poked her fork into her chocolate croissant and frowned.

"Do you get motion sickness on buses?"

"It's not that."

"Then what is it?"

"They'll put me in remedial classes. In eighth grade I tested at the high school level for reading and still they made me take sentence-building."

"Sounds dreadful."

"Yeah. It made me want to stab myself in the eyes."

Learning Juniper's code was going to take some time. "Well, we can't have that. I'll make sure you're placed in the right classes. I get off work at four most days. I'll be home as soon as I can. Can I trust you on your own until I get home?"

Juniper gave her a "duh" look. "I promise I won't set your couch on fire if that's what you're worried about."

"I'm not," Glory said, though a part of her was scared silly at the idea of Juniper in her house without supervision. She sipped her latte and studied the trees in the center of the grassy, outdoor plaza filled with enormous oaks. It was a typical California winter day, eighty degrees, despite the predicted rain that rarely fell. Young mothers walked by toting kids who didn't understand why they had to wait a month for Santa to show up. Glory wondered how she and Juniper would celebrate Christmas. She used to accompany Dan to midnight mass at the mission, a festival of candles and carols in Spanish. The service was always packed. They'd sleep in Christmas morning, drink Irish coffee for breakfast, and take a long ride with the horses and the dogs. How had Juniper's family celebrated anything after Casey went missing?

Right now Juniper flipped through the free *Central Coast Weekly* that listed entertainment from here to Sacramento. Did she long for tickets to Beyoncé, or Roller Derby? Did she like those rap artists who looked to Glory like car mechanics or criminals? What was her idea of fun? A woman walked past with two Italian greyhounds in harnesses, one seal and the other blue. Glory almost spoke up to compare notes about Edsel, but then for no reason at all, she was blindsided by a memory of the back of Dan's neck. Whenever he was driving the truck and she was sitting beside him, she noticed the sun-darkened skin on the back of his neck, middle-aged and craggy. She had loved to place her fingers there, where time had taken its toll. For a moment she could almost feel a slight tickle against her fingers, but as soon as she tried to will the sensation closer, it departed, taking another nip of her heart. Shoppers and diners came and went, kids on skateboards wove in and out of pedestrians, and middle-aged men sped by on racing bicycles with tires so thin they looked as if they could cut grooves in the asphalt.

"We should get going," Glory said, and stood to bus their trash.

"I need to use the restroom."

"Go ahead. I'll wait here." While Glory waited, she noticed a T-shirt in the bookstore window, a deep purple shade with a Celtic graphic of two rearing horses. She thought of Juniper feeding Piper and Cricket. On sale for $10, two for $15. She bought one, as well as the other books in the *Shōgun* series. When Juniper returned from the restroom, she handed her the bag. "Early Christmas present."

When Juniper looked inside the bag, she said, "Why are you being so nice to me?"

Glory looked at Juniper's face piercings and saw a fearful girl trying to look grown-up. "Just say thanks and let's go. We need to walk the dogs."

"Thanks."

Later, when they were cruising along in the weekend traffic, Juniper turned down the radio and said, "Mrs. Solomon?"

"*Glory*, kid. As in 'glory, glory, hallelujah.'"

"Is that your real name?"

Glory grinned. "It is. My father went a little nuts when his daughters were born. My sister got the worst of it. Imagine twelve years of roll call for Hallelujah Smith."

They laughed. Juniper said, "I know the voucher Ms. Proctor gave you was only good for Target. Thank you for buying me the shirts and the books. I know they cost extra."

"Books are always worth the splurge. Of course, that means we'll be eating beans and rice all week."

"I don't mind."

"Juniper, I'm kidding! I can't tell a joke to save my life. When I hear a good one, I have to write it down and read it in order to get the lunch pine. I mean, *punch* line."

When Juniper laughed, it was as if someone had pumped helium into the truck's cab. So many things were funny on the drive home. The black cows chewing their cuds, a jacked-up pickup with a nerdy driver at the wheel. The oldies station playing the Norman Greenbaum song "Canned Ham."

Eight thirty A.M. on the Monday after Thanksgiving, Glory dropped Juniper at King City High and spoke to the woman at the attendance desk about testing and placement and bus schedules. Over the years the Solomons had gone through this ritual many times, registering their foster sons. King City was a good school, and though Glory didn't know the new people working at the front desk, they were all smiles and warmly welcoming to Juniper.

"That went well," Glory said as she said good-bye for the day.

Juniper scowled. "Appearances can be deceiving."

Glory patted her shoulder. "Don't be so gloomy. The day will be over before you know it. See you tonight."

Juniper stood and watched her go, waving as if Glory had left her at the pound.

Glory drove to the Butterfly Creek General Store to buy a freshly made doughnut, and to say a quick hi to her friend Lorna.

"Glory Bea!" Lorna said when Glory walked in through the squeaky screen door. Lorna shooed aside her husband, who was restocking the countertop display of topography maps popular with hikers. "Juan, sweetie. Go cover the register while I visit with our *hijastra*." She looped a mug through her finger. "I hosed off the chairs this morning, so check before you sit down in a puddle. I can't wait to hear all about the wedding. I hope you brought pictures."

"Soon. I'll post them on the Web site."

Lorna sighed. "Oh, well, that's something to look forward to then, isn't it? I gotta get me one of those laptop computers. My great-nephew Elliot carries his everywhere he goes. My niece is worried he'll end up working for the Geek Squad, but I say more power to him. So, what was it like? Do pirates party like bikers or Girl Scouts? Did they make anyone walk the plank?"

"Actually, it was fairly sedate."

"That doesn't tell me a thing. Come on, girl! I need specifics. Surely there was a smidgen of debauchery. Did a bridesmaid dance on a tabletop in her slip? Did anyone stand up at the 'give a reason these two should not be married'? Just once in my lifetime I would dearly love to see that happen. I guess that's only on soap operas, right?"

Glory told her about the gunman.

"Now that sounds promising. Was he tall, dark, and handsome? Brown eyes or blue?"

"Just a regular-looking guy, maybe forty, and I think Latino. His eyes could have been brown. I wasn't really paying attention, Lorna. I was trying to run a reception."

"Well, wake up." Lorna gave Glory a smack on her arm with the order pad. "How about his voice? I bet it was that rumbly kind of bass that hits you right in the—"

"Lorna, we probably exchanged ten words. The most attractive part of this guy was that he had a camera and he knew how to use it."

She chuckled. "That sounds a little naughty."

"To a person with a dirty mind, maybe."

"Guilty as charged," Lorna said. "I may be old, but even old ladies have fantasies."

"Too much information."

"Relax, I'm not going to tell you about my sex life. Though it is—how is it the kids say it? Smoking hot?"

"Lorna!"

"Relax, Glo. Now, did he have on a wedding ring?"

"No, he didn't. He was just a nice guy who happened to be in the right place at the right time—for me, due to his camera. I'm sure I'll never see him again."

Lorna reached into her pocket for her cigarettes. "Never say never. Life just loves to surprise the heck out of you. So what's up with Queenie?"

Every time Lorna invoked her nickname for Halle, Glory pictured her sister lying on a red velvet fainting couch ringing a bell to summon a maid. "The same old same old. Actually, I'm keeping a secret from her, and since it's almost Christmas, I have to tell her pretty soon."

Lorna exhaled blue smoke. "Now you're talking. Tell me all about this secret and I'll help you come up with the perfect plan. Say, I could go for a piece of leftover pumpkin pie. How about you?"

"I'm craving your maple doughnuts."

"Juan!" Lorna hollered. "A couple Vermont life preservers, pronto! One cup of blond sand for our girl here, and refill my cup while you're at it."

Glory had long ago given up learning Lorna and Juan's private language. "I thought your doctor put you on the diabetes diet."

"Maple comes from a tree, dearie. That makes it a vegetable in my book. Plus I make the icing with brown sugar. That's not as bad as white sugar, you know."

"You might want to double-check that," Glory said, but let it go. "Okay, here's my news, and it's big. Caroline Proctor called me just before the wedding." Juan brought the doughnuts. "*Hola*, Juan. Good to see you."

He set the plates down, then gave Glory a kiss on the cheek. "Good to see you, too, Glory. Here's your coffee, extra cream and two sugars." He put the can of Reddi-wip on the table and set down Lorna's oversize mug of black coffee. "*El azúcar* for my *azúcar*."

"*Gracias*," Glory said. "Did you two have a nice Thanksgiving?"

He sighed. "Day in, day out, Lorna works me like a dog."

"Oh, shush," Lorna said. "Get back inside before somebody shoplifts the Slim Jims." Lorna thumbed the red cap off the whipped cream. "I know these are bad for the environment," she said, squirting swirls of sweet cream on top of her coffee, "but I'm old and I work hard and I deserve some sweetness. Oh, maybe just a smidgen more." The tower of cream grew taller. "Go on. What did Caroline have to say? Is this the secret that's going to get sister's undies in a bundle?"

"Actually, it is." Glory told Lorna about Juniper. "Can you believe it? What are the chances of our paths crossing again? At first I said no, but when I introduced her to Cadillac, something happened. I don't know, it felt wrong to send her on her way. I dropped her off at King City High School this morning. It's strange to have another person in the house, but I like it. I forgot how much of a racket kids make."

Lorna nodded. She cut her doughnut into pieces, speared one with her fork, then ran it through the whipped cream before putting it into her mouth.

"It's not like you to have nothing to say," Glory said.

"That's because I'm listening."

Glory felt the bite of doughnut turn to a lump in her stomach. "Lorna, do you think I made a terrible mistake?"

Lorna took hold of both Glory's hands and looked her in the eyes. Lorna's steely gray hair was braided, then wound into two buns above her ears. Her sharp features and hairstyle made her look like an Indian maiden on an antique postcard. "*Terrible* isn't the word I'd use."

Glory's face went hot. "Then what word would you use? It's not like I traded my pickup in for a Hummer or bought myself a Picasso. She's a kid who needs a home for four years. When Dan was alive, we always had fosters."

Lorna let Glory's hands go. "*Estimado*, you have a big heart and I know you mean well. Plus you get a check for taking her in. That's got to help your present situation, but—"

Glory's back stiffened. "It's not about the money."

"*Calmarse*. But, Glory, the burden rests on you alone now. It hasn't been a full year. Are you sure you're ready to add a teenager into the mix?"

"Was I any more ready for those boys Dan and I fostered?"

Juan hollered out the door, "Lorna! *Teléfono. Ven aquí, por favor!*"

Lorna smiled because that was what a good friend did, but Glory could tell she was biting back her words. That felt worse than having her come right out and ask, "Are you *loco en la cabeza?*" Lorna took Glory's hand again. "Did I show you my newest pig statue? It's a cast-iron boot scraper. Won't that come in handy the next couple of months?"

"You bet." Lorna's affection for the javelina was evident everywhere, from the pig brooch on her sweater to the patterned fleece vest she wore in the wintertime. Every rancher and farmer in the area hated the beasts. They ran amok, rooted up gardens, and terrorized farm animals.

Glory put her coffee down. A group of hikers had arrived and were discussing their expensive hiking shoes. Glory figured she could have bought a month of groceries with that much money. "Lorna, your approval means the world to me. I'm going to try this. I think Juniper and I might be good for each other."

"She's a lucky girl. Be sure you bring her to the Christmas party. She can socialize with my great-nephew. Elliot has a face like a pie, but he's a nice boy, and she could use a friend, right?"

Glory stood up. "Definitely." She took out her wallet, but Lorna pushed it away. "Thanks for the coffee and doughnuts."

"I'm always here for you." Lorna took a few steps toward the store, then turned back to Glory. "I'm just going to say this one thing and then I promise I'll drop it."

"Here we go," Glory said under her breath.

"Seriously. Glory, teenage girls have *pantaletas* on fire. I see them here in the summertime. They think nothing of shoplifting a package of gummy bears when they have money to pay for it right in their pockets. They parade around in stringy bikinis and the poor boys get all worked up. They're too embarrassed to buy rubbers so they have unprotected sex, and who ends up pregnant?"

"Lorna, I love you with all my heart, but right now you're sounding a lot like Queenie."

"Consider this practice for telling Her Majesty."

Glory folded her paper napkin and set it down on her empty plate. "I'm already in trouble for buying my mother romance novels for Christmas."

"Put a bow on the girl's head and a tag reading, 'To Queenie, with love from Glory.' She'll be so relieved it's a joke that she won't care you took the girl in. Are we still friends?"

"Of course." Glory hugged Lorna good-bye. She wanted to tell Lorna that in the past couple of days she hadn't cried one tear. That she'd skipped her regularly scheduled Closet Time and actually laughed a few times. Who better to show her how to survive loss than Casey McGuire's younger sister? But Glory looked at her watch and knew she'd be late for work if she didn't leave right then.

Tuesday, Glory was sent home from work at noon, having worked only two hours. The store manager sent Larry O. to deliver the news. "The recession has everyone scared and hanging on to their money," he said.

"Can you explain that in plain English?"

Larry looked around the store as if he were the manager, considering rearranging everything. "What can I say, Gloria? Last one hired, first one—"

"Am I fired?"

"No. But unless you decide to work graveyard, your schedule will be a day-to-day decision for the present. Sorry if that messes up your plans."

He actually sounded sorry, Glory thought as she drove home, trying not to cry, making mathematical calculations in her head. Was it was too late to apply anywhere else? With Juniper home on the weekends, that limited Glory's availability even more. She could park Juniper at the store's snack table with her homework while Glory worked her four-hour shift, but the county might frown on that. What the heck. She'd use the free time to experiment with fondant cakes. Put flyers up in the market: "Beautiful, homemade cakes in holiday themes. Pirate ships a specialty." Why stop there? She'd make some brochures, distribute them to B&Bs to advertise her culinary skills in addition to a charming wedding location. Did a person need a business license to sell cakes? How did you charge? By the inch?

The phone rang and Cadillac ran to it and began barking. Glory danced around him, trying not to fall down, and grabbed the receiver. Her hand was so slippery with buttercream icing that she dropped it, sending Edsel yipping down the hall in fright and Caddy running to clean up what Edsel missed. "Leave it," she said, but Caddy had already lost interest when the phone stopped ringing.

Glory was out of breath when she finally said hello. Whoever was on the other end had probably hung up by now. "Excuse the racket. I accidentally dropped the phone, and the dogs—oh, never mind. This is Solomon's Oak Wedding Chapel, Glory Solomon speaking. May I help you?"

"Glory, it's Monica Phelps."

Since all of their foster sons had attended King City High, Glory knew the principal well enough to call her by her first name. She was probably calling to say hello, since she hadn't been in her office yesterday when Glory registered Juniper for classes. "Hello, Monica. How are you?"

She heard the sigh in Monica's voice. "I'm fine. I'm afraid there's been an incident with Juniper."

"Oh, no! What happened? Is she hurt? Does she need to go to the hospital?"

Principal Phelps cleared her throat. "Not an accident, an *incident*."

That didn't sound good. Glory worked her apron off with her left hand and was already reaching for the car keys hanging on the rack next to the sink. "Is she all right? Anything broken?"

"No, no. She appears to be fine. But the student she struck is a little shaken up."

"She hit someone?"

"Apparently she had to be held back from doing it again. I'm sorry, Glo, but you know the rules. Matters such as these constitute an automatic—"

"Three-day suspension," Glory finished for her. "Wow, Monica. I'm shocked. She's been nothing but gentle since she arrived here. Doesn't seem to have a mean bone in her body. Were there any witnesses?"

"Quite a crowd, evidently."

"You're sure? We both know how teenagers exaggerate."

"Any other circumstances I'd be the first to suggest that. The girl she hit has a red mark on her face I'm praying doesn't turn into a bruise, or things might get ugly."

"I don't know what to say. Could you give her another chance?"

"I'm just as sorry as you are. But her suspension is statewide policy. If there's a repeat offense, she could be expelled."

Heat climbed Glory's neck. Over the years, when their foster sons got into various scrapes fueled by hormones, Dan's policy was to back off. Let them learn from their mistakes what it means to be an adult. Glory agreed, but Juniper was a girl. What kind of fourteen-year-old girl hits someone, and on the second day of class? "What was Juniper's side of it?"

"She refuses to say. Maybe you can drag it out of her. I have her sitting in the front office. When can you come get her?"

"I'll be there in twenty minutes," Glory said, and hung up the phone.

She covered the fondant poinsettia leaves—or were they petals?—with waxed paper and put them in the fridge. Until the phone call, she was happily experimenting with detailing fondant and sculpting chocolate. Her fingertips were stained red, and her shirt had powdered sugar and luster dust all over it. She put Edsel in the bedroom and whistled for Cadillac to get in the truck cab. "Time to go to work, buddy," she said. "I have a feeling it's going to be a long day."

All Glory's dogs had high self-esteem. Edsel was a bit of a narcissist, Dodge believed to his marrow that everyone in the world was put there to welcome his slobbering kisses, but only Caddy was a master at détente. Glory knew it was wrong of her to pass him off as one of those service dogs allowed in public places, but in his defense, he was certified to visit convalescent homes. She snapped on his vest in the school parking lot and walked into the high school office with him at her side.

Immediately Cadillac went to work on the office ladies, offering his paw for high fives. The woman at the front desk fell for him instantly. "Oh, what a cute doggie! Any chance you're going to breed her? My kids would love a puppy for Christmas. Do they come in smaller sizes? My daughter would adore a purse dog."

The phrase raised Glory's hackles. For some reason, people believed that tiny dogs were born housebroken and obedient, when the truth was they needed as much training as the hundred-pounders. She smiled. "Thanks. He's neutered, actually. Have you thought about a shelter dog? Full grown? They're so grateful. That's where he came from."

"Oh. That's certainly an idea to consider."

Glory smiled harder. "I'm here to pick up Juniper McGuire," she said, looking around the office. Among the blond wood and tall, beige filing cabinets there she was, slouched in an orange chair just outside Principal Phelps's office, staring into space. Glory wondered when she'd found the time to paint her nails purple, and furthermore, where she'd got the polish. Shoplifting, the other day at Target? There was plenty of opportunity to slip a small bottle like that in her pocket. But why? It only cost a couple of dollars. Glory would have bought it for her had she asked. And fighting on top of that? Like all teens, Juniper was quick-tempered, and Glory had to admit the girl was sarcastic beyond her years, but she was so gentle with the animals that Glory couldn't picture her hitting anybody.

"Monica," Glory said when Principal Phelps walked toward

her. She was dressed in a blue pantsuit and silver scarf, the school's colors. "So nice to see you, Monica. How's your mom doing?"

"Good to see you, too. The hip replacement did wonders. Mom's back out on the golf course three times a week."

"That's great. Say hello to her for me."

The principal reached down to pet the dog. Her smile disappeared. "How are you holding up?"

Glory tightened her grasp on Cadillac's leash. Despite the fact that she'd never shed a single tear in public since Dan died, it felt as if everyone expected her imminent meltdown. "I'm keeping busy. So, you have some papers for me to sign?"

"Yes, here's her official suspension," Principal Phelps told Glory, who took the pen and looked at Juniper. The girl looked away, her face empty of emotion. Glory took a second set of papers, stapled together. "If Juniper returns to class, she'll need to return both of these, signed and witnessed, preferably by me."

"If?" Glory said. "Is she in that much trouble?"

Principal Phelps came closer and lowered her voice. Her reading glasses hung from a gold chain decorated with tiny Christmas ornaments. "Juniper is a smart girl, Glory. Of course we want her back, but until she can get herself under control, I'm not sure KC's a good fit for her. Have you considered counseling?"

Was Glory supposed to admit that the girl was already in counseling? That apparently her problems ran so deep she should agree the girl was a societal misfit? For the first time ever, Glory felt ashamed, as if Juniper's unacceptable behavior was her fault. "Monica, I appreciate your honesty. Give us a few days and I'm sure she'll shape right up."

"That's the idea." Monica patted Cadillac, who whimpered at being ignored by Juniper. "Take care, Glory."

Juniper stood up and walked over to Glory, then knelt down

to give the dog a hug. Cadillac took that as permission to erupt into a howling chorus of *I love you*s. The ladies at the desk swooned. "Did you hear that? It's like the dog can talk."

Juniper took his leash. "Can we get out of here?"

"In a minute," Glory said. "Pull up your sleeves."

"Why? You're embarrassing me."

Principal Phelps gave the girl a weary smile. "Juniper, last chance. Stand up for yourself and tell us your side of the story."

Juniper looked at the principal, then back at Glory. "I don't have anything to say, so would everyone please stop asking me?"

"It's all right," Glory said. "We'll talk on the way home."

The principal turned back to her office. A phone rang, then another. The admin staff returned to other tasks. Glory reached into her pocket for the keys to the truck, and Cadillac took hold of his leash, walking all of them toward the glass double doors adorned with the King City mascot, a galloping mustang next to a powder blue horseshoe. This is a blip, Glory thought as she passed secondhand cars kids like her foster sons had scrimped and saved for. A onetime incident. She's getting settled is all. They left the sunny office that smelled faintly of whatever overcooked veggie the hot lunch offered. Broccoli, Brussels sprouts, or green beans rendered the texture of clay, a vegetable kids would use as ammunition because no one in her right mind would eat it.

As they seat-belted themselves into the truck, Glory cued Cadillac to "be sweet," which was what she did when they visited Dan's mom at the convalescent home. To Cadillac, that meant placing a paw on someone's knee and waiting for further instructions. Let the old folks pet you. Give a kiss, but only if they ask. The elderly also enjoyed visits from Edsel, though his only trick was spinning in circles when Glory twirled her index finger. Caddy had a closetful, from the *I love you* howl to standing up on his hind legs and dancing backward. That move alone could evoke laughter from the most isolated patient.

But Glory's favorite of Cadillac's antics was "grin" on command, when he lifted his upper lip until his teeth showed in what appeared to be a smile. Dan had shown Glory a book that explained it as submissive behavior, but Cadillac learned the command in no time, and Glory chose to believe the collie smiled. She started the truck, and before they were out of the parking lot Cadillac pawed Juniper's shoulder, whined softly, and, sensing she was amenable, threw himself at her, licking her face. "Eww, gross," she said, holding up her hands.

"Border collies are such a popular breed that artists have painted them into Van Gogh's *Starry Night*, Monet's *Lilies*, and I forget the artist but that picture with the old people and the rake."

"*American Gothic*," Juniper said in a monotone.

"Right. Those ladies in the front office sure liked your dog. Your principal, Mrs. Phelps, is a cat person."

"I feel sorry for the cat."

Glory couldn't help laughing. "She's trying her best."

"She looks at me like I'm trailer trash."

"No, she doesn't."

"No offense, but you're blind if you can't see that." After five minutes of silence, Juniper added, "Aren't you going to make me talk about what happened?"

"I figure you'll tell me when you're ready. Are you ready?"

"No."

"Then I'll wait."

Juniper had no idea that Glory was counting on the drive home to figure out what to do next. She had to figure it out correctly and effectively, if only to prove to Lorna and Halle that she could handle things. Until then, she maintained her composure. Just like Dan, she'd be firm and consistent, the authority figure—but kind and soothing, the kind of mom every kid wanted. Caddy spilled out of Juniper's lap and pressed against her.

Juniper cried so softly Glory almost didn't notice. Juniper turned her face away, but her raised shoulders, shaking ever so slightly, betrayed her calm demeanor. What had happened that would change the girl from acting like an ordinary freshman into physically assaulting someone she'd known for one day? Glory sighed. Life would be a lot simpler if everyone grew tails and began walking on all fours. She switched on the radio, tuned it to a classical station, and drove on autopilot. The miles passed in silence until Caddy recognized the turn for the farm and began squealing. As they pulled up to the house, Glory shut off the ignition and turned to Juniper.

"Go wash your face and change into some work clothes. There's a box of old clothes in the barn."

Juniper held Caddy close and hiccuped. "Why?"

"Because we're going to clean out the chicken coop and it's messy. Bring a bandanna to tie over your nose and mouth. There should be some in the top drawer of my dresser. After we finish the coop, we're going to set mousetraps."

"Mousetraps?"

"When you live rural, they come with the territory."

"But mice carry the hantavirus. It's contagious."

"In New Mexico, maybe. This is California."

"I'm not touching a dead mouse even if it's in a trap."

"I promise, all you have to do is set the traps."

Juniper jumped down from the truck. "What do I do about Caddy?"

"Check his water bowl and put him in his kennel."

"Isn't that mean?"

"Not at all. It's his safe place. Sometimes he goes in there voluntarily."

Glory sat in the truck, watching Juniper walk into the house. Suddenly she remembered the wad of cash sitting on her dresser, and her pearls.

Part II

JOSEPH VIGIL

*I didn't want to tell the tree or weed what it was.
I wanted it to tell me something and through me
express its meaning in nature.*
—WYNN BULLOCK

Welcome to the Butterfly Creek General Store!
Your one-stop shop for the comforts of home
away from home
Voted Best Darn Pizza in Central California since 1988
(& we deliver)
Official meeting place for The Butterfly Creek
Intellectual Society
Bicyclists and Bikers welcome
Open Monday–Thursday from eight A.M. to nine P.M.
Friday–Saturday until two A.M.
CLOSED on Sunday, no matter what!
Sundays are for visiting with the grandbabies.
Juan and Lorna Candelaria, owners
FOR SALE BY OWNER: Inquire Within

Chapter 4

DECEMBER 2003

T HE FIRST TIME Joseph walked across the parking lot to the Butterfly Creek General Store, he was impressed by the number of signs tacked up on every square inch of the building. It reminded him of the Sign Post Forest on the Alcan Highway. You could stand here and read signs all day.

The store was an oasis of icy cold Coca-Cola and penny candy, and then there was the pizza. You could have it delivered to you at your house, office, or campsite. If you were a hiker, biker, birder, climber, camper, lunatic, or a local, this was your meeting place to plan hikes, to unwind from rock climbing, or to recharge before the drive back to Los Angeles. DECAF IS FOR SISSIES declared a red-and-white enamel sign to the left of the doorway. SEAT YOURSELF read another. Busing your table was implied. According to Lorna, kids regularly stole the sign she and Juan had especially made by a local carpenter, Dan Solomon:

Today's Special: the Swamp Juan pizza
Tomorrow's Special: the Swamp Juan pizza
Looking for a great meal? Try our Swamp Juan pizza

Pilfering the sign had become a tradition with Cal Poly students. They'd take it for a week, hang it above their fraternity
door, have a Swamp Juan party, then return it. A week later, another fraternity took it, and so on. Juan finally put it on hooks for
easy removal.

The general store had a turning rack of picture postcards, toy
fishing rods, hand-tied flies, bait, Seventh Generation diapers,
playing cards, flip-flops, beach towels, coloring books and Crayolas,
sacks of marbles, old-fashioned jacks with the red foam ball, pork
rinds, five flavors of Doritos, red vine licorice, sunscreen from
SPF 5 to 70, aloe vera gel, baby powder, toothbrushes, travel-size
shampoos, and much more. The moment Joseph stepped onto
the creaky wooden floorboards inside the store, he traveled back
to when he was ten years old, here with his grandmother, buying
a slab of bacon for breakfast.

The Butterfly Creek smelled like coffee, french fries, and pies
just out of the oven. It had been his first stop after the long drive
from Albuquerque to Lake Nacimiento. That day his back ached
so badly that his left leg was dragging, and he worried whoever
saw him might think he was drunk. The long drive was really
too much without pain medicine, but he refused to drive while
he was on it. He shuffled into the store to buy bread, cheese,
eggs, and a quart of orange juice to tide him over until he was
ready to face a chain market and shop. Lorna took one look at his
road-raggled self and sat him down at the outdoor table with the
Budweiser umbrella. She nuked him a homemade breakfast burrito and poured him a cup of coffee that had just about blistered
the soles of his feet.

"On the house," she said. "Now, tell me, who are you?"

"Joseph."

"Where are you from?"

"New Mexico."

"How long are you staying and what do you plan to do while you're here?"

She would have made a great detective, Joseph thought.

On she went, leaving the questions hanging. "Juan and I have lived here all our lives. We know spots the tourists don't. Caves you'll never find on a map, fishing holes—" Right then Juan had yelled for Lorna, and she patted Joseph's shoulder. "Better go see if he set the kitchen on fire again. You finish up that burrito and I'll be back to check on you presently. Save room for pie; I baked a chocolate silk this morning. I top it with whip cream and chocolate bits."

The warm pie reminded him of the pudding his grandmother used to cook on the woodstove in the cabin he was about to move into.

Lorna sat down with him while he ate it. She smoked a cigarette. "What are you doing out here in our little neck of nowhere? I don't see a boat trailer on your car. You aren't all gigged up in North Face clothing. I freely admit I'm a nosy old lady. Hearing other people's stories is my only fun. Tell Lorna your secrets. I can keep them."

Joseph laughed. "We've met before. You probably don't remember me, but I bet you remember Penny Vigil."

"I sure do. The green A-frame cabin on the Oak Shore of Dragon Lake."

"My grandmother. She left it to me."

"Lord Almighty, you're Penny's grandson! I can't wait to tell Juan. Are you here to fix the roof? It's in bad shape."

Joseph was reluctant to answer. He wanted solitude, not dinner invitations, but he believed people were put on earth to be polite to each other. "I'm here for a few months. At the end of

April the cabin will be torn down so the developers can finish the project. They're building a 'weekend retreat' on the land. I'm not sure what that means exactly, but it involves giving me a lot of money."

Lorna snorted. "Another six-thousand-square-foot 'cabin' in the woods. Explain to me why people need five bathrooms and granite countertops to 'get away from it all'?"

"That's a good question."

Lorna wagged her order pad at him. "I suspect there's more to this situation than what you're telling me. That place has a woodstove, not central heat. You could have done everything by fax machine. Are you going to sit in the cabin until the bulldozers arrive and stage a protest? Write the great American novel? You look like you might be a writer type. Though you'd need to wear a black turtleneck sweater and one of those French berets if you really want to convince people."

The choking feeling that accompanied a turtleneck drove Joseph crazy. "I've never been much good at writing. Give me a camera, different story."

"Oh, that's right—Penny was always taking pictures. Must have made a big impression on you to choose that for your career. So what do you take pictures of, if I might ask?"

Crime scenes and dead people? Wounds and bullet casings? Bloody palm prints on walls and tire treads in mud? "While I'm here, I plan to take pictures of trees."

"Trees? Why trees?"

"California has giant redwoods."

"But a tree just stands there. Why not take pictures of pretty girls?"

He smiled. "I find trees more interesting."

"Someone broke your heart, didn't they?"

More stories she didn't need to hear about. "I'm just taking some time for myself. A vacation, I guess."

Lorna got up to leave, picking up his empty plate. "I'm going to tell you something, Joseph. In between trees, I suggest you start doing some push-ups. Get that broken heart of yours back in fighting shape or you could miss out on something wonderful."

"Sound advice. Thank you for the meal, senora."

"Oh, call me Lorna. Everyone does."

How could you not find comfort in a place like that? Cream-sicle bars. Bottles of root beer so cold and slushy it hurt your teeth to drink. Return the empty, you'd get a nickel back. Also, a large-size Swamp Juan came with four Tootsie Pops. Even left-over, the pizza was good.

On Monday, December 1, Joseph got up at dawn, still not accus-tomed to the time difference. He looked out the cabin window and saw frost on his car windshield. The air steadily warmed up in what he'd come to think of as a California-style winter, much warmer than Albuquerque. He drank coffee and reviewed his photos of the pirate wedding. He photoshopped the red eyes on the bride back to brown. He cropped the sword-fight pictures to zero in on the groom's steel and grimace, and occasionally he looked at the picture he'd shot of the frowning woman who was running the show, Glory Solomon. She was a good cook. But her expression—what did she have to be pissed off about? He'd saved her bacon with his camera. He could not imagine showing his face there again, but that's where the white oak tree was, the only one like it in the entire state. He'd seen it once before, the summer he was ten.

That summer had been the second year in a row that the oak

trees had failed to produce acorns. When squirrels and chipmunks began to raid trash cans and boldly challenge campers at
the lake, the Forest Service investigated. That the oak trees might
be dying out was one of the explanations. UFOs, pollution,
secret government projects, the coming of another ice age . . .
those were the explanations discussed at the Butterfly Creek. The
predictions terrorized a ten-year-old boy's heart, giving him his
first taste of insomnia.

"What will the squirrels eat, Grandmother? Where will birds
make nests? If there's no shade, won't the animals die?"

"Come with me," Grandmother Penny said. She drove her
pickup truck to Solomon's Oak, chatted with the man who came
to the door of the farmhouse, then she and Joseph walked over to
the white oak, a tree with one strike against it already. This variety
of tree wasn't supposed to grow here.

"This tree is over two hundred years old," she said. "Does it
look sick to you?" she asked him, bending down to collect a few
of the beautiful nine-lobed leaves.

Joseph remembered his heart racing as she placed the sturdy
leaf in his fingers. "It could be sick deep inside. With something
you can't see."

His grandmother held up a leaf so that the sun shone through
it. "See those lines, Joseph? Those are the tree's veins, just like the
ones in your body. Blood flows through your veins. Sap flows
through the tree's veins."

"But what about the missing acorns?"

She smiled and smoothed his hair. "Nature follows its own
rules, *nieto*. We can say a prayer for the acorns if that will help you
feel better."

He couldn't remember if they prayed or not. Probably. Grandmother Penny covered the bases. In case the acorn drought was the

death knell, she made sure he saw Solomon's Oak. Taking a safety pin from her purse, she pinned the biggest oak leaf on his shirt, over his heart, like a forest ranger's badge. That summer he wore it until the leaf crumbled, leaving only the pin. This year, before driving to California, he read up on oak trees for his photography project. Among the many tree stories, he found this: *Pin an oak leaf next to your heart, and you will be protected from lies and deceit.*

If he'd worn the leaf all these years, would it have saved his marriage to Isabel?

When your family stretched across the state from Crownpoint, New Mexico, to Dona Ana County in the southern part of the state, to the green-chile capital, Hatch, you went to weddings every month. A dozen bridesmaids and groomsmen was not unheard of. Formal dress was *necesario.*

He thought about their wedding—his and Isabel's—such a far cry from the pirate wedding he'd been to a few days before. Video, a full mass at Saint Francis Cathedral Basilica in Santa Fe, and tamales were three essentials Isabel insisted upon. She wore a handmade, lacy, white dress with a six-foot train. Joseph wore the tux he owned rather than rented, because every Vigil male owned one. Isabel placed the traditional bouquet of white roses at the feet of Blessed Mother's statue. In front of 180 guests, maximum seating allowance for the sit-down, formal dinner reception to follow at La Fonda, they spoke their vows twice, first in Spanish, then in English.

A mariachi band led them and all their guests out of the cathedral onto San Francisco Street, playing music as they walked the short block to the hotel for the reception in La Terraza Sala and garden patio. From there they could see the basilica, the Plaza, and the Sangre de Cristo mountains. Isabel's family was conservative. They served fruit punch instead of champagne. Alcohol was consumed clandestinely, in the restrooms and in the Bell Tower Bar. People stepped out for a bit of fresh air and returned ready to dance for hours with no one the wiser. For sure there were no crazy wooden barrels of grog. There had been no swords, either, though it struck Joseph as the perfect metaphor for his brief marriage.

Isabel could not get pregnant.

The tests showed nothing wrong with either of them. After mass every Sunday she asked the priest to bless her *útero. Nada.* Joseph was *mala suerte,* bad luck, her mother told her. Best to part now, before she grew too old to bear children. Isabel annulled their marriage on the grounds that as a practicing Catholic, Joseph had failed to "establish a community of life and love with another person."

She married in the same church six months after their official divorce was final and gave birth to twin boys the following year.

Joseph's cop friends and fellow crime-lab techs set him up with sisters or cousins, but he hadn't clicked with anyone, and to be fair, he hadn't really tried. After the shooting, he considered it divine intervention that he was alone at this time of his life because no woman deserved to go through this ordeal with him. Yes, it was a miracle that he could walk, that he was alive, but he was miles away from whole. That was part of why he was spending the winter here instead of in Albuquerque.

Not only was he was on permanent disability, but the lawsuit payout was so ridiculous that Joseph could comfortably live the rest of his life without working, if he chose to. He'd given himself six months to photograph those enormous trees. Maybe those two acorn-free summers had initially piqued his interest in trees, but he was also fascinated by the root systems they sank into the rockiest earth, and the way some could survive earthquakes, fires, and drought years, with so little water.

He organized the pirate-wedding photo thumbnails, culled, and ended up with five halfway decent shots for each segment of the wedding, and dozens of candid shots that captured the spirit of the party. The picture of the cake made him laugh. Vigil wedding cakes were about snowy white layers and silver-frosting bells and pale pink roses. The pirate ship cake had ambition. He pictured Glory Solomon with a library book on pirates in one hand and a spatula full of buttercream in the other, and still wearing that pissed-off look. He laughed again.

He downloaded the photos onto a disc and printed out the best one of the bride and groom to slide into the front of the empty CD jewel case. On the back of the case he used one of his tree shots, imposing the bride's and groom's names and the date over it, a touch he knew the couple would like. He e-mailed Glory Solomon:

Dear Ms. Solomon,

If I send the photos to you as attachments, it'll take all day to download, so I mailed you a CD. Let me know if there're any problems. Here's my cell number.

Regards,
Joseph Vigil

Okay, so he was sending the CD by snail mail because after the gun he didn't want to embarrass himself further, but her tree was another story. Of all the trees in California, he wanted particularly to photograph Solomon's Oak. Now that Grandma Penny was gone, and the cabin soon to follow, he wanted a last reminder of that tree and his summers.

On Thursday, Joseph woke to rain, made coffee, and sat down with a book. By eleven the rain turned into a torrential downpour. His grandmother had told him that pounding kind of rain was "male," according to the Navajo. All Joseph knew was that the damp made his bones ache even more, necessitating an early-morning pain pill. When he couldn't find a comfortable position sitting or standing, he lay down and shut his eyes, reliving the shooting that caused the aches he now had to find some way to live with.

He and Rico had met in a pre-law-enforcement class at the community college and discovered they were both on track for AA degrees in criminology. With the degrees in hand, they would work their way up to the better-paying jobs immediately. Both joined the force, finished training, and began as beat cops in Duke City. But where Rico thrived on dangerous circumstances, Joseph hated them. He worried he'd freeze at some critical moment, end up responsible for somebody's death, so when a technician position in the crime lab opened up, Joseph applied. Enamored of the nifty equipment for analysis of crime-scene findings, he found a use for his high school geometry, learned to foreshorten photographs and to do ID fingerprint recovery in the field. Rico and the guys gave him a ration for it:

"Buy a chemistry set to play with on weekends."

"You'd rather take orders than give them?"

"Less chances of meeting cute women."

"You'll have to turn in your gun."

Those things were true. The job turned out to be more of a science than the art he imagined, but there were always new tools and systems to learn, and the difference they made in conviction rates satisfied him. Three years later, Rico was promoted to detective, and while most detectives scorned lab workers outright, Joseph and Rico remained close.

They met for beer after work sometimes. On the weekends, Joseph went to Rico's kids' soccer games and family barbecues. Rico never let up trying to pry him out of his lab chair. "Come along on one of our busts. It's exciting. Nothing feels as good as cuffing some jackass and throwing him into the paddy wagon."

Joseph got up. His back pain nagged him so that he couldn't concentrate. He poured himself a cup of coffee, then noticed a trickle of rainwater seeping down the inside of the kitchen window. It wasn't worth fixing, but it would be nice if he had the option to. On the back porch was a stepladder. If he tried to carry it indoors, he would spend the rest of the day lying on a heating pad, popping pills. For a task other men could do one-handed.

The Oak Shore was so deserted this time of year that all it needed was a couple of wandering burros to qualify as a ghost town. At one time there had been trees in every direction, fir, oak, cottonwood. Clear-cutting had created three hundred acres for custom homes. Once Penny's cabin was bulldozed, entrance through the double gates to the area would require a punch code. Homeowner fees kept the landscape at a civilized distance.

Joseph had learned to swim in this lake. He had rocked in the green canvas hammock on the front porch while Grandma Penny sat on the steps shucking corn for their dinner. One of the three sisters was always present: corn, squash, or beans, often the creamy Santa Maria *pinquitos* she'd simmer for hours in her beloved micaceous-clay pot. They'd fold them into fresh tortillas and feast for days.

Grandma Penny collected rainwater in a barrel because why

waste such a precious resource? When a rainbow appeared, she reminded Joseph, "It's bad luck to point at a rainbow with your finger. Best to use your thumb, otherwise you might catch arthritis." She had her opinions on the birds, too. "That bluebird right there? Angry bird. Thinks it's a hawk."

Like Lorna at the general store, his grandmother wanted to know his life plans.

"What are your ambitions, Joseph?"

Stuntman. Pro basketball player. Race-car driver. Pilot. FBI agent.

"Yes, *nieto.* I know you can do this if you put your mind to it."

The cabin had no television, so every night he reread the books she'd given to him as a kid. From their mildewed pages he learned about the California Gold Rush, the migrant farmers, and the positive side of the Spanish missionaries, yet the book that burned within him was the tale of Ishi, the last California Indian living wild. One day, Ishi walked out of the forest and agreed to spend the rest of his life as an aboriginal artifact living in a museum exhibit people could visit. In his youth, Joseph thought that was beyond cool. Now it sickened him to think of any Native person living his life on what basically amounted to a stage set. But since the shooting, Joseph understood Ishi. In some situations all you could do was make a place for yourself and wait for time to pass.

"Without a job, a man is no better than a horse," Joseph's father had often told him during his growing-up years. "He might look handsome, but God gave us muscles to use, not admire." His father gathered piñon nuts the old-fashioned way, laying a tarp under the tree and climbing a ladder to strike the open cones to dislodge the nuts. He took his twenty-five-pound limit every week and parked his truck off the interstate and sold bags. He grew Hatch chiles and hauled his barrel-roaster-and-propane-torch contraption to Albuquerque to broil green chile to sell at the farmers' market.

"Fire up!" he'd call out as he lit the flame. The roaster tossed the chiles around like bingo numbers. "Chiles coming out!" he'd holler when the blackened chiles released their skins. He sold them in sandwich-size Baggies all the way to fifty-pound sacks. Driving anywhere in late summer or early fall, Joseph rolled down his window just to smell the smoky, spicy scent unique to his state.

His mother grew tomatoes and corn and tended her orchard of stone fruit. She braided chile *ristras* and sold them through a mail-order catalog. These days she needed a magnifying glass to braid neatly, and it took longer to make her quota. The last letter she'd sent to him made her feelings about the upcoming holidays clear.

Primo,

I am making and freezing tamales though my hands get numb after only an hour. If you were here, you could help me with the cornhusks. I forgot to dot the dessert tamales with food color, so I guess Christmas dinner will be a surprise. Your father and I wish we were all together to go to Mass, open presents, and enjoy visiting friends.

Love from your *madre*, who is *triste y solo.*

When the rain let up, Joseph washed out the cup and spoon, checked to make certain the propane was turned off, and put on his jacket. He drove to the post office, mailed the CD to Glory Solomon, then headed out toward the highway. To get to the city of Carmel, you drove Highway 68 to the two-lane Highway 1, which was always crowded from Salinas to Monterey, and finally arrived in Monterey, with the excellent aquarium and Fisher-man's Wharf. Today he bypassed the tourist attractions and headed to the doctor's office, where he had an appointment with an orthopedic specialist. The office was in the gallery-filled village of Carmel, known for its world-class golf course and expensive cottages.

Afterward, if the weather stayed dry, he'd drive south to the Big Sur redwoods.

"You need to get things looked at every three months, sooner if any of your symptoms worsen," the surgeon in Albuquerque had told him. The California doctor looked more like a surfer than a surgeon. Joseph sized him up. Maybe thirty-five, 160 pounds, caramel leather deck loafers with a Goodyear-tread sole. He had one of those sticking-up hairstyles that made him look as if he'd just woken up. On his way to the exam room, Joseph passed doors to X-ray machines and other equipment he couldn't identify. He lay down for the X-rays, which were digitally delivered to a flat-screen television monitor in the exam room.

The doctor took time out to shake his hand. "Nice to meet you, Mr. Vigil."

"Same here."

The young doctor frowned as he studied the films.

"Bad news?" Joseph asked.

"We should do an MRI. If you can come back this afternoon, we can do it today."

"That fast? Is there a life-and-death problem?"

The doctor chuckled. "Sorry. I didn't mean to alarm you. I have my own machine, and I like to get fresh films. Waiting around for CHOMP to get an opening just isn't practical. I'll give you some Valium intravenously, of course, and you'll need someone to drive you home. Can you call your wife?"

"No."

"Can you arrange to spend the night in town?"

Joseph sat back on the exam table. "I'm in the middle of a project. How about we do it after the first of the year?"

"I know your type," the doctor said.

"What type is that?"

"The type of man who thinks an MRI is a waste of time."

"Is it going to change how my back feels? Heal the broken parts?"

"No, it isn't."

"Then why do it?"

"With the MRI in hand, I can assess other avenues we might explore to manage your pain. There are new procedures every year."

It sounded to Joseph like "A cure for—insert disease here—is just around the corner."

"I've been wondering, how long will it take before I can get off the painkillers?"

"What's your discomfort level on a one-to-ten scale?"

It was a solid eight and a half and had not changed one iota since Joseph had left the hospital. "It's not totally immobilizing. Some days—" He stopped himself. "It's pretty bad sometimes. Especially when it rains."

"Common reaction." The doctor typed into his laptop computer before looking up. "Disturbed tissue takes a long time to mend, but that's only part of it. Cases like yours, I shoot from the hip. You okay with that?"

"I prefer it."

"All right, then. Barring a miracle, you're never going off the pills. I can't predict when, but you will likely build up a tolerance and eventually need to use a stronger medicine. Your liver's working overtime processing the pain medication, so avoid alcohol."

Joseph nodded. "I don't drink."

"Good. Okay if I examine you, give you your money's worth?"

Joseph sat still while the surgeon tapped on his back. It hurt, but it always hurt, so he didn't say anything.

When the surgeon was finished, he said, "Mr. Vigil, you must have been born on a lucky day. Most patients with your injury are in a sip-and-puff wheelchair for life. To say that your spine's compromised is putting it mildly. I'd say you're looking at least two more surgeries down the line."

"Terrific."

"Did your doctor in New Mexico not explain all this to you?"

"He did. This being California, top-rate doctors, I hoped you'd see things differently."

"Sorry I don't have better news for you." The doctor typed the prescription refill into the computer. "You can pick this up at the desk. It's schedule II, so it needs to be hand-carried to the pharmacy and accompanied by ID."

Joseph knew all this, so he said nothing.

"I've read the particulars of your accident. How are you doing emotionally?"

"Fine."

The doctor closed the computer and set it on the counter. "Mr. Vigil, may I be frank?"

"Sure."

"Survivor guilt is a bitch. I've seen patients trying to tough it out alone end up in the psych ward. You should see a therapist. I'll write you a referral for this great guy in Santa Cruz."

"Appreciate it." Joseph pulled the paper gown away and put his arms into his flannel shirt and buttoned it up.

The doctor walked out the door behind him. "Think about seeing the therapist."

"You bet."

As soon as he reached the parking lot, Joseph threw the business card into the trash can. He drove to the nearest drugstore to fill his prescription. The pharmacist himself came to the counter. "Picture ID, please."

Joseph showed him his New Mexico license with the red Zia on the yellow flag.

"You're from out of state?"

Joseph showed him the letter from his New Mexico doctor, the California doctor, and answered, "Yes, on an extended visit."

"This drug carries a high degree of addiction," the pharmacist said.

Suddenly it was all too much for Joseph to be explaining this every month. He turned his back on the pharmacist and pulled his shirt out of his jeans and bared his shoulders. Spinal disk C4-5, that had left the worst scar, twisting like a centipede from his neck to his shoulder blade. Below that, thoracolumbar 10 wasn't much prettier. "I'm not an addict."

"Of course you're not, sir. I apologize. We get so many people abusing this drug we have to be hypervigilant . . ."

As the man's voice trailed off, Joseph's hard feelings increased. Did they think he was too stupid to read the information sheets they stuffed in the bag with his pills? "I'll take this, too," he said, placing one of those nutritious meal bars on the counter. The clerk took his money and asked if he wanted the bar in another bag. "Not necessary." Then he said, "Thank you," because if he hadn't, his mother would have been ashamed of him.

He got into his car and sat in the parking lot while the blinding rain beat down like fists. The first bite of the nutrition bar tasted like dirt. So did the second. He ate it anyway. Then he leaned his head against the steering wheel and cried. This day was done. No way he was taking pictures of redwoods in a mood like this.

The following week it rained every day. Going stir-crazy in the leaky cabin, Joseph drove to the Woodpecker Café five miles north of the cabin in the town of Lockwood. They had fourteen red leatherette booths and six tables. Wagon-wheel light fixtures hung low over booths that were usually occupied by locals. Every time Joseph walked into the restaurant, it seemed as if the same five guys were having the same argument in the booth by the window. The café stayed open year-round and was near enough to the Mission San Antonio de Padua that customers included lost motorists.

Sixteen days from Christmas, though, and twenty miles from shopping, there were plenty of empty seats to choose from. The locals had checked Joseph out the first time he'd come into the restaurant and dismissed him as a fool who couldn't read a map. Each time he returned, though, a few more people nodded hello, especially women. He figured the Lorna Candelaria grapevine was responsible for that.

Single ladies take note: Divorced Latin male, owns a cabin on the lake (for a while, anyhow). Nice guy. Comes from good people. Has some money. Artistic. Check out the fancy camera.

He sat in a booth and opened the newspaper while he waited

to place his order. Page one: A Los Angeles school district let eighty teachers go. Senator Barbara Boxer advocated a new tax on businesses that polluted the environment. Magic Mountain theme park announced the opening of their sixteenth roller coaster. On page two, out of habit he checked the weather in Albuquerque, a surprisingly warm fifty degrees. He couldn't break the habit of reading missing-children stories and obituaries. How Rico lived with that day in and day out, Joseph did not know. The lab was bad enough. It killed him to ID bodily fluids on kids' clothing.

After an especially hairy case, Rico had confided in Joseph over a beer at the Zinc Bar. "Some nights I can't sleep. Their faces haunt me. You were smart, dude. Wish I had a job where I put in my hours and go home at the end of the day."

Joseph's department had no openings, and even if there were, Rico would take an enormous pay cut and need to go back to school to qualify. "You have seventeen years in," Joseph told him. "Retire and become something else."

"On a pension so small I can't support my dog? I might as well go work at Starbucks."

"I don't know what to tell you, man. Places like that have health insurance. What's the worst that could happen to you? Spill coffee on somebody?"

"When we make a major bust, the rush is incredible," Rico said. "If I transfer to another department, everyone will call me a wuss."

"Come on, Rico. Isn't that like the old saying 'Sticks and stones will break my bones, but names will never hurt me'?"

The conversation ended when Rico got a call. Two weeks later both Rico and Joseph ended up in an auto-salvage-yard crime scene south of Duke City. It turned out that the industrial building off SR 47 wasn't culling and selling usable car parts; it was meth lab central. Satellite labs were dotted throughout the city, in mobile homes advertising new housing developments. These weren't the work of gangs or wannabe gangsters, but of serious manufacturers dealing product, going after young people with potential and leading them to addiction. The warehouse lab was the brain that organized the moneymakers. It was typical to find assault weapons at the scene of a drug operation, and even bomb-making materials. Protocol was rigid and followed for good reason. CI had pronounced the warehouse clear an hour before Joseph arrived. Rico was celebrating the bust with his new partner, Isaac, and several other detectives who'd been involved. Joseph was on-site to record evidence with his Nikon D80, and the atmosphere was intense, like American Indian night at UNM when the Lobos were on a winning streak.

Somehow between all of them and the bomb squad, though, they had missed a guy hiding in a cupboard, and he had a gun.

"Afternoon, Katie Jay," Joseph said to the waitress, a natural blonde of average height in her twenties wearing a Christmas-tree pin next to her name tag. She was a sophomore at San Luis Obispo, studying environmental science, and always had a ready smile for Joseph.

She got out her order pad and pen. "Let me guess. BLT on rye with extra mayo?"

"Yes, please."

"Joseph," she said, filling his coffee cup, "you really ought to try something else on the menu. We have a great tri-tip on sourdough, chicken salad to die for, and the tuna melt's all those knuckleheads ever order." She pointed with her pen to the cattlemen squished five to the booth. "Do you think they ever work?"

Joseph laughed. "They're probably cattle barons. Someday I'll take you up on the menu recommendations."

"Just not today," she said, shaking her head.

"Nope. Today feels more like a BLT day."

The Woodpecker was for BLTs. The King City Truck Stop was for breakfasts, 24-7. Butterfly Creek was for turkey on sourdough and pizza. Chicken salad was for women.

"Coming up," she said, and took his order to the cook.

Joseph waited until she brought his sandwich before popping the cap on his pain meds. He shook out his lunchtime pill. If he took it now, he had thirty minutes before it kicked in, and he could be home by then. Outside the rain continued to pour.

Katie came by with the coffeepot again. "You got a headache today, Joseph?"

"Something like that. Thanks for asking."

She laid his check facedown next to the salt and pepper. "Have a good one. Stay dry if you can."

So much rain fell that December that the earth couldn't absorb it all. On his forays out for food, Joseph watched roads flood that had been bone-dry when he arrived. One morning he woke up and decided the heck with waiting for nice weather. He'd make the rain work for him. A single drop of water pooled on a leaf created a second camera lens, a natural magnifying glass. Veins, pores, pigment, and stem sharpened to hair-thin detail played a trick on the eye. A leaf, or abstract art? Set the shutter speed down to one eighth, depress and pan left to right over wet leaves, and the result was motion and color so complex that it would have taken an artist's paintbrush to reproduce it.

Chapter 5

Rain followed Joseph down Highway 1 toward Big Sur. Between the sheer cliffs and narrow road, he tensed his hands on the steering wheel. He drove directly to Julia Pfeiffer State Park, parked in the visitors' lot near the lodge, and began walking, his windbreaker hood over his head and his camera cloaked in its own raincoat. Signs indicated trails in every direction, the river, the beach, lookout points, the waterfall, and the groves. Back the other way was the albino redwood he didn't want to miss. He opted for the canyon trail marked EASY, ONE-QUARTER MILE, GENTLY ASCENDING PATH TO THE FALLS because it was lined with towering, cinnamon-colored redwoods. Underfoot, the rain matted the thick forest duff, making his steps springy. Green ferns, bent by the rain, lined the trail. He planted his feet carefully and kept track of his time so he didn't get caught in a deluge when he drove the coast highway on his return home. When he crossed the footbridge, the noise of the waterfall was deafening. He leaned against the handrail, waiting for the strain in his back to pass, and studied the trees.

His grandmother had taken him here several times. They'd stood on an earlier version of this bridge to look at the towering giants. She pointed out "goose pens," openings at the base of a redwood where fire had hollowed out the trunk, but the tree continued growing. Some of them were five feet across. "A long time ago," she told him, "settlers housed their livestock in those pens. A few cows, goats, and geese. I heard a story that a hermit made his home in a pen so big he had three stories, a woodstove with a chimney, and a front door."

"Was he a kid, like me?" Joseph asked.

"No, he was an average grown-up man."

"Didn't his family miss him?"

Grandmother Penny laughed. "Maybe so. You know, Joseph, even with all their college degrees, scientists don't know what causes the cones to release their tiny seeds. But I know the secret."

Anything mysterious had Joseph's name on it. "Tell me," he said.

She took his hand and they went off the cut trail to stand beneath one of the giants. Grandmother placed her hand on the tree's spongy bark and began to sing a wordless song he knew he'd never be able to repeat, so he listened with his whole heart. When she finished, she smiled down at him.

"The tree can tell from a woman's song that it's a time to let the seeds go."

Joseph hoped to hike until he reached the falls. He wanted silvery water traveling ninety miles an hour to spray his face and jacket, but he couldn't make it to the top. He took pictures of trees growing horizontally out of the rocks before he started down. On the way back to his car, he photographed smaller redwoods growing in a circle surrounding a single large tree. They reminded him of Pueblo storyteller dolls, children circling a grandmother. Between the dripping rain, forest scents, and the age of the redwoods, he felt as if he were standing in a cathedral.

A Steller's jay broke the silence with his scolding. After that, he heard the trill of a winter wren and watched a six-inch yellow banana slug cross his path. He took a picture and tried to imagine the sense of touch in the creature as it rolled its body over the forest floor. From the parking-lot turnaround, he saw the Big Sur River thrashing its way through boulders the size of Volkswagens.

He drove to the Fernwood Campground down to the Old School House to photograph the albino redwood. The twelve-foot tree depended on a host redwood for survival. He knew the scientific reasons behind it—it didn't process chlorophyll—but the longer he stood there, the more it seemed like an unhappy ghost, so he returned to his car.

Because that dreadful nutrition bar was a memory now, he stopped at the Big Sur Bakery before heading home up Highway 1 to buy a Danish and coffee for the long drive home. He tried not to stare, but the woman at the counter had long, silver hair like Glory Solomon. He had no intention of cashing that check she sent him. It was only a couple dozen pictures, paid for with the leftovers. Cut, dried, connection ended. But as he drove up the highway, finished with the redwoods, her oak tree was on his mind. With luck, she had a day job that left the place deserted for a few hours while the daughter was at school. He could pop in, take pictures, pop out, and no one would be the wiser.

A minor mudslide across the highway forced Joseph to keep his speed at twenty-five miles per hour. At this rate, he'd arrive home well after dark. It had been hours since his last pain pill, and if there was ever a reason not to take one, driving in these conditions was it. Joseph wadded up his jacket and stuck it in the small of his back up against the seat. When after a few miles he came to the backed-up traffic jam before the Bixby Creek Bridge, he wondered if there'd been a car accident. The two-lane road had been no problem on the drive down. After five minutes and no movement, Joseph turned his engine off. The car behind him pulled a U-turn and headed south, toward San Simeon. Since there was no radio reception, Joseph waited, feeling sorry for the Department of Transportation worker standing out there next to such a sheer drop on this cold day. The trademark fog was rolling in. It started to rain, making it difficult for drivers to see each other, let alone the DOT worker's fluorescent vest, sign, or the orange traffic cones set in the lane. While Joseph waited, he thought of how Rico often used his detective status to get out of traffic jams on Menaul Boulevard. The guy loved taking chances.

During Joseph's brief time on the force, he ticketed dozens of drunk drivers every week. But no amount of fines, suspended licenses, or DWI blitzes stopped them. Every year some fool drove drunk the wrong way on the highway and took out an innocent family, a carful of teenagers, or an elderly woman minding her own business. Those wrecks stayed in his mind, adding up.

When Rico was assigned to the Exploited Children division and, later, Missing Persons, he was so hopped up on adrenaline that at times he seemed manic. "This is it," he told Joseph, "the most important kind of police work there is. Dude, come back to the force."

Was Joseph a coward for keeping his distance from all that ugliness? He told Rico, "If it wasn't for us microscope jockeys, you wouldn't have the necessary evidence to convict those *cabrones*."

When Rico went to Missing Persons, he confided, "I'm not sleeping much. Fidela and the boys don't know, but some nights, after they're asleep, I walk the dog a couple miles to tire myself out."

Even when the odds were against the detectives, the work was addicting. You mainlined stress. Solving cases depended on timing, paying attention to inventory, and things could change in a second. A hiker finds a missing person's necklace and provides a grid to search. A construction site comes to a halt with the discovery of a single human rib bone.

The DNA identifications Joseph performed allowed detectives to close cold files open for decades. To narrow the age of a human bone to within ten years, prove the gender of even a partial skeleton, gave detectives a better chance of identification. Joseph's work was nothing like that television series with the ridiculously dim set. The techs wore polo shirts and lab coats, not skintight T-shirts cut to reveal six-packs or movie-star cleavage. Most of them were underpaid working stiffs with more tasks to do than a day allowed. DNA results took months, not moments.

Missing Persons located wandering elderly people and guided them home. Runaway teenagers turned up. But when a child went missing, no matter which division you worked, everyone hustled, because there were two golden time frames, two chances for a positive outcome.

The "golden hour" was the optimum time allotted to find a missing child alive—sixty swiftly ticking minutes. She could be at the neighbor's without permission, at the school playground dawdling on the swings, or hiding from her parents in a closet while they hollered themselves hoarse so she could punish them for denying her cookies before dinner or the all-essential cell phone. The "golden day" was the block of twenty-four hours during which the Amber Alert went into effect, and organized searchers might be able to find the body of the missing child. It was imperative that family stay by the phone because there might be a call, either from someone with knowledge or rarely, but it did happen, the child herself. But family wanted to post flyers, make pleas on television, offer rewards; basically do anything other than sit there waiting for the inevitable, and who could blame them? Yet the worst was actually a positive outcome because finding the body at least provided the family closure. A body had a face to kiss good-bye. Having a body to place in a grave was ecstasy compared to wondering the rest of your life. Could she be alive? Was she cold, hungry, afraid, injured, lost? Rationalizations took over logic. She was a tough kid and could survive just about anything. They'd recover as a family. If it was a one-in-a-million chance that she'd return, that meant it had happened once; therefore it could happen to them, too. Whatever horrible experiences she'd had could be a turning point, not an end.

Rico told him, "There's nothing worse than delivering the news."

Joseph watched Rico's career take its toll on his face. His friend had switched from beer to whiskey shots. "How much weight have you lost? You're starting to look haunted. If it's this hard on you, I bet it's affecting your kids and Fidela."

"Their little bodies," Rico said. "It's like they're saying, 'Why didn't you find me sooner, before he did this to me?' "

"You're human, Rico. A person can only take so much before he has to look away. Maybe it's time to ask for a transfer."

Albuquerque was laid out like a Scottish-clan plaid, busy streets crossing each other, pausing to erupt in strip malls and newly gentrified neighborhoods such as Nob Hill, where old storefronts were going condo. The city had turned into a business hub, not just because of the new hospitals or the undeveloped land or even the arts for which the state was famous. Casinos were the draw. Tourism went steadily up. Chain hotels quickly moved in, Doubletree, Marriott, and the Hilton. But look up and the blue sky still went on forever. Every day, cloud formations called up Peter Hurd's paintings. From Bosque del Apache's annual bird migration to the Bandelier ruins to the sold-out, tendays-long balloon fiesta, the state had as much beauty as it did grittiness.

One of New Mexico's abundant natural resources was the year-round wind that traveled at face height filled with grit and prairie dust. The wind covered tracks, ruined crime scenes, and scratched camera lenses. It made winter colder. In spring, it tossed juniper pollen like confetti and provoked bad behavior in a city full of allergy sufferers. Recovering alcoholics fell off the wagon. Rehabilitated burglars found other people's wide-screen televisions and iPods irresistible. Auto smash-and-grabs tripled. Graduates of anger-management class relapsed and domestic calls rocketed. Registered sex offenders kept a lookout for the solitary kid taking a shortcut, and though such acts were unacceptable in every way, to work in law enforcement you had to be realistic. Rico Torres had never broken down on a crime scene that Joseph knew of. He could not say the same for himself. Their business had plenty of happy endings, but the losses were devastating.

Suddenly the cars in front of Joseph began to make U-turns, heading south. When Joseph reached the orange cones, he saw why. Just over the bridge Jack Kerouac had made famous, and around a steep curve, a quarter of the highway had tumbled down the cliffside into the ocean.

When he reached the DOT worker, he said, "What happened?"

"Same thing that happens every year," the man in the fluorescent vest said. "Too many vehicles on a road that wasn't designed for heavy traffic. Rain plus hillside equals landslide equals road closure. You'll have to turn around and go the other way."

"But I'm trying to get back to Jolon."

"Look for the turnoff to G18. It's kind of a twisty road. Dumps you out near the mission. Go slowly and you'll be fine."

Joseph stopped in Big Sur to gas up. Finding some minute area of coverage, his cell phone bleated. While he filled his car, he listened to the voice mail from Lorna Candelaria, inviting him to the upcoming Christmas party at the store. "I won't take no for an answer," she said, and coughed. "I know where you live, buster," she said when the coughing fit ended. "It's potluck, so bring something, even if it's just crackers."

WINTER HOLIDAYS
ENGLISH 100
BY JUNIPER McGUIRE

   December twenty-first is Winter Solstice, the shortest day of
the year. On Solstice, the Earth's tilt decides how much sun
we'll get. Various cultures across the world celebrate Solstice
with songs, poetry, and religion. So it's easy to see where
Christmas came from. Even in the years before Christ was
born, or before there were trade routes or even the wheel,
people marked the day when the season turned to winter.
   Why is because when the sun set so early farmers couldn't
grow crops or feed animals, and people and animals starved. So
they would have done anything to lure the sun back. Once
people figured out that they could plan ahead and save enough
food by paying attention to the calendar, Solstice became a
reason to par-tay. The shaman or chief or priest decided that day
was for praying, drinking alcohol, reciting stories, dancing, and
sacrificing animals (total genius move for hungry people if you
ask me) and the best way to make the sun feel welcome. Like the
sun cares? The sun is a dying star! In five billion years it will turn

into a red giant triggering stellar winds and sucking Earth into its core and then it will go white dwarf, and who knows after that because we won't be here, duh. Solstice? Probably enough people believed that if they didn't throw the party, then the sun would get all offended and shine on some other planet.

Juniper—while I applaud your idea here, this is not a freshman-level essay. What exactly is your thesis statement? Your diction is uneven. Surely there is more to say about the Christmas season than two paragraphs! Regarding the "scientific" information included, there are more effective sources than the Internet. C+

Chapter 6

GLORY

On Friday, December 19, Glory sat in a psychologist's office for the first time in her life. A couple of their foster sons had needed counseling. Glory drove them and sat in the waiting room. Whatever went on behind the closed door had been between the therapist and the boy. This was the first time Glory had been invited into the inner sanctum, and frankly, she missed her weekly dose of *People* magazine. It was nothing like what she'd imagined—no hypnosis, no ink blots, no lying on a couch free-associating. No. It was three people trying to force each other to say things they did not want to say. For every minute that ticked by without a solution, Glory felt worse.

"This is about telling the truth, not punishment," Lois Anthony, MFCC, explained for the fourth time since the counseling session had begun. Glory had called her ahead of time to fill her in on Juniper's lies and the petty theft. Ms. Anthony was a red-head with the kind of freckles that from far away made her look tan. Up close, Glory had never seen so many all in one place. If she could count how many there were on the woman's right cheek, she might be able to leave the office feeling as if the three of them had accomplished something instead of circling the same subject for forty-five minutes of their state-paid hour.

"Your mom wants to work with you on this," Ms. Anthony said. "Can you try to meet her halfway?"

Mom—was it a mistake to let her call her that? Three weeks ago, Juniper was suspended, and in her three days at home, she had again and again said how grateful she was to Glory for not sending her back to the group home. "I love it here," Juniper said. "I love the animals and I love you, too, Mom. Is it okay if I call you Mom?"

What could Glory say besides yes? The foster boys called her that, and they called Dan "Dad." It touched Glory's heart. She thought it meant things were going well. Maybe in some alternate universe they were, but here on earth, Glory knew things were not going well. She had no idea how to fix the situation. Juniper's behavior was like a virus. Glory's attempts to steer her back to the right path were like antibiotics. As soon as she found a medication that worked, the virus mutated into something else.

Juniper continued braiding the fringe on a throw pillow. They sat a foot apart from each other on the couch, but Juniper leaned so far away from Glory that an ocean might as well have been between them.

"Time to put that pillow down," Lois said. "Your mother has something to tell you. Glory?"

"I'd like to talk about the Percocet," Glory said, and waited.

She was going for shock on Lois's advice. Even though she'd found the missing bottle, all six pills accounted for, she hadn't confronted Juniper until this moment. Juniper was turning out to be such an accomplished liar that Glory wanted to call Monica Phelps and apologize for doubting her description of the fight.

Instead, she enlisted Lois's help, hoping that with nowhere to hide, the girl would confess. Then Lois could take over, guide them to the truth, and change things for the better from this moment on.

Silence.

"Glory," Lois said, "why don't you tell me how this all came about."

"I was on a dusting rampage." When faced with not enough money coming in during the holiday season, Glory cleaned house. She batted cobwebs out of corners and carried spiders out to the barn. "I took the shades off lamps and dusted the lightbulbs. I picked up the lamp in Juniper's room to dust underneath and that's when I found it."

"Found what?" Lois prompted.

"My missing bottle of Percocet. Wrapped inside a tissue. Under Juniper's desk lamp. A long time ago the bottom came off the lamp, so it's hollow inside."

Which meant Juniper had probably stolen the bottle the first day she came to Solomon's Oak, and knowing that she'd had it all along just shredded Glory's heart.

"Juniper, every story has two sides," Lois said. "What do you have to say for yourself?"

Juniper looked up from the pillow. As she always did when Glory caught her in a lie, she blushed and went stony. "Drop me off at the Monterey detention center."

Lois didn't flinch. "Were you planning to take the pills so you could get high?"

"Of course not."

"Good. The medicine was prescribed for your mom, not you. Not only is that dangerous, it's substance abuse, kiddo. I'm supposed to report it to the county."

"What if I don't know how it got there?"

"What if I don't believe you?" Glory said.

"What if I don't want to talk about it anymore? Is this session over? If not, I'd like a bathroom break."

"You can wait five minutes for the bathroom," Lois said, looking at her clock. "What else, Mom?"

Glory sighed. How had Dan decided what was important and what was trivial? Did she start with the cash on her dresser being $40 short the day she sent Juniper in to check Edsel's water dish? The broken cereal bowl—a chipped piece of Franciscan pottery, you could find one just like it at a thrift store—that Juniper had hidden in her dresser rather than just throw out in the trash? Why hide it? No matter what Glory found or said, Juniper had "no idea" how it had happened. Glory had lost it. "You're telling me that a broken cereal bowl walked out of the kitchen, made its way down the hall, opened the door to your room, opened your dresser, and then wrapped itself in your black T-shirt?"

"Maybe."

"If you won't talk about the Percocet, then let's talk about the money you took off my dresser," Glory said.

Juniper jumped up from the couch and flung the pillow to the floor. "It's not my fault I'm this *damaged*," she screamed. "This *proves* you hate me, just like every other foster parent in the world. Fine, then. Call Caroline and tell her to come get me. Then you can go back to your regular life and your stupid dishes." Juniper picked up the pillow again, sat down, and hugged it to her chest.

How one girl could create such drama was mind-boggling. "Four years from now you'll be eighteen," Glory said. "Do you want to go to jail over six stupid pills or forty dollars? I never said I wanted to send you away. I just want us to get through this and move past it. I want you to learn to tell the truth."

Silence.

"Juniper, go on to the restroom," Lois said. "Your mom will meet you in the waiting room. We won't be long."

Juniper was out the door so fast her hair whipped behind her.

"She has all the hallmarks of a liar, Lois. Constant face touching, changing the subject, a tonal shift in voice, high-pitched and defensive, overt attempts at humor dripping with sarcasm."

Lois chuckled. "Darn that Internet."

"What's so funny? Do you think I'm making this up?"

"I think you're a concerned parent who's trying her best. Glory, forget what you've read online. This is not as bad as you think. She's trying to figure out who she is. That simply comes with being a teenager. Remember, in addition to hormones, she's experienced monstrous losses. It's not surprising that she takes things. Creating a stash probably makes her feel secure. Look at what she's taken. Painkillers. Money. Maybe she thinks she'd better prepare for the day all this stability comes crashing down on her like it has in the past, so when she's back on the streets, she's got provisions."

"How does a broken cereal bowl fit into that scenario?"

"It's part of a set, right? She probably thought it was worth a lot of money. She's used to guardians caring more for their personal property than her. But consider this. Notice she didn't ingest the pills or spend the money. She stockpiled everything. Like a raven decorates his nest. Ravens are smarter than people give them credit for."

"Well, bully for ravens. I still don't see how this applies to Juniper."

"She's using denial as a tool, so she can feel powerful. This week, be casual. Don't pretend the money wasn't taken. We all know it was. If you want to take things away as a consequence, make sure you give the period a finite, fair time frame. Go about your normal week and give her extra chores. Let her live with her actions for a while. Let her make up fables. Sooner or later, she'll be caught in a lie and humiliate herself. Embarrassment can be a powerful motivator for change."

INCLUDING YOUR FOSTER CHILD IN HOLIDAY TRADITIONS!

ENGLISH 100

EXTRA CREDIT

BY JUNIPER McGUIRE

Too often foster parents expect the foster child will
automatically feel the same joy that they do about Christmas.
Shrinks say that a foster child's stress "expresses itself in
swearing, striking out, crying jags, isolating, and even stealing."

People! Do you really think all it takes is a couple of candy
canes, ornaments, and a plastic Nativity scene to make your
Christmas feel like the kid's Christmas? Look, the kid is
trying. Christmas isn't some game like Monopoly where you
stand a chance of winning if you follow the rules, though. The
foster parents think, "What is wrong with her? Doesn't she
appreciate all the trouble we've gone to with the tree, lights, and
the stockings?" They introduce her to their relatives and say,
"It's Juniper's first Christmas with us!" and everyone is
thinking, "The poor thing. Did you hear what her biological
parents did to her? Honestly, some people should have to get a
license to reproduce. How can she miss her family when we are

taking so much better care of her? She has a bed, three meals a day, nice clothes, and we let her watch our big screen TV. Now it's Christmas and all we want is a nice holiday and she is off crying for no good reason."

It's like telling the Indians to be grateful for reservations.

Ask the child about her past Christmases. Don't worry, she isn't going to tell you the story of how her mom got drunk before breakfast or her dad smacked her when she woke him up to give him the tie or shaving cream or wallet for Christmas because what else do you get a dad?

She wants to remember the good stuff, and the tradition of putting an orange into her gym sock because that meant Christmas once and it still could if you'd let it. She could be afraid that if she tells you it will make her sound like white trash. She might not know the Jesus and Wise Men story and to her frankincense sounds like the name of a really bad rash.

Ask her what her favorite Christmas song is and if it's the one of the dogs barking "Jingle Bells," then would it kill you to play it a couple of times?

Also, the kid might not know how to say thank you for an iPod or a bubble bath assortment because when she leaves your home for another one they might not let her take that with her. Usually they take it away because if the other kids don't have it they could get in fights.

If you ask a shrink they will say by age seven a child knows 90% of the coping skills that will get her through life. A foster kid just wants things to feel stable.

1. Don't get in fights with your extended family.
2. Don't get all hammered on alcohol.

3. Don't let people ask questions like "What happened to
   her?" because the kid already feels like a bug with a pin
   stuck in it, waving her arms and legs and going
   nowhere.

Psychologists like to use analogies instead of just saying things
straight out, like "When you go to plant your garden don't drop
in a kernel of corn and expect roses to come up." Now I'm not
saying every foster kid is corn but sometimes when you get all
ready for corn it might not come up either. You just have to
wait and see what grows.

*Juniper—I can see the effort you put into this essay, but you missed the
deadline I gave for makeup work by two days. No credit allowed. Grade
for the semester: C-. Happy Holidays!*

A Winter Solstice Wedding
Lily Grant/Chris Reston
December 21st, 2003
5:00 P.M.

Menu

Champagne
Mulled cider
Roast beef with Yorkshire pudding
Twice-baked potato casserole
Roasted baby carrots, haricots verts, *pearl onions*
Cranberry/orange gelato
Snowflake sugar cookies
Fondant poinsettia red-velvet cake

Glory was on her sixtieth fondant poinsettia flower—ten more than she needed, but she was on a roll—when she straightened up and felt the sharp zing in her lower back from leaning over for so long. It made her think of Joseph Vigil, his limp, and that he still hadn't cashed the check she'd sent him. She meant to call him to find out why, but as busy as she was preparing for the solstice wedding, he was at the bottom of her list. Juniper had created an online album of his pirate-wedding photos. Thanks to her computer skills, Solomon's Oak's Web site now had a My-Space page that was racking up fans. Best of all, they had a wedding set for April, a plein air painters' gourmet luncheon in May, and they were tentatively booked up for June, with a wedding every weekend, and two more pending for August. Even with the money Glory had spent on the color brochures, after Christmas she could quit Target, unless her money continued to disappear. Juniper had returned a twenty—found it in the laundry—but another was still missing.

Glory went out the back door to find her. Today's chores involved mucking stalls, grooming both horses, and scrubbing the dog kennels out with disinfectant. Tomorrow morning, they'd dress the tables for the sit-down reception in the barn. In the chilly air Glory saw the hose running on the cement kennel floor. Cricket was tied to the post and half-groomed. The manure pile was composting, which meant it hadn't been raked. Meanwhile, Juniper was teaching Cadillac to leap through her outstretched arms while throwing the ball for Dodge. From a distance, they made a family portrait. How could Glory scold a teenager who looked this happy?

"Hey," she called. "Looks like you're having a lot of success there."

Juniper grinned. "Cadillac's so smart."

"You bring out the best in him. Could you turn off the hose, finish the horse, and let the dogs in, please? I need help with the cake."

"Okay," Juniper said, as if things were perfectly fine, and Glory marveled at how quickly her mood shifted. Hormones, as Lois said? Or was this more of her act and Glory had yet to find out what she was covering up?

Fifteen minutes later, she heard the dogs scrabbling over the floor racing into the living room, where a nice fire was going. Juniper washed her hands and dried them. "What do you want me to do?"

"Put on an apron, and then let's assemble the layers," Glory said, handing Juniper the spatula of buttercream icing. The first cake layer was on the glass pedestal. "Put down an inch of icing at least," Glory said. "We don't want this cake going anywhere."

"Except into the guests' mouths."

"Right."

They carefully peeled away the parchment and stacked the other four fondant-covered layers atop the first one. They were each slightly off center, which gave the cake a kind of whimsy, which the bride had requested. "Chris and I are a little quirky," Lily had informed Glory over the phone.

Juniper stood back. "That looks weird."

"Once we put the poinsettias on, it will be beautiful. Come on. You put down the red ones."

Juniper set down the spatula. "How do I know where they're supposed to go? You should do this part. Can I go do my homework now?"

"Don't give up before you've tried. You can do it. Look at my drawing." Glory pushed the paper across the counter to Juniper. "It's a cake, is all, not rocket science."

"I'd rather not, Mrs. Solomon."

Glory sighed. Since the therapist visit, whenever Juniper was angry or felt that she wasn't getting her way, she called her Mrs. Solomon instead of Glory or Mom. Glory was determined not to react, but sometimes it stung. "Okay, I'll do it." Juniper sat down at the kitchen table and opened her math book. She was good at the homework part, but did poorly on the tests. Glory thought Juniper might have "test anxiety." While she worked numbers out on ruled paper, Glory affixed the red and green fondant petals/leaves and, after the berries were secure, finished the cake by dusting it with a coppery, edible luster-dust product she'd found online.

"What do you think, Juniper?" Glory said, turning the cake to slide it into the box.

Juniper glanced at the cake. "It's not a pirate ship, if that's what you're getting at."

"They can't all be pirate ships."

"Weddings are for chumps."

"Paying chumps," Glory reminded her.

"Whatever."

Now would be the perfect time for a Percocet, Glory thought. Where were they? Locked up in Dan's tackle box out in his also-locked workshop. It wasn't worth the effort right now. Maybe after the wedding tomorrow. She put the cake into the cooler and pressed her hand against the glass, thinking of the hours spent on the cake versus what she charged. It was never enough.

"Juniper?"

She sighed. "For the jillionth time, I *didn't* steal the money."

"How did you know I was going to ask about that?"

"Because you get that look on your face like you just ate prunes."

It was true. Juniper stuck to the story that she'd found the money in the clothes to be folded, specifically the jeans load of laundry. For some reason, Glory could not let it go.

"How many times do I have to tell you? It was on the floor. I picked it up and absentmindedly stuck it in my pocket to give back to you, and then I forgot about it. Call me when you're ready to take me to the library. I need that copy of *Tess of the d'Urbervilles.*"

With that, Juniper retreated to her room, Cadillac following behind. Dodge got up, then decided he was fine by the fire and lay back down. Glory supposed some parents would take away the dog as punishment, think that was the way to make an impression.

Not her. Caddy was Juniper's constant companion. Glory didn't want to tear her room apart like some pulp detective character each week, so she'd given the responsibility of cleaning it over to Juniper. The thing she couldn't let go of was that twenty still missing. In her budget, $20 meant buying enough dog food, or paying the truck insurance. She tidied up the kitchen to make the rest of the reception food, but before she started cooking, she went to Juniper's room and knocked on the door.

"Library?" she said, looking up from her desk.

"Stand up and turn out your pockets."

Juniper stood up and did as she was told. The paler denim lining of her jeans pocket exposed a crumpled twenty that fell to the floor. "Oh, my gosh," she said in a monotone. "Will you look at that. It must have gotten stuck way down in my pocket. Here you go. Twenty effing dollars." She bent down, picked it up, and handed it to Glory. "Wow, *Tess of the d'Urbervilles*—and what kind of name is that?—sure had a sick life. She worked crappy jobs, got raped and pregnant, and then the baby died! She loved this guy named Angel, but he couldn't forgive her for having the baby, so he hauled ass to Brazil or Colombia like she was ruined for him forever. *Then* he decides to forgive her, but by then she'd married the rapist guy, so she kills him for true love and Tess and Angel go on the run and at Stonehenge the police catch her, and before she gets executed she makes Angel promise to marry her sister. Then she dies! What is the point? Love makes people make the stupidest choices. I'm so not getting married. Not ever. I don't care who the guy is, it's just not worth it."

Glory rubbed the wrinkled twenty, so thin it *could* have gone through the washer and dryer. She'd need CSI to prove otherwise. What else could she do but let it go? The theft had changed everything. She took her purse with her even when she took a shower.

"How can you know anything about the book yet? You haven't even read it."

"I went online and read the reviews. If I know the high points ahead of time, it's easier to read books from the olden days."

"Olden days? It was written in the 1890s."

"Over a hundred years ago!"

"Doesn't knowing the ending spoil the surprise?"

"It's not like I'm reading it for fun. I just want a good grade. That English teacher hates me. Did you know there were seven movies made about Tess? Except the 1913 version doesn't exist anymore because the film rotted. It starred Minnie Maddern Fiske. No wonder no one remembers her. If that was your movie-star name, wouldn't you change it?"

"Thank you for returning the money."

Juniper blushed furiously and began scribbling on her notebook paper. "I did the self-test on my math chapter and got a hundred percent," she said without looking up. "Now if I can just do that in class. Algebra's all about memorizing. How does that help you in real life? Or is it just something they do to make students torque their brains?"

"That's enough homework for today," Glory said. "Let's go ride the horses before it starts raining."

"What about my book?"

"The library's open until eight."

"What about Cadillac? Can he come, too?" The border collie looked up at Glory. He'd gone from an outside-only dog to the buddy of a girl whose moods swung like jungle vines. His other activities included herding Edsel down the hallway when the opportunity arose, and nipping at Dodge when he didn't follow directions. Glory thought of all those homes she'd tried Caddy in and still couldn't believe that he'd belonged here all along. He was a buffer between them and didn't mind being "the DMZ." When each had a hand on the dog, it was easy to talk, to laugh even.

"Both big dogs are coming on the ride. It's too cold for Edsel. Why don't you find some boots and start tacking the horses. I'll meet you out by the barn in a few minutes. I have to phone the florist to confirm tomorrow's delivery."

Glory had already made the dough for the cookies. Tonight she'd bake them and do the prep for tomorrow. An evening wedding with only thirty guests meant that she only needed two servers, so she'd called Robynn instead of Gary or Pete. Juniper relaxed around Robynn, but Gary and Pete made her nervous. In the kitchen she called Beryl Stokes at DeThomas Farms, whose wholesale poinsettia sales in Carmel Valley were legendary. In five short years, Phoebe DeThomas, niece to the late master gardener Sarah DeThomas, had taken a defunct farm and brought it back to life. In addition to the Sarah's Legacy poinsettia strain, the all-women-run farm had perfected a creamy ivory-green named Juan's Spirit. By candlelight, it glowed. The minute the bride told Glory how big the flower budget was, she'd called DeThomas Farms. The phone rang twice before Beryl answered.

"Glory!" she said. "Caller ID has dissolved our anonymity forever. How are you doing?"

"I'm fine, how are you?" she said, thinking no one ever asks that question and wants to hear the truth.

"Can't complain. We make the bulk of our money on poinsettias, so this is our best time of year. I have your flowers ready. I'm just finishing up the bridal bouquets. They came out beautifully. I hope you'll post a link to us on your Web site and we'll do the same for you. I have about an hour's work left. I'll drive over tomorrow morning if that works for you."

Though they only knew each other through mutual friends,

Beryl had sent Glory a note after Dan's death, with a print of the rows of flowers at DeThomas Farms. Glory kept it on the windowsill because every time she looked at the hollyhocks, bachelor's buttons, and the mammoth sunflowers, she was reminded of the multitude of colors there were in the world. If not here, somewhere in the world a woman was looking at flowers that distracted her from life's struggles for a moment. Inside it read, "If you ever need to talk," and Beryl had printed her number below.

"That will work just fine."

"Excellent. See you then. Happy holidays."

After Beryl hung up, Glory took a breath and blew it out slowly. Twenty lousy dollars and she'd forced the girl just like a prison guard. Just do the next thing, she told herself. Don't think about anything but this minute. Fetching her boots from the closet, she bumped against the box of Dan's things. It had been a month since she tried to pack it, but she still couldn't let go. She slid into her boots, pulled on a barn coat, and went outside. Both horses were saddled. She checked Piper's cinch and loosened it two holes. "Hey, muscles," she called to Juniper. "If you can slide two fingers under the strap, it's perfect. If you can't, you're bruising his ribs."

Juniper's shoulders sagged. "Did I hurt him? Should we call the vet?"

"Piper's fine. Just be gentle. Treat them like you want people to treat you."

"Buy him Red Vines licorice and a cell phone and an iPod and stop accusing him of stealing?"

Do not take the bait, Glory told herself. "Very funny. If you have any horse-related questions, ask."

The Solomon horses had taught many a foster boy that

practicing kindness, calmness, and thinking from the horse's point of view made the world an easier place to understand. In the short time they'd been together, Glory thought that was happening with Juniper, but now that she knew Juniper was lying, she wasn't sure. She figured time with the animals was the best thing for Juniper, so Glory had her ride and groom the horses daily.

She boosted her onto Cricket, then used the fence rail to pull herself onto Piper's spotted back. He nickered a little as her feet found the stirrups and his muscles tensed. He loved going into the oak forest and could somehow tell that was where they were headed. Glory scratched his neck and smelled salt, earth, and sweet hay breath—if only she could bottle that. The dogs were already waiting by the honeysuckle-covered gate. If you didn't know where to look, it was hard to find the latch. Glory missed on her first try, leaning down from Piper so low she nearly fell off. Before she could balance herself for a second try, Cricket nosed in and opened the latch.

"Whoa," Juniper said. "How did you train her to do that?"

"I didn't," Glory said, "but that explains the times the horses have gotten out. We'd better install another latch at the bottom of the gate."

"Horses rule."

"Not if they get hit by a car. Remind me when we get home so I don't forget."

They kept the horses at a walk until they crossed the county road. Then it was down an incline into a usually dry arroyo that this year ran with a few inches of water. "Keep hold of Cricket's reins," Glory warned. "She's a mudpuppy."

"What's that?"

"She likes to roll in it, just like a pig. I don't want you falling or getting mashed."

"Really, Mrs. Solomon? I didn't know you cared."

"Oh, I don't care. I took you in so I could have a smart-aleck slave. As soon as we get back home, there's a generous supper of stale bread and water waiting for you."

"Har de har, har. Next thing you'll tell me is Justin Timberlake called to see if I was free this weekend."

Glory let her have the last word. "We can trot now."

"We're not going to gallop, though, right?"

"Not now, but someday."

"Nope. Not ever."

Juniper was terrified of the lope, the gait most riders adored. After a ten-minute trot, Juniper clutching the saddle horn the entire time, they reached the grand valley oak stand, a place so thick with trees that the horses could proceed only at a walk. The dogs, however, knew the terrain so well that they wove in and out of trees like ribbons, racing each other. The waning sunlight dappled their coats and Glory's hands on the reins. The weather had definitely turned, and horse breath plumed out in front of them. The forest had its own smell, a pungent powder that lined Glory's nose and seeped into her pores. The land was protected, but if the population continued to increase the way it had over the last twenty years, then a hundred years from now, when stories such as *Tess of the d'Urbervilles* were considered Paleolithic, there could be condominiums here. Sewage systems. The ugly gray of asphalt parking lots. She wished the Spanish had let things be.

"What are you thinking about?" Juniper asked.

"How great you're doing on your riding. How about you?"

Juniper's face crumpled. "That if I hurt Piper, I'd kill myself."

"First of all, if talking about suicide is your way of kidding, stop it immediately. Say something like that in front of Lois or Caroline, you'll be in the hospital on a 5150 involuntary psychiatric hold for a seventy-two-hour observation before you can take your next breath. And believe me, they have really lousy food. Piper's fine."

"But now when I go in the barn to tack him, he'll think I'm going to hurt him."

"Horses remember just like we do. So do dogs. But they also sense your intentions. What you did was no big deal. Look at Piper's ears." They were pricked forward, interested in his surroundings. "See? He's happy. Let's switch horses."

"No. I'm scared of Piper. He's so tall."

Glory dismounted and held Piper's reins. "Come on. You have to learn to ride all kinds of horses."

Juniper slid down from Cricket. Piper was happy to change riders, and Cricket was happy to lead him anywhere. "Hey, where's your right glove?" Glory asked before giving her a leg up.

"Must've lost it on our last ride."

"We'll keep a lookout. In the meantime, give me the other one." She called Cadillac, held it to Cadillac's nose, and said, "Find."

"What are you doing?"

"A while back, to counteract his boredom, I taught him the rudimentary bits of tracking."

"I didn't know he could do that," Juniper said.

"I'm not sure he can. We haven't practiced it in a long while. Go on, boy. Find."

Cadillac waited until Juniper was settled on Piper, then ran ahead, Dodge following. Glory used the opportunity to really study Juniper's riding progress. She'd eased her death grip on the reins. Her shoulders were no longer hunched up by her ears, which meant she was relaxing a little, but not much. "Pretend you're a sack of potatoes," Glory told her over and over. Light brown roots peeked out from her dyed-black hair. She'd lost at least five pounds, probably from eating healthy meals, and her jeans were loose on her. She wore a flannel shirt of Dan's, miles too big for her, from the old-clothes box. She had knotted the shirttails around her waist. For a moment it was like catching a glimpse of a child of his, and Glory regretted letting all those chances to have a baby go by. The last time Dan asked, Glory had said, "I'm just not ready." A stupid answer she regretted every day. While he lay there dying, did he think about what he'd missed? Were the foster boys enough? Glory was afraid of being a mother. Look how crappy she was doing with Juniper. She was afraid to share her husband for one minute, even though he seemed to have an endless supply of love. She was afraid he might die and leave her with kids the same way her dad had done with her mom. She was terrified of having a daughter who'd end up like Casey, or who hung out at the minimart by the Chevron station, every day stuffed full with opportunities that could turn out fatal. Now here she was with Juniper, who'd had all those things happen to her and more. The fact remained, if she hadn't waited, she might be riding with a part of Dan that had more life than a piece of clothing.

Then she noticed Juniper's boots. They were Dan's Red Wings. Which meant she'd been in Glory's closet to get them. Juniper had large feet, but surely his size-ten boots would swim on her. Probably while Glory was talking to the florist, Juniper had gone into her room, searching for boots. She rode up beside her to give her what for. But the girl had her eyes closed and was letting Piper lead the way. She was so scared she was trembling. Glory decided the talk could wait until after their ride.

Dodge ran back and forth as they rode, checking in, then taking off at a dead run. He barked his head off, and Glory hoped that would tire him out enough that he'd sleep quietly in his kennel all night. Would Dodge ever be right for anyone? Kids made him hysterical, and excessive barking was the number two reason people left dogs at shelters. The first was failure to housebreak, and usually the owner's fault, leaving a dog cooped up for nine hours at a time. For a long while Juniper and Glory rode without speaking, falling into the horses' rhythm, the sun filtering through the oaks, nothing around them but the trees.

"This must be what heaven's like," Juniper said. "I could stay here forever."

Glory had no idea what heaven could be like for anyone. All she knew was if heaven didn't take dogs and horses, she wasn't going. "It'd be great for a little while."

"Why not forever?"

"The woods get cold at night, kiddo. And all kinds of creatures come out."

"We could wear jackets and gloves."

"Yes, if we could keep track of them. Speaking of, have you seen Caddy?"

She shook her head no. "Whistle. He'll come back. He always does."

Glory blew through her fingers, listened, and heard nothing. "We'll give him a few more minutes, but then we need to head back. Our first traditional bride-and-groom wedding tomorrow. I'm excited, even if you aren't."

"I'm excited about a piece of cake. Everything else is just like watching some boring old play I've seen a hundred times." She pitched her voice high. " 'Do you?' 'I do, I do.' What a bunch of b—"

Glory pointed her finger at her. "Language."

"I was going to say *bull pucky*."

"Glad to hear it." They rode a quarter mile more, to where

the oaks thinned out and the road began. It was a good place to turn around because you had all those wonderful oak-filled miles to follow in the other direction. Glory whistled two, three times more, but no black-and-white bullet came flying through the trees. "Let's stop our horses and listen," she said.

"It's my fault," Juniper said. "I should have kept better track of him. What if something happened? What if he's hurt or someone took him home because he's such a pretty dog? What if I never see him again?"

"Caddy knows the woods. He'll be back. Let's keep the horses at a walk for a while, though."

As they rode, Juniper's head turned from one side to the other, searching. Glory wasn't concerned—yet. If he didn't come home tonight, then she'd worry about a coyote or mountain lion encounter. There were worse ways for a dog to go, and that was how you had to look at it or you'd go nuts.

Ten minutes later, he shot out of the trees, a dirty glove in his mouth.

"He found it!" Juniper yelled. She jumped off Piper and ran to her dog. "Good boy! It's my glove! It has the same tag and everything. Isn't he the smartest dog ever?"

"Smart dog," Glory said. It looked as if the glove had been from here to the coast and back again. "Be sure to wash it when we get home. Home," she said, and Dodge turned to follow Cadillac.

"Wait for me!" Juniper said, and all by herself pulled herself into Piper's saddle.

As they drove across town, merging into traffic, stopping for traffic lights and Christmas-shopping pedestrians, Glory broached the subject casually. "I noticed you took Dan's boots."

Juniper fiddled with the radio, trying to find a station that wasn't playing rap, which Glory outlawed, not only because of the lyrics, but because it gave her a headache. Classic rock: There they had common ground. As Janis Joplin sang "Piece of My Heart," Glory remembered Halle belting it out into her hairbrush as if it were a microphone when Halle was the same age as Juniper was now. It was an oldie back then, so what did that make it now? An *eldie*?

"Uh-huh."

"Dan's boots that were in my closet."

"So?"

"Remember, we made a rule that you need to ask before you go into my bedroom? And for permission before taking something?"

"But you had them in the box marked for Goodwill."

"True, but that doesn't change anything. We made a rule, you broke it."

"But you told me to find boots! I went through the old-clothes box but there weren't any in my size because I have elephant feet."

"Then you should have told me. And your feet aren't that big."

"You were on the phone!"

"For about five minutes. You could have asked me after I hung up."

"Maybe I did ask and you just don't remember it."

Here we go, Glory thought. "Tell me the truth right now and that will be the end of it."

Juniper went silent while Glory drove down residential streets, looking for the library. Once she found the entrance, she dropped Juniper off and went in search of a parking place. Inside the library, she used what was probably the last public telephone on planet Earth to call Caroline.

"It's stupid stuff," Glory told her. "Making up stories about her teachers praising her, and then I get the robo-call from the school that she isn't turning in her homework. She takes a hand-ful of change off my dresser, and then denies it. Today she took a pair of boots from my closet."

"Glory, I have to say that doesn't sound like that big of an issue."

Glory hadn't mentioned the Percocet because she knew that would result in Juniper's being returned to the group home. Her rationale? As Lois said, she hadn't *taken* the Percocet.

"It sounds pretty normal to me," Caroline continued. "You've been through all the standard foster-care stuff with boys. Juniper's no different. She's testing how far she can push the boundaries. We both know her issues go deeper than that, but an abandoned kid usually goes one of two ways. She idolizes her parent, won't hear one bad thing said about him. Or she believes the reason he left is because she's not good enough."

"Couldn't there be a third alternative? Something easier to figure out?"

Caroline laughed. "Glo, every foster kid I've ever known has a quirky view of the truth. And I don't mean that Juniper's expe-riences make up for lying. We both know she's had a hell of a time and a long way to go. It's just that lying is a tendency we see a lot. They 'spin windies,' as my cowpoke brother used to say. Maybe to imagine themselves as something better than they are. If I had to guess, I'd say that deep down, she believes her father left her because she could never measure up to Casey. Take that up with Lois and I bet you'll find some answers. Meanwhile, keep it simple. Just state the obvious. Remind her she's not to go into your room again without permission and walk away."

"Right," Glory said, though she'd already tried that. "Hey, are you going to the Butterfly Creek Christmas party?"

"Wouldn't miss it."

"What are you bringing?"

"The biggest bottle of vino I can find and a corkscrew. What are you making?"

"Oh, I don't know. Something."

"Well, if you need any suggestions, let me know. Your biscuits come to mind. Or cake. There ought to be a traditional Christmas cake."

"There's stollen."

"That's German."

"Marzipan?"

"Italian. But I wouldn't kick either one out of bed."

They said good-bye and Glory hung up the phone. Was she wigging out over a stupid pair of boots? She found a novel on the NEW ACQUISITIONS rack and sat down in one of the easy chairs the library had purchased circa 1980. The book was set in Albuquerque, New Mexico, and made her think of Joseph Vigil.

"I'm sorry," Juniper said when they got in the car to go. She reached down to unlace the boots.

"Change when we get home," Glory said, too tired to say more.

"So is this my third strike?"

"What?"

"You know, like felons. The pills were strike one, the money I swear I didn't steal was strike two, and now the boots are strike three, and when we get home, you'll call Caroline?"

"Is that what you want?"

"No."

"Then follow the rules, Juniper. Don't take things, and tell the truth. If you're worried you've done something wrong, come talk to me. I don't count mistakes like the penal system. I'd rather concentrate on what you're doing right, which is almost everything."

"What I'm doing *right*? Really? You mean it?"

Glory, determined to look on the bright side, clicked on the turn signal and drove out of the library parking lot and said, "Yes, really."

After McDonald's drive-through for a Coke and fries, they stopped at the big-box electronics and appliances store to pick up Glory's new camera. It cost enough money to make her knees knock as she stood at the counter waiting for help. She either had to learn to take better pictures or contract out that part of weddings, which meant putting money in someone else's pocket. She also needed to upgrade her computer so it could run more sophisticated programs. If the business continued, the money she was spending here today would pay off. If not, there was always Craigslist. The salesperson who came to help her was probably sixteen years old, stocky, wore glasses, and walked splayfooted; therefore he was of no interest to Juniper.

"I hate this place," Juniper said, fidgeting, and knocking over a display of Word program discs. She straightened them up, sighed, and finally said, "This is boring. Can I go to the pet store and look at the parrots?"

"Sure, go on. Be back in half an hour." The clerk's eyes gleamed when Glory told him everything she intended to buy. "Don't get too excited," she told him. "Before I write the check you have to show me how to use it all."

Thirty minutes later her head was spinning with instructions, but she was positive she could use the camera. She bought two backup batteries, a charger, an upgrade to her current program, and *Photoshop for Dummies.* She took the clerk's card and the schedule for classes. After she wrote the enormous check and waited for phone approval, whatever that entailed, she found Juniper by the DVD section, looking at horror movies for sale. "Don't those give you nightmares?"

"They're so fake." Juniper put them back on the shelf and took one of Glory's bags. "This is heavy."

"I'm going to need your help with everything. I'm also thinking I could increase your allowance because of that."

"Really? That'd be great."

Could she tell that Glory's heart was going ninety miles an hour? That she had no idea if the allowance increase would help Juniper get over stealing? Maybe they were both acting.

They drove home listening to NPR, both tired and hungry. "Does Terry Gross only interview authors of books about genocide and terrorism?" Juniper asked.

"Those are important things more people need to know about," Glory answered. "I'm sure she covers a range of subjects."

"Well, never when we're driving places. Someone ought to tell her that not everyone wants to think about Rwanda driving home every night. How about talking to an author about regular people doing regular things?"

"Send her an e-mail," Glory suggested.

"What's the point? No one listens to people my age."

Glory patted Juniper's shoulder. "I listen to you. I'm sorry if me reminding you about the boots contributed to that. Or is it something else you want to tell me?"

Juniper didn't answer.

"I'll feed the dogs," Glory said, "so you can get started on poor, doomed *Tess*."

"It's my night to make dinner. What are we having?"

Glory laughed. "Macaroni and cheese, I guess. Any remarkable parrots at Petco?"

"They're all pretty great. I wish I could get an African grey. A baby I could teach to talk."

"You could. You're good with animals."

"I'm not all that great. Ask Piper."

"Look at how much Cadillac loves you."

"You don't know that for sure," Juniper said, looking out the window at the streetlights and Christmas decorations. "Probably he thinks I'm Casey."

At home Glory needed the time it took to measure out dog food, vitamins, and additives to come to terms with Juniper's remark. She'd immediately told Juniper she was wrong. That Cadillac had bonded with her that first night, not because Juniper was related to Casey. But deep down she had to admit he might remember Casey. *Never raise your hand to a border collie because they never forget,* Glory had read in a sheepherder's book. Did that mean they remembered fear, or did they recall the actual trauma, the way a human would? Miracle of miracles, were Casey to come back, would Caddy dump Juniper to return to her? Caddy was smart, but some of Glory's dogs in the past were big, dumb lunks, like Toyota, who wanted nothing more than food, a daily game of ball, and long walks where he could mark trees and roll in dead-animal stink. Others had affection to spare, like Dodge, who so desperately wanted that in return. Ford never did trust men. Glory had never hit any of them, although they tested her plenty by killing chickens and scratching doors to splinters.

Smart ones such as Cadillac were always the most difficult to place because they needed variety in their days, lots of interaction, and challenging activities. She tried to match temperament to temperament with owners who understood that a bored, intelligent dog could become a destructive dog. Cadillac would still herd goats when asked, and he'd found Juniper's glove, but he'd devoted himself to being Juniper's companion. While she was at school, he spent his day waiting for the minute she'd walk in the door. If Glory was home, at three thirty P.M. he'd get up, stretch, go to the door, and ask to go out. Glory watched him from the kitchen window. When he caught sight of the bus, he started wagging his tail, and by the time Juniper came walking up the drive, his whole body shook with excitement. He was hers and that was all there was to it.

He still ate his meals with Dodge. Dodge raced around the yard, the horses staked out their hay flakes, but Glory could tell that Cadillac considered himself beyond all that. In the grand scheme of life, saving death-row dogs from euthanasia was next to nothing, but when Glory placed one successfully, it felt like the most important thing she'd done.

Across the way, the wind blew through the trees, and Glory pulled her collar up. She headed for the barn as a spattering rain started to fall. Because of the wedding, the tack, feed, and equipment had temporarily been relocated to Dan's workshop. Five tables covered with white linen cloths stood in the place of sawhorses and saddles. In the center of each table she'd placed tall, mercury-glass hurricane lanterns with pale green candles that matched the poinsettias that would arrive tomorrow. A second-hand, red Oriental rug from the thrift store warmed the wood floor considerably and gave the place a threadbare, funky elegance. Earlier in the week, Juniper had helped her nail together a set of risers for the chapel, so that when the poinsettia plants were placed upon them, it would look as if the couple were standing in a winter garden. Flanking the flowers on both sides were potted, five-foot-tall fir trees she'd "rented" from the Christmas-tree lot.

In two days she'd pack them into the truck and return them so they could be sold as Christmas trees. In the *Thrifty Nickel*, she'd found a used space heater to warm up the barn. Once she switched it on, it would be toasty in here, perfect for dancing and dining, and hopefully no gunplay.

"Is it okay that I made us hot dogs and baked beans for dinner instead?" Juniper said when Glory came to the table.

"I love hot dogs," she said, reaching for the pitcher and pouring water into their glasses. She sat down. Juniper's library book sat beside her plate.

"Okay if I read at the table?"

"Not right now. First I want to talk about Christmas."

"That won't take long," Juniper said. "If it's just us, it will be like a regular day, unless there's a wedding. It's not like we're exchanging presents. Are we?"

"I may have picked up a little something for you."

"But I don't have anything for you! Will you take me shopping? Can we go to Target? I could shop while you're working. Then maybe I could get you a halfway decent present. You should have told me."

"How about the used-book store instead? But you can't spend over a couple of dollars."

"That's not even the price of a decent paperback! I'll need twenty at least. And how do I know what you like to read?"

"Calm down," Glory said. "You'll earn twice that at the wedding. I'll give you a list of my favorite authors." Then Glory dove into the difficult part. "We have two options. Lorna Candelaria has a yearly Christmas Eve shindig at the general store. And my sister, Halle, invited us to her place for Christmas Day.

She lives a couple of hours north, so we'd have to leave early to get back to feed the animals. You're going to meet my whole family, even my mom. There will only be one man there, Halle's husband, Bart. Halle serves fancy food and you'd have to dress up."

"In what?" Juniper asked.

"Nice jeans and a shirt."

Juniper laughed. "Mom, you have no clue what goes on in the real world if you call that dressing up."

Mom. Glory tried not to smile. "Thanks a lot. I was thinking we might ask them over here on Christmas Eve. That way they can meet you in a place where you feel at home."

"It's your house," she said, reaching for the ketchup.

"It's our house. After that, maybe we could all go to Butterfly Creek."

"Do you have to dress up for that?"

"You can get away with a clean shirt. Lorna usually has a band playing."

"I'd rather do that. Now is it okay if I read my book?"

"Sure."

They ate dinner quietly. Tomorrow Glory would cook the roasts and time things so that she could make the Yorkshire pudding just before serving, bring it tall and golden, steaming hot out of the oven. She told herself this wedding was no different from one of her old Christmas parties, when the neighbors gathered, except it wasn't a potluck and most of the guests would not have horse manure in their shoe treads. And Dan wouldn't be there to carve the meat.

Closet Time.

While Glory did the dishes, Cadillac lay by the fire soaking up the warmth. Juniper put down her book to play with Edsel, a first. He raced around the living room chasing a canvas toy, tied to a strand of yarn, that Juniper kept just out of his reach. It was shaped like a fire hydrant. When Glory didn't recognize it, her stomach sank. "Where'd that come from?"

Juniper continued the game without looking up. "I bought it at Petco."

Immediately Glory thought of asking to see the receipt. Would she doubt Juniper for the next four years? Was she willing to send her back into the system over a toy with a plastic squeaker that Edsel would break before the night was through? But if she'd been caught shoplifting, the store might've pressed charges. Called the police. Put this on her record—a second shoplifting offense made a pattern. The county could decide Glory wasn't foster-parent material after all. She unwrapped the thawed cookie dough. It was ready to roll and cut into dozens of snowflakes. She mixed the powdered egg-white icing and added pale green food coloring drop by drop until she was satisfied she'd matched the poinsettias. It took maybe ten minutes, and by then she could stand it no longer. "Juniper, if you shoplifted that dog toy, and I pray that you didn't, that could be a strike three."

Juniper allowed Edsel to catch the toy and said, "Game over, little dude." For a while, she petted Cadillac, taking his black-and-white head into her lap. He groaned with pleasure when she scratched his neck. "Suppose a person did steal a stupid ninety-nine-cent clearance dog toy. How would they go about making it right?"

"The person would go back to that store and give them the money or the toy or both. And apologize."

"Couldn't the person just send it in the mail, anonymously? Like people do with petrified wood in the Painted Desert? I read online that people who stole those rocks all had bad luck until they mailed them back to the park rangers. They have a whole room of them and letters from the people who took them telling all the bad things that happened to them after."

"That sounds like guilt to me. Let me ask you something. How would a person learn their lesson without facing the store manager they stole from, and hearing how shoplifting affects their business? Stealing a dog toy—what, a nickel's worth of fabric?—could get a person charged with a misdemeanor, which goes on a juvenile record. That kind of stuff adds up. Pretty soon everyone will look at you and say, 'There goes sticky fingers.'"

"I wash my hands as much as you do."

"It's a figure of speech, Juniper."

"What does that mean?"

"Look it up."

They took a time-out while Juniper consulted the computer's dictionary. "'Departing from a literal use of words, metaphorical.' And before you ask me what that means, I already looked it up, too. Comparing something to something else that isn't really like it at all. Like 'the moon is a silver coin in the sky' when really it's a cold, dead, hunk-of-rock satellite that stupid people pretend is romantic." She feigned gagging.

Glory concentrated on rolling out cookie dough and cutting perfect snowflakes. Juniper made a big point out of washing her hands, then, without being asked, she began to load up the cookie sheets. Such a feeling of incapability washed over Glory that she didn't know what else to say. She handed Juniper the rolling pin. "One secret to making perfect cookies is to always let the oven heat up for an hour before you bake. I don't know why, but the cookies turn out better."

"Who taught you that?"

"My grandmother Denise Smith."

"Where's she live?"

"She used to live in Santa Fe, New Mexico. In a house made of adobe bricks. She died when I was a teenager."

"What's adobe?"

"Clay, soil, water, straw, and, in the old days, ox blood."

"Ick. Who'd want to live in a house with the walls made of animal blood?"

"They used it on the floors, not the walls."

"Oh, my gosh, you could never go barefoot. Wouldn't it stink? So do you miss your grandmother like you miss your husband?"

Whenever Juniper asked her about death, Glory struggled to phrase her words carefully, because she knew Juniper was really talking about her sister, Casey. "Grandma Denise lived her life with a serenity I wish I'd inherited. She could bake anything. Her *biscochitos* were out of this world. She had a good, long life, though I wish we'd had her around longer." Glory handed Juniper the spatula. "Take your time when you put the cookies down onto the baking sheet. If you hurry, they fold over on the edges. We don't want crooked snowflakes."

Juniper slid more cookies onto another tray. "It's lame," she said, after stopping to pop one of the silver dragées into her mouth, "when the people you love are somewhere else."

"You mean dead?"

Juniper nodded. "I don't believe in heaven."

"I'm not sure I do, either. And that makes it even harder, doesn't it?"

Juniper said nothing, so Glory took a chance. "Is that why

you take things? To have something permanent of your own? I'd understand if that was the case, honey, but it would still be wrong."

Juniper slid the cookie sheets into the oven. She set the timer, then stepped back from the counter and reached into her back pocket, pulling out a wrinkled piece of paper, which she flattened out on the counter. It was a receipt for a clearance-item, ninety-nine-cent dog toy, paid for with cash. Then she turned, patted her leg to call Cadillac, and went to her room, ignoring the apology Glory called after her.

At three A.M. Glory woke from a dream in which Juniper was heavily pregnant and in handcuffs. *Tell them I didn't do it,* she begged her. Juniper was dressed in tattered clothing, looking homeless. Her facial piercings had multiplied until Glory could hardly see her expression. Try as she might, Glory couldn't fall back to sleep, which was maddening, because she really needed to. She went into the closet, sat down, and pulled the door shut. She pulled her knees up so she could rest her face and arms on them and hugged Dan's shirt to try to muffle the crying that came out of her as easily as blood spilling from a wound. Edsel scratched on the closet door. "Go back to bed," she whispered. He whined, and Glory knew he'd wake up Juniper if she didn't let him in, so she opened the door so he could slip inside. Immediately he began butting his head against the hem of her nightgown, wanting underneath so he could burrow for a warm spot like the one he'd left under the covers. Good to know that while my heart is breaking, my house dog thinks only of his own comfort, Glory thought. She hated the way her heart beat erratically and how the tears were unstoppable. Stupid grief had a system all its own, governed by something larger than her willpower. Some days it was as if the tears needed to be shed only to make room for a fresh supply. Would this ever end? There were days she hated Dan so much she could have socked him in the nose. What kind of loving widow fantasized about such things? She told herself that a pregnant Juniper was a metaphor, a symbol of something, and the dream had come out of the dictionary discussion. Metaphor, the moon . . . but of what, besides a teenaged mother? Casual sex, as Lorna warned, a future that was on its way, like it or not? She leaned back and felt something against her butt. When she looked behind her, she saw that it was Dan's boots, polished to a sheen, laces tied, set back exactly where Juniper had found them. Glory wanted to scream. Once again, Juniper had gone into the closet without permission.

That did it for the possibility of sleep. She showered, dressed in work clothes, and went into the kitchen to start cooking.

The couple had a special request: handmade, sweet-cream butter and freshly baked sourdough bread. As soon as the sun was up, Glory called her mom, who had never slept past daybreak in her life.

"Whip heavy cream in a stainless steel bowl over another, larger bowl, filled with crushed ice," she said. "Then rinse it and gently press out the liquid in a sieve. I used to let you girls make it for holidays. Kept you busy and out of my hair. Failproof."

"I wish you hadn't said that. Now I'm jinxed. How long do you beat it? All I have is handheld mixers."

"Then you are going to get yourself one heck of a workout. I'd drive over and help you, but you know how my hands are," Ave Smith said, referring to her inflammatory arthritis. The term sounded inconsequential, like pain aspirin should take care of. But because her body was constantly inflamed, her organs functioned under stress, and worse, her joints hurt her so much that she'd had to give up her passions, gardening and knitting, and needed a special card holder when she played bridge.

"What's the doctor say these days?" Glory asked.

"Oh, he wants me to go on some new kind of medicine. They give it to you in a drip, like chemotherapy, once a month, but one dose costs more than a used car! I told him no way. If I hurt real bad, I take half a Tylenol."

"Half? Mom, does that really do anything?"

"I don't intend to get addicted to drugs, Glory."

Glory knew better than to argue when her mother got huffy. "So what do you think about Christmas? Having a cup of cider here so you can meet Juniper, and then we head over to the Butterfly Creek? There'll be a bluegrass gospel band. I know how much you love gospel music."

"Sounds good to me. It's Halle you have to convince."

Glory sighed. "I think Bart'll enjoy it."

Her mother laughed. "He won't if Halle tells him not to. How did you two girls turn out so differently?"

"I don't know, Mom. Maybe my genes got tweaked. We ate a lot of hormone-enhanced beef."

"Don't start with that. We bought what was affordable. I don't see it had much of an effect on your bosom."

That was it. "I'd better hang up. The florist is here."

"Good luck, honey. Call me when the dust settles and tell me all about it."

"Christmas Eve, I can pick you up if you don't want to drive."

"Halle just got a new Volvo. If I don't let her drive me over, I'll never hear the end of it. Besides, I'm right on their way."

"Love you, Mom," Glory said, and hung up just as Beryl Reilly Stokes opened the front door. "Hey," Glory said, turning. "Ever made twenty pounds of butter by hand?"

Beryl laughed. "Actually, I have. In a convent home for unwed mothers. Easter butter lambs to sell to support the church. Got a second mixer?"

Glory handed hers over and fetched the other one. "I'll pay you for your time."

"Not necessary," Beryl insisted. "This'll go fast. Then we can concentrate on the flowers. Which came out beautifully. You're going to be so pleased."

Juniper skulked by, a peanut butter sandwich in hand.

"That your daughter?" Beryl whispered.

"Yes. My foster daughter."

"Handful?"

"Oh, she's a good kid. I just wish she'd develop a relationship with the truth. But her mood's my fault. I accused her of something she didn't do. Not even blackberry pancakes with whipped cream can make up for it."

"You need more ice in your bowl," Beryl said.

Glory looked at her. "I don't know. My bowl feels pretty darn icy already."

Beryl laughed. "Things'll warm up. When I turned forty, I thought that my love life was long over, but in the last five years I've had three boyfriends. Of course, one was a liar and another a bird whisperer with practically no income."

"A bird whisperer?"

"Handsome, half-Native raptor rehabber, broke, a different drummer, but what a lover."

"What about the third guy?"

"Retired detective who followed me here from Alaska. He saved my life, so I had to marry him."

"Tell me if it's none of my business, but it sounds like you have some regrets?"

Beryl looked out the window at the wintry scene Glory had watched change from dark to dawn to a morning so chilly she'd needed Dan's down jacket while she broke the ice on the horses' water trough. Underfoot, the grass crackled. Snow wouldn't stick, but they might get a dusting in time for Christmas.

"How does a woman answer that question?" Beryl said. "I mean, my first marriage was terrible, but like an idiot I hung in, and I paid for it dearly. When I was single, living with the women on the farm, I don't think I've ever been happier. Yet, like a moron, I left them for the wealthy liar who seemed too good to be true. Guess what? He was. Well, I got to see Alaska, the last frontier. And I met Thomas Jack, who was happy living in a Quonset hut with a single woodstove for heat. I love Mike. He treats me gently, but lets me go my own way when I need to. We never run out of things to talk about. He's a good cook and he likes my parrot. I'd miss him if he were gone the same way I know you miss your Dan. But truthfully, there's a part of me that longs for exclusively female company across the kitchen table. We worked beside each other, raised each other's kids, laughed over old movies, and there were days we ate crème brûlée for breakfast."

"Crème brûlée? I didn't know what I was missing."

Beryl smiled. "Come visit the farm sometime. Help out for an afternoon. It's hard work, but nonstop fun. Instead of keeping them locked inside, we share our sorrows. That makes it so much easier to go on."

When the butter was finished, Glory used the melon baller to scoop out curls, setting them on a platter and covering them with waxed parchment. When it was full, Beryl helped her find a spot for it in the fridge. They were just finishing the final tray when Juniper walked back into the kitchen.

"I set the poinsettias up in the chapel and I put the roses and bouquets in the cooler."

"Thank you, sweetie," Glory said. "That was awfully nice of you. Juniper, this is Mrs. Stokes."

Juniper sighed and would not make eye contact with Glory, but couldn't resist the opportunity to zing her. "I have to *prove* myself," she said to Beryl. "Mrs. Solomon doesn't trust me."

"Juniper, that's not so," Glory said. "And please stop calling me that."

"Life, Mrs. Solomon, as you so often like to point out to me, isn't fair."

Glory sighed.

Beryl looked right back at Juniper. "Sounds like you're in charge of the flowers, so here's what you need to know. The rosebuds need to rest in the bucket of water in a cool, dark place. That's called conditioning. When you're ready to make the centerpieces, be sure to cut them at a forty-five-degree angle and do the cutting *underwater*. Fill the vases with equal amounts of lukewarm water and lemon-lime soda. Don't worry, I brought some. Make sure the waterline is below any leaves or they'll rot. If you need to cut them to fit the vase, put them back in the soda immediately so they'll soak up the solution."

"That's a lot to remember," Juniper said.

"That shouldn't be hard for you. Even without your mom telling me, I knew the minute I saw you that you were smart beyond your years."

Glory wanted to cheer at Beryl's subtext. Had that come from living communally, too? Sign me up, she thought.

"What about the bouquets?" Juniper asked.

"Don't hand them out until the last minute. Glory, you should go take a look before everything gets too busy. I've never seen a maid of honor's bouquet as beautiful as the bride's, but this one is. What do you think of them, Juniper? What kind of flowers do you want to carry when you get married?"

Juniper touched her finger to a spot of liquid that had beaded up on the rim of the sieve. She put her finger in her mouth and made a face. "Eww. Worse than yogurt."

"That's whey," Beryl said. "As in curds and whey."

"I'm never getting married," Juniper said.

"Why not?"

Glory tried to gesture behind Juniper's back to get Beryl's attention, but there was no way other than to interrupt and change the subject. "She's too young to think—"

Before Glory could finish, Juniper said, "I don't like men. They can be so mean you wouldn't believe it."

Beryl said, "Actually, I'm unfortunately familiar with that. I've given up way too much of myself in the name of love. It's so much easier to see your mistakes at my age, not that it changes anything. But I'm happy to report that there are a few good guys out there, and I married one of them." Beryl looked at Glory. "Nobody knows when they'll pop up. So think about letting a few in someday."

"Not me," Juniper said.

Because all the arrangements for this wedding had been made over the phone and via e-mail, Glory hadn't met the bride or the groom. She was just putting the potato casserole in to brown when Robynn called out, "Bridal party's here."

"Juniper," Glory called. "Can you show them to the den so I can finish here? My hands are full. Juniper!"

"I heard you the first time, Mrs. Solomon," Juniper hollered back.

That mouth of hers, Glory thought. Here I am watching the casserole through the oven door to make sure it doesn't burn like Dan's yams because it means the difference between paying the feed bill or calling Target to beg for more hours and she's giving me flack. Most inconveniently, the truck needed new tires now instead of after the first of the year. The casserole's sharing the 1960s-era oven with the roasts did unpredictable things to the temperatures and the food. She didn't dare leave the room. As she sat on the floor and peeked through the glass door, she prayed the only kind of prayers she ever prayed: Please come out perfect. Red polo shirts do nothing for me. I'm not old enough to wear khaki pants five times a week. I can't fall asleep until I've counted out every dollar coming in and where it has to go. Roasts, please be evenly browned and pink in the middle, and, Cupid or Eros or whoever is responsible for making couples fall in love, let those arrows fly. Bring more weddings my way. God, our Creator, or whoever or whatever you are, please help me with Juniper. And bless me even though I don't deserve it.

Just then Edsel came flying into the kitchen and dropped the canvas toy at her feet. He trilled in that strange, catlike way of his, and she picked up the toy and threw it into the living room, guilty all over again.

The roasts continued cooking, but as soon as the casserole came out of the oven, Glory tented it with foil to keep it warm.

She knocked on the closed door of the den. "Lily, it's Mrs. Solomon. Need any help?"

"We're good" came a chorus of female voices.

"Great. Let me know when you're ready. Everything is right on schedule. Your guests are arriving, and thank goodness, it looks like the rain has stopped."

Glory showed the guests into the chapel and clicked off a few shots with the new digital camera and reviewed them. Perfect. She checked the batteries and clattered over the patio in her good shoes. She powdered her cheeks and smoothed the collar on the same blue dress she'd worn for the pirates. Back in the house she returned to the kitchen. Juniper had changed into the black pants, white shirt, and burgundy apron that identified her as a server. She stood in the doorway, frowning.

"What's the matter?" Glory asked.

"You seriously need to go shopping."

"What's wrong with this dress?"

"Nothing if it was 1980. Also, ever heard of a curling iron?"

"Thanks a heap."

"I'm just *telling the truth*," Juniper said.

The phone rang and Glory grabbed it. "Solomon's Oak Wedding Chapel, this is Glory speaking. How can I help you?"

"Hi," said a female voice. "I found you on Yahoo's 'Pick of the Week.' You have a great Web site. I don't suppose there's a chance that Valentine's Day is still open for a ceremony?"

Yahoo had featured her Web site? Glory took a breath. Of course it was open. Every day was fair game. If someone wanted to marry in her chapel on Christmas Eve she'd dump her family plans in a heartbeat. But she didn't dare let this bride-to-be think she was some kind of desperate farm widow. "Let me check.

Hold on a second, please." She put her hand over the receiver and caught Robynn heading out the door with the buffet trays. "Juniper! Yahoo featured our Web site! We may have another wedding if you two don't mind working Valentine's Day."

"Sure, Mrs. Solomon," Robynn said. "I'll work any day of the week I'm not in class."

"Juniper?"

"Do I have a choice?"

"Yes, you do."

"Can I have a raise?"

"I just raised your allowance."

"I spent one-twentieth of it on a toy for a needy dog. That's called *altruistic*. Look it up. Seven fifty-five more per month is fair."

Glory didn't have the energy to argue. "We'll talk about that later."

The two girls collected serving pieces and went out the back door to the barn.

Glory picked up the receiver. "What time of day were you thinking of?"

"We'd love a lunchtime ceremony if you have it open."

"You're in luck. I do have that time open. Let me mark my book. I'll need a nonrefundable deposit, and your contact information." She scrawled with a pen across the calendar for a year that hadn't yet arrived. February 14 was two weeks before the anniversary of Dan's death. "Let me take your number and call you tomorrow. I'm just about to start the loveliest evening ceremony, it's a solstice wedding."

"Are they Wiccans?" the woman asked.

"Not that I know of. Why?"

"I saw the pirate sword-fight picture. You sound open-minded."

"So long as no animals are harmed and your check doesn't

bounce." The woman laughed and Glory said she'd secure her spot as soon as the check cleared.

"It'll be in the mail tomorrow."

"You better get out there," Juniper told Glory as she hung up. "Everyone is in the chapel and hap-hap-happy. They're ready to start."

Glory rushed to the chapel, which was scented with pine boughs and transformed by the creamy poinsettias and potted firs. In the back of the chapel stood the bride and her maid of honor, no other attendants or flower girl. They were dressed in the palest green satin and taffeta. Their dresses matched the poinsettias so well that Glory felt certain the new camera would do them justice. "Everyone has the correct bouquet?" she asked. They nodded, and Glory cued Juniper, who nodded to Robynn, who told the guitarist to begin.

Glory hadn't known that Pachelbel's "Canon" could be played on the classical guitar. The two women linked arms, and she thought, how lovely that these two are such good friends they want to share this special moment together. But when they walked down the aisle together, and the guests who stood for them were mainly women, Glory realized she'd misunderstood. They stopped at the minister—Nola van Patten, Beryl's recommendation—and faced each other. Standing up for them were two other women. The one with close-cropped hair was dressed in an off-white tux and stood in the place the best man traditionally occupied. The maid of honor wore an ivory dress with long, lacy sleeves that looked vintage.

"Who gives these women to be joined in marriage?" Pastor van Patten asked, and one of the brides laughed and said, "Well, it sure isn't the State of California."

"Yet!" someone called out from the pews.

A few guests chuckled, but the couple were solemn when it came to their vows, just as the pirates were. In the benches, people draped arms across each other's shoulders and murmured. Two kindergarten-age kids couldn't wait to throw confetti, which Glory knew would show up in the floorboards for months, but that was fine.

Juniper tapped her shoulder. "Where're the grooms?"

"Shh," she said, and lifted the camera.

"Are they, you know?"

"It appears to be the case." Glory concentrated on the clerk's instructions for the camera and went after capturing the perfect moment, a photograph the couple could show to their great-grandchildren, to prove how backward and narrow-minded people once were in this Golden State of theirs.

Glory poured champagne since Robynn and Juniper were underage. Instead of buffet style, this time they served full plates. Not a quarter hour into the reception, Robynn gave Glory a panicked look. "Mrs. S. They're asking for seconds. We're not going to have enough food."

"More bread," Glory said, and raced into the kitchen, where she microwaved four frozen loaves of sourdough bread and sliced them raggedly. She sent two trays out with Juniper, along with bottles of olive oil, balsamic vinegar, and sprigs of rosemary, since the butter was gone. "Start up the music and encourage dancing," she said, and was about to bake another two dozen cookies when she remembered Halle's good-for-brunch, lunch, midnight-snack, and main-dish recipe she made every Easter: Chile Egg Puff. Glory took out this week's bowls of eggs meant for the co-op and five cans of New Mexican green chile she'd bought mail order. She'd begun buying cheese already grated, to save time, and all she needed now was flour, baking powder, and salt. She filled her largest casserole dish and set it in the oven to bake. In forty-five minutes, the warm puff would be perfect after the dancing, and before the cake. She'd send them on the road home feeling well fed and as if they'd never enjoyed themselves more, and hurrying to recommend the chapel to all their friends.

The cake had so many pictures taken of it that Glory worried it would melt before they got around to cutting it.

"Look at the wee petals," one person said.

"It's askew, just like you are," Chris told her new wife, and they laughed and fed each other a forkful. Glory set the top layer into a small box for the brides to take home. When a gray-haired woman who looked like her mother's bridge partner, Opal, asked her to dance, Glory danced. Juniper stood there gawking at her openmouthed. When Robynn brought out the egg dish, the guests lined up holding their plates. Glory realized she'd better have backup plans from now on.

At the end of the party, nothing was left over, not even a broken cookie. Juniper sulked in the living room, her arms around Cadillac.

"Are you still mad at me about the dog toy?" Glory asked. "I made a mistake. I'll apologize fifty more times if it will help."

"I never got any cake."

"Aw, I didn't get any either."

"But I was looking forward to tasting it."

"Juniper, it was their cake. They paid for it."

Juniper's lower lip stuck out like a five-year-old's. Glory told herself a sugar habit was better than drugs.

"I'll tell you what," Glory said, though she was bone-tired and wanted nothing more than to lie down on the couch and go directly to sleep. "If you say you forgive me, I'll go into the kitchen right now and make you some cupcakes."

"Red velvet?"

Glory sighed. "I suppose."

"With chocolate buttercream frosting? That really good kind of dark chocolate and maybe a little white chocolate on top?"

Glory laughed. "How about you make the frosting? Besides, you can't ice the cupcakes until they're cool."

"I don't care. I'll use it like dip. Will you put the silver things on top?"

"Hey, I'm still waiting for my apology to be accepted. I really am sorry."

"I forgave you already, I just hadn't said so out loud."

"Well, a person likes to hear it," Glory said, dragging herself to her feet.

"I officially absolve you for assuming I was an adhesive-digited purloiner of canine baubles." Juniper smiled.

"A dictionary becomes a deadly weapon in your hands, doesn't it? Okay. Now let's go beat some butter and sugar. I hope I have an egg left or you might have to crawl into the henhouse and give Heather a squeeze."

Close to midnight, after the cleanup was done and the dogs let out, Juniper came and sat on the couch next to Glory. She rubbed her foster mother's neck and shoulders a little too hard, but Glory endured, knowing it was important that she appreciate the gesture. When Juniper was done, she laid her head down in Glory's lap, looking into the fireplace. The dogs had flaked out on the hearth rug, absorbing the heat like four-legged solar panels. Glory held her breath, wondering how to respond to this quantum leap in affection.

Glory placed her hand on Juniper's hair. Pretty soon they were either going to have to dye it or cut it. Two inches of pale brown hair against the black was not this year's new look.

"Mom?"

Mom. Even with all the trouble, Glory loved this kid. "Yes?"

"How do you know if you're gay?"

"I guess you just know. Do you have emotional or"—Lord, how did she say this?—"physical feelings for women?" That lame description made it sound as if you wanted to be volleyball partners.

"I don't have any feelings for anyone, except Cadillac."

"Not even mean old Mrs. Solomon?"

"That's *not* what I'm talking about."

"Then what are you talking about?"

"Seeing those women tonight. Some of them dressed like guys, some looked totally normal, like you'd see on the street. That one you danced with looked like Principal Phelps, the bee-oche supreme."

"You're right, she did. But Principal Phelps is nice, even if you can't see it right now. Juniper, every person at the wedding was 'normal' no matter their preference in partner."

"So I went on the Internet and looked up causes of being gay."

Glory tucked Juniper's hair behind her ear, revealing the bluebird tattoo on her neck. "Somehow I doubt the Internet is the best source for answers of that nature. There are people out there who say and do hateful things out of fear."

"Duh! I know what prejudice means. What I mean is, I still hate those boys at my last home. All they did was make fun of my

boobs and sometimes grab my butt and not let go until I cried. I
hate them. Every guy I look at I think, will he be the next one
who tortures me? Does that mean I'm going to be gay?"

Glory sighed. She thought of Beryl's husband, saving her life.
Dan had exuded the kindness of a monk. Why hadn't God, or
whoever, kept him alive to continue to provide a role model for
teenaged boys? "Juniper, what those boys did to you was wrong.
It has nothing to do with being gay or straight or undecided.
They're just adolescent brats with too many hormones and bad
behavior."

"Like me."

"You can be annoying sometimes, but you're not a brat."

"Every time I think about what they did, I get so mad."

Cadillac sat up, sensing Juniper's tone. Dodge rolled over to
warm his other side and groaned. Edsel climbed on top of Dodge,
lay down, and shut his eyes. This family, Glory thought. It was
past time to go to bed, but Glory knew she couldn't be the one
to break the tentative embrace of—she guessed this was what it
felt like, having a daughter—mother and child.

"Maybe that's for the best," Glory said. "Sometimes anger's
healthy. Next time you talk to Lois, ask her about it."

"Sometimes I have nightmares."

"I know you do. I hear you crying."

"I can't help it."

Glory rubbed her arm. "A lot of things that have happened to
you would have done in a weaker person. Me, for example.
You're so strong. Boy, do I admire that. When I'm mad or sad, I
sit in my closet and cry. How dumb is that?"

"I know. I hear you, too."

"What a pair we are."

"You don't like men, either. I can tell. Are you gay?"

"No, sweetie. Some people like women and some people like men. Some like both and some like none, for always, or just the time being. Worrying about it is borrowing trouble. Let life unfold and surprise you. Who knows? Maybe you'll be as happy as Lily and Chris were today. Maybe it'll turn out that was your path all along."

"Something more for the kids at school to hassle me about."

Starting Tuesday, it was holiday break. That meant Juniper 24/7, until January 2. "Have they been bothering you?"

"Oh, you know, they call me 'tree freak' and 'ass kisser.'"

"That's not very nice. Shouldn't you tell Principal Phelps?"

"Are you *kidding*? Do you know how much worse that would make things?"

"I wish you'd change your mind about this, Juniper. I really do. There are laws against bullying."

"No."

The fire popped and crackled as it burned through the logs. Glory was so tired she couldn't get up. Working hard for herself was one thing, but was life any better for Juniper since she'd moved to Solomon's Oak? Was this Christmas going to be a disaster? Could she ever stop worrying about money? Edsel twitched every once in a while, triggering a groan from Dodge, and earning a look from Cadillac, who slept with one eye open. Juniper grew heavy in her lap. When she was certain the girl was asleep, she sang her a Neil Peart song, "The Trees." The oak trees, selfishly hoarding sunlight, were no match for the maple trees that organized like Teamsters bearing hatchets, axes, and saws. Glory substituted junipers for the maple trees, and though that ruined the rhyme scheme, the song held up just fine.

Chapter 7

JOSEPH

When Joseph felt the thundering under his feet his first thought
was *earthquake*. Then came the wild-eyed horse, reins flying out
behind, and the girl hanging on to the saddle horn for dear life,
screaming, "Stop! Stop!" at the top of her lungs. He recognized
her immediately. It was the teenager with the earrings in her
face, the one who'd grilled him at the pirate wedding. Her name
was odd, Spruce or Birch or some other tree species. "Somebody
help me!" she yelled, and he guessed that somebody would have
to be him.

To stop a runaway horse, you needed to project authority and
remain calm, something a horse this worked up rarely noticed.
Your best bet was to grab a rein and turn the horse's head to one
side, causing its neck to bend, and its whole body to move in an
arc or a circle. Such a move slowed the horse down, and when
things were in crisis, it was beneficial to go slow. Lucky for
Joseph, the girl looked steady enough; she had a death grip on the
saddle horn. Lucky for everyone, the horse hadn't stepped on a
rein and brought them both down. Joseph ran toward the horse
and grabbed hold of the left rein, pulling hard. He stumbled,
afraid he was going to fall down, but found his footing again and

pulled. The leather burned his palm, but the horse slowed from a gallop to a trot, mere feet from the part of the oak grove thickest with trees. Any branch could have knocked her off that horse. Broken her neck, maybe. But the horse wasn't stopped yet. Joseph had no choice but to run alongside, his back be damned. "Grab his mane!" he told her.

"I can't let go!"

"Yes, you can!" With all that bending the horse was forced to make, he slowed down to a walk, which allowed Joseph to convince him to halt. Poor guy was as scared as the screaming meemie on his back. His sides heaved, and a scrim of lather had risen on his neck. Joseph kept his voice steady, saying, "Ho, ho," over and over. The horse's nostrils flared, but his breathing was slowing down. In a few minutes, Joseph would be able to help the girl down and walk the horse back to wherever they'd come from. "See?" he said. "I knew you could do it. Good girl."

Now that the horse was still, the girl released one shaking hand and grabbed the horse's mane. "N-now what?"

"Hold on a second." Joseph caught the second rein and walked the snorting horse in the other direction. The worst of it was over, but he knew better than to relax. "Ho, buddy. That's right." Then he told the girl, "Okay, slide your right leg across his back and dismount."

"I can't."

"Sure you can."

"I'll fall."

"If you do, I'll catch you." His heart pumped with adrenaline; he could only imagine how the girl's was behaving. He'd lived rural long enough that he'd seen his share of horse wrecks. It was a mystery to him why so many people believed they were born knowing how to ride. The emergency stop was the first lesson he'd learned, and the most valuable. He wondered why Glory Solomon hadn't taught her daughter that lesson.

The girl was crying hard now. He patted her leg. "Come on, take your right leg out of the stirrup. Put your weight in the left."

Finally she slid her other leg over, and he grabbed her waist to help her to the ground. Immediately after the dismount, she screamed, "Take your hands off me, you pervert!"

This startled the horse again, and he crow-hopped, which nearly yanked Joseph's left arm out of its socket. He patted the gelding's muscular neck to calm him down. More luck. Inexperienced rider plus freaked-out horse equaled darn lucky he was in the woods taking pictures. Then he noticed the border collie, wagging his tail as if this occurred every day. "You there," Joseph said, "looking so calm and all. How come you didn't herd this animal back home?"

The dog wagged its tail.

The girl was still crying, so Joseph handed her a napkin from his pants pocket to wipe her eyes. Every café he went to, they gave him too many, and he hated throwing them away, so wasteful, that he ended up with wads of them in his pockets, which made for problems on laundry day. "Remember me from the wedding? Ex-cop picture taker? I sure liked the leftovers you sent home with me."

She wiped her face. "Joseph? What are you doing out here on Christmas Eve?"

"Oh, the usual. Pulling my gun on reindeer. Looking for a solemn ceremony to crash. Saving girls on runaway horses." The horse was breathing normally now. He'd recovered and so had the girl. Joseph looked around. "You're not riding alone, are you? Where's your mom?"

"I'm not alone. Cadillac's with me. My dog."

"I see that. Now, pardon me for sounding like a cop, but ride in pairs or a group until you're more experienced. Your horse could've stumbled, thrown you, any number of unfortunate scenarios."

She had stopped crying, but not trembling. "I'm not a beginner! I'm fine now."

You're a beginner until you can keep control of your horse, he wanted to say, but didn't. "You lost your reins and you were screaming your head off."

She smoothed her two-tone hair back behind her ears. "So? What if you stumbled all alone here on Christmas Eve and nobody saw you?"

It was a good point. "You still haven't answered my question. Where's your mom?"

She looked away. "Aren't you supposed to be at church or home with your family? I don't have one, so I can do what I want."

"That might come as news to your mother."

He turned and walked the horse in the opposite direction. "My family's eight hundred miles away. I miss them."

"So then why aren't you at the movies with your girlfriend, or helping out at the homeless shelter? Serving up instant mashed potatoes with that canned brown gravy."

She laughed her head off after that. In moments she'd gone from big sobbing tears to hysterical laughter, and he wondered if she was high on some drug or drunk, or if that was her normal behavior.

"Homeless people are funny?"

"Of course not," she said. "But two holidays out of the year is all they get?"

"It's better than nothing."

"Oh, yeah. Right. Like people want to be reminded they have

no family so they go into the shelter expecting something halfway decent. It smells good; it looks like it should taste good. But put a spoonful of gravy in your mouth and it's like eating brown snot." She laughed again. "Sorry. Guess you had to be there."

"Sounds like I'm glad I wasn't. Juniper, like the tree."

"What?"

"Your name. I just remembered."

"Give the man a prize. How about some extra gravy?"

She was laughing again. Juniper wasn't such an odd name. Where he came from, people had last names like Spottedhorse and Twohills, or hyphenated mouthfuls like Valle-Sanchez-de-Gallardo-Iglesia-Montoya. "Your mother doesn't know you're out here, does she?"

Juniper patted the neck of the now calm horse. "She's at the store buying crackers and a cheese ball. Tonight is a very big deal. *Blood* relatives."

What did that mean? "Do you have permission to ride by yourself?"

Juniper shrugged. "So I broke out of jail for a half hour. Big wow. I'll be back before she gets home, the horse will be cleaned up and she'll never know. Are you taking pictures today?"

"I was."

"Of what?"

"All these oaks."

"I bet I know why. If you photograph trees in an orchard to make a pattern, the negative space becomes just as important as the subject. That's what Michael Busselle did."

Joseph was shocked to hear her mention Busselle. Knowing that name meant she'd been looking closely at photography, exploring the greats. "Well, no more trees for me today. I'm going to follow you home. My car's the yellow—"

"Land Cruiser, I know." Juniper gave him a dirty look. "I'm very disappointed in you, Joseph. You look cool on the outside, and the gun is major bonus points, but open your mouth and you sound just like every other adult. You don't trust teenagers."

"I trust 'em. It's the rest of the world I have trouble trusting around them. Come on, I'll give you a boost up. You keep that horse at a dead walk."

"I'll lead him home by hand."

Joseph knew if she did that, she'd never get on another horse again. "Oh, no. You wanted to ride, so you'll ride."

"Why should I listen to you? We hardly know each other. Technically, you're a stranger."

"Did you forget I'm armed?" He patted the left side of his jacket, where the gun used to be snug in its holster. The day after the wedding he'd bought a lockbox for it and put it under his bed, finally admitting that the likelihood of getting mugged at Lake Nacimiento was low unless the chipmunks had taken up arms. "I'll rat you out to your mother in a heartbeat. Once a copper, always a copper."

"Copper." Juniper laughed at that, but she let him boost her right leg up and over the saddle.

"Relax," Joseph said.

"I am relaxed!" The horse startled.

"Stop yelling."

"I'm not yelling! Let's go, Caddy." The stealthy, blue-eyed dog led the way, the horse following like a thousand-pound magnet.

Joseph drove alongside her at five miles an hour. They crossed the county road and went up the Solomon Ranch driveway. He parked by the vine-covered fence in front of the barn and got out. Juniper was through the gate before he shut his car door. She groomed the horse at Mach 1. She was still so young that she expected if she brushed hard enough, no evidence would remain to convict her. Joseph knew from his years in the crime lab that most criminals left glaring calling cards. Well, riding horses without permission was her problem, not his. The pinto horse behind the fence whinnied and screeched as if her best friend had threatened to move cross-country. "Those two look inseparable," he said. "What made you take the horse out by himself?"

Juniper didn't answer. She offered the mare a handful of oats, but the horse let them fall to the ground. "Cricket, shut up!" she yelled. "How was I supposed to know Piper would flip out like some nutcase?"

"Imagine if Cricket jumped the fence and ran to the county road. A horse that freaked-out isn't going to stop and look both ways. Your mom could've come home to a real train wreck."

"That's such a cliché."

Ouch. The tyranny of teenage girls, Joseph thought. It's a wonder anyone gets married.

Once Piper was settled in the turnout arena that led to the stalls, Juniper turned to Joseph. "You can go now."

She'd left the grooming tote outside the barn, which Mrs. Solomon would spot right away. Should he tell Juniper, or let her bust herself? "Because it's Christmas Eve, I'm going to give you a present. But I want something in return."

"What? Sex?"

He sighed. "That's not funny. I want your solemn promise that you won't go riding by yourself anymore. Deal?"

"Depends on the present."

He pointed to the tack tote, spilling brushes and a cake of saddle soap. "Put that back exactly where you found it or your mom will know immediately what you did."

Juniper packed the tote and carried it into the barn, where,

Joseph imagined, every single piece of equipment had its assigned space. "Thanks," she said. "It's weird how you show up every time there's a problem."

"Coincidence."

Juniper shook her head. "I'm totally exhausted. Already today I've fed the dogs, the goats, and the chickens, I've scrubbed the kitchen tile grout with bleach and a toothbrush. I waxed the mantel and buffed it, swept the floors, and folded the laundry. I even put the cider and spices in a Crock-Pot so it'll be ready when the *relatives* arrive. I should change my name to Cinderella."

He chuckled. "What's so bad about relatives? We all got 'em."

"They're *her* relatives, not mine. I'm a foster."

"Lucky you," he said, and meant it.

"Yeah, well, she treats me like a slave."

"Do you get an allowance?"

"Yes."

"How much?"

"I'm not telling you that just so you can beat me up with it."

"Some kids grow up without an allowance."

Any gratitude she'd shown was replaced by a dead, icy look in her eyes. "Some kids don't grow up at all, Joe. Merry effing Christmas. Now get out of my sight or I'll tell Mrs. Solomon that you tried to touch me."

"Remember the story about the kid who cried 'wolf'? Merry Christmas, kid."

GLORY

"Come in, come in," Glory said, taking hold of her mother's arm while Bart held the front door open. Chilly winter air mingled with the heat from the fireplace, and the smell of the hot cider was everywhere. "I made appetizers," Glory said, leading her mother, who was wearing a red pantsuit and her silver squash-blossom necklace, to the mission-style rocker. The oak chair back and arms made it easy to get in and out of. "Mom, you look lovely tonight."

"Thank you, honey. It's so good to see you. I haven't been to your place in I don't know how long."

Glory knew. Nearly ten months. The day after Dan died, her mother, who rarely ventured past a ten-mile-radius comfort zone, had braved the freeway and back roads to stand at the stove and make her daughter "milk toast," a childhood tradition whenever Glory was convalescing. After that she sat on the couch and hugged Glory, singing her all four verses of "The Gate Ajar for Me."

Glory motioned Juniper closer. "Mom, I want you to meet Juniper, my foster daughter. Juniper, this is my mother, Ave Smith."

For her Christmas outfit, Juniper had chosen the black sweater that was miles too big for her and black jeans. Over the sweater, she wore the purple Celtic horses T-shirt. She refused to add a scarf, a necklace, or Christmas-tree pin; this was her outfit and she was sticking to it. She also had all her face jewelry in place. "Nice to meet you, Mrs. Smith."

"Hello there, Juniper."

Juniper brought her a mug of hot cider with a cinnamon stick. "Have some. It's really good."

"Juniper made it," Glory said.

"Thank you," Ave said. "You look very festive with those ornaments in your eyebrow and such. Tell me, did it hurt when you poked the holes?"

"A little."

"Do they let you wear them to school? Glory told me you're at King City High now. A freshman."

"They don't, but I put them in the second I get home."

Bart held the door open for Halle, who balanced a huge gift basket wrapped in green cellophane in her arms. "Noel, Noel," she said, and set the basket on the kitchen counter, where it dwarfed the plate of crackers and the almond-encrusted ball of sharp cheddar. She slipped out of her suede coat and handed it to Glory, who hugged her sister.

"Thanks, Halle. Merry Christmas to you, too." Glory pointed to a box wrapped in brown paper with a pinecone ornament tied into the raffia bow. "I've got five kinds of jam to send home with you." She looked up at Bart, the only one who looked comfortable in his clothes, faded jeans, scuffed loafers, and a green sweater that actually fit. "Halle, Bart, meet Juniper, my foster daughter."

Bart shook Juniper's hand, moved closer, and asked about the graphic on her T-shirt. "We've been to Ireland twice," he said.

"Did you see Stonehenge?"

"That's in England," he said. "But, yes, we did, and pretty much every stone circle and plinth we could find on a map. I hope someday you can visit."

Halle said, "Hello," but kept her distance.

Glory watched her sister survey the room and tried to see things from her eyes. No doubt she counted every stray dog hair and scratch in the worn wood floor. It made no difference how much Glory scrubbed, the old house would not pass Halle's inspection. When Halle came to visit, Glory saw the flaws so plainly. It wouldn't take much to snazz things up, a coat of paint, new cabinet hardware, and slipcovers to cover the slipcovers, a few new floorboards. The problem was that Halle left, and once she was out of sight, Glory got busy with more important things. Juniper ladled a mug of cider for Halle. Glory watched her sister try to unobtrusively inspect the rim of the cup. One lousy time Glory had accidentally given her a used wineglass, and that did it, twenty years of the lay health inspector's distrust unleashed.

"Glory," Halle said, "your house reminds me of one of those Christmas cards put out by Leanin' Tree. Everything is so homey and cozy and Western. But where's your Christmas tree?"

All of that was code for "run-down, cramped, and tacky." Glory felt sure Halle would rather be at a world-class performance of *The Nutcracker* somewhere in the Bay Area than here in Glory's derelict homestead. "We bought a live tree so we could plant it after Christmas. It's by the chicken coop. I can take you out there if you want to see it. We decorated it with popcorn strings and cranberries. The other day birds were all over it."

"That's okay. Did you do something to the cupboards? Refinish them?"

"No, but I plan to get around to that soon. Come and sit down here, on the throw. I vacuumed the couch. I promise, no scabies."

"Glory," Ave warned. "Don't bait your sister."

"What? This throw is cashmere." Glory held back the information that it came from T.J.Maxx and was marked down to $9 because it had been opened and had an easily repairable pulled thread. In the background, Edsel yipped and scratched at the bedroom door. "Juniper? Would you mind getting the dog?"

Juniper excused herself, returning with Edsel in his holiday outfit, a black fleece hoodie with silver bows, one-two-three down his long back. "Be sweet," Juniper whispered, and he headed straight for Glory's mom.

"There's my little Eddie!" Ave said. "Come here, you cutie-pie!"

"I have to show you my new car," Halle said. "It's got a hands-free cell phone, built-in GPS, and side air bags."

"Sounds great," Glory said.

"Glory," Ave said. "He looks like Frank Sinatra in that outfit. Eddie, you'll have to jump up by yourself, I'm afraid. I can't trust these old claws of mine to catch you anymore."

"Mom, don't let it snag your new clothes," Halle said.

It. Glory felt her heart clench. Every holiday reminded her that her mother's arthritis was advancing. In one fluid leap, Edsel was in her mother's lap, holding up one paw for a high five, working Ave's soft heart in hopes of treats. Out back, as if they could hear what was going on, Cadillac and Dodge began complaining.

"Isn't he overheating in that outfit?" Halle said.

"Believe me," Glory said, "if he didn't want it on, it would be in shreds."

"He can't have crackers," Juniper warned Mrs. Smith. "Let me get you one of his special biscuits. Mom taught me how to make them."

Halle's head turned at the sound of "Mom."

Glory stared a hole in her. *I dare you to say something. Just try. Nothing would make me happier than watching you put your size nine Naturalizer in your mouth.*

Bart put his arm around Halle. "Glory, that little dog of yours is such a character. He must be great company for Juniper."

Juniper shook her head. "Edsel's all right. But he's not Cadillac."

"I'd like to get a dog someday," Bart said. "When I retire."

"Why wait?" Glory asked. "I've got one out back ready for adoption. A housebroken, Frisbee-playing, come-when-you-call, watchdogging sweetheart named Dodge. You can take him home tonight. I'll even throw in a bag of kibble."

"Over my dead body," Halle said.

"Halle! Don't talk like that on Christmas," Ave said, letting Edsel nibble at the dog biscuit. "Don't either of you ever wish time away, and never joke about death."

The room went quiet. The Smith sisters were instantly reduced to teenage girls bickering over who had used whose mascara one minute and the next minute crying streaky black tears in each other's arms because their father was dead of a heart attack. Twenty-three years had gone by, but every Christmas Glory expected her gentle giant of a father to walk into the room wearing his Santa hat, silver boxes in his hands with new charms for the bracelets they were too old to wear, but treasured. When Ave raised her voice in the slightest, her daughters went silent.

"Juniper," Ave said, "would you mind bringing me a few of those people crackers, please?"

"Okay." Juniper began loading up a plate.

Glory wanted to hug her.

Bart gestured to the computer sitting on the desk where Glory had moved it so that Juniper could use it for homework and Glory could supervise what she was doing. The screen saver defaulted to solomons-oak-chapel.com, a slide show of cakes, trees, the chapel interior, and musicians. He jiggled the mouse and whistled. "Someone has done a heck of a good job on this. Glory, did you take a class or something?"

"Juniper did it. Isn't it great? And in no time at all. Have her show you the link to the pirate wedding."

"It's great you're having such luck with this wedding business. Dan would be proud."

All day Glory had known the moment was coming. Someone would say something about Dan, then she'd feel her throat constrict and taste salt in her mouth and fight the longing to rush to the closet. Instead, she took a breath, then let it out slowly. "Thank you for saying that, Bart. I hope if he can see how we're all faring, that he's proud of all of us."

"Course he can see us," Ave said. "He's sitting next to His Heavenly Father and they're both having cider spiked with a little dab of whiskey."

"A big dab of whiskey," Bart said.

"The cheese ball looks so tasty," said Ave. "Did you make it, too, Juniper?"

"I unwrapped it from the package."

"Well, good for you, dear. I can tell you're a big help to my daughter. It's hard to be without our loved ones, but we should be rejoicing that they've gone to be with the Lord in eternal love."

That was the second thing Glory had been dreading, her mother bringing up God, implying that Dan was happier there than he could have been here, and, by including Juniper in that conversation, implying that God was all right with lives ending in unspeakable violence. "Bart, can I get you more cider?"

"Thanks, that'd be great."

While Glory ladled the spicy drink into his mug, Ave and Edsel cuddled in the rocker. Juniper delivered the plate of goodies, and immediately Halle set down her cider. She shooed Edsel away and plucked an imaginary hair off her mother's shoulder. She also took the plate from her. Halle was practically hand-feeding her the crackers and cheese. "Be careful, Mom," she said, holding a napkin under her hand. "You don't want to spill on your nice new pantsuit."

Glory tried not to roll her eyes. This was her cue to compliment Ave on how nice she looked in the expensive red Christmas present Halle had given her early so she could wear it tonight. Subtext: Halle can afford this. Glory cannot. "Mom," Glory said, "Grandma Denise's necklace looks great with your outfit. Did you polish it?"

"Your grandmother would have my hide if I let silver polish near any of her Indian jewelry. She liked everything to look like dead pawn. That's old jewelry that was pawned by the owner, but never redeemed," Ave said to Juniper. "She said that was how you could tell the real New Mexicans from the people who moved there from out of state. Polished *concho* belts so bright they could blind a person, hah! There's nothing like Christmas in New Mexico. You girls are too young to remember the *farolitos* atop adobe walls, candlelight blinking against the snow, and the smell of piñon in the air." Ave turned to Juniper. "Folks would light small bonfires in their driveways and everyone walked up Canyon Road. It's magical, Juniper. Maybe someday soon your new mom will take you to see it."

"I'd love to," Glory said. "But right now I think it's time to head over to Butterfly Creek."

"Mom, let me know if tonight's too much for you. Bart and I can take you home whenever you feel like it. You can sleep in the backseat of the Volvo without a worry," Halle said, looking at Glory. "It has heated seats."

"Well, let's go see the fabulous car before it gets dark," Glory said. "You guys can follow my truck over to the party."

"I just hope it won't be too cold for Mom," Halle said. "I've never heard of an outdoor party in December. Not to mention held at a general store."

Bart helped Ave to her feet and she kissed Edsel good-bye.

Glory bit her tongue.

JOSEPH

"Ladies and gentlemen, thank you for coming out tonight to celebrate the annual Christmas Eve tradition of turning the Butterfly Creek General Store into a honky-tonk Christmas," the banjo player said into the microphone with the word BLUE in chrome across its front. "We've been playing together since Adam was a pup. Our sets are eight songs long, danceable, and we don't get fancy unless Clyde over there gets into the sangria. If you have any requests, take it up with Senora Candelaria, who is gracious enough to keep asking us back every year. Okay, boys. Let's get down to business."

Joseph watched the banjo player step back and turn to the guitarist, who in turn nodded to the fiddle player, and seconds later a bluegrass version of the gospel tune "Are You Washed" drifted out into the night air, rocking the Chinese lanterns strung overhead from table to table. Joseph held his camera in front of him, considering. Live music gave a photographer the opportunity to get creative with low stage lighting. Using the flash was taking the easy way out. Worrying about it so much you missed the shot was "chimpy." A fast shutter speed was essential, unless you were going for some artsy outcome, but all he wanted was a reminder of this evening, something he could give to Lorna for being so nice to him while he was here.

"*Cámarografo*, you're holding that little box in front of your heart like a shield," Lorna scolded him. "Put it in your vehicle and ask some hottie to dance while you're still young."

Joseph smiled at Lorna, who was gussied up in a pink, pearl-snap cowboy shirt, a pink suede fringed vest over that, jeans with rhinestones down the sides, and pink python boots. "You're the only hottie on the scene."

"Nonsense," she said close to his ear, and pointed out several women who had overdone the makeup and wore stiletto heels. "Any one of those girls would be *encantada* if you asked them to dance."

Joseph leaned close to her ear and said, "*Bajaron la calle dando brincos.*"

"That's not true. They aren't expecting 'happily ever after,' Joe. It's Christmas. Nobody wants to be alone." Lorna let go of his hand and went off to manage other folks' lives.

Joseph looked around at the oil-drum barbecues grilling Santa Maria tri-tip beef and at the tables laden with side dishes. The *arroz con pollo* looked great, and tightly rolled *taquitos* with guacamole also beckoned. The *nopales* salad disappeared before he could get a plate, but there were no pineapple dessert tamales like those his mom always made. Maybe he should have flown home for the holidays, but he wasn't ready for a roomful of relatives' concern, his mother's babying him, his father wearing that look that meant "*¡No seas niño o crío!*"—when are you going to snap out of it! He'd call them tomorrow, then call Fidela, Rico's wife, and the boys, Hecktor and Antonio, to make sure they'd received the presents he'd splurged on—mountain bikes for the boys, a fancy ice-cream maker for Rico's widow. Transparent gestures, he knew, but he had to do something.

He felt a hand on his arm and turned to see Juniper pushing Glory Solomon toward him. Glory was wearing the blue dress again and had a barn coat draped over her shoulders. What with the oil-barrel bonfires and heat lamps, it was warm enough out here on the patio deck that a light jacket sufficed. He smiled and said hello, but it was impossible to hear her talk, so he followed them over to the food tables, carefully weaving in and out of guests and dancers.

"I didn't know you knew Lorna," Glory said when their ears stopped ringing. "How are you, Mr. Vigil?"

She hadn't brought up the runaway-horse rescue, which meant Juniper hadn't told them about their earlier meeting. Interesting. Should he bust Juniper on Christmas Eve? When he made eye contact with her, she made the slightest shake of her head no.

"Call me Joseph, and I'm decent. How's the wedding business? Or did I ruin your reputation?"

Glory smiled. "Not at all. We have bookings in February and April."

"Excellent news. Happy holidays." He turned to move along, but she stopped him.

"Wait. I was wondering. We're kind of a ragtag bunch, but would you care to meet my family?"

"Lead the way," he said, because what kind of *tarado* said no? He placed his hand on her shoulder, steering through the crowd. Coming up on her family, he was surprised to learn Ave Smith was much shorter than her daughters and frail-boned in a way that spoke of long-term illness. When she held her gnarled hand out to shake, he placed both of his around it and felt the heat that emanated from her bones.

"Glory told me that you made the pirate wedding day interesting."

"Yes, ma'am. I'll never live that story down."

"It's good to have stories that make us laugh at ourselves," Ave said.

Joseph looked at Juniper, and he knew she was thinking of the horse debacle only hours ago. "That's so true, Mrs. Smith. What do you think, Juniper?"

"I guess," Juniper said, looking around, he could tell, for somewhere else to be.

She reminded him of the kids he'd worked with back in Albuquerque. If they could take one tenth of the energy they put into acting cool and divert it into schoolwork, 100 percent of them would graduate instead of only 43 percent. He turned to shake Glory's sister's hand. She gave him the royal fish-eye, but he smiled and said, "Lovely to meet you, Halle. Your sister told me about you."

"Really? What did she say?"

"That you're her best friend and role model, and I can see why."

Juniper giggled, and Glory looked dumbfounded. Eh, so what if he was feeding her *abono*. It was Christmas.

"Well, I don't know what to say."

"No need to say anything," Joseph said. "This must be your husband? How do you do, sir?"

The brother-in-law seemed warm and engaging, but he also looked as if he'd rather be watching ESPN. He stepped up and shook Joseph's hand and asked him about his camera.

"It's a Canon EOS 40D 10.1 megapixel SLR."

"Sweet," Bart said. "Are you here in an official capacity?"

"Excuse me?"

"Bart means, are you taking pictures for Lorna?" Glory said, saving him.

"No, just for fun. Would you like a family portrait?"

"I thought you didn't like photographing people," Glory said.

"I make exceptions for holidays."

"In that case we'd love it," Glory said. Halle stood with her side to the camera, and Joseph smiled because so many women used that trick, believing it made them appear slimmer. Halle was nowhere near fat; in fact, she looked a little scrawny to him. Juniper stretched her arms around her mother and foster grandmother as if she'd known them all her life, but steered clear of the sister/aunt, who steered clear of her. Ah, families. Joseph framed them in various ways. Juniper's face piercings caught the light, and Joseph took advantage of it. He took five or six pictures, then a portrait of Glory alone with Juniper. Juniper leaned over Glory's shoulder, her two-tone hair falling forward. Glory put her hand up to hold Juniper's. When she smiled, Joseph knew it was a keeper the second the shutter clicked.

"Remember just how you posed for this picture," he said. "If you take the same pose every year, you'll create a story."

"Of what?" Juniper asked.

"Of how much everything changes."

"Or stays the same," Glory added.

"Ooh, that sounds so mysterious," Halle interrupted. "Take one of Bart and me. Maybe we can use it on a future Christmas card."

Joseph obliged. "Any more?"

Glory turned to her brother-in-law. "No offense, Bart, but could we take one of just us ladies?"

"A great idea," he said.

Halle stepped into the shot, turning sideways.

"Move closer together," Joseph said. He took shot after shot, looking for the moment that revealed each of their personalities. Glory, getting the job done. Her mother, Ave, gracefully existing with pain that shaped her days. Halle, smart, efficient, dressed to the nines on the outside, insecure on the inside. Then there was Juniper, the wild card.

"This will be a lovely addition to my family album," Mrs. Smith said.

Juniper had had enough. "I'm going to find the restroom," she said, and walked away.

"Stay close," Glory called after her.

Even with the hormones and boy craziness that came with her age group, Joseph envied Glory time with the smart-mouthed kid. But why was he thinking about teenagers? Lorna would say, "A perfect opportunity to get close to a pretty woman and what do you have to show for it? A camera full of *their* moments." So he stayed and made himself talk. "Where do you folks live?" he asked Halle and Bart.

Halle answered for the two of them. "We live in the North Bay area, Santa Rosa. Have you been there?" With her sequined top and black trousers she could have been on her way to see some Russian ballet with $200 theater tickets.

"No, but I know your trees."

"Our *what*?"

"Santa Rosa trees. The controversy over removing eucalyptus."

"They're like candle wicks," Halle said. "You don't want them in your backyard, that's for sure."

"What trees do you have on your property?" Joseph asked.

He'd given Bart an entrance. "We have crab apple and an ornamental plum, but my pride and joy is our Spring of Equinox cherry. It grows like a weed, and every year when it blooms, our yard hums with bees. I always wanted to give beekeeping a try."

"I'm unfortunately allergic," Halle said.

"This is true," Bart said.

"Do you know about the ancient Japanese cherry tree Yamataka Jindai Zakura?" Joseph asked.

"Come again?" Bart said.

"Sorry. The Yamataka Jindai Zakura, estimated to be eighteen hundred years old. Story goes that the second-century folk hero Yamato Takeru Nomiko planted it. It still produces fruit."

"That is some kind of miracle," Bart said.

"Oh. You're a gardener?" Halle said. "I can't tell you how many gardeners I've hired who quit without telling me."

"Halle!" Glory said.

"What? I just asked a simple question. Did I offend you, Senor Vigil?"

Senor.

"Not at all," Joseph said. "I'm not a gardener, but my father is a fifth-generation farmer. I'm interested in unusual trees, which is how I met your sister, because of Solomon's Oak."

"Did you grow up in the area?" Halle added.

"No," Glory said. "He comes from New Mexico, just like Mom."

Joseph looked at her, surprised.

"Juniper told me," Glory said. "Joseph, our mother was born in Clovis."

The thin woman said, "Girls, I may be an old lady, but I can still flap my jaw without assistance. Joseph, I don't suppose you know my hometown?"

"My family comes from Hatch and Santa Fe. But, sure, I know Clovis. There's a lot of new development going on there. I bet I know what you miss about it: Tucumcari Mountain, the Buddy Holly museum, and the State Theater."

"Does that ever bring back memories. I miss the smell of piñon fires, but I don't miss the thunderstorms."

Joseph laughed. "My grandmother used to tell me that storms were caused by birds flapping their wings."

"Is that right?"

"Yes, ma'am." He could tell Ave Smith had been away from New Mexico so long she'd forgotten what weather could do. Late snowstorms, lightning strikes, lack of rainfall. The conversation stalled, and Joseph struggled for a graceful exit. "Where did

Juniper go? I was hoping to tell her merry Christmas again. That is a great kid you have there, Glory."

The surprised look Glory gave him said it all—Juniper was a handful, Glory's family wasn't 100 percent behind the foster-daughter business, and add that to the first Christmas without her husband, she was hanging on by a thread. He continued to hold her gaze longer than was polite. It occurred to him that after separating himself from his own family, here was the person he wanted to tell his story to, but the place was too crowded, and besides, it was Christmas. She might not understand about the prescription medicine; there was Rico's death. Too much, really. Would her smile turn to glacier ice, or would she look away as Isabel had near the end of things? He couldn't take the chance.

"Juniper is over there." Glory pointed. "Looks like she's visiting with Elliot, Lorna's great-nephew. Oh, dear. I think she's flirting. Maybe I should go get her before things get out of hand."

"Let her have some fun," Ave said.

Glory looked at Joseph and he smiled. "Your mom's right. She's a good kid."

"If only you knew," Glory said softly, so that no one caught it but him.

The band had played a couple of songs already, "Jerusalem Ridge," "Up and Around the Bend," and now began "Doubting Thomas," the first slow-tempo song of the night. "Thanks, I'd love to dance," Glory said, pulling Joseph away from her family.

"Uh, thanks?" he said, when she had placed her left hand on his shoulder and offered her right hand to him.

"You're saving my sister's life because I'm about ready to duct-tape her mouth shut and cut off her air supply."

He laughed. With small steps they moved around the crowded deck. The strength of her hand in his surprised him. She smelled like a kitchen, something between cinnamon and just-baked bread. All the sensations made for an enormous contrast to the ache in his back. When he caught sight of Lorna, he smiled, expecting a thumbs-up for his efforts. Instead of applauding, she folded her arms across her pink vest and gave him a hard look. Now what? Maybe her suggestion had an exclusivity clause. He was free to dance with any woman *except* Glory Solomon.

When the music stopped, they let go of one another and clapped, standing shoulder to shoulder. "Thank you," Glory said. "I think my blood pressure's back down to normal."

"You're welcome. If the next song's slow, want to dance again?"

Before she could answer, the band launched into "Foggy Mountain Breakdown," and Mrs. Smith got to her feet and began clogging. Glory's face went from shock to worry to delight. Everyone around her mother began to clap in time to cheer her on. Everyone except Halle, who was scowling.

"She won't be able to get out of bed in the morning," Glory whispered to Joseph.

"It'll be worth it."

Ave Smith stopped herself before Halle could scold her. She was red in the face but smiling.

Joseph shook her hand. "Ma'am, that is definitely some Clovis-style clogging."

"Shh." She pointed to the stage where Lorna now stood in front of the microphone.

With Lorna, you never knew what might come out of her mouth. Joseph hoped she was about to say merry Christmas, or that the Butterfly Creek was happy to give a ride home to anyone who'd drunk too much, but when Lorna opened her mouth, out came a song Joseph had never before heard. Her raspy voice sawed through the night air, gathering strength as she sang. "Oh, man," Joseph said when she was halfway through the first verse.

Glory said, "It's called 'I'm That Sparrow,' by Chaz Bosarge. Lorna sang it at my husband's memorial service."

Some songs invited dancing, others clogging. The song Lorna belted out demanded a witness. By the end, Joseph was too choked up to look Glory in the face.

She touched his arm. "I'm sorry my sister called you Senor Gardener. I'd say she means well if it were true, but I don't think that's the case. If it helps, you dancing with me will have her digesting her pancreas for months. And thanks for what you said about Juniper. You see things in her I don't, at least not yet. She admires your pictures, and there isn't much she does admire. Any chance you might give her a photography lesson sometime?"

"It would have to be soon. I'm out of here in April."

"Oh, I didn't know that."

He found his composure before he looked at her. "My cabin. As soon as the rainy season ends, they're taking a bulldozer to it."

"That's criminal."

"Nah, it's inevitable. Place is falling down anyway."

"And you're all right with it?"

"What else can I be?"

"Right." She hesitated a minute. "Look, I don't mean to sound crass, but if there's anything there you might be willing to part with, like old floorboards, cupboards, or an old woodstove, I'd love to buy them from you. I'm trying to fix up my barn for parties."

"Sure. Come by after Christmas. Tell Juniper I'll give her a camera lesson if she keeps out of trouble."

"Joseph," Glory said before she gathered her family to go, "are you ever going to cash the check I sent you?"

He smiled. "Outlook doubtful."

She looked at him, puzzled. "Merry Christmas."

She left him standing there. He watched the family make their way across the parking lot, Halle's spiky heels tap-tapping like a woodpecker.

Lorna stood next to him not two minutes later. She marched him over to a picnic table. "That one is off-limits, José."

"Why?"

"I never saw two people more in love with each other than Glory and Dan. Her sorrow runs deep and she's vulnerable. Take advantage of her and I'll shave off your eyebrows."

"Just so you know, she asked me to dance."

She tsked. "I am going to tell you something you don't know about Glory Beatrice Smith Solomon. She is blind to that jealous sister of hers. I swear, Halle is so envious of what Glory had with Dan that when she chews gum, her teeth squeak. No trips to Europe or diamond wristwatches can make that go away. Glory, bless her heart, confuses her sister's remarks with disapproval. No matter how many times I tell her Halle's jealous, she doesn't hear me. And that Halle! Bosses that poor husband of hers around so much, you watch, someday she's going to lose him. I ought to know. I have sisters and ex-brothers-in-law coming out of my cornucopia."

"Glory's fortunate to have you as her friend."

Lorna straightened Joseph's jacket. "Are you going to push her into something she isn't ready for, such as your bed?"

"Furthest thing from my mind."

"Tread carefully, Joe Camera. I may be a *vieja*, but I can *vapulear a alguien* as good as the next person."

He had no doubt that she could kick his ass. "*No te preocupes*, not to worry. I'm headed back to New Mexico. I have nothing to keep me here."

Lorna laughed. "How the heck can you be Penny's grandson and so seriously deluded? You're not going anywhere. You've just arrived. *Feliz Navidad*, Joseph."

"*Y próspero año* to you, Lorna. You sang the *culo* off that song."

"I sure did, didn't I?" She walked away.

Just before Joseph got out of bed on Christmas morning, he experienced a brief glittery moment when he wondered if during the night he'd crossed from the mortal coil to the hereafter. Until he moved his body, the pain was absent. He could pretend the shooting never happened. Though this phenomenon had occurred enough times for him to no longer be surprised by it, he still expected that when he opened his eyes, he'd see Rico sitting on the foot of his hospital bed. *Hey, amigo,* he'd say. *Some people will do anything to get out of work.*

The last time he'd seen his friend, Joseph lay on a hospital gurney hooked up to three IVs and a heart and blood-pressure monitor. All around him piles of bloody gauze turned from bright red blood into mulberry dark stains. Rico had been examined, treated, and released. He had a through-and-through in his biceps and a grazing flesh wound from a bullet that had glanced off a rib in the lower left quadrant of his belly that was pronounced "superficial" and covered with a large Band-Aid. He patted his shirt pocket where he'd tucked his prescription for antibiotics. "Joe, all I have to do is flex my arm and show this bad-boy scar. Fidela will swoon at my bravery, make my favorite dinner, let me have the television remote, and later, when the boys are asleep?" Rico clicked his tongue. "You, on the other hand, will have to take off your shirt, turn over, and explain your injury. Women don't have that kind of patience anymore."

"What do I care?" Joseph remembered saying as he floated in and out of the drug-induced state that kept him free of pain until he was rolled into the OR. "After Isabel, I'm off women."

"You don't mean that."

"I do so."

Rico laughed. "Isabel would have made a terrible old lady. That is how you find the perfect woman. You look at her and think, fifty years from now she is making you a tuna fish sandwich and begging you to take her to Sandia Casino. If that makes you smile, you have found your soul mate. Someday soon you're going to need that heart, buddy. Tell them to fix it, too, while you're under the knife."

The orderly arrived and pulled up the side of Joseph's bed until it locked. He knew it was serious when they did not remove the board from the paramedics' gurney. His neck was immobilized in one of those collars that reminded him of his high school football uniform. They only wanted to move him once, transferring him to the OR table.

The surgeon hadn't said much. "Son, I will get you through this surgery, but I'm not going to sugarcoat it. Your chances of walking are optimistically twenty-five percent."

Joseph recognized the accent, Texas Hill Country. With surgeons and airplane pilots, you wanted a fearless Texan in charge. "I don't want to be Christopher Reeve. Something like that happens, accidentally shut off a machine."

"You have an advance directive?"

"No, sir. But I'll sign one now."

"Doesn't work that way, I'm afraid." The surgeon plunged a syringe into the IV tubing, and a small amount of clear liquid made Joseph's head swim. The surgeon called out to the techs standing by, "Fentanyl on board. Let's roll. Guess I'm going to have to save your life. I'll do my best with your legs." He turned to Rico. "You family?"

"I am. How long will the surgery take?"

"However long it takes. Give the nurse your name and phone number and we'll call you as soon as he's in recovery."

"Go home," Joseph told Rico. News cameras were trying to angle their way into the ER, and too many people were rushing around as it was. "Go kiss your wife and show the boys your war wounds."

"Nah, I'm staying. I want to be the first person you see when you wake up. *Hasta la vista, compañero!*"

See you later, partner. As if Rico considered their bond intact.

At discharge Rico had been ordered to see his family doctor in a week. They gave him his X-rays in a manila envelope. Any shooting put a cop on desk duty for a while, but Joseph knew Rico would find a way around that.

Joseph's surgery lasted four hours. The bullets were delicately removed and saved in a plastic evidence baggie. He was put into traction and parked in the ICU until he stabilized. The first two days post-op passed in a blur—he remembered his mother's face, the priest she dragged into the room to pray over him, his co-workers allowed in for a few minutes every hour. Joseph concentrated on moving his toes when ordered to, though he wasn't always sure he succeeded. Every time the doctors ran the tuning fork over his soles and whispered to each other, Joseph pictured Grandma Penny's cabin by the lake. Blue water. Horsetails. Pollywogs. The feel of the wind, the lap of the water.

When his head had cleared enough for him to become aware of his surroundings, three of his cop friends and the captain came into his room with the look on their faces that meant they'd been waiting to tell him the terrible part.

Joseph swore under his breath. "Tell me everything," he said. "I have to know."

Christmas morning and no *canciónes*, no Christmas carols or hymns. Jóseph moved his legs and the pain bracketed his spine like the metal teeth on an animal trap. He sat up, waited for things to adjust, then hobbled into the kitchen to nuke a bowl of instant oatmeal so he could take his pain pill. In exactly forty-one minutes, the time it took to fully kick in, he called his parents. "Happy Christmas, Mami," he said when she answered.

She started crying and handed the phone to his father, who said, "Your mother misses you," which was code for when are you coming home? This foolish idea of staying in a falling-down cabin all winter with no heat? Bah.

Feliz Navidad.

Ya'at'eeh Keshmish.

Merry Christmas.

Good-bye.

He didn't want to make the call, but it would be cowardly not to call Fidela on Christmas Day. He pressed the speed-dial number for his friend, wishing for the millionth time Rico would answer.

In Albuquerque, if you left your tree at the curb with trash, the city would pick it up for a few bucks. The collected trees were ground up, made into mulch, free for the taking. Maybe the newly elected governor, Schwarzenegger, didn't have the budget, because in the weeks after Christmas, in Joseph's daily meanderings from the Butterfly Creek to the Woodpecker to the Chevron station, he saw tree after tree tossed into what had formerly been an open meadow, a farmer's field, the beginning to the oak forest where he'd saved Juniper and received a ration for it. After the fifth tree, he stopped, took out his camera, and began taking pictures. Some still had tinsel on their branches. One was strung with lights and had a few broken bulbs. When possible, he propped them up, but mostly he photographed them as they lay, symbols of America's favorite holiday, abandoned. Why cut down a tree to throw it away?

OFFBEAT WEDDINGS INCREASINGLY POPULAR

Los Angeles Times—January 5, 2004

When Central Coast carpenter Dan Solomon died unexpectedly last year, his widow, Glory, faced surmounting hospital bills in addition to their mortgage. Her passion for rehabilitating death-row dogs and finding them families looked as if it might have to end.

The Solomons' ranch is known for the unusual tree growing there. Specifically, a white oak, the only one in the state, estimated by UCSC horticulture professor Jane Frederick-Collins to be two hundred plus years old.

Last October a visitor knocked on Mrs. Solomon's door with an unusual request. Would she permit a band of modern-day pirates to use the chapel on her property for their wedding ceremony?

The stone-and-oak chapel her husband built on a whim has quickly become a coveted locale for couples planning unconventional nuptials. . . .

Joseph studied the picture accompanying the article. The photographer had imposed a tic-tac-toe grid over the shot, dividing it into nine squares. Where the lines met were the "points of interest." He had posed Glory just right of center. Behind her, the chapel, slightly out of focus, looked like a scene from a fairy tale. Her long silver hair lay across her shoulders. The story this photograph told was this: You cannot own this magical place, but you can rent it, make memories, and take them with you when you go on home.

"What'll it be today?" Katie Jay asked Joseph.

"Tuna sandwich, please."

"Excuse me while I get my nitroglycerin."

When the rain let up, Joseph drove to the Chevron station and gassed up his car. At the market, he grocery-shopped for paper towels, toilet tissue, a six-pack of Coke, and birdseed. Two hours from sunset, he headed to the Solomon Ranch intent on photographing the damn oak tree once and for all. He parked his car by the house and knocked on the front door. No one answered, but the dogs started barking. Maybe Glory was in the barn. Around back of the house, a few brave chickens doddered in the rain, but most of them were in the coop staying dry, and who could blame them. The two horses he'd seen on Christmas Eve when he escorted Juniper home crowded the fence, hoping for handouts, and he wished he had apples. The little brown dog in his kennel sat on top of his doghouse, howling as if rain falling meant the end of the world. "If you don't want to get wet, go inside," he said.

The dog only barked louder. He was pretty worked up.

Joseph tried the vine-covered gate, but it wouldn't open. Like a fool, he boosted himself up the fence, then sat down on the top rail, his back muscles clenching so badly he had to push his fist into his side to stop the cramp. Okay, so he'd have to sit awhile for his back to settle down before he could get down. A few minutes—that was no big deal.

Except to the little brown dog spinning circles in his kennel. To him this man on his fence was cause for absolute hysteria. After Cadillac started howling, Joseph worried his eardrums would burst. When a dog barked on his father's farm, it meant coyote, horse wreck, or cow/ewe/dam/mare having trouble calving. Joseph tried to ease down from the fence, but when he leaned forward, the pain was worse. He gritted his teeth and pushed himself forward until the ground was under his feet. He went down on his knees and stayed there awhile, winded from the pain. When he could stand upright again, he unlatched the brown dog's kennel door. The dog went immediately for the barn, returning with a tennis ball.

"That's all you wanted? Don't expect much. I can only pitch underhand."

After a half hour of fetch, the brown dog was tired out and panting, and Joseph felt feverish with pain. He let the dog have a long drink from the hose, then returned him to his kennel. From inside the fence, surely the latch would be easier to unlock. He ran his hand along the vines until he came to the gate. Yes, pulling the upper latch was easy, but to reach the one on the bottom of the gate, he could neither squat down nor could he trust that if he went down on all fours, he could get up from there without help. He wasn't climbing the fence again. While he pondered the dilemma, he stroked the horses' necks for a while, missing his dad's farm and remembering how in winter a light snow would fall, dusting the horses' backs, and quickly melting. He was photographing the horses when Glory pulled up.

She threw the pickup into park and ran to the fence so quickly she left the driver's door hanging open. She was up and over the fence in no time, a shotgun in her arms. "Whoa," Joseph said.

"What the hell are you doing in my yard?"

He could see someone else in the truck. He raised his hands. "Passing time waiting for you. That's all."

"Oh, it's you." She pointed the shotgun to the ground. "Joseph, you shouldn't be on my property when I'm not here. What if you'd gotten hurt?"

He couldn't help smiling, because could he get any more hurt? "I grew up with horses, dogs, and sheep. I know what I'm doing."

"That doesn't matter! You could have gotten bitten, stepped on, let the horses loose . . ." She was killing mad, her face tight. Where was the woman he'd danced with on Christmas Eve?

"I'm sorry. It won't happen again."

"Please just leave."

"Mom, what's going on?" Juniper said, leaning over the fence, but Glory held up her hand to silence her.

"Believe me, I've tried," Joseph said. "It's too long a story, but here's the gist of it. I can't open the gate."

"How did you get in here?"

"Got this youthful notion I could climb the fence. I could, but apparently it was a onetime deal."

Glory walked to the fence, knelt down, and opened the lower latch, revealing the camouflaged hinge.

Juniper opened the gate from the other side and walked in. "Hey, Copper, guess I'm not the only one getting in trouble today.

Oh, my gosh, how cool is it that you're both packing heat? Did you ever see that movie *Tombstone*? Both of you could totally be in it. Joseph, will you show me your gun just once? I'd love to hold one, to see what it feels like, and Mrs. Solomon won't even let me know where she keeps the shotgun shells. How was your Christmas? Did you get any good presents? How come you never came back to give me a photography lesson?"

"Juniper," Glory said. "Go indoors."

"No way. Joe's my friend. He came to visit me."

Joseph hobbled toward the gate, embarrassed for them to see his limp. "Nice to hear I have a friend. But I came to see your mom."

"Why her?"

He held up the camera, feeling stupid. "To ask if I could photograph the tree today."

Glory looked at him. "It's forty-five degrees out, muddy, and the sun will be down in an hour. Why would you want to take pictures today?"

"I know, I know," Juniper said. "Because when the shadows are long, the light's better. That makes it the best time of day to take pictures."

"Look, I'm sorry," he said again, shifting his weight in an effort to escape the pain that crawled up his spine and squeezed. "Truthfully, I read the article in today's paper, thought of the tree, and Juniper's correct, this is the optimum time frame to shoot the tree. I should have called."

"What article?" Glory said.

The shotgun was nearly as tall as she was, and Joseph wondered if she'd ever fired it. "The one in today's *Los Angeles Times* about your chapel. Great publicity. You'll get a ton of calls from it. Didn't you see it?"

Glory pushed her hair back from her face and tied it in a bun. "The reporter said he'd call me if they ran it."

"Eh, you know reporters," Joseph said. "Deadlines."

"Am I in it?" Juniper asked.

"There's a copy in my car. You're welcome to it."

"I'll get it!" Juniper was out the gate in seconds. It looked as if her hair had grown another inch since the last time he'd seen her. She'd grown, too. In the high desert of New Mexico, junipers were hardy trees the color of a pup tent. The dusty blue berries they produced were good for cooking venison and making gin, but not so many knew what his grandmother had told him: Plant juniper trees by your front door. No *brujas* can pass without counting the exact number of needles on the tree, and as everyone knows, witches lack patience. In this case, it was Juniper who lacked patience. She opened the car door and leaned over until she was on her stomach, reaching for the paper he'd left on the passenger side of the floor. Joseph smiled because kids did what they felt compelled to do without running it past manners first, and when they could no longer get away with it, life became a lot less fun. Glory rubbed her chin, one finger pressed against her mouth as if she were keeping something that wanted to come out penned up and vine-covered like the gate. Yet as soon as Juniper opened the paper to show her the feature article, Glory's expression changed entirely. The hand pressed against her mouth went over her heart. The tension in her face departed. She no longer stood in her backyard reading a paper while two dogs flung themselves against the kennel door to get out. Lorna had told him on Christmas Eve that she'd never seen two people more in love than Glory and Dan. Glory was in the cupped hands of grief, reading the facts of her husband's death typeset in a newspaper for the world to see.

After she stopped reading, she looked up at Joseph and she was a different woman, calmer, her anger tamped down like pipe tobacco, but still there. "Thank you for bringing us the article, Joseph. Go take your pictures. If you'll excuse me, I have work to do inside."

"Can I go with him?" Juniper asked. "Please, Glory, please? I promise I'll be back in time to set the table. Please? I want to learn to take pictures so bad."

"Go ahead. But we're going to talk later."

"I can go? Really?"

A kid admittedly in trouble for something that sounded serious getting a reprieve? It was no surprise to Joseph. His father saved all the articles about Rico so that Joseph could read them when he was well enough. Glory Solomon needed that alone time to digest the newspaper story privately. She needed it more than she needed to keep a rein on her handful-and-then-some foster daughter.

"I'm just going to ask you straight out, Joe. Why do you limp?" Juniper asked on their hike toward the oak. "I mean, I noticed it at the pirate wedding, and at the Christmas party, but it's way worse today. Did you sprain your ankle? Sometimes a sprain hurts worse than a break. Do you think using a cane would help?"

"My legs are fine. I'm out of shape is all. When I couldn't reach the bottom latch, I did a foolish thing, climbing your fence."

"So are you in pain?"

"A little, but I can handle it."

"Do you want some aspirin, or ibuprofen?"

"No, thanks."

"So if it doesn't hurt killing bad, then why are you gritting your teeth?"

"I'm gonna take a wild guess here. Your hobby is asking questions?"

"Only rich people have hobbies. How else can a person find things out if they don't ask questions? Now tell me about photography. What is your plan with the tree? Do you like the 'lonely tree' kind of composition, or are you looking for the patterns the branches make?"

"You know something? Sometimes being quiet and observing teaches you more."

Juniper pulled her jacket tighter. "That is totally something a cop would say."

"I already told you, I'm not a cop anymore."

Juniper pointed her finger at his chest. "That doesn't mean you aren't one in your heart. You can't unlearn how to look at stuff. Believe me, I know."

Hoping for some quiet, he didn't answer. They slogged a hundred feet or so over muddy ground. Joseph tried not to limp. Though aspirin upset his gut, he would have chewed up a dry handful just to take the edge off. Instead, he studied the tree. Ansel Adams would see a stark tree, with the sky as definition. Wynn Bullock would pose a nude woman by the tree and turn her into a wood spirit. Jerry Uelsmann would plant a human fist inside the tree and sheep floating across the sky. Joseph Vigil couldn't see past anything other than branches that seemed to pierce the darkening sky so jaggedly you expected it to drip blood.

"The Christmas pictures you took came out great," Juniper said. "My foster grandmother really liked them, so maybe you should change subjects from trees to people. I mean, under a tree's a good place to sit for shade, but what else is there? They don't do anything exciting except maybe once in a while get struck by lightning."

He spoke without looking at her. "This isn't any tree, Juniper. It's Solomon's Oak."

"Stop right there because I've heard all about it being magical and improbable and good luck and having a spirit and all that. It didn't help when Mr. Solomon got sick, did it, and his family took care of it all these years so you would think if it was going to help anybody, it should have been him." She placed one hand on the trunk and twirled around, getting her shoes even muddier, demolishing any interesting patterns the rain had left behind.

"Can you be still? We're burning daylight. If I get the picture I want, I won't have to come back again or annoy your mother."

"Okay, okay." Juniper tucked her arms under her armpits for warmth. "If I stand still, I still get to talk, right?"

"No, you may not. Not for a few minutes. Be silent." Joseph took several pictures from a distance, then he zoomed in his lens for close-ups. The rutted bark was home to dusty green lichen. Up close it looked as if someone had ripped the fabric of the universe, and the tree had no choice but to continue its journey. But he couldn't communicate its height. "Stand next to it," he said.

"But I thought you only wanted pictures of the tree."

"You're only in the picture to be perspective."

"Thanks a lot." Juniper stood there, hands in her pockets. "You know what I think? I think your back hurts more than you let on. I think it's a good thing you brought me along, because what if you hurt yourself on that fence and we were maybe out of town and you needed help getting up? It's kind of like riding a horse in the woods by yourself. Dangerous."

"Hey, did I bust you with your mom?"

"No."

He turned around to go back to his car. "Then cut me a break."

She hurried up beside him. "I will if you stay for dinner. It's my night to make the salad."

"Somehow I doubt your mother would be up for that."

"But you're *my* friend." She stuck out her lower lip. "I could really use the support."

"Why? Are things not going so well? You looked pretty happy at the Christmas Eve shindig."

"I got suspended for fighting today."

"Fighting, as in fists?"

"It was a total misunderstanding."

"Why do I doubt that?"

"I don't know because I'm telling the truth. Sure, I've messed up in the past, but I only did the things I did for really good reasons. Like when I accidentally took some money, I gave it back. I gave back the pills, too."

"Are you talking about street drugs?"

Juniper looked away. "Be serious. They were prescription, just not my prescription."

"So why steal them?"

She sighed. "I was worried, okay? My real mom OD'd, and when I met Mrs. Solomon, she was so sad I thought she might try it, so I had to hide the pills. I should have flushed them. Then she never would have known. I was stupid not to think of that, but you know what they say, 'All drains lead to the ocean,' and drugs in the water are bad for the environment. But it sure got me in trouble."

"I'm not convinced you should be talking about this to me."

"Why not? You're my friend. You're kind of her friend. You guys danced. She's nice. Dogs love her. She works really hard. I guess you can tell that without me saying. But I know lots of stuff that wasn't in the article, like, her hair went gray when she was my age, so she's not as old as she looks, she's just tired from working and dealing with me and needs hair dye and a makeover really badly. Her dad died before she could have him walk her down the aisle at her wedding. Then her husband, who was like some kind of saint, died. Stay to dinner, Joseph, please, please, please?"

Joseph felt as if he'd walked into some kind of cubist-painting dream where goats floated by, and people jabbered in a language he didn't understand, and the fractured parts didn't connect. He put the lens cap on his camera. "I'll stay for fifteen minutes and we'll talk about photography, nothing else. You can get me a glass of water."

"Excellent! Download your pictures right now on our computer. You can show me how you decide which one is the best. Or you could tell us all about your life, like when you *were* a cop and why you stopped being one."

Joseph wondered if some physical act went beyond sighing because his entire body felt as if it were doing that. "How many times do I have to say this? I'm not interesting."

"Dude, we don't have a television or a stereo or even an antique Game Boy. Trust me, any story you tell will be more interesting than what we usually talk about, which is how often I mess up and what am I going to do about it. Especially tonight. Can't you stay for an hour? I'll make guacamole. Do you like potato chips or corn chips?"

"Either."

"You don't have a favorite snack?"

"Not really."

"Liar. I bet I know what it is. Ruffles and onion dip."

"I'm lactose intolerant."

"Give me three more guesses. I bet you ten bucks I guess it right."

"Have at it."

"Teriyaki beef jerky?"

"Nope."

"Olives stuffed with blue cheese."

"If you were paying attention, you'd realize the lactose intolerance factor rules out cheese."

"Salted peanuts?"

"I believe you owe me ten bucks, Juniper. I'll take it in quarters if you have 'em. It's laundry week."

"I can't believe I didn't guess it. At least tell me what it is."

"Sardines in oil."

"Are you kidding me? That would give you cat-food breath. Does your girlfriend make you gargle Scope before she lets you kiss her?"

"Don't have a girlfriend."

"Why not?"

"Don't want one."

"Seriously?"

"Seriously."

They walked toward the back porch. Juniper showed him where to scrape the mud off his shoes. "Guess I won't ask you to help me pitch hay flakes to the horses," she said, "but you can mix up the dogs' dinner. Stapled on the wall above the kibble bins is the recipe. Cadillac gets a scoop of Platinum Performance Plus, and Dodge gets Serenity."

"What's that?"

"Joint protection for Caddy, and calming herbs for Dodge. If you ask me, that's not working, but Glory says we have to give it a month."

"Your dogs are lucky. I know people who don't eat this well."

"Oh, no. I'm the lucky one, Joe. Cadillac would do anything for me."

Between the excited nickering from the horses, he heard her sweet-talking the one who had scared her silly.

"Hey there, Piper. Hey there, Piper man. Whatcha been do-ing, what is your plan?"

Joseph had to smile. That old saw about women and horses was true. He carried the dogs' dinner bowls to Juniper and waited for her to finish with the horses. "From my stupid fence stunt I can't bend down right now," he said. "Otherwise, I'd be . . ."

She took the bowls and grinned. "No problem. Thanks for helping me."

Joseph waited on the back porch, inhaling the smells of his fa-ther's farm. This was the time of year when daylight increased a few minutes each day. Farmers went nuts trying to decide when to plant. Winter was on its way out, but would take a few licks before it gave up. Memorial Day was the earliest you could com-fortably plant, but if you waited until then, your crops might be too late for farmers' market. Farming was like gambling. His mother's apricot trees always bloomed too soon and got hit by a killing frost. She'd get up on a ladder and drape bedsheets over the flowers in vain. Standing still, Joseph's back hurt worse than when he moved. He wanted nothing more than to lie down on his bed with icepacks. He counted how many hours it had been since he took his last pain pill and realized he'd forgotten his lunchtime dose. Genius move. Now it would take him a couple of days to get ahead of the pain.

"I love my dog more than anyone on earth," Juniper said, walking toward the back porch. "My Cadillac Coupe de Ville!"

"He's a good-looking animal."

"Animal?" She looked at him as if he'd called her dog a mangy cur. "The Cad-man is my best friend. He's so smart that he can find lost things. Whenever Glory loses her keys, she says, 'Keys, please,' and he finds them. You should see him herd the goats, only right now he's not allowed because one of them's pregnant. He sleeps next to my bed every single night."

Joseph nodded at her convoluted story, thinking how tired down to her bones Glory Solomon must be at the end of the day. "Can I get that glass of water now?"

"Sure, just go on in. The cupboard's to the left of the sink."

He didn't want to. It felt like trespassing. The back door opened into a laundry room with an old white washer and a newer-looking beige dryer. On the shelf above the appliances were detergent, bleach, and a tub of OxiClean. Next to them, a stack of folded cleaning rags. The door in front of him opened to the kitchen. It was outdated and the cupboards could use refinishing, but what struck him was the tidy way every object occupied its place. On one counter sat cake pans, decorating equipment, and an industrial-looking mixer. He wondered if Glory was getting ready to make one of those cakes, like the pirate ship.

She gave him a look that asked, why are you still here?

Juniper walked in behind him.

"May I use your restroom before I go?" Joseph asked, and Glory pointed the way down the hall. Even with the door shut and the water running, he could hear them arguing. He cupped his hand beneath the water faucet and tried to swallow the pill, but it stuck in his throat, and he needed a second gulp to get it down.

"I invited Joseph to have dinner with us," Juniper said.

"Without asking me? Juniper, what were you thinking? The house is a mess and we have work to do. I was planning on making tuna fish sandwiches tonight. That's not a dinner to serve to guests."

"It's not like he expects a three-course meal. He's a guy and they're always hungry. Why don't we have spaghetti? That's a cinch to make."

"If it's so easy, then you make it."

"Maybe I will."

"Go ahead, then. Make it. Be sure you measure out the pasta for five people instead of two. Men eat more than women."

"Jeez, Mrs. Solomon! Don't you think I know how much spaghetti to cook? Once upon a time I had a dad. He could eat so much spaghetti that we had to cook two whole packages every time!"

"I'm sorry. That was thoughtless of me. But don't get the idea that Joseph being here gets you out of the massive trouble you're in. It's a postponement of our discussion, that's all. In the mean-time, think about what you did. Since you don't have to be up early for school, I guess we can talk all night about why you got suspended."

"It wasn't my fault!"

"Tell me how am I supposed to believe that when you won't talk about what happened?"

Mrs. Solomon? Joseph could hear the tears in the girl's voice eclipsed by the anger in Glory's. After the stubborn pill finally went down, he waited a few minutes to allow them to finish. He'd tell them he'd take a rain check on dinner. But while he dried his hands, he realized he shouldn't have taken the pill if he wasn't going to eat immediately afterward. Once the queasiness arrived, it was hard to quell. Already he'd had one bleeding ulcer from the drugs, and he didn't want another. When he returned to the kitchen, he apologized for intruding. "If I could please have a slice of bread or a roll, I'll be on my way."

Glory looked at him. "You want a slice of bread."

"Yes, if it isn't any trouble. My stomach—"

"For Pete's sake, who are you? Oliver Twist? If you're that hungry, stay." She threw down the dish towel she'd been holding. "Juniper's making dinner. I have some work to do in the barn."

"It's not that I'm—"

"Excuse me, may I get by?"

He and Juniper watched her go out the back door and let it slam. "She doesn't really have anything to do out there," Juniper said.

"Yeah, I got that impression. I should go."

"No, I want you to stay! She just gets moody sometimes. Plus that article upset her, though she'd never let on. Mrs. Solomon's private. She won't cry in front of anybody. She cries in her closet where she thinks no one can hear her, but the walls are thin."

"I'm leaving. I don't want to upset her any more than I have, and neither should you."

"No, no, no. The worst thing you can do right now is leave. You can distract her. Tell her about your cop experiences. That's what she needs. Someone new who'll perk her up. You like spaghetti with meat sauce? Mine's really good. I am so the bomb at cooking now. Makes up for the horrible food we had at the group home. You'd think it's impossible to ruin macaroni and cheese, right? But they did, I swear. Some nights I'd just make a couple of peanut butter sandwiches, take them back to my room, get narked on by some mean girl, demerits for hoarding food, have to . . ."

He nodded. No escape was in sight and he still needed a piece of bread. Juniper handed him the grater and some Parmesan cheese and never once stopped talking. He checked her pupils to see if she was on some kind of upper, but they appeared normal. While the sauce simmered, he ate a homemade, buttered Parker House roll and his stomach quieted. He looked out the window at Mrs. Solomon playing with her dogs. She threw a glow-in-the-dark Frisbee for Cadillac. The nervous brown mutt she had weaving in and out of her legs while she performed a simple dance step. They definitely had the routine down. She made a loop with her arms and the brown dog jumped through, then trotted back in the other direction. Joseph tried to think of some music that would make it all fit together, some kind of background for the rhythm of their movements, but nothing seemed right. Juniper babbled on. He tore romaine lettuce into pieces and sliced avocado for topping just as he had a million other times back in New Mexico, wondering what would happen when Glory came back indoors. He heard a scratching on the door down the hallway. "What's that?"

"Edsel," Juniper said. "If I let him out you have to be prepared for a speeding bullet."

"Edsel is a gun?"

"An Italian greyhound." She loosed the beast, who ran laps around the kitchen and living room as if he were on the track in Ruidoso until long after Joseph was sure the dog had made himself dizzy.

"He's so small," Joseph said, and Juniper shushed him.

"Don't let Mrs. Solomon hear you say that. He's her baby. She makes all his food special."

After the salads were eaten and the plates mopped dry of vinegar-and-oil dressing, Juniper ladled out the spaghetti with ground-beef sauce and Glory held a bottle of wine up toward Joseph. "Want some? It's not all that great but not all that bad, either."

"Wish I could, but it interferes with this medication I'm on. Thanks, though."

"What kind of medication?" Juniper asked.

Glory sighed. "It's impolite to ask such a personal question, Juniper."

"But how am I going to learn anything if I don't ask questions? It's the Socratic method."

Joseph laughed.

"You'll live if you don't. Now apologize to Mr. Vigil."

"Please, it's okay. I wish you'd both call me Joseph."

Juniper set her fork down. "Mr. Vigil, I am sorry I asked such a personal question, even though I still want to know why you take pain pills, especially since you said your legs were okay. I'm betting it's your back. I'm also betting you hurt it being a cop, am I right?"

Glory poured more wine into her glass. "Juniper, change the subject, *now*."

"Okay. So, former officer Vigil, how do you make spaghetti sauce? Do you use the stuff out of a can? Do you put meat in it? Sausage? Carrots? Tofu? Mrs. Solomon says everyone has a family recipe. What's yours?"

Joseph smiled. Glory looked at him as if it were news to her anyone could smile under these circumstances. "My grandmother used to make it with chile."

"Like chili con carne?"

"New Mexican chile, I bet," Glory said.

"*Exactamente,*" he said. "Southern New Mexico green chiles, roasted over a wood fire. You know all that because of your mom, right?"

"My grandmother, actually. She taught me to cook."

Juniper cleared her throat. "Isn't that really Mexican food and not Italian?"

"Good question," Glory said. "Which is it, Joseph?"

Now that she was on her second glass of wine, every so often she smiled, too.

"Grandma Penny always called it spaghetti so that's what I thought it was. First time I ate spaghetti in a restaurant, I thought they had a terrible cook."

Glory laughed, nearly choking on the wine. Juniper laughed, too, but then she said, "Tell us some gnarly cop stories, please?"

"There isn't anything to tell. I wasn't on the force long enough to be there in the action."

"I don't believe you. What was your hairiest crime ever? Did you ever pull a gun on someone? Kill anybody?"

Joseph took a sip of water. "I didn't like it. The second I could, I switched to the crime lab. I analyzed evidence, wrote reports, and took pictures of crime scenes."

"But that's cool, too," Juniper said. "Just tell us a story."

Joseph ducked his head and looked at the china plate smeared with meat sauce. A chip was on the rim, and had this been Isabel's kitchen, she would have thrown that dish out so fast it would break the sound barrier. "Cops pull guns so infrequently you wouldn't believe it. Just having it on your hip is usually enough, but sometimes things happen. I got shot."

"Oh, my gosh," Juniper said. "That's why you have the limp! What happened? Was it a bank robbery? A suspect fleeing the scene? Grand theft auto? A meth lab employing underage children?"

"Meth lab, but the shooter was eighteen."

"Whoa," Juniper said. "You got shot by a teenage meth addict? No wonder you carry a gun. Do you have flashbacks? PTSD? Scars?"

Glory interrupted, "This is why you wanted a slice of bread, isn't it? The medication upsets your stomach unless you take it with food. You must think I'm a shrew. I'm sorry."

"You were just being a careful mom." He hoped that was the end of things because he didn't want to talk about Rico.

Glory looked at him steadily. "If that were my job, I'd be afraid every day of my life."

"So did you at least shoot him back?" Juniper asked.

"No, I did not. I'd stopped being a cop a long time before this happened. I was there to take pictures of the scene. That's all."

Juniper leaned in on her elbows, rapt. The wind rattled the kitchen window. Joseph looked toward it and wondered if putty would silence it. Glory set down her wineglass.

"Oh, come on," Juniper said. "You're leaving out the good parts. We can take it."

"You're a pushy one, aren't you? My grandmother would call you *testaruda*."

"What's that mean? Hormones? Adults blame everything on hormones."

"Bullheaded."

"Your grandmother doesn't know the half of it," Glory said.

Joseph's pill was making him mellow, and with the absence of pain and an interested audience, he relaxed a little. "I'll only tell one cop story, you understand? Don't ask me again."

"I won't," Juniper said. "I can get a Bible if you want me to swear on that. We have a King James."

"I started out as a cop. I ticketed speeders, drunk drivers, and went on domestic-violence calls. Every day was difficult. In the lab I thought I'd be insulated from all that. There was a missing person's case, where we found the girl too late. There are some pictures you don't want in your head, trust me."

Glory, who had just taken a drink of her wine, suddenly had a coughing fit. Juniper looked down at her plate, stunned.

"You wanted to know," he said. "I warned you."

Juniper got up from the table so quickly her chair nearly toppled over, but at the last moment Joseph stood up and caught it. She booked it down the hallway and into her room, slamming the door. Cadillac followed her, then came back to Glory. She let him out the back door. Joseph looked at Glory. "Man, this place is like the Bermuda Triangle. I mean well, but everything I say around you two comes out wrong. I'm sorry." He started to get up but she placed her hand over his arm.

"Let me explain. You're new here, so you probably don't know. Juniper is Casey McGuire's younger sister, the girl who went missing in the late nineties."

Joseph felt the weight of all that food in his gut. "¡*Qué idiota!*" he said under his breath. "How can I apologize to her?"

"I'm not sure you can."

"But this is terrible. I have to apologize. I reminded her of what happened to her sister, and worse, I implied the level of violence . . ."

"Casey being gone is a fact of life. Juniper's learning to deal. She's come a long way since the pirate wedding, but, oh, her back-slides are Olympian. Today, I can't even go into it. Want some decaf? I make great decaf. That's because on nights like these I pour a big old shot of whiskey into it. You can have one shot, can't you?"

"I can have a sip. Will you let me clear the dishes?"

"As long as you let me load the dishwasher. It would be too much for your back to bend down to the racks. I don't even like doing it." She turned on the tap to fill the saucepan to let it soak. Suddenly she put her hand across her eyes and Joseph could tell she was trying not to cry. "Why does everything have to be so hard for that girl? Why can't she catch a break?"

He touched her shoulder and felt it tremble. "Seems like she caught a huge break, finding a home with you."

Glory looked at him, rubbing her eyes with soapy hands. "I don't know. Trying to get her to behave, do her schoolwork, you have no idea. I think I'm making things worse."

"Doesn't look like that from where I stand."

They worked alongside each other quietly, with only the click of dishes and silverware fitting into their slots to break the si-lence. Not a sound came from Juniper's room. When the coffee was brewed, Glory poured Joseph a cup and added cream. "Oh, gosh. I didn't ask, I just—"

"Made it just like your husband would have liked it," Joseph finished. "It's all right."

"No, it's not." She poured it out. She filled another cup for him and fetched a bottle of Scotch from the cupboard above the fridge.

They sat down at the table again, waiting for the coffee to cool enough to drink it. Under their feet, the brown dog sighed.

Juniper came out of her room, her eyes puffy and her face flushed. In her hands was a large manila envelope.

"Hey," Joseph said, standing. "I didn't mean to dredge up sad memories. I hope you'll forgive me."

Juniper said nothing. She undid the clasp on the envelope and poured its contents onto the kitchen table. Out spilled newspaper articles, flyers, and bumper stickers reading BRING CASEY HOME. They just about covered the tabletop. Juniper looked up at Joseph and smiled. "It's like you were sent here to help me," she said, just before she started crying. "You can be the one to find my sister."

Part III

JUNIPER T. MCGUIRE

A dog will never forget the crumb thou gavest him,
though thou mayst afterward throw
a hundred stones at his head.
—Sa'dī, *Gulistan*, A.C.E. 1258

Chapter 8

"HONEY," GLORY SAID as Juniper pushed papers toward Joseph, "we've been all through this. After such a long time, it's unlikely—"

"There's always hope. Miracles happen sometimes. Elizabeth Smart came home. That could happen to Casey. Right, Joseph? Cops solve hopeless cases, don't they?"

Joseph ran his hand over his mouth, trying to find words that wouldn't drive the shattered bits deeper into this girl's already broken heart. "How old are you, Juniper?"

"I'm nearly fifteen."

"Then you're an adult. Sometimes adults have to face facts."

Her hopeful expression crumpled. "Facts aren't right a hundred percent of the time! What good are they? I hate facts. I hate whoever took my sister. And I hate you!" She swiped the table clean with her right arm, brushing all the papers to the floor before she put her head down, sobbing.

"I'm sorry," Joseph said, bending down and picking up the papers one by one, even though it hurt him to do so. He straightened the wrinkled pages and automatically began sorting them by date, latest to oldest, until he reached that first bold headline in the *Monterey Herald*:

LOCAL GIRL MISSING—FOUL PLAY SUSPECTED

When Casey McGuire's dog returned from a walk without her, police issued an Amber Alert . . .

Joseph's hands automatically reached for the beige file folder with the police department logo on the front, but it wasn't there. This wasn't his job anymore. Besides, only the details the public was allowed to see were here in Juniper's possession. Certain aspects were purposely held back. When a case went cold, usually one detective close to the community kept it on his desk and checked every couple of months for anything possibly connected to it. Occasionally the police got a break. Joseph took a breath. "We're friends, Juniper. True friends don't lie to each other. Nothing good ever comes of lying or secrets. That's why I'm being straight with you, as much as it hurts you to hear it."

Glory put her arms around the girl. While Juniper sobbed, Joseph sat down at the table, scanning the papers as he went. He couldn't stop himself from reading. It was all there, the hopeless stench of a bad ending, beseeching parental pleas printed on newspaper that had dried out and turned brittle. Rusted-paper-clip imprints. The delaminating plastic edge of a button with Casey's school photograph smiling out into her short future. Detectives pretended not to let such things affect them, but stories ate at them, the same way they had Joseph. He carefully straightened the pages, knowing how sacred they were to Juniper, slid them back into the envelope, and rewound the string closure. Then he looked at Glory, who returned his glance with so bleak an expression all he could think to do was motion toward the door and mouth, *I'll go now.* She shook her head no, so he waited, as uncomfortable as he was listening to the girl's weeping.

"If I could, do you know what I'd do?" he said, touching Juniper's shoulder.

"Besides make it not have happened?" she mumbled.

"Of course, but since I can't do that, I would make you some *ch'il ahwéhé.*"

"What's that? Some kind of memory-erasing potion? Why not just give me a lobotomy?"

"Cota tea from the green thread bush. It's good for stomachaches, it purifies the blood, and when my grandmother made it for me, just looking at the golden liquid in my cup always made me feel braver than I really am." He looked at Glory. "What are the chances of you having Navajo herbs in your spice cabinet?"

She chuckled. "Not good."

"Next time, I mean it, when you guys come to my place for *espagueti* dinner, I'll make us a pot of cota tea. You should plan to arrive early so we can go down to the lake and look for arrowheads. There's a good rock to sit on and watch the sun set, and right now is too early for tourists to spoil everything with their Jet Skis and motorboats."

"Oak Shore," Glory said. "That's where you live? I haven't been there in a while, but it used to be such a pretty place."

"Still is, so long as you look toward the lake and not the houses. When I was a kid, I thought that rock was where all the sunsets went, like solar collection. I figured it slept in the lake all night, then seeped out by morning to become the dawn. It was alive to me then. I'll make us green-chile spaghetti, New Mexican style."

"That sounds nice, doesn't it, Juniper?" Glory asked.

Juniper lifted her face from Glory's arms and looked at Joseph. Her skin was blotchy and her eyes as swollen as if she'd been in a fistfight. "You really can't help?"

"No," he said, maintaining firm eye contact. "Losing some-one you loved so much never stops hurting."

"It sucks beyond sucking," Juniper said, standing up and wob-bling a little. "I think I'll go to bed now. Where's my dog? I want my dog."

"I let him out back," Glory said. "Go wash your face and I'll fetch him for you."

Joseph said, "Thank you for inviting me to dinner, Juniper. I like your spaghetti recipe, but I have to say, I think mine's better."

Juniper laughed for real, but one of those fake smiles he con-sidered a plague of the Caucasian race followed. If you're sad, be sad, he wanted to say. She walked down the hall. He heard a door click shut, then water running. At the back door, Glory whistled for Cadillac and brought him to Juniper when she came out of the bathroom. She took her dog with her and closed her bed-room door. Joseph and Glory sat at the table, their coffee cold. She took both cups and emptied them in the sink.

"Why did you ask me to stay?" he asked.

She turned around, her silver hair falling loose from its bun, strands swinging one second behind her. He saw a glimpse of her true self then, and how she made herself plain on purpose, proving Lorna's words. Glory was scraped-raw vulnerable. As if someone had removed her outer layer of skin. She was always going to be prettier than she let herself believe, and this ability to ignore that natural beauty was what made the older sister so criti-cal of her life. Maybe keeping a distance was part her grieving, a way to stave off feelings. Though how it was possible to remain distant with Juniper on board he could not imagine.

"Because I want to talk to you."

"So talk," he said.

"Let's go outside and let Dodge out for a run. That way we

can have privacy. Back soon," she called out to Juniper, who didn't answer.

Glory opened the kennel door to let Dodge out, then returned to the back steps and sat down. Joseph walked down the steps and past the barn-red chicken coop, Dodge pushing to get in front of him. The hens were inside for the night. He wondered how she'd trained the dogs to let the chickens alone. Dodge raced toward the corral and disappeared in the dark. Joseph waited for Glory to say whatever it was she needed to tell him.

"I appreciate you letting her know up front, like you did about her sister's case, where things stand. She's battling demons you can't imagine, or maybe you can."

Joseph nodded.

"And thanks for keeping the details of that case you were on to yourself."

"Wild horses couldn't drag it out of me."

Glory got up, walked to the barn, and pulled the sliding door shut. One of the horses whinnied. "It's difficult sometimes. Juniper's so defensive. She won't talk about things. She lies, and I don't know what to do about it."

"I hope you don't think that's your fault. Hormones do make them a little bit nuts. I've witnessed kids stab each other and at the end of the day they're best friends."

"Do you have kids?"

"I haven't been too lucky in that department."

"Then how do you know all this?"

"I tutored kids like her back in Albuquerque, smart kids who dropped out of school because what else could be more fun than breaking and entering? At that age, their circuitry is all fouled up. Juniper told me you had foster sons before her."

"We did."

"Then you know that things'll get better. All I did was listen and try to help them pass their GEDs. What you're doing is so much harder, but ultimately it's the kid's choice. At the end of the day you have to go home to yourself." As Dodge completed a lap of the yard, Joseph could just make out his shape in the darkness.

Glory leaned against the fence. "After she goes to bed I lie there and think, what am I doing? Either I'm making decisions for her, or she makes bad decisions by herself." Glory turned to face him. "Juniper really likes you."

"I like her, too. She's a smart kid."

"Then I'm just going to come right out and say this. Men have only let her down. The police, her dad abandoning her, boys in her last placement, it's all been negative."

"Okay, but what's that got to do with me?"

Glory rubbed her temples. "I don't want you to hurt her, too. You said you're leaving in April. I'm worried that if she bonds any more with you, it will kill her when you go."

Joseph paused before he spoke. "Glory, you may not be Juniper's biological mother, but you are a good mother. My back injury's changed my life. I can't coach soccer. I can't do the job I was good at. One thing I know is, I'm good with teenagers. From now until April, I have nothing but time on my hands. If you'll allow it, I'd like to give Juniper some photography lessons. Does it have to be an all-or-nothing thing? When I return to New Mexico, we can e-mail photos back and forth."

"But you saw how unglued she got tonight. You'd subject your life to that kind of emotional drama?"

"That was grief coming out is all. Everyone's been there."

"Doesn't make sense. Your accident, the pain you're clearly in, your cabin being torn down—why take on this, too?"

"Sometimes you meet people and you just know you've crossed paths for a reason."

Suddenly Dodge returned, ran a circle around Joseph, then jumped up, hitting him hard on the chest. The dog was a good fifty pounds, heavier than he looked. All that force pushed into Joseph's chest and knocked the breath out of him.

"Dodge, down!" Glory said sternly, and took hold of Joseph's arms. "Are you okay? Did he hurt you?"

"I'm fine," he said, gasping until his lungs filled again. It hurt like the dickens, but until the dog's paws connected with his sternum, he'd been experiencing a minor miracle. His back pain had existed separately from their conversation. Put aside. No spasm, no dull ache, just a sense of being alive in the way he used to be. Living in the moment.

"Excuse me a minute while Dodge and I have a little lesson," Glory said. "Dodge, drop." The dog lay down. "Good boy. Now stand."

The dog was on all four legs in an instant.

"Sit. Good boy, now lie down. Roll over. Stand, and circle."

Joseph saw how the dog read her body language, and how she was partnered with him so well, it reminded him of formal dance competitions.

"Good boy! Now weave! Zigzag!"

Then she began to walk backward, bending her legs at the knees, lifting each one to the side, making a quick opening for the dog to duck under. Joseph couldn't believe this was the barking, jumping, rowdy dog that had almost knocked him down. It was more than obedience; it was a woman dancing backward with her dog in the moonlight. "Where did you learn that?" Joseph asked.

Glory changed direction so that Dodge was now the one

backing up. "It's called freestyle canine dancing. There are competitions for it. You should see it when it's set to music. I haven't figured that part out yet, but someday." She held her arms up. "Jump!" she called, and Joseph couldn't believe she could catch fifty pounds of dog without hurting her own back. She gave Dodge a kiss and set him down. "Okay, Dodge. Free dog. Go do your business."

"Very impressive."

It was fully dark now. Dodge was visible only when he ran under the barn light. The dog bumped his nose against Glory's leg, a tennis ball in his mouth. "We'll play tomorrow." She rubbed his head. "Dodge has a ways to go. I'd always thought of myself as a pretty good dog trainer, but I've never been so wrong about a dog as Cadillac."

"How so?"

She switched on the outside porch light, one of those compact fluorescents, and he saw her frown deepen. "My husband could read kids like they were books. Not me. I like to think I have a gift at sensing a dog's talent, helping it to hone its skills, learn manners, and eventually find the right forever home. Cadillac was Casey McGuire's dog. The one she was walking the day she disappeared."

"*Predestinado.*"

"Are you serious? You believe in fate?"

"Why not? *La mano poderosa,* the work of the mighty hand belonging to our Creator, is always at work. All the time things happen that are larger than we can understand."

"You really believe that? What kind of God allows a girl to be kidnapped and murdered?"

"*No se.* I don't know. We're mortals. But who says we have to know everything?"

"Because there are *some* things we need to make sense of. For example, I could tell from the start Cadillac needed kids. He'll play ball or Frisbee all day long. The McGuires were his first placement—Juniper was barely ten, Casey fourteen. They were a happy family, a stay-at-home mom and a hardworking dad with two adorable little girls. Caddy instantly clicked with them. They had a fenced half acre, pretty much ideal. I did home visits, trained them, trial weekends, and then Cadillac was officially theirs. Another happy ending, I thought. At Christmas I'd get a card with a picture of the dog wearing felt antlers, stretched out in front of the family fireplace. The night Casey went missing, Cadillac came back here. He passed half of the Lassie test."

"I don't understand."

"Oh, you know. Dog travels countless miles to return to its original home, leads the family to the kid in trouble. But Cadillac couldn't tell us where Casey was." Glory began walking to the back porch.

"I'm sorry."

"Thank you for saying that. The last thing the family needed was to be reminded of their loss, so I took him back, expanded his training. The cattle rancher he went to next told me that one afternoon he just stopped herding. As if he'd reached his quota, or something. He turned around and walked out of the man's property and walked five miles back here. Then I thought, well, perhaps he's a candidate for search and rescue."

"Sounds difficult."

"Not really. You start out the same way you do with any dog, the basic commands. Then you teach 'find,' using a brinsel—a fancy word for a stick you tuck under the dog's collar, which he places in his mouth to let you know he's found something. Then you complicate things, graduate to a piece of clothing, and eventually people, or corpses. Cadillac loves bones. Once he brought home the rotting leg of a cow, so pleased with himself, and believe me, the smell was awful. Took days to get it away from him." She looked at Joseph. "Sometimes I can't get over the fact that this dog ended up touching both girls' lives."

"I'd like to hear more about this search and rescue training."

"Are you sure you're not just making polite conversation?"

"Aieee. What do I have to do to prove to you I'm one of the good guys?"

"Forgive me. It's just when it comes to Casey . . ." She stopped. "I'll never get over feeling like there was, or should have been, something I could have done."

Glory blinked and he could see the tears in her eyes. "Search and rescue," he said. "Talk to me."

"You teach the dog to discriminate between scents, and to cue the handler in different ways, to let her know exactly what he's found. 'Digging' for skeletal remains, 'jump up' for live human scent, 'sit and bark' for cadavers. We never got as far as cadavers. Obviously, opportunities for that were not readily available."

"Why'd you stop?"

Glory shooed Dodge to his kennel. He immediately climbed on top of his doghouse. Joseph felt the chill of the night air at work on his back. He wondered if he offered his jacket to Glory, could he keep the conversation going?

"Besides it being a full-time job, and expensive? Training a dog for S and R is a lifestyle. Unless you work for the county, there's no money in it. Then my husband died. Plain and simple, I needed money to live on. When I got hired at Target, there weren't enough hours in the day to get everything done."

"The newspaper article made me wish I'd known your husband."

"Dan would have liked you, too."

"In Juniper's papers—I assume the police tried dogs to hunt for Casey?"

"Police, sheriff, firefighters, civilian volunteers. They tried everything. Bloodhounds used in the Murrah bombing flew up from Oklahoma and Georgia. The trail ended on a pullout on a road twelve miles from here. All the dogs stopped there. It was as if she vanished on that spot."

Abducted in a car, Joseph thought. Two kidnappers. There'd have to be one to restrain her, one to drive. Drugged her, took her elsewhere, and then dumped her body. With so many acres of wilderness, the Santa Lucia Mountains, the ocean, she'd probably never be found.

"It breaks the dog's heart when he can't complete the 'find,'" Glory said. "They get depressed the same as humans." She rubbed her arms. "I've kept you outside so long I'm embarrassed. But it helped, just talking to you."

"I'm glad."

She looked at him. "You want to know the cherry on the top of this awful day? Today was Juniper's first day back at school after the holiday break. A fresh start. So what does she do? Gets suspended. For the second time. I have no idea what consequences to give her. Nothing I did the last time seems to have made an impression. Here I go again. Can we shelve this discussion for another time? I should check on Juniper."

Joseph smiled because the phrase "another time" meant there would be one. "The right thing to do will come to you."

The wind came up moving through the tree and they heard the kennel gate clank open. "Oh, no. I forgot to latch it. Where's Dodge?" she said. "Dodge?"

Joseph put two fingers in his mouth and whistled, and the

dog came trotting over, tail wagging. Glory took hold of the dog's collar and sighed. "Thank goodness." She looked at Joseph. "Cameras, guns, meth labs, and dog whistling; Joseph Vigil, you are full of surprises."

"Don't forget my superior spaghetti."

"We'll see about that."

Joseph couldn't figure what it was about Glory that interested him. She was the antithesis of Isabel, who went for traditional furniture and cultivated roses in her garden. She wore dresses, not denim. The soles of her Sunday shoes somehow never scuffed. Though head coverings were no longer a requirement in the Catholic Church, she wore a shoulder-length mantilla to mass anyway. She would not consider surrogacy or adoption. Glory Solomon was like prairie roses allowed to wander. Kids drifted in and out of her life like changing seasons. He didn't want a romance, but how this worked into a possible friendship he did not know. "Thank you again for the dinner."

"You're welcome."

He had only walked about three feet or so when she called out, "Joseph!"

He turned, careful not to pivot. "Yes?"

"Have you ever owned a dog?"

Joseph thought of the red and blue heelers on his father's farm, all working dogs, named Bambo or Gallo, or Estrellita that one time his mother had got her way. When it snowed, they slept in the barn, and when it was hot, they slept under his dad's truck. Reservation mutts, "brown dogs," sometimes strayed onto the property, mangy and antisocial. They wouldn't even take dog food you put out. They rested awhile and went on their way. "No," he said. "I never did."

"Dodge would make a good dog for you. He's young, and

when he's not being a brat, he learns fast. You could train him to pick things up that you have trouble reaching. I can tell he likes you."

"Glory, you know I can't give a dog the treatment he deserves."

"Why not?"

"For one thing, I can't take him on long walks."

"Saying 'for one thing' implies there's a second thing. So what is it?"

"How about the fact that I own no cattle?"

She laughed. "There's a first time for everything."

Joseph reached into his pocket and took out his car keys. He looped them around his finger and tried to think of the right thing to say. *I'm moving out of here in less than three months? I don't want to be left twice? I don't want to love something that will die before I do?* The words wouldn't come.

"Come to my house for dinner next week and we can talk about it." He could see that his boldness flustered her. "It's up to you. If you get a chance, e-mail me how Juniper's doing. And good luck with the suspension consequences."

"Good night, Joseph."

"Good night." When he opened his car door, he heard her call out, "Think about Dodge."

Man, she did not let up.

In the Land Cruiser, he started the engine and let it idle while he clicked his seat belt into place. Oh, his back was punishing him now. It felt as if the vertebrae were grinding bone on bone, like a basalt *molcajete*. The lights in the barn went out, but through the kitchen window one continued to gleam. He imagined Glory working on a fancy cake for, say, Valentine's Day. Surely at least one wedding was scheduled on that day of sweethearts and roses. The bride in the traditional white dress, her man in a black tux with the pink *faja*, cummerbund, surely one of the silliest words on the planet in English or Spanish, which literally translated to "panty girdle."

He doubted Juniper would make it to her senior year without getting expelled. Some kids were better off going for the GED. Glory reminded him of that white oak tree. Something thriving that shouldn't be, a force to be respected, and photographed to document, lest people assume you were telling a fish story.

While driving home he thought about Casey McGuire and the pages he'd scanned. People blamed the parents for not instilling the proper fear of strangers into their children. They ought to log on to missingkids.com and check out the faces. Look past the makeup, the piercings and tattoos, the age-enhanced photos. Violence could never be a child's fault. Fault lay with a fundamentally loose spring in the human mind. Some freakish intersection of circumstance and opportunity that tapped into the reptilian depths of the brain, a place that had yet to be mapped or remotely understood. An area that, thank God, slept in most humans. In his opinion, a place someone ought to stick a needle into, deeply, and fry it so it could never wake up.

That next morning, back pain be damned, Joseph decided to attempt a walk around the lake. He'd taken his medication at breakfast, in anticipation of the effort. He put on hiking boots he hadn't worn since the accident. Every step into the leafy mulch made a satisfying crunch. The lake rippled silver, and a blue heron was wading in the marshy shallows. He kept his focus well ahead of his feet. The chill air tasted crisp. But after only fifteen minutes, needing a rest, he had to stop at the same boulder he used to dive from when he was a kid. Someone had dumped beer bottles. He picked them up and put them in his jacket pockets. The wind here hit his face gently; in Albuquerque, it was abrasive. In the middle of cold, gray winter, you'd see a shock of yellow forsythia on the prairie and it felt like a promise. Here, flowers bloomed year-round and you needed a calendar to tell the season. While pain corkscrewed up his back, he shut his eyes and listened to the water lapping the shore. Mysterious birdsong came from the evergreen trees. There was no way to decipher what they were saying. But once he thought of it, he couldn't stop wondering.

Casey would have been eighteen years old now. She'd have worked her first job, fallen in love, and in a few months she'd graduate high school, then head off to college. Last night, despite his efforts not to, Joseph Googled Juniper's sister. Every article, every picture, every tribute written in her memory. Sixteen months after the disappearance, the father moved out. When the divorce was final, Mrs. McGuire overdosed on sleeping pills. How could she be so selfish, leaving Juniper? Maybe she thought the dad would take over. Joseph surprised himself wishing he could confront the father and give him an earful. Only cowards skipped out on kids. What did the dad think? That if he left her behind like an abandoned pet, some kind heart would feel sorry for her and take her in? Thank God someone had. That someone was Glory.

All this while as he leaned against the rock, his back throbbed and his muscles cramped so badly he had to lean over and grit his teeth. Zipping up his jacket, he limped back to the cabin to lie down on two heating pads. Before he did, he applied a transdermal pain patch. He lay flat on his back for three hours before he dared get up again. All that time the only sound in his cabin was his own breathing, the occasional scratching of a camp jay at the feeder. Maybe Glory was right. Maybe a dog would help.

A week and a half passed and Joseph heard nothing from Juniper or Glory. Was Juniper angry with him for telling her he could not help find Casey? She'd be back in school by now, taking exams, working on science projects the way the kids in Albuquerque did this time of year. Was a telephone call too forward? Every morning he ticked another day off the calendar and marveled how, once the sun came out, the soggy mess that was his front yard returned to firm ground. The occasional tulip his grandmother had planted popped up from the greening grass. On weekends, college students descended in cars blaring rap music, pitched tents, challenged each other to swim in the cold water, and hung out at the Butterfly Creek, drinking beer and getting rowdy, and daring each other to steal the pizza sign.

An envelope arrived in Joseph's post office box, the official notice that the demolition crew was coming the first week of April, weather permitting. He e-mailed the Solomons.

Glory—

If you're still interested in floorboards, ancient appliances, and wicker furniture, come over soon with your truck.

—Joseph

She didn't respond. He e-mailed the delinquent.

Juniper—

How about that photography lesson? I got time—but the clock is ticking.

—Joseph

On February 5, a chilly but sunny day that had started out well enough, Joseph was at the Butterfly Creek waiting for his turkey sandwich when a group of bikers pulled up. The second they removed their helmets, they began arguing the merits of various engines. One guy—with BION embroidered in silver letters on the back of his jacket, short for "bionic," Joseph presumed—waxed on about his "1957 FLH Harley chopper with the shovelhead top engine." His bike, parked at the steps onto the deck of the Butterfly Creek, alongside the four others, reminded Joseph of old western-movie horses at the hitching post. He wondered what these fellows did for a living that they could drive their bikes to the middle of nowhere to have an argument. Ah, be fair, he told himself. Maybe they were on disability, too.

This mishmash of pontificators was what Lorna referred to as a meeting of the Butterfly Creek Intellectual Society. It wasn't MENSA. Members included European hikers who upon emerging from the forest ordered and consumed five large Swamp Juan pizzas. And fly fishermen. The passionate fishing-rod discussions— bamboo versus graphite—would never be settled. Hikers argued long underwear—silk or Gore-Tex or Capilene? He saw the faces of the fed-up-to-here-with-family campers, pining for mindless television when a whole lake and family were right there in front of them. Every now and then a lonely old-timer who'd had been around so long he swore he remembered wagon trains sat down at Joseph's table and started up a conversation about the state of the union, which sometimes implied Confederate.

As Joseph sipped his high-octane coffee, Lorna brought his sandwich and sat down at his table. She was wearing her fleece vest with the javelina print, and she swiped her bangs from her blue-shadowed eyes. "Joe Camera," she said, sighing. "My engine's running slow this morning. How is life treating my favorite shutterbug so far this new year? Come on, spill. I got eight more hours to my shift and Juan is boring me so bad I'm about ready to make myself a kite out of a cereal box."

"Nothing new. Still taking tree pictures."

"What is it with you and the saplings?"

He smiled. This was their prologue and he would miss it. "A tree stays rooted, which is more than I can say for most people."

"The human race would die out if folks didn't get restless. You're here, aren't you?"

"Only two more months."

"We'll see about that." Juan hollered for Lorna and she ignored him. "He doesn't really mean it until the third or fourth time," she said, and lit a cigarette.

Before Joseph could say a word, Lorna spoke. "Do not lecture me on my one enjoyable vice or I will put a wormy tomato in your sandwich." Then she laughed, and the laugh turned into a cough. From their various conversations he'd learned that Lorna had survived breast cancer, had a son in prison, lost her dad to Alzheimer's, and that she could trace her roots back to the Salinan Indians, one of many tribes decimated by the missionary era but which was making a comeback. She also had the misfortune not to have inherited a pile of money to retire on. Unless some-

one bought the Butterfly Creek, she and Juan would keep working until they dropped dead.

"Smoke two cigarettes at a time," Joseph said. "Doesn't matter
if I approve."

"Oh, honey"—she blew out a plume—"I stopped caring about
what people thought of me when I was seven years old. Every
September my mom bought a bolt of material and made me five
identical school dresses out of it to wear all year. If I grew, she'd
add an inch of material to the hem. I was one tough cookie before
I hit eight."

"That had to be painful."

"Ancient history." Lorna tapped a finger on Joseph's camera.
"We were talking about trees before you got all sidetracked on
my cigarettes."

He laughed. "Can I show you something?" He clicked his
digital camera screen to REVIEW and showed Lorna the photos of
Solomon's Oak. Until the photo with Juniper in it, the tree was
just a tree. Once the girl stood next to it, the tree struck up a
conversation: *I'm enormous, I've survived against all odds, and my
plan is to make the world rewrite the science books.* Then it added a
postscript: *You have no idea the things I've seen.*

Lorna tsked. "That girl's poor face looks like she went through
a windshield and a blind doctor put it back together with an office
stapler. I knew you wouldn't stay away from them."

"Actually, I have. The last time I saw either of them was the
day I took this picture."

"Now that surprises me."

"Why?"

She mussed his hair, which had grown out since November to
the point where he needed to comb it. "Oh, Joseph. What are

you? A mole rat? Get your nose out of the camera lens. Can't you see that you're first-class husband material?"

"How's me taking a picture of a tree tell you that?"

Juan hollered again, this time in Spanish. Lorna set the camera down on the table and stood up. "I have exactly six puffs left before he blows a head gasket. Joe, you're polite and a good tipper. You made a connection with that teenage *paquete de problemas*, the overflowing package of problems, and how many men would voluntarily step onto that minefield? I'd have to kiss you to find out if you're any good at that, but since I'm old enough to be your grandmother, I'll take your word for it."

"That's all a woman needs to know about who would make a good husband?"

She straightened her collar and took a last puff. "In my estimation, things boil down to that."

"Is that how you chose Juan?"

"Juan? I felt sorry for the poor hombre, he was so clueless. He had such clodhoppers he couldn't dance a lick. He didn't have a nice car, or money to burn, or much else going for him, but he followed me around like a duckling and threatened to maim anyone who said a bad word about me. First chance I got I married him. Then I taught him how to scrub a floor, wash windows, make a sandwich, and count out correct change. Trained him pretty darn well, don't you think?" She patted Joseph's shoulder and leaned in close. "Tell me if I need to mind my own business, but the white pills I see you popping like Tic Tacs have me worried. Do I need to put you on my prayer list?"

"No, but I appreciate the concern. They're prescription."

Juan's next holler was deeper in pitch. Lorna stamped out the cigarette, picked up the butt, and deposited it in the trash. She looked up at the dark clouds, clearing briefly before more moved in. "Hallelujah, a patch of blue sky." She handed Joseph a UPS pen from her pocket. "Here, start off the new year with a new pen. Look at that darling truck inside. Tip it and it slides back and forth! Endorse your checks with this gem and it'll bring you good luck. Remember, we got Riff Raff, that jazz band from down south, playing this weekend. Real good guys, and clean-cut music. You should invite the widow and the delinquent and come have a listen."

When Lorna was gone, the biker conversation filled the void. "The shovelhead," Bion said to his pack, "is so pretty it's a shame to cover it up." Joseph threw his bread to the chipmunks and bused his trash. He walked to his car. Lorna reminded him of his mother, who saw miraculous omens in crippled sparrows. She had no problem giving him a smack on the head. Lorna probably did have a wormy tomato behind the counter, and a lot of other things you were better off not knowing.

On the drive home, he stopped not far from the Butterfly Creek to take a photograph of yet another massive oak, its roots exposed and threading toward the creek bank like the gnarled foot of an old man. It looked as if the tree had decided to cross the water to join the oaks on the opposite side but had maybe waited too long, and that was why it was the only tree on this side of the creek. He wondered what pushed the roots upward like that, and what was under the tree. Given the history of the place, surely there were bones and potsherds and the remains of woven grass baskets. He thought of Glory training Cadillac to find things, and Casey's remains still missing. Earth was its own museum, admission free of charge until you died. Then you became part of the exhibit.

At home he downloaded the pictures, culled the worst ones, and placed the keepers alongside his best shots, the ones that would go into his album. With the UPS pen, he made notes on what order he wanted the tree pictures in because it was time to print them. He enlarged the picture of Juniper standing by Solomon's Oak and studied it. None of the other trees required people. Was the oak the picture that finished the series? Why did he feel as if it might be the beginning of something else?

He shut his eyes and dug down deep in his pocket for his afternoon pain pill. He looked out the window while he waited for the pill to work, trying to imagine a yellow bulldozer parked in the spot where his car was. There would be a Dumpster, too, and a demolition crew taking the cabin apart as quickly as they could. Time was money to the developers, but to Joseph, money bought time. Lots and lots of it.

As soon as the pill kicked in, he thought, damn that oak. All he wanted was a portfolio of California's unique trees. His giant redwoods? Decent, but not spectacular. The silvery green eucalyptus of Santa Rosa? His composition brought the menthol scent to mind at once. Solomon's Oak? He had to face facts. Every picture he'd taken of it, even the one with Juniper that showed its size, fell so far short of what the tree conveyed to him that Joseph could only conclude that ambition was at fault. The tree reminded him of Ship Rock up in the Four Corners, another lone natural wonder in the middle of nowhere. The Navajo nation considered it sacred. But every once in a while some dumbass rock climber tried to climb it and fell to his death. The disrespect shown to the rock formation met its punishment. Joseph wondered if his own hubris had offended the oak tree. Did he have to give up?

But the moment the thought came to mind, he knew he

would pursue the tree until the day he got it right. He picked up his cell phone and called Glory Solomon's number before he chickened out.

"Solomon's Oak Wedding Chapel," Juniper said. "Can I help you?"

"*May* I help you," Joseph said. "How come you're not in school? Don't tell me more monkeyshines?"

"I kind of got suspended again."

"You mean the suspension the night I came for dinner, right?"

"Nope. A different one."

He whistled. "What happened?"

"It was a totally stupid thing."

"Do I want to ask?"

"Not unless you promise not to yell at me after."

"No can do. Your mom there?"

"Nope, she got called in to work at Tar-jay. I still have two hours before she gets home, so I'm cleaning the house. I think that'll make her go easier on me."

"Juniper, I don't think that house could ever be made clean enough to work the kind of miracle you're hoping for. How many times does this make you've been suspended?"

"Three."

"Once more and you're expelled permanently."

"How do you know?"

"Because that's the universal thing about high schools. Why do you sound so proud of getting suspended?"

Juniper snorted. "You want to know what my school day is like? First-period PE they make you run a *mile* because they don't have enough money for gymnastics equipment. I hate getting all sweaty and tired, and whether I walk or run, I come in dead last every time. Second period, algebra! Numbers and characters and theorems mush together and I can't get above a C on the pop quiz no matter how hard I study. Mrs. Solomon says I should join a study group! But how can I when I have no friends? Not even the geeks will talk to me. Third period, and I'm starving by this point but lunch is still one period away, I reek from PE, I want to cry about flunking math, it's time for social science! Right now we're studying pre-Columbian history. Bering land bridges, maize, and using fire as a tool. What am I ever going to do with pre-Columbian history besides forget it?"

"You're right," Joseph said.

"You agree with me?"

"Sure do. You'll never use algebra serving fast food. And pre-Columbian history? Sheesh. You might as well quit school today. I wonder, though. Do you have to graduate high school to be the manager at the burger joint? For sure, whatever your position ends up being—change maker, salad chopper, fries fryer, you do get to wear a nifty visor. And minimum wage, everyone knows it's easy to live on that."

"Very funny, Copper. I thought you were my friend."

She'd forgotten that the last time she saw him she'd said she hated him. A jay landed on the deck outside Joseph's window and cocked its head toward him, looking for a handout. What was wrong with the seed in the birdfeeder? he wondered. "I'm a friend who doesn't much care for watching you throw your life away."

"It's my life. Why are you calling Mrs. Solomon anyway?"

"Permission to take more pictures of the tree. My last batch didn't capture what I was aiming for."

"You're friends now. You don't have to ask permission."

"Yes, I do. That's called manners."

"Manners. Give me a break. What were you trying to capture?"

"It's hard to explain. I'll know it when I see it."

"That sounds like something out of a kung fu movie. I thought you were Navajo and Mexican. Isn't there cooler wise sayings in Navajo?"

"*Aren't* there. I'm mestizo, mutt, like that brown dog Dodge. The wisest things I know are common sense, and I'm sharing them with you. The question is, are you listening?"

Juniper was quiet for a minute. "I got your e-mail but I couldn't write back since I was grounded from using the computer. When are you coming over to teach me how to take pictures for real? I really do want to learn. Polishing lightbulbs is boring."

"Polishing lightbulbs is a good skill to master for the job you're going to get without your degree. Practice turning off your mind when you're flipping burgers and saying, 'Have it your way.' Ask Glory if I can come over tomorrow, or on the weekend."

"What about that spaghetti dinner? You promised us you'd cook."

"I'm still willing. It's up to your mom. Hey, Juniper. What kind of student was your sister, Casey?"

"She got straight A's."

"When you lose somebody, take a lesson from their lives. That way their dying doesn't erase them entirely."

"I hate you."

"I hate you, too. Shine the lightbulbs real good. Don't forget to tell Glory I called."

"I won't. Bye, Copper Joe." She hung up.

The rest of the day he found himself smiling now and then, thinking about Juniper on a stepladder unscrewing bulbs to get at the dust and that little greyhound racing around the house as if it were a track while the black-and-white collie zoomed behind, trying to herd him from one imaginary pasture to another, and Dodge barked his high-pitched, supersonic bark that made Joseph's ears ring. Lots of crazy stuff went on in that house. He imagined Glory waiting on people at Target while her mind whirled around trying to figure out what to do about the third suspension. There would be more than raised voices when she got home. He cropped and touched up his pictures, trying to talk himself into believing the bad ones weren't ready for the bone pile. Before heating up his dinner, he printed out the photo with Juniper against the tree. At lunch Lorna had remarked on her torn-up face, but in color on the paper, Joseph saw a resemblance between the girl and the oak he hadn't noticed before. Against the gnarled bark, Juniper in her ripped jeans and grim smile looked as if she'd lived two hundred years' worth of life already, too, witness to terrible things. She was so mad at the world you prayed she didn't have matches in her pocket.

At ten that night his cell rang, jarring him out of the Ishi book he practically knew by heart.

"Hello?"

"Sorry to call back so late. I've been—" Glory sighed—"a little busy."

"It's not too late. I stay up until midnight, usually."

"Juniper said you called. I guess she told you about her latest suspension."

"She didn't tell me why."

Then it was as if Joseph had turned on the faucet. "What do I do, Joseph? She's smart, capable of good grades, and she even studies without me harping at her. But try to get her to stay out of fights and she reacts like I'm asking her to go cliff diving. California passed anti-bullying laws for a reason, I told her. Those kids torment her about Casey, but she refuses to let me intervene. I tell her over and over, they're immature and petty, wait until they lose someone and eventually they will. I tell her, don't let them push your buttons and never let them see you cry, so what does she do? Throws a punch. Pulls a plastic cafeteria knife out of her pocket and *threatens* a cheerleader with it. A knife!"

"A plastic cafeteria knife is what, about five inches long? If she were eighteen, she could be charged with felony assault."

"I know that. You know that. Juniper—well, something happens every week, and the principal is fed up and I don't blame her. Why does my kid have to be such a hard-ass? Oh, gosh. Excuse my language, I meant to say—"

"Sometimes *ass* is the only word for it."

"I don't mean to dump all this on you. I just get so frustrated. I can't talk to my sister. She's on tenterhooks waiting to prove that I've made this monstrous mistake."

"Tenterhooks?"

"*Escarpias*. Hooks, holding fabric together carefully so it doesn't rip."

"Like a clothesline?"

"Never mind. It's just an expression. Even Lorna thinks it's a mistake."

"Do you think it's a mistake?"

Glory went silent for a minute. "No. I can't say exactly why, but I believe in this kid."

"So do I."

"You must think I'm some kind of nutcase, calling you up to unload like this. I know you have enough problems of your own, but you said you used to work with teenagers, so if you have any ideas, I'd sure appreciate hearing them. If you feel like sharing. Jeez! I'm sorry. Just ignore all that. Let's start over. How are you?"

"At present, the good in my life outweighs the bad."

"Juniper said you wanted to come by again and photograph the tree."

"It can wait. How about chile spaghetti for dinner tomorrow?"

"We have to start cooking for the Valentine's Day wedding tomorrow."

"You asked for my advice. This is it. The day after Valentine's, come to dinner here. Arrive early. Bring the dogs and the desperado. If it doesn't rain, we can walk around the lake. If it does, we can play Parcheesi. My house is four miles from the Butterfly Creek. The dark green A-frame with the dilapidated roof surrounded by the mini-mansions."

"I know where it is. I've driven past it."

"So come to dinner. Give yourself a break."

"Okay, Joseph. See you then. Good night."

"Good night, Glory."

He felt the old reflex rise to say "Sweet dreams," the way he used to when Isabel turned away from him to sleep. But when he discovered she was dreaming something else entirely, he vowed never to say it again. After the call, insomnia set in. He named and filed his pictures, ran a diagnostic program on the computer, then walked around the cabin, looking at the cobwebs in the ceiling corners, dust bunnies under the furniture, and worst of all, the rag rug. It needed to be taken outdoors and shaken, but he couldn't lift it by himself. Lorna said Juan was good with floors, but the man was seventy-nine years old. Joseph thought of the bikers; they would have no trouble hauling a rug down porch steps. It was amusing, this conundrum of his. It did not involve a woolly mammoth or the jaws of a mountain lion, or a train jumping its tracks; it was a six-foot-by-nine-foot rug as old as he was, and set against him, it would always win.

Saturday night he lay in the dark, mentally composing his grocery list:

Anaheim chiles (sub. for smoked Hatch chiles)

Ground pork (try to find fresh?)

Garlic (New Mexico garlic was fresh and plump, not dried out as in the California markets)

Cumin. This stopped him completely. Grandma Penny used to buy the seeds whole and grind them into powder. She insisted on giving Joseph a hankie filled with seeds to carry on the day he got married. "Carry cumin on your wedding day," she said, "and your wife will stay true. It also keeps chickens from wandering off." Joseph was pretty sure he'd had that hankie in his pocket the whole ceremony. He'd never had chickens, but maybe it was time to try that out.

Cilantro (available fresh anywhere)

Noodles (best to make your own)

All that sounded as if it would taste like a pathetic bachelor with a dirty rug threw chopped peppers into regular old spaghetti and then sat down to watch NASCAR. He got up, looked through the cupboards, and found the last two packets of dried corn of his grandmother's stash. He opened one and poured it into a saucepan full of water and lime to soak overnight. Posole was a never-fail dish, as soothing as mashed potatoes and just as filling, plus with the kick of hot peppers, it was a lot more memorable than spaghetti.

Just as he expected, Glory brought Dodge with her, and Juniper had Cadillac by her side. The poor little greyhound missed out on everything. They parked their truck a ways from his cabin and let the dogs run off-leash. Juniper looked happy. Glory's frown looked etched into her face. Joseph opened the screen door and brought out the teapot of cota tea and three mugs.

"This is hot," Juniper said when she took a sip.

"It's winter," he said. "Hot drinks are called for."

"Mom, you have to taste this. It's like, I don't know, really good." So it was "Mom" again. Juniper was pulling out all the stops.

Glory sat down at the picnic table on Joseph's porch. She was dressed in jeans and a purple fleece jacket, the collar pulled up. "Thanks," she said listlessly, and accepted her mug.

"You're welcome." Joseph watched the dogs nose into bushes and take off running toward a couple of jays on the branch of a pine tree. Cadillac abandoned the chase quickly, but Dodge's bark button was activated, that painfully recognizable cattle-dog shriek that truly insulted human ears.

"Dodge! For crying out loud, will you be quiet for two minutes?" Glory said. "I have a headache." The brown dog stopped at once, cringing at her side. "Down," she told him, her voice uncharacteristically harsh. Joseph reached down to pet the dog. "Don't," she said. "He's being a brat today. Like somebody else I know."

"Can I walk around the lake?" Juniper asked. "Mom, will you come with me? Joseph?"

"The further you walk, the muddier the path," Joseph said. "You could slip and fall, hurt yourself."

"I won't fall. I'll be careful."

"We'll need a flashlight."

"Walking won't hurt your back?" Glory asked.

Of course it would. Joseph looked across the lake where the last light of the day illuminated the ripples. Soon the sun would sink into it and the water would go pitch-black, but for the next twenty minutes there would be a glorious explosion of orange and magenta. He looked at Glory. "You think I'm going to miss a perfect sunset with two special ladies because a couple of my vertebrae are quitters? Come on. If I can't make it, you two can bring down a deer, skin it, and scrape the hide to build a travois and drag me back here."

That made Glory smile. Juniper was already down at the pebbly shore, picking up rocks. "Where are the arrowheads? You said there were arrowheads!" Without waiting for an answer she ran off.

"She's never heard of patience." Glory sighed. "Maybe we should let her go ahead of us. She's probably as tired of my company as I am of hers."

"How was the Valentine's wedding?"

"It went well, but you know."

"Know what?"

She looked out toward the water. "It wasn't a pirate wedding."

He smiled. "Nothing could compare to that."

"Can I help you with dinner?"

"Sort of. You can help me haul out my rug and shake it, if that isn't too lame to ask."

"Most men wouldn't even notice the rug was dirty."

"I'm not most men."

Juniper and the dogs ducked out of sight, then reappeared behind a fir tree. "Are you guys coming or not?" she hollered.

"In a minute," Glory yelled back.

"It embarrasses me to ask for help."

Glory stood up and walked into the cabin behind him. "I'm the same way. Maybe we both need to get over that."

"Do you think it's possible?"

"I don't know. But I can honestly say no man on earth has asked me to shake out his rug. Oh, my gosh. I didn't mean that to come out so wrong."

He smiled. "It's okay. I won't tease you about it."

Her cheeks stayed red as she pulled the bulk of the rug out his front door. Together they draped it over the railing and slapped at it until the dust clouds made them cough.

"This probably hasn't been cleaned since my grandmother died," Joseph said. "You know what? Leave it here and the construction crew can haul it away."

"It's a nice rug. I'll take it if you don't want it. Meanwhile, I'm happy to shake it whenever you need me," Glory said, grinning.

"First time a woman ever said that to me." He smiled back.

"You've led a sheltered life."

"Apparently."

After that, it was as if they shared evenings together all the time. Juniper, bored of her solo walk, threw the ball for Dodge. Caddy pranced at the water's edge, transfixed by fish he could see but could not figure out how to herd. Dodge jumped in the lake and splashed around. "Mom!" Juniper called. "Joseph! You guys promised we'd walk around the lake!"

"Come on," Joseph said, setting his tea down on the table. "We can watch the sunset."

"All right. But as soon as we get back, I'm opening the wine I brought."

"Fair enough."

Halfway down the path visitors ran into ruts all summer long, Glory knelt down and prized up an arrowhead. "It was just sitting there," she said, holding it up for Juniper to see. She handed it to Joseph and he rubbed the dirt off it.

"Chert," he said. "See how uneven the flakes are here at the point? That's called 'fast and dirty,' a point made on the spot for a job, then discarded. I'm surprised to see it here. I used to find arrowheads in my grandmother's garden when she dug up the potatoes, but not this close to the lake."

"I want to find one," Juniper said.

"Take mine," Glory said, but Joseph reached out and took Glory's hand, closing her fingers around the point. "You keep it. It's special. Let Juniper find her own."

"I bet I never find one," Juniper said.

"You won't with an attitude like that," Joseph said.

"I'm going closer to the lake," she said, and Joseph lifted his hand to warn her to be careful. "The shore drops off," he said as a wet Dodge raced by him. "It's really slippery. She could fall in."

"Let her," Glory said. "It appears to be the only way she learns."

When Juniper fell, Glory reached over and squeezed Joseph's hand. Juniper was screaming and Cadillac ran in circles around her, trying to make things better. "I'm all wet!" she cried as she staggered back to them.

"Where's my flashlight?" Joseph asked.

"I could have drowned and you're worried about some cheesy flashlight?"

"It's a cop flashlight. Expensive."

"I think it went in the lake."

"You can buy me a new one with that hefty allowance you get."

"What am I supposed to do?" she said. "I'm all wet!"

"There's clean towels in the bathroom," Joseph said.

"Go dry yourself off," Glory said. "Be sure you leave your muddy boots outside."

"Duh, I do know a few manners."

"That you somehow manage to forget at school," Glory said.

The girl ran ahead of them, pretend-screaming, both dogs racing behind her. Glory and Joseph waited until she was out of sight before they started laughing. Joseph noticed how Glory threw her head back when she was in the thick of it. Unless they had a couple of martinis under their belt, people didn't usually let go like that. He made himself a promise to make her laugh like that once a day until he left.

"You going to let her learn all her lessons that way?" he asked.

"It did seem to work."

"Mud's soft, but water can be tricky. We have all these arroyos in New Mexico. Places hikers are advised to stay out of. It's *importante* because even on the hottest day of the year rain can come out of nowhere, flooding the gully, carrying people off like that." He snapped his fingers.

Just before he served the salad, Joseph took a pill and a half. He quickly folded a piece of sourdough bread in half and ate it. He wanted to enjoy the dinner instead of grimacing his way through it hoping that his expression passed for a smile.

"My grandfather planed these floorboards by hand," he said as he passed vinaigrette dressing to Glory. "I'm sorry I can't pull them up for you, but maybe Lorna knows someone who can."

"It's weird when you think about it," Juniper said. She was wearing a pair of Joseph's sweatpants and a flannel shirt. Her wet clothes hung outside on the porch rail.

"What's weird?"

"How many feet walked here in the cabin's lifetime."

"You're right," Joseph said, as a flash of memory of himself lying in bed, lantern light flickering in the dark while his grandmother tidied up, came into his head. Afraid he'd miss something, he fought going to sleep but never won. Tonight's meal was the last one he would cook on the propane stove. A few of the old windows might be salvageable. Without people inside, all there was to the cabin was parts.

"It must be hard to say good-bye to all this," Glory said, looking around. She took a sip of wine.

The three of them at Joseph's table reminded him of the sepia photos in the Woodpecker Café. That moment in time became history because a photographer had collected it. His fingers itched to get his camera, but he thought Glory would find it rude, so he didn't. He turned off the stove and lifted the lid on the Dutch oven.

"Soup, or is it stew?" Glory said, putting down her glass. "Whichever that is, it smells wonderful."

"Technically it is soup, but it's a lot more than that. This is posole. My grandmother learned it from her grandmother and so on, all the way back to"—he looked at Juniper—"pre-Columbian times."

Juniper sighed. "I thought we were having spaghetti."

"We can have spaghetti any old time," Glory said. "Isn't it exciting to try something new?"

"No. I was all ready for spaghetti."

Joseph ladled the posole into the bowls. The scent of chicken stock, pork, cilantro, and oregano filled the room. Underneath all that, the distinct scent of cumin came through. He handed the full bowls to Glory, who set them at their places. "Every family has its own recipe," he said. "*Cacahuazintle*."

"Gesundheit!" Juniper said.

"Juniper," Glory said, "that's rude."

"That's all right," Joseph said. "It's a funny-sounding word."

"What's it mean?" Glory asked.

"Dried white corn for making nixtamal, fresh masa. Depending on the cook, posole can be different every time. I like onions and pork in mine, radishes and sliced avocado for toppings. But you can make it meatless, *blanca posole*, or with canned hominy, although I don't recommend it."

There was a moment of silence, an awkwardness they each realized at the same time. Here they were eating dinner together, laughing, making inside jokes as if they were connecting to each other's life forever, yet how little they truly knew of each other. No wonder his family went so overboard on food, Joseph thought. Good food shared with new friends created an opportunity to hear everyone's stories.

Glory broke the silence when she lifted her wineglass. "I don't really say grace, but how about we toast?"

"To what?" Juniper said. "My wet clothes, or this dinner not being spaghetti?"

Joseph lifted his water glass. "What else? To *amistad*. To friendship."

BEGINNING PHOTOGRAPHY

FEBRUARY 2004

BY JUNIPER McGUIRE

All Michelangelo needed to sculpt *La Pietà* was a chisel and a rock. Supposedly, he was inspired by Dante's *Divine Comedy* (1308–1321). Who spends thirteen years writing a poem? In that amount of time a person can go from birth to teenage, from teenage to the most fun years of your life, and from getting old to dead. I have not read the poem, but it is One of the Greatest Works of Literature, which means that it is going to be Really Hard to Understand and Probably Very Boring and something I will be Required to Read and Pass a Test On before I am released from this netherworld, this infernal region, this abyss, this damnation, this perdition, this fire-and-brimstone, Hades, *Sheol, Acheron, Gehenna,* or *Tophet* that is home school.

All I can say is thank God for Wiki for "interpretations" of what *La Pietà* stands for, because when you are in high school you can't just think something is beautiful because it's super realistic. Oh, no. Art and literature and music have to mean more than one thing in order to be great. One theory is that

what the *Pietà* means is that *inside* the Mary part of the statue is
actually a *young mother* looking down at her *baby* Jesus. This
means that only smart people looking at the statue can see the
truth, which is that the Jesus in her arms is a dead grown-up
because he has already been crucified by John, Mark, Luke, and
Pilate. Why can't Jesus' mother see that? Because Mary's lost it.
Her son is dead and she can only stand to see her baby the way
he once was, safe in her arms, full of warm milk and sleepy.
Reality—she just can't go there.

Think about that idea for a while, and then try going back to
regular life. Things you thought were pretty, such as a horse
eating its alfalfa or how yellow daffodils are growing around a
white farmhouse will never be just flowers. After Mary and Jesus
and Michelangelo, get ready for the worst headache ever.
Because from that moment forward not only will you wonder
how other people see the things you see, including basic stuff
like the color blue, but it will occur to you that maybe you're the
one seeing things wrong. How is that art? It's just messed up.

If everything in the world means more than one thing, how
do you ever know what is what?

And what if you don't?

Then all the true stories could be false. The world might not
be the planet we think it is. Earth could just as easily be a tennis
ball being chased by some giant random dog, running ultra-slo-
mo across a gassy galaxy that is really only someone else's side
yard, a part of something so big you can't take it all in.

This is why when you go to take a photograph, the first
thing you learn isn't how the camera works. It's about accepting
that the picture you end up with will never be the picture you
were trying to take. Right off you have to be okay with that or
don't bother. Like say you were taking a picture of a rose in

bloom and just when you press the shutter, a bee flies into the picture. What's your picture of then?

JTM: I see you working your brain muscles here! Good work. Keep it up and you may get through high school yet. —JCV

Chapter 9

GLORY

The morning of February 27 Glory sat in her closet with the door open, staring at her unmade bed. Tomorrow was the one-year anniversary of Dan's death. He had slept next to her for almost twenty years, and counting the days he was in the hospital up to now, she had now slept without him for 367 days. Last night she'd had a dream about Joseph Vigil that would have made Lorna Candelaria blush. A person could chalk that up to the body crying out to have its needs met, but Glory had to admit Joseph Vigil made her feel—comfortable? He was a good sport when Dodge tried to hump his leg, just pushed the dog away and continued talking. He worried about a dusty old rug and asked for help with it. It wasn't so much that he said surprising things, because he was a quiet man, but in his photographs he was clearly saying much more than could be spoken aloud. She had known him four months and he was leaving in two and suddenly that bothered her.

Dan had been her world. She shut her eyes and shook her head.

Out of nowhere, Edsel leapt up on her, causing empty hangers to crash and several to hit her in the head. She wanted to scream at him, but the poor dog only wanted his breakfast. Her outdoor animals had ESP as to when she woke up. Cricket began that panicked neighing she did every morning as if the dreaded day had come when that flake of hay would fail to materialize. Her last-chance dogs had learned too well that life wasn't always fair. They waited as excitedly for breakfast as the horses, but if the food didn't arrive, they'd let the matter go.

Juniper liked to make her own breakfast, sickly sweet cereal and gobs of real butter on dark toast. Was Glory supposed to force-feed her steel-cut oats? Quiz her on the food pyramid? Being a mother to a daughter was like boot camp. Some days, like today, even though the pangs of hunger torqued Glory's own stomach, she could not bring herself to swallow food. Only coffee.

With her robe tied tight around her and her feet in rain boots, she fed the animals, checked on Nanny, the goat that would soon deliver, made coffee, and took a cup back to her bedroom closet. She shoved the fallen hangers aside. By now she had a comfortable pillow in here and an old quilt to wrap herself in. She sat down next to the box of Dan's clothes and put her arm around it. In several places the cardboard was smooth from her rubbing it.

"Explain something it to me," she said, as if Dan could somehow hear her. "You wouldn't let so much as a bookend go out of your workshop unless it was sanded to perfection, buffed with beeswax, and had your signature on the backside. You couldn't tolerate a dripping faucet for a minute before you got out the wrenches. So why couldn't you take care of yourself like you did everything else? Look at what you left behind for me to do! How am I supposed to manage? I swear, if it wasn't for the animals, I'd set fire to the place and be done with it."

She pictured blue flames, white at the core, devouring the

shingles, blowing out the sticky windows, blackening the bathtub
with its rusting faucets and chipped enamel revealing crumbling
cast iron. The cobbled-together fence that blew down once a
week? Let it blaze. In her mind, what was left when the smoke
cleared was empty land ready to launch someone else's dream,
the same as Joseph's cabin. Except for the chapel. Oh, the beams
might scorch, but oak that thick was slow to burn, and the stones
used in the walls would take one look at the fire and say, "Please.
Can't you do any better than that?"

When Dan died, Glory's plan had been to stay here until she
drew her last breath. Why? She woke up every day in a lumpy,
old bed. Sure, she'd made love with her husband there, shared
twenty years of dreams, but now she slept with a dog that wanted
his breakfast by eight A.M. and didn't mind walking across her
face to let her know he was hungry. Every morning she got up
and walked barefoot down the hallway and what did she see? The
oak tree, first thing, from her kitchen window. And what good
had it done her? After a few minutes of musing that over, she made
coffee and waited for Joseph to drive up in the yellow Toyota and
trudged through another day. The reward? Witnessing the look
on Juniper's face when Joseph brought her something, even if it
was just a library book on Ansel Adams.

But Joseph was leaving in April, and soon it would be March.
Thirty-one days and he would be gone.

Lorna had assured Glory that when a year had passed, she
would look at the world with new eyes. That she'd find strength
in herself to go on. That she was young; another life was waiting
for her out in the world. Caroline Proctor said that missing Dan
would always hurt, but life didn't give a hoot about grief. It went
spooling along; that was how foster children had to look at things
or they'd curl up and die. Halle thought Glory should sign up

with eHarmony and find another husband. She'd left three messages this week alone, and Glory had ignored every single one of them.

Hey, Sis. How about meeting me at Macy's? They're having a trunk show . . .

Glory? Any chance I can hire you to make a cake for Bart's secretary? She loves anything Juicy Couture. I can e-mail you a picture of her handbag.

Have you used your gym gift certificate yet? Call me back.

Before Glory lost her nerve, she telephoned Lorna.

"Feel like lunch tomorrow?" Glory asked when she picked up.

"So long as I don't have to make it."

"I could pick up some Chinese food. Moo shu or fried rice?"

"Either sounds good. Don't forget the fortune cookies. Ask for extras."

"I thought you were on that diabetes diet now."

"A cookie or two isn't going to kill me. In fact, get some of those almond cookies, too. For Juan. You know how he loves them."

Glory knew that one cookie would turn into three or four cookies, and that five cookies would lead to ten. But why not eat what you love and die early? Hadn't life proven itself fickle and sour as all get-out? One minute Lorna would be there and then the next she wouldn't. No more taking orders from smart-mouthed kids. A chance to put her feet up for good. Glory would lose her corporeal friend, but in all other ways Lorna would be with her, just as Dan was. That feeling of him alongside. Maybe this was how life was supposed to work. People came into your life and made you fall in love with them so that when they left, you never stopped appreciating them.

"See you around noon tomorrow," Glory said, and hung up.

She wondered why she didn't hear the noise of Juniper's morning shower. Usually she wouldn't get out of it until Glory knocked on the bathroom door, reminding her it took twenty minutes before the water heater filled back up and other people wanted to take showers, too. She tapped, then opened the door to Juniper's room. The girl was sprawled across her bed, snoring, Cadillac beside her. He thumped his tail hopefully.

"Go eat your breakfast," she said, and shooed him outdoors where his kennel was open, his dish inside.

The clock was on its side on the floor. Juniper was supposed to set her alarm for eight and to be ready for homeschooling by nine. Glory did the morning farm chores; Juniper tended to the evening feedings. Joseph promised to show Glory how to manage homeschooling before he left so that she could step into the role comfortably. Or uncomfortably. One thing was for certain: Juniper was not returning to public school.

"Hey, Juniper, get up and dressed," Glory said, giving her shoulder a shake. "Joseph will be here any minute."

Chapter 10

JOSEPH

T. S. Eliot had declared April to be the cruelest month, but Joseph knew better. February was the worst, with that awful sweetheart holiday tucked in the middle, mocking all the people who weren't in love. Also, it was short on days, moving up his deadline for leaving.

"Joseph is doing this out of the goodness of his heart," Glory whispered to Juniper, who stood there yawning. "No more sleeping late. Tomorrow you get your butt out of bed earlier and be ready to work, and I mean it."

Joseph stacked the homeschooling books on the old picnic table. Glory was snorting like the old bull on his father's farm, way past doing anything about whatever made him mad, but clinging to habit. How could she be this angry when spring was just around the corner? It was the first dry day in a week. The rain had beaten down so hard that part of the Oak Shore's hillside had slid away, exposing the foundations to several of the fancy lake houses. The developers were more preoccupied with reinforcing things with rebar and concrete block than they were with tearing his cabin down. But with the bitter came the sweet. Everywhere Joseph looked, flowers budded and bloomed.

A sweet taste was on the wind that rustled through the greening tree branches. Cadillac was rambunctious, racing around the property when Juniper was occupied with her studies, not above bringing the girl "gifts" in a plea for attention. He dragged fallen tree limbs up to the table and stood there panting, waiting for praise. He regularly found dead things to roll in; he was thrilled with the baths that followed, but the worst thing ever was the day he ran up to them with a hunk of a cow's jawbone, teeth intact, in his mouth.

Juniper screamed and screamed, convinced it was human, even though the teeth were immediately recognizable to Joseph as used for grinding grasses into cud.

Cadillac, so proud of his find, would not let it go for a piece of lunch meat, his beloved Frisbee, or his favorite treat, a "bully stick," a more socially acceptable term for what it was, which was a steer's penis.

Glory, the luckiest woman on the planet, had been off working at Target that day, which left Joseph to deal with the hysteria, so he went onto Wikipedia to look for an anatomical illustration of a cow's skull, intent on proving to Juniper that it was a bovine mandible and not a human's. But try finding a lateral view that showed enough of the *Margo interalveolaris* to convince her that it was part of a larger structure. The Internet often disappointed him. It was either too easy or lacking. He thought fondly of the bookmobile that drove up to his elementary school once a week and wondered where those old blue vehicles had gone. Car heaven. Scrap metal.

Home school. He'd assured Glory that she'd be able to take over when he left, that it was manageable, when in fact every day seemed to include one commotion or another. The A Plan often went awry, and sometimes the B Plan did, too. Frankly he couldn't imagine Glory coping with it day after day.

At the end of one especially grueling day he'd opened the door to the Land Cruiser to find Dodge in the passenger seat. Joseph tried to shoo him out, but the dog was having none of that. "Fine," Joseph said, "but don't expect the kind of life you get here." He took him home.

Dodge *insisted* on a walk around the lake every day, and a swim. Joseph could only make it so far—but indeed, a little farther each day—before he had to stop and wait for the clutching pain to release his muscles. On the days he homeschooled Juniper, Joseph brought Dodge along and tried to convince him it was a better deal all around to relocate back to Solomon's Oak, but at the end of every day the dog was waiting in the car for him.

"You probably think that Joseph's such a nice guy he'll let you slide," Glory said that sunny morning of February 28. "Trust me, Juniper. You're going to earn your high school degree. By doing the work."

The kid was learning when to keep her mouth shut—around Glory. Everyone else Juniper had problems with, which meant Joseph, which meant he had to find a book on etiquette, and that was no easy endeavor in the year 2004. Joseph began to think that every high school teacher deserved a six-figure salary and free spa treatments for life.

Glory put her hands into her pockets. "After I finish my errands I'm going to have lunch with Lorna. You behave yourself. I will call every hour to check in."

Juniper, stone-faced, folded her arms across her chest.

"Say good-bye to your mother," Joseph said.

"Buh-bye, Mrs. Solomon."

Glory huffed, "That's right, be snarky. Fools that we are, we're only trying to save your educational life. Joseph, call my cell if there's any problem, no matter how small."

Juniper said, "I still don't get why I can't have a cell phone if you can."

Looking as if she might snap in two if a good wind blew through, Glory turned her back on them and walked toward her truck. Edsel, that teaspoon of a dog with the goofy outfits and toys, howled like a monkey when Glory left, and Cadillac joined in. Outdoor-dog rules did not apply to that dinky pup. Personally, Joseph thought the dog could use more dinner—his ribs showed—and the opportunity to urinate on trees. It made Dodge happy to leave his calling card on every leaf or bush or rock bigger than a baseball. "Joseph's dog," Glory called Dodge now, even though the dog minded only Glory.

Juniper tapped her pencil against her open notebook. "Did you get a good look at Mrs. Solomon? How much weight she's lost? Seriously, what if she's sick?"

"Only kind of sick she is, is sick of your shenanigans, and guess what? Me, too. Open your Spanish book. Let's get started."

"You know what she does at night?"

"Juniper, focus. Your Spanish book."

"She's back to sitting in her closet every night. Cries really quietly. For exactly ten minutes. Isn't that weird?"

"That's her business."

"You're wrong. It's your business because she's your friend. Isn't she?"

Joseph turned the chair around and straddled it so he could stretch his back while he worked. "Did you think having to take you out of high school before you got expelled was her dream come true? She had to do some fancy talking to keep the school from pressing charges. What were you thinking?"

"They totally overreacted. A plastic cafeteria knife would break if you stabbed real human skin. It's physics."

"Actually, it's intentional assault, and the knife qualifies as a weapon. Haul in the history of your fights with this girl, present your case in adult court, the DA could argue premeditation. These days plenty of judges try juveniles as adults. Come to think of it, you'd look great in an orange jumpsuit."

"Lois says that you making fun of me isn't good for my self-esteem."

Joseph looked toward the barn, envying the animals living *la vida sencilla*, the simple life. When he'd researched homeschooling, he'd become a vocal convert as soon as he read John Holt's words: *Learning is not the product of teaching. Learning is the activity of learners.* Now he'd like to dig the man up and have him try to work with Juniper.

"Okay, forget about the knife for a second. What did you say to her, your exact words?"

Juniper liked saying it: " 'You'd be a really great person if there was someone there to kill you every day of your life.' "

"That's a threat."

"It's not a threat, it's kind of from a Flannery O'Connor story."

"No matter who said it, when it comes out of your mouth, it's a threat."

"She deserved it."

"So tell the principal what she said to you."

"I don't feel like it."

Joseph sighed. "Do you know how lucky you are, *chica*? I know kids in Albuquerque who went to juvie camp for less. Terrible shit happens there."

"Terrible shit happens everywhere! I never heard you swear before. Why now?"

"Some situations require it. Now open your Spanish textbook and *vamanos* or I'll make you run hills."

Juniper sighed, groaning dramatically at how heavy the book was and how many pages there were to read through. "What's Spanish good for besides bossing your maid around if you're rich, which I'll never be? I can order a taco dinner and cuss in Spanish already."

Tempting as it was, Joseph refused to take the bait. "Do you know who Ponce de León was?"

"Not really."

"He brought the Spanish language to America."

"Big deal. Someone was bound to, eventually."

"The deal is big. In fact, it's *muy grande*. From 1990 to the year 2000, the number of Spanish speakers in America grew by sixty percent. It's the fastest-growing ethnic group. It's estimated that by the year 2010, over thirty-five million Americans will speak Spanish."

"So? That's only ten percent of all the people who live in the U.S."

Joseph rubbed his jaw. "Do the math. How many Spanish speakers will that make a hundred years from now? By the way, if you were trying to hurt my feelings by disrespecting my heritage, you failed. Sticks and stones, that's the biggest lesson you need to learn. Now turn to lesson four and read the dialogue."

"I thought we were going to take pictures today."

"We are, when you memorize the dialogue and show me that you know the math problems in chapter four."

"You're not a real teacher," Juniper said, and bent her head and began reading. "*Hola, Carmen. Vas a la bib-li-oh-tee-ka?*"

Joseph looked up into the oak tree, which was green and full of birdsong. Juniper and Glory were part of his life now. Dinner companions, dog training, late-night phone calls. When he thought of it like that it sounded like a single's ad:

DLM ISO SF (troubled teenage children okay),
for short walks, long talks, and distraction
from the pain in his back.

"*Bib-li-o-tec-a,*" he pronounced. Poor old Juan had been asking for directions to the library for fifty years.

GLORY

Lorna let the Butterfly Creek General Store door slam shut behind her and handed Glory a shopping bag.

"Jeepers. What's in here?" Glory asked. "Granite?"

"Don't sass me, child. It's just a few additions to our picnic doings, that's all." Lorna pointed to the sign for the creek trail. "Let's take the path to the water. The spring runoff is the highest I've ever seen. Come on. What's got you moving so poky this morning? I've seen crippled snails outpace you."

"I couldn't sleep."

"Insomnia's the sign of a guilty conscience. What do you need to confess?"

"Nothing a pound of Valium couldn't cure."

"Then walk faster. That'll get your endorphins pumping like an oil rig. Plus, you sweat out all your sorrow if you put your back into it. Know what I do when I feel down in the dumps? I walk it off. Some days it takes five miles, but it's never failed me yet."

Even with her cigarette habit, Lorna could keep up with New Yorkers. "Walking" to Lorna was racing to anyone else.

"Just smell this spring air," she said. "What a treat to sit with my favorite girlfriend on Butterfly Rock and have lunch."

Though Glory had been up half the night, she plodded down the trail until they reached the railroad ties, arranged like stairs in the earth, leading to the creek bank, which was rutted with tree roots and stones. The hard-packed dirt was stubbly with native grass that had already turned green. In a few weeks, when temperatures rose another twenty degrees, the landscape would turn golden and as flammable as a gasoline-soaked rag. Dan would still be dead. Joseph would be gone. Juniper would have a whole new bag of tricks with which to torture her foster mother.

"This is a nice spot," Lorna said. "Hand me a napkin so I can wipe the squirrel poop off that boulder."

Glory collapsed more than sat, her breath heaving. "I told myself to live this day like any other. But that turned out to be worse than making a big deal out of it. How can grief take so much out of a person?" The shallow creek had a swift, noisy current as it flowed down the creek bed on its way to the river.

"Did you run Dan's anniversary obituary like I told you to? Ask the mission church to say a mass in his name?"

"No," Glory said. "That's part of your culture, not mine."

"Well, then, Miss Smarty-pants, what is your culture?"

"I'm white and religion-free. The absence of culture creates its own culture."

"I never heard such a load. Actually, you're pinker than white, and something as ordinary as blow-drying your hair qualifies as a ritual. Time set aside to remember, to mark certain days as special, that's what makes us function. You know I'm always willing to lend you my culture."

"I'll survive," Glory said, and that was the problem. Survival was being stuck in the same place for months without a shred of comfort—except for Joseph, who was a great comfort—but not for long.

"Fine." Lorna sat down to open her red-and-white food container. "Ah, fried rice. Tastes as good as it smells, and how many things can you say that about? So what do you have planned for today?"

"Nothing."

"That's not so. You're lunching with your friend, who's known you for almost twenty years. We're sitting by a precious resource we can't live without. If that's not enough for you, go sit in the chapel your husband built for a while. Silence is holy."

"So's a nap." Glory yawned. She set the container of moo shu pork down on the rock. Inside the bag Lorna had given her was a gallon jar of pickled eggs. Glory had lugged a gallon jar of pickled eggs down the trail for what? Dessert? Was Lorna's mind starting to go?

"But you won't do either, will you?"

"I might. I might even do both."

Lorna snorted. "Glory Bea, do you think that if you wait grief out, it will just go away?"

"That's what I've been counting on."

Lorna rattled off a heated response in Spanish. "*Encontrarse como un pulpo en un garaje!*"

"What?" Glory tried to translate, but surely she was mistaken, otherwise, her friend had just accused her of behaving like an octopus in a parking place.

"Look," Lorna said. "If you live in chaos, I can't stop you. But I don't have to listen to it. Let's change the subject."

"To what?"

"Well, my son's still in prison and nobody's offered a dime to buy the store. You have the misbehaving teenager and the company of a certain New Mexican who, if I'm not mistaken, has feelings for you that are veering off that friendship trail into uncharted territory."

"Lorna, you read too many tabloids. There's nothing there except this notion that he can reach Juniper."

"Oh, that's right. What do I know? I'm just an old lady who makes sandwiches and sweeps up after bikers and says 'Thank you for your patronage' a thousand times a day."

"I know how hard you work. If I had the money, I'd buy your store. Your life is much more interesting, believe me. Mine's like trying to separate necklaces when the chains get knotted up."

"That's what happens if you don't put things away carefully."

Glory leaned back against the rock and put her unwrapped chopsticks down on a napkin. When she began to cry, Lorna patted her leg. "You know we are sitting in the very spot. Before everything was dammed up, this creek was ten feet deep and one wild river. It grabbed up Mrs. Michael Halloran and her baby daughter like they were toothpicks. The *testarudo* husband refused to listen to the Indians and tried to cross the river after they told him how rough it was. What a mistake! So much lost, all from distrust. If he'd waited just a few more weeks, who knows how those three lives would had gone? The mother might have had more children, the daughter could have grown up to be a famous architect like that Julia Morgan. If only he'd listened."

"The Constitution says people are entitled to make their own choices, even if they're stupid ones."

"*Sí*, but sometimes it pays to do something someone else tells you to do, even if you're not certain of the outcome."

Analogies made Glory's head ache. What was there to say? The story of Michael Halloran's headless wife was probably a fable, a warning to young girls not to stray far from home. Glory wanted the river back, to jump in and have the current deliver her anywhere else. She wanted to sit here until it was dark, so still that she wouldn't frighten the deer that came out of the woods to drink from the creek. Maybe an owl would fly by. It didn't have to be a great horned, necessarily, but that was her favorite kind. She picked the almond off one of the cookies but didn't eat it. When Lorna finished her lunch, she broke apart a fortune cookie and fed Glory the sweet, curved cookie. Because it was too much effort to turn her head and spit it out, Glory chewed and swallowed and felt the juices in her mouth turn sour. What had she learned in a year? That grief was saying good-bye constantly. If she knew that, why didn't it help?

JOSEPH

"Time for lunch," Joseph said. Juniper had butchered Spanish and cried over algebra, leaving biology and language arts for the afternoon. As always, Glory had left a meal for them—this time peanut butter sandwiches, chips, and Diet Vanilla Pepsi, Juniper's favorite soda. Glory had not telephoned. Joseph hoped the break from Juniper would lift her spirits.

"I'll bet you a hundred dollars you don't know who invented peanut butter," Joseph said, cutting his sandwich in half.

"Bet I do," Juniper answered, then crammed hers into her mouth. "George Washington Carver," she mumbled around the lump of sandwich. "Pay up."

Joseph smiled. "You're wrong."

"I am not!"

"Prove it." If there was one thing Juniper hated, it was being wrong.

"I read it online."

"How many sources?"

"One's enough."

He shook his head no. "*No, ése*. Guess what ethnic groups we know for sure ate peanut butter?"

Juniper slumped in her chair and groaned. "Let me guess. Pre-Columbian."

"Bingo."

She peeled the crusts off her sandwich. "Do you spend your nights researching Pre-Columbian facts to spank me with?"

"That's a good idea. Should I add a hundred dollars to the fifty K you already owe me?"

"Not until I check two or more sources," Juniper said, going to the computer.

When the information came up, Joseph watched Juniper's lips moving as she read. When she took her hands off the keyboard, he said, "Remember this moment for the rest of your life. Admitting you're wrong is the first step in educating yourself. Come on. Let's clean up and go take pictures."

"What about language arts?"

"We'll combine it with photography. You'll see. It'll be fun."

"I seriously doubt that."

"We could sit here and write a five-paragraph essay if you'd rather."

"No, no." She quickly bused their dishes, fetched Cadillac, and was back before Joseph had time to swallow his pain pill. Feeling her watching him, he wanted to tell her, I hope you never get to this place, but compared to his kind of pain, hers was off the scale.

Out walking around the ranch, Juniper pointed out an old fence post missing its rails. Midway up, inside one of the notches, was a bird's nest. "I think that nest has eggs," Juniper said. "The bird flies away the second I come near."

"Take a picture," Joseph said. "See if you can identify her by her nest."

They visited the goats next, and it was a good thing that Cadillac and Dodge were both leashed because Caddy was sure it was time to herd the hugely pregnant Nanny. Joseph held both leashes while Juniper photographed the goat's eye, with its strange, slotlike pupil. Then he handed Juniper nail clippers. "Cut a lock," he said, and held out an envelope for her to deposit the hair into, then sealed it up.

"Why would I want hair from a pregnant goat?"

"Because UC Santa Cruz can run a DNA panel and I thought learning about genetics this way might be more fun than reading about it."

"Well, it isn't so far."

"Do you think you know all there is to know about DNA?"

"I think I know enough to get me through life."

"Really? Suppose you came on the scene of a murder before the cops arrived. They'd automatically arrest you for looking guilty. DNA analysis could clear you, but, oops, it's a waste of time. Yeah, you know all you need to know. Forget it. Throw the goat hair away, and I'll drive you to the nearest McDonald's so you can apply for a job. How's that sound?"

"Do you know how much worse homeschooling is than high school?"

Joseph smiled. "I know you're using your mind instead of your fists, and that's all I care about."

Later, Dodge provided a canine hair sample, and Joseph plucked hair from his own scalp. They sat on the porch studying

them under a cheapo microscope, and he told Juniper to draw
what she saw.

"Get serious," she said. "I'm not an artist."

"If scientists had to draw like artists, we'd still think the earth
was flat. Draw."

As the afternoon wore on, they classified the white oak by
phylum, genus, and species, copied down the Latin names, and
tried writing in calligraphy. They consulted a Bible concordance
for mention of oak trees, which led to the folklore of trees, which
led to Greek myths, which led to the politics of oak trees in
California, endangered-species laws, and lastly Joseph brought
out his secret weapon: poetry. He read aloud "The Oak Tree," by
Matsuo Bashō.

" 'The white oak / sees cherry blossoms / in the river.' What
do you think?" he asked Juniper.

"Is that the whole poem?"

"It's called haiku."

"I don't care if they call it sushi, it sounds more like a joke
than a poem. I thought poems were supposed to be *about* something."

"That poem is about plenty of something. Think about it.
That's all I ask. Open your mind. Now let's go take pictures."

"Finally!" Juniper crowed, but Joseph made her put her books
indoors before they took off with cameras and dogs. He put Edsel
on leash, feeling sorry for the dog, cooped up all day like a house
cat. Edsel strained at the leash with all of his ten pounds and peed
on anything more than an inch tall, proving Joseph's theory that
given the opportunity, the little dog would man up.

Did it qualify as a miracle that Juniper had made it one entire
day without cussing or punching another human being?

Joseph made sure that they photographed the visual component of everything they'd studied today. Close-ups of the color patterns on the goats' hides; panoramic shots of the ranch; the three dogs vying for the lead position; the two horses' heads straining over the fence, their tails swishing in unison; and when they'd filled up the memory card, Joseph made Juniper sit and cull the pictures on the computer. "Dump any picture you consider pretty," Joseph said.

"But I want to keep those."

"Nope, get rid of 'em. They're only pictures. You'll take thousands more. But first you have to cut them apart, find out how they work. Save your most intriguing shot, and the ones you hate."

"This is not how to learn to take pictures."

"How do you know if you don't try it? It's an *assignment*. Take ten minutes to study them. Be prepared to explain why you feel that way. I'm going to stretch out my back."

While he walked around the house, he took inventory of Glory's things. The pitcher collection started with a two-inch-high creamer and ended with what he believed was called a ewer, made of a blue calico-pattern pottery that looked old and heavy. Dog-eared cookbooks were stacked on the tile counter. She had an array of pots and pans that hung from hooks on the wall. A life in objects that would fill a moving van. Meanwhile, his life fit into a suitcase. With the warm weather drying everything up, Joseph's clock ticked. Only a few more weeks.

"I'm finished," Juniper called. "I hope the ugliest photographs ever taken give you a thrill. They make me want to hurl."

He was pleased to see the landscape of the goat pasture, the ground bare except for scattered turds and a toppled-over bucket. The background showed a stretch of road and the faint blur of a car passing by. Up close and also out of focus was the mailbox, protruding into the shot, ruining everything. Juniper said, "This one is so bad it makes me want to scream."

"What makes it bad?"

She shrugged. "Everything's fighting to be the important part. Plus it's all ordinary stuff. Ugly. Pictures should be pretty."

He ignored her comment. "Okay, Juniper. You photographed that composition by accident. Now let's try doing one just like it, on purpose."

"You want me to take ugly pictures on purpose?"

"I sure do."

The light was beginning to fade when Glory drove up in the truck. She saddled up Cricket and ponied Piper alongside and headed up the hillside. The dogs were straining to join her, but Joseph kept them back. "We're done for today," he said once Glory was out of sight. He handed Edsel and Caddy off to Juniper and took hold of Dodge's leash. "Better go get dinner started. I have to go."

"Don't you want to have dinner with us?"

"Not tonight. I'll see you on Monday. Practice your Spanish."

He drove away with Dodge sitting in the front seat and hoped Glory didn't see that he'd abandoned her rule of crating the dog when he drove places. Dodge whined a little when they pulled onto the highway, but quickly settled down when Joseph turned up the radio. "That's right, you're an NPR dog. Let's listen to 'All Things Considered.'"

At the post office, a package was waiting, a large box that weighed little. The return address was his parents'. He set it into the back of the Land Cruiser and drove home. Inside the cabin while he heated up water for coffee and leftover Swamp Juan pizza for dinner, he prepared Dodge's supper, adding canned pumpkin and a few sardines; fish oil for a shiny coat; pumpkin to keep him lean. After a quick trot down to the lake, a swim, and a game of fetch that could never go on long enough so far as Dodge was concerned, the dog lay down in front of the wood stove and Joseph heaved a sigh of relief.

After dinner, he slit the tape on the package and opened the box. On top of many crumpled Hatch, New Mexico, *Citizens* was an envelope addressed to him written in his father's handwriting. He opened it and a disability check fell out. He'd had his mail forwarded to his parents, rather than here. He looked at the numbers on it, thought of Fidela opening her check, and how they would both burn them to bring Rico back. Finally he set the check aside, pulled off the newspaper article paper-clipped to the letter to read later. His dad wasn't big on letters or talk.

Primo,

We have had some nice weather. Still, your mother worries about her apricot trees almost as much as she worries about you.

Your padre

Under more crumpled paper was a three-foot-long, dried chile ristra enclosed in Bubble Wrap, clearly his mother's handiwork. Hang one on your *portal*—porch—and good luck would come to you all year round. He bent his head and inhaled deeply. The faint burn in his nose made him shut his eyes. He could almost smell the sage. The pull to get in his car and drive east was visceral. Why send it to him when he was returning in a few weeks? Maybe he'd leave it with Lorna. She could use some good luck.

He unfolded the newspaper article. From the *Albuquerque Journal*: MORE ARRESTS IN LAST YEAR'S METH LAB SHOOTING: JURY TRIAL SELECTION TO BEGIN IMMEDIATELY.

After the adrenaline rushed his bloodstream, Joseph set the article down, absently smoothing its edges.

GLORY

It was eight P.M. March winds blew, rattling the windows, reminding Glory she hadn't washed them since the last wedding, that Valentine's Day event with the heart-shaped, four-layer, pink fondant cake that dyed her fingernails fuchsia for days. Juniper sat at the table taking notes from a library book that Joseph suggested she read. Glory sipped her second glass of red wine, impatient for the slight buzz that made her edges blur. More annoying than waiting for that numbness was that she had made it two weeks past the anniversary of Dan's death and hadn't died of grief.

She snapped her fingers when Edsel tried to distract Juniper with the once-controversial, paid-for-in-full canvas fire-hydrant toy she'd bought him, but Juniper merely reached down, patted the dog's head, and kept on reading. Eventually he lay down on the floor next to Cadillac, groaning to let everyone know the extent of his disappointment. Joseph took the dog on walks the days he came to homeschool, and now Edsel insisted on a daily walk versus his previous pastime, couch loafing. He'd muscled up, and Glory had to admit, his coat looked great.

Glory held her library book open on her lap, reading the same two sentences over and over: "The heat is a presence. Palpable and relentless, it rolls over Albuquerque like a hot iron."

Maybe Joseph lived in a different part of the city, somewhere higher in elevation, and instead of like an iron, the temperature was more like a warm hand against your neck. With a mountain view and spectacular sunrises. Less traffic. And the scent of a piñon fire warming adobe bricks. And strolling mariachis. I have to stop drinking wine every night, she thought, and set down the glass.

Juniper shut her book and stretched her arms. "All this stuff Copper Joe wants me to do is way harder than public school. I'm ready to go back now."

"Very funny."

"What's funny about it?"

Glory shut the library book. "If it's that simple for you to change your behavior, why didn't you do it months ago?"

"Maybe I wasn't ready, okay?"

"Not okay. It's selfish. Do you know what you put Caroline, Lois, and me through?"

Juniper ignored the question. "What if I sign a paper saying I promise I won't hit anyone ever again?"

"It's too late. I officially withdrew you from school. The subject is closed."

"That's *real* understanding of you, Mrs. Solomon."

"What can I say? Actions have consequences."

"What is that? Some kind of old saying that doesn't mean anything? Whatever. I'm going to bed. Come on, Caddy."

"Let him out to pee first, Ms. McGuire," Glory said to the girl's back as she walked down the hall, the collie following. Time alone sounded great, and it was, for about fifteen minutes. Then the alone part hit. What she needed was someone to chat with about anything that *was* going right. She thought of Joseph, but tipsy as she was, she feared she'd say something stupid, like "I want to sleep with you," and then she'd have to explain it wasn't about romance, it was about ten minutes of feeling something other than this endless yearning for something she couldn't even name.

Definitely not calling Joseph.

She called Caroline and got her service. She called her mom, then remembered it was her bridge night at the Senior Center and she wouldn't be home for an hour. She called Halle. "Hey, Sis. You have a minute to talk?"

Her sister sighed. "Gee, I don't know. Do you think I left you all those messages for the fun of it?"

"I'm sorry."

"Why didn't you call me back?"

"Because I didn't want to hear you say, 'I told you so.'"

Halle was quiet for a moment. "Is that what you think I do?"

"Not every time I see you," Glory hedged, regretting the words already.

"Oh, please. Don't try to soften the blow when you've already delivered it. The truth is, I'm never sure how to talk to you, Glory."

"Why not?"

"Because you don't really open up to me anymore. Not just me, either."

"That's not true. Is it?"

"Let me say this before I lose my nerve. You won't ask for help. You act ridiculously stoic, and, trust me, you're not fooling anyone. Even Mom agrees with me."

Indignation rose up, making Glory's heart beat faster. "Halle, my husband *died*."

"He sure did, and that sucks. What I want to know is, how long do you think you can get away with ignoring your family by using that excuse? I for one don't think Dan would appreciate it."

SOLOMON'S OAK   *313*

Glory picked up her wineglass again and studied the ruby red liquid in the glass. Halle might as well have stuck a baling hook into her heart. "Never mind. I actually called to see what was up with you. Bye." Glory hung up the phone, and suddenly the wine tasted wonderful, so she shut the phone off and finished her glass. Whether Halle called back or didn't, any conversation would be like the iron in Albuquerque, *palpable*, *relentless*.

She folded laundry, made and refrigerated shortbread dough. Checked her e-mail in case someone wanted to get married. Not this week. Edsel followed her every move, and finally she took a good, hard look at the little dog and admitted she didn't give him enough exercise. Yes, he was tiny, but, no, that didn't mean she could skip his walks on days she felt sorry for herself. It wasn't fair to the dog she'd adopted and called her own. "Harness," she said, and the greyhound launched himself, landing in her arms, and began licking her face. "We'll do this every day from now on," she promised him, and took him outside. The little dog pranced, not minding the wind or the darkness.

They walked to the oak tree. From there, the chapel looked more like a lodge than a church. Edsel peed upon the tree for so long Glory had plenty of time to ponder her sister's words.

Was Halle right?

On the year anniversary she'd expected some sense of closure. She'd said good-bye. Meant it when she said she hoped heaven was everything Dan dreamed it was. Other people had uncanny experiences when someone died. Comforting signs, good omens. Did her loss have to be so freaking ordinary? She tried to imagine Dan walking back into her life again. Would he be angry she'd turned his private refuge into almost as public a place as the oak tree? Allowed pirates into the place he prayed his most private prayers? Certainly he would have straightened things out with Juniper. She'd be on the honor roll, learning woodworking, sitting on the corral fence laughing at something he said.

She let Edsel back into the house and checked the goats. Nanny was miserable, and who could blame her, her sides stuck out eight or nine inches more than usual. Days ago, Glory had forked straw and shavings into an empty stall, creating a birthing place for Nanny that was five inches deep, but Nanny wasn't having any of that. Tonight Glory herded her inside with water and pellets, shut the gate, and listened to Nathan bleat. He could stand nose to nose with her. Mesh wire was the only barrier, but try explaining that to a billy goat. Nathan wanted *Monday Night Football*, meat loaf on Thursdays, sex three times a week whether Nanny was interested or not. "Get over it," she told him, and turned his oat bucket upright, throwing in a handful of feed, which distracted him immediately. She went indoors, locking locks and shutting off lights, trying to think of a way to apologize to her family for shutting them out. Maybe she'd never get over losing Dan, but as painful as it was, life did go on.

At six, Juniper came running into Glory's bedroom, bounced onto the bed, and grabbed hold of her shoulders. "What is it?" Glory said, sitting straight upright. "Is the barn on fire? Did you call 911?"

"Nanny had twins. Adorable baby twins! Get up, Mom! You have to come see them right now. You have to."

They sat on the barn floor, shavings clinging all over their pajamas. Juniper took pictures of the teetering babies. "Two girls," Glory said. "Would you like to name them?"

"That depends. Are they going to end up as Easter dinner?"

"Nope. They're going to give us milk and help us make goat cheese to sell, and you know what that means."

"More chores."

"What if it meant a raise in your allowance?"

"That would be a miracle."

"Juniper, why do you always think of the worst possible outcome?"

"I'm just following your example."

Glory was struck mute. When the barn phone rang, it startled her. It had been so long since she'd used it, she'd almost forgotten it was there. She got to her feet to answer it, and on the way she spotted one of Dan's gloves lying across the fence rail, stiffened into the shape of his hand. She slid her fingers inside it, then picked up the receiver. Who on earth calls before seven A.M. unless it's bad news? Please not Lorna, please not her mother, and please not Halle or Bart or Joseph or Caroline or anyone who wasn't ninety-nine years old and ready to go.

"Honey, it's Caroline."

"My goodness, you're up early."

"Sleep is just a good idea. I bow to the god caffeine. I'm afraid I have some news that can't wait for a reasonable hour."

"Caroline, you're scaring me. What is it?"

"It's Juniper's father."

"Oh, no. Did he die, too? How much more does that girl have to go through?"

"No, he's very much with us. As in here, in town, apparently. He wants to see her. You're going to have to break this to her somehow."

"But he abandoned her. He can't waltz back into her life when he feels like it, can he?"

"I've already scheduled their meeting with Lois. She and I will act as support during the session. Glory, you still there?"

"I'm here." Glory leaned around the post to look at the babies. The kid with the latte-colored blaze made her way out of the birthing pen. Suddenly she discovered the springs that all goats seem to have in their hooves. She reared up, fell down, got back up, and then she had it—what Dan called "a case of the sproings." The only thing funnier than newborn goats leaping around were baby ducks discovering their first puddle. "Yes," Glory said. "Give me a while, Caroline. I'll call you back."

She hung up and pressed Dan's glove against her cheek. He would have gone straightaway to Juniper and told her, *Your father's back. Let's go talk to him and see what he has to say.* Not Glory. She would rather stop breathing than break Juniper's heart one more time. She watched from the stall entrance as Juniper baby-talked and gently stroked an exhausted Nanny. After a while Glory would figure out how to say it, but right now, all that mattered were the newborns. She opened the stall gate and walked inside. "Looks like they're getting the hang of things."

"Oh, my gosh, Mom! I thought of the perfect names. Wait till you hear."

"Tell me."

"Karma and Patience. From *Shōgun*. It was Blackthorne's karma that he had to remain in Japan, and it was his patience that allowed him to capture Ishido. In the book, it says that the moment you accept your karma is when learning begins. Kind of like what Joseph told me. Let one wild feeling take over and it will lead to another. Patience makes you strong. Isn't that great?"

"It's terrific," Glory said, putting her arm around the girl with the impossible grin. "Now tell me what you want for breakfast."

THE WESTERN BLUEBIRD (*SIALIA MEXICANA*)
BY JUNIPER MCGUIRE

You might expect to see a bluebird in a meadow, but your chances are better if you look in the forest.

Bluebirds are not entirely blue. Gray, white, and dull blue for the females provides camouflage. Deep cobalt blue on the males, except for the drapes on his shoulders that make him look like he's wearing a chestnut brown shawl.

In the 1939 movie *The Wizard of Oz* Judy Garland sang "Somewhere Over the Rainbow," which the American Film Institute ranks as one of the best songs of all time.

When sailors log 5,000 miles at sea, or cross the equator for the first time, they mark their passage by getting a bluebird tattoo on their right hands. When they come back the other way, logging 5,000 more miles, they get one on the left hand.

Bluebirds are "secondary cavity nesters," which means they move into other birds' abandoned houses. The entrance must be no larger than an inch and a half in diameter or starlings can get in and steal their eggs. Look three to five feet aboveground for a bluebird's nest. Chances are the nest will face south or east.

The bluebird is the state bird of Missouri, New York, Idaho, and Nevada.

One Navajo story says that two bluebirds stand sentry at the Creator's door.

Bluebirds have long been associated with happiness in essays, plays, novels, and memoirs, which means that you write the truth about your life, no matter how unpleasant.

JTM: Now this is more like it. —JCV

Chapter 11

JOSEPH

Joseph sat on the front porch of his cabin, throwing the tennis ball for Dodge. He worried that if he didn't make the dog stop and take a drink now and then, he would collapse. All around them Joseph felt spring pitching hardball. Too bad there wasn't a way to warn the plants. All that sun feels great at first, but in no time it'll crisp your leaves and there won't be enough water to go around.

In three weeks his family expected him to drive up, park his car next to his father's truck, and to sit down while his mother fed him twenty thousand calories because it was common knowledge that a forty-year-old man couldn't be trusted to feed himself. He needed to wrap things up here, which prior to Glory and Juniper meant packing a suitcase and gassing up the car. But Juniper was responding so well to the homeschooling he hated to go.

He threw the ball long, watching Dodge run toward the lake. The dog loved to swim. He nosed around the shoreline upending turtles and displacing frogs. But with children racing by and campers taking walks wherever they pleased, Joseph would soon have to keep Dodge leashed. The dog brought the ball back and dropped it at his feet, looking at him hopefully. "Give me a break," Joseph told him.

Should he drop him at his father's farm, where he'd have to fight his way into the herd hierarchy? If Joseph moved back to Albuquerque, would walks in the ninety-degree heat suffice? There were eleven dog parks, but he'd driven by those places, sun-beaten and grassless. Dodge lived for his daily swim. He didn't mind that Joseph had to go slowly on hikes. All that meant was that he could race back to check on Joseph and cover twice the distance.

The matter of Glory was not so easily resolved. Imagining a day going by that they didn't talk was difficult. Juniper, that wild streak in her, her street smarts and courage . . . she was an embryonic autodidact if ever there was one. While Dodge slurped water from his bowl, Joseph walked to the lake's edge, where segmented horsetails shot up, their stems marked by distinctive brown rings. Dodge raced by him, crashing through bushes and scaling rocks, and jumped in the water. When you pulled the sections of horsetail apart, they made a popping noise. Juniper would rattle the keys on the keyboard and report to him:

Equisetum is a rogue in the plant world because it reproduces by spores instead of seeds. It's non-photosynthetic! One-hundred-million-plus years old! A survivor of the Paleozoic era. As close to a living fossil as any plant can be, and guess what? It's Pre-Columbian!

He could tell her that when Grandma Penny ran out of steel wool, she sent Joseph to the lake to pull up a handful of horsetails to show him how good a job they did on her cast-iron kettle. *Like* papel de lija, *sandpaper, its abrasiveness can turn a rough thing into a smooth thing. Not everything comes from a store.*

Examining Nanny's DNA profile led Juniper to research the Dead Sea Scrolls, written on goatskin. DNA results had proven that the pieces of skin had been taken from the same goat, or its relative, and allowed scientists to order and date the holy text of the Jewish religion.

I don't believe in religion, Juniper said. What has God ever done for me?

But Joseph watched Juniper singing to the dogs and currying the horses. Looking at the past was warming her up to the idea of a future. God was patient.

"The girl is coming around all on her own," he had told Glory yesterday, which was code for "I have to leave you both and I don't know how to do that."

In return, Glory said, "Butterflies are hatching," which was code for "I can't talk about your leaving because then it will be real."

Weddings, butterflies, goats, and dogs; Glory would be fine after he left. She was the kind of person who soldiered on. The abundance of female energy in his life made Joseph dwell less on his aches and pains. The impossible oak tree resisting his efforts to capture it on film couldn't compete with a homemade peanut-butter-and-jelly sandwich and an hour of conversation filled with laughter.

Back at the cabin he sat down on the porch steps, and Dodge, stinky and wet, whined. He looked at the ball and then up to Joseph, as close as they got to a common language. "Thirty-six more times." Joseph counted down until he reached zero and stood up and walked inside to the kitchen. "We're putting the ball into the drawer now," he explained, showing Dodge and closing the drawer.

Joseph sat in front of the computer, looking at the photos he'd chosen to finish his project. The disc was at the copy shop, and soon they'd call and say the prints were done. He'd ordered five comb-bound sets. One for Juniper, one for Fidela and the boys, one for Lorna, and two spares.

He didn't need to look to feel the dog staring at him as he waited for his beloved ball to reappear. How the heck did Glory get any work done? What did she know that he didn't? Dodge sent out *pleasepleaseplease* vibes and Joseph gave up. *"No mas today, comprende?"*

Clearly Dodge did not *comprende*.

When his cell phone rang, Joseph was thrilled. Any call was preferable to another game of ball. *"Ya'at'eeh,"* he said, in case it was Juniper. He was trying to enlarge her knowledge of languages.

"Joseph?"

He heard the catch in Glory's voice and knew it was bad news. "What happened?"

"It's Juniper's father. He's come out of hiding."

"Isn't that a good thing?"

"Probably not. He left her once already. What if she gets her hopes up and he disappoints her again? What if he wants to move her someplace like Baltimore or Scranton or Milwaukee? What if I never see her again?"

"Go get in your truck," he said. "Drive to the Woodpecker Café. I'll buy you lunch."

"I can't eat."

"You can watch me eat. What did Juniper say when you told her?"

"That's the problem. I haven't told her yet. Besides, I don't want to leave her alone here. I'm out here in the barn calling you so she won't hear me."

"Juniper's ready for a chance to prove herself. Woodpecker Café, fifteen minutes." He ended the call before Glory could come up with another reason to stay stuck in her pickle and felt his own heart sink. Poor kid.

He'd forgotten that the café's mantel was Dan Solomon's wood-work, but it was the first thing Glory noticed. She walked right by the table Katie Jay led them to and placed her hand against the chiseled oak. Joseph watched her while he waited at the table for her to return. When she did, he said, "I like the BLTs here."

"What's the soup?" Glory asked the waitress.

"Vegetable barley."

"Guess I'll have the BLT."

"Sounds good to me, too," said Joseph.

Katie Jay shook her head. "Watch yourself around this one," she told Glory. "Wheat, white, or sourdough?"

"Sourdough," they answered in tandem, then laughed.

"Tell me everything," Joseph said when their drinks arrived.

Glory related Caroline's phone call. "Unless they're members of the Manson family, biological parents win out over foster care. The courts don't overlook abandonment or abuse, and they insist on counseling, but he could take her away, this very week." Her face was impassive. She wouldn't look directly at him, but her gaze kept returning to the fireplace mantel. "Dan was a great car-penter."

"Yes, he was." Joseph folded his hands and placed them on the table. "Maybe I have something you can use."

"What?"

"Juniper's homeschooling. She's getting caught up with high school requirements. I've been to family court dozens of times. I can go as her guardian *ad litem*. The judge will agree it would be a shame to interrupt such progress. He could be swayed."

"I doubt it. Anyone can homeschool. And there are good schools everywhere. Thanks for trying, but I think I'm sunk. I'm a coward, Joseph. I can't tell her."

"Yes, you can."

"How?"

He reached across the table and took her hand. "Let's walk around the lake. Sometimes when you let your mind go blank, your subconscious comes up with solutions."

Probably it was Joseph's taking Glory's hand that changed things. The hug she gave him when they walked along the familiar path around the lake was also part of it. Then they both spotted the pair of herons wedding-marching their way through the horse-tails, and that was it. Maybe the connection began way back when she found that arrowhead, but Joseph was pretty sure that what tipped them over was the pain in his back that stopped him. "I have to rest a minute," he said, and leaned over a boulder, both arms bracing him.

"Of course." She whistled for Dodge and practiced a few dance moves with the dog until Joseph could straighten up. He leaned on her shoulder as they walked slowly back to his cabin.

Indoors, she helped him to his bed, brought an icepack, and handed him his pills and a glass of water. "I can stay awhile," she said. "What else do you need?"

She needed to tell Juniper; he needed to tell Glory he was leaving and that he no longer wanted to. But first he needed the painkiller to hit his bloodstream, and he needed to count down the minutes until it did. "Talk to me. About anything. After thirty minutes, I'll be okay."

"No, you won't," she said. "After today, nothing will ever be okay again."

He watched her tidy his cabin according to standards a woman found necessary that a man did not. Dusting, for example, when the house was slated to be torn down. *And then Caroline called and it was like this hole in my heart was waiting for Juniper . . .* Putting the clean dishes back into the cupboard when the cupboard and the dishes were destined for the Dumpster outside. *Cadillac, saying he took to her is putting things mildly, and what if he won't let her take the dog? . . .* Giving Dodge a good brushing, which sent hair flying, which didn't matter, but then she swept up with a broom and dustpan. *Maybe I'm drawn to difficult people . . .* He'd never noticed the broom in the closet. Because his back wouldn't allow the movement necessary to sweeping, the broom stayed in the shadows, invisible. *And it isn't like this is forever, she has three years and change before she's legally an adult, we could e-mail, right? . . .* When there was nothing left to do, she washed her hands, then came to sit beside him on the bed. "How's your pain?"

"Better." He felt the bed give to accommodate the extra hundred pounds. The weight was nothing. It didn't change anything, but it changed everything. "Either way, whether she goes to her dad or she doesn't, I want you to come with me to New Mexico."

"I can't travel."

"Why not?"

She raised her arm and gestured widely. "The farm, the weddings, and who's going to take care of my animals? The dogs are on special diets, Edsel's seizures are what landed him in the shelter in the first place—"

"How about asking one of your foster sons? They're old enough, reliable, and they know the place. You said Robynn was sweet on Gary. I'm sure they'd welcome the opportunity to be alone together. If you're worried about Edsel, bring him with you."

"How can I leave California? It's my home."

"I don't think they revoke your license for an out-of-state visit. A week or two. When's the last time you had a vacation?"

"A couple of years ago Dan and I drove to Yosemite. Dan wanted to see the giant sequoias—just like you, he loved the trees. We stayed at the Ahwahnee hotel, which was incredibly expensive, even off-season. It was fall, the leaves, my gosh, were they pretty. Did you know that Ansel Adams used to show up there every afternoon to practice the piano? So many people came to listen, the hotel started serving high tea."

She was operating on raw nerves, close to stammering. Their mutual attraction was expanding. The elephant in the room. High voltage if they dared touch. His heart, which he was certain had hardened to steel, unfolded one wing. If things caught fire, he'd have to let them burn . . . Joseph reached out and took her hand. He pulled her fingers to his mouth and pressed his lips against them. "Like sparks," he said, "under your skin." When he took both her hands to pull her toward him, she hesitated, but only for a second. Then she lay down next to him, murmuring, "This is such a bad idea," while he kissed her shoulder, which tasted of salt, and the hollow in her neck, which didn't, and her cheek and finally her mouth and said, "Give me one good reason to stop and I will."

Whether she could or couldn't hardly mattered because she didn't. For a while she kept her eyes shut, and he wondered if that was her way, or if were she to open them, the connection would shatter. Either way, right when their breath was coming the faster, he had to stop her. "This is terribly embarrassing."

"More embarrassing than a rag rug?"

"Yes. If things go any further, I have to ask you to be on top. My back."

"Is that all? I thought, oh, no, Joseph's going to tell me he's not *that* kind of guy and call me a *picarona*."

He laughed. "A hussy? Where the heck did you learn that word?"

"Lorna."

They locked eyes and giggled, then laughed nervously, then full out, until they both had tears in their eyes that were an equal mix of sadness and happiness.

From that moment forward, every time he looked at her there was more bare skin to explore. He admired the gentle rounding of her breasts, her flat, muscular stomach, and the sharp hip bones to either side, which were the warmest parts of all. As first-time lovers they were clumsy, bumping heads, saying "Ow" and "Sorry," and his stupid back limited their positions. Every time he grimaced, she moved a few inches and asked, "How's this?" and he could not help laughing. So much to be learned, when all parties were willing. "Hussy," he said again, then he was inside her and nothing else mattered.

A Farewell Dinner Party Menu

Spaghetti
Romaine salad with blue cheese dressing
Diet Vanilla Coke over crushed ice
Red-velvet cupcakes with chocolate buttercream frosting
Vanilla pudding/flan

Glory broke the news to Juniper over dinner. "Your father wants to see you," she said, holding on to Joseph's hand under the table.

Impatient, sarcastic Juniper put down her fork and listened until Glory finished the particulars, then said, "What if I don't want to see him?"

"Well, it doesn't really make a difference," Glory said. "Legally, he's still your father, and he could go to court to make sure everyone knows that."

Juniper looked from Glory to Joseph. "Do you think I should give the loser a second chance?"

Joseph said, "Whatever happened in the past, he's still your father."

Of course he didn't want her to meet with the man. In the short while Joseph had known Juniper, the teenager had grown as fast as the baby goats. She was developing curves and her voice was kinder; she asked questions now, before blurting out her opinion. In their homeschooling, she put herself out there a little more each day. She made educated guesses and spectacular mistakes, but she was so excited about learning he wanted to write John Holt a fan letter, only to remember that the man died in 1985. On the other hand, maybe the father didn't deserve her, but family was family. He thought of Rico's kids so often. What they would give to see their father again. "You should see him," he said.

"What if he wants me to move back in with him?"

"Let's see how the meeting goes," Glory said.

Juniper looked down at her favorite dinner, but didn't move to pick up her fork. From that angle someone might think she was praying. Joseph took the opportunity to study that bluebird tattoo on her neck. The artist was professional. It was good work, not a cartoon, yet not entirely realistic. He knew that armed with a photo he could track down the guy who did it in hours—three at most—and smack him around for taking advantage of a young girl who'd spend the rest of her life trying to forget it.

"May I be excused from doing the dishes tonight?" Juniper asked.

"Sure."

She scooted her chair back, then stood. She pushed the chair back in until it touched the table. She folded her napkin and set it alongside her plate and headed for the back door, Cadillac behind her.

"Where are you going?" Glory asked.

"Out to the barn to check on Nanny. I want to pet the babies."

"That's a good idea," Glory said, forcing cheer into her voice that wasn't fooling anybody. "It's cold, so take a jacket."

"I've got one in the barn."

They listened to the screen door swing shut and looked at each other. Sex made a person absolutely crazy, Joseph thought: the goofy looks they tried to hide, the way he cherished muscle aches in places he didn't normally feel anything, and the heat her skin gave off when they came within five inches of each other. It blotted out common sense. When he thought of her face, inches above his, he was pretty much useless.

"I feel guilty," Glory said.

"We didn't do anything wrong."

Glory looked away, and when she looked back, her eyes brimmed with tears. "I can't help it. In my heart I feel like I cheated on Dan."

"Come here." Even though it wasn't comfortable, Joseph held her on his lap. He leaned his head against her breast and listened to her pounding heart. "Right now in New Mexico, the lilacs are blooming. For a few short weeks, the smell in the air is spellbinding. Then on its heels comes the blasted juniper pollen. The UPS driver has to wear a dust mask to make deliveries. Every day the sun shines a little longer; the sky is a little bluer, and the clouds that scud across the prairie are prideful and never the same twice. On my dad's farm, the onions are in. He'll stay outside so long my mother will threaten to give his dinner to the dogs if he doesn't come inside."

"It's your home and you miss it," Glory said.

"Just a week. I meant what I said, I won't touch you again if that's what you want. Come for one week. Perspective. It'll clear your head."

It was a long time before Juniper came back into the house, and by then Glory had retreated to her own chair. Without a word Juniper headed to her room, Cadillac right behind her.

JUNIPER

When Mrs. Solomon woke me, Joseph was with her. I figured, here we go, I'm gonna catch hell for oversleeping again. But something about the way they stood next to each other—almost touching—made me wonder if he'd spent the night.

Mrs. Solomon said, "Today is all ours. We're going to drive the back road to the coast, have a picnic, and take photographs and beachcomb. There will be no talk of fathers. We're going to live in the moment."

"Can Cadillac come?"

"All the dogs are coming. Now go take a shower and get dressed."

I washed my hair, and when I looked at it in the mirror, I thought maybe I'd get it cut short so the brown and black didn't look so stupid. Mrs. Solomon trimmed Ms. Proctor's hair, so she could do mine. But with my hair cut short, my tattoo showed, and I hated when people asked me why I got it, what it meant, did it hurt, and do you have others and in what places?

The minute I came out of the bathroom I smelled chicken frying. Mrs. Solomon wrapped it in foil while it was still warm, and even though it was early morning, I wanted to eat it right then. That apple, carrot, and raisin salad I loved was already in Tupperware. We put on T-shirts, long-sleeved flannels, sweatshirts, and packed raincoats and hats, because the coastline here is always foggy.

Joseph brought the cameras.

Edsel had to wear a coat. I hoped he didn't have a seizure at the sight of the waves. Cadillac and Dodge loaded into the back of Joseph's Land Cruiser all excited because dogs are clairvoyant when it comes to going somewhere. I brought towels, a gallon jug of water, and two bowls because when it comes to food and water, Cadillac doesn't like to share.

Joseph drove. When Mrs. Solomon found something interesting, she read out loud from a book on marine mammals. Before we drove through the oak trees, we passed the road where my family once lived in a green house with white trim and a gray shingled roof. The houses were torn down as part of the Dragon Lake planned development, but other than a billboard saying how great everything would eventually be, there weren't any houses. G18 is an old road, cut in 1971, way before I was born, and paved only a while back. It travels through microclimates, like oaks and scrub to ferns and rain-forest kind of plants before it ends at the Pacific Ocean. I guessed Joseph didn't know that this route took us past the place where my sister's trail ended. Mrs. Solomon was busy staring at the book in her lap when we passed it, reading elephant-seal facts so we could pretend this was homeschooling, not some last best day before my dad came to get me and ruined everything.

"One bull weighed a record eleven thousand pounds," she said.

"Wonder how they convinced it to get on a scale?" Joseph said.

Mrs. Solomon laughed at that, but today, she was laughing at pretty much anything he said. How could she, when he was leaving? Whenever I thought of never seeing Joseph again, it felt like someone was stabbing me.

A jay flew across the front of the car and I thought of Casey's blue sweater and felt sick to my stomach, but I kept it to myself because I could tell Mrs. Solomon needed this day to go perfectly.

"*Animalia, Chordata, Mammalia, Carnivora, Pinnipedia, Phocidae, Mirounga.* Hey, listen to this. Elephant seals molt every year, but instead of growing new fur on the same old skin, they grow *entirely new skin,* pushing cells from the blood vessels through the blubber and outward. That has to hurt," Glory said.

"Probably not if you grow up that way," I said. "Probably you get so used to it that it feels like peeling after a sunburn."

The drive seemed to take forever, but when I checked the odometer, it turned out we'd only gone about twenty miles before we reached the sand and surf and so many seals lolling on the beach that I said, "From here they look like a box of spilled cigars." A simile.

"Six-thousand-pound cigars made for a giant's fingers," Joseph said.

A metaphor.

The dogs wanted more than anything to jump the chain link and give the seals the business. Edsel barked the most of anyone. I pulled up the hood on my sweatshirt and tucked Edsel inside the pocket for my hands, his head peeking out to make sure nothing good happened to anyone else unless he was a part of it.

"Is anybody going to eat my chicken?" Glory asked.

Joseph ate two pieces, then said, "This is the best chicken ever. Of course, you haven't tasted my green-chile chicken *ench-i-la-das*."

Inch-ee-la-thas. He said each syllable distinctly, just like our Spanish dialogues. Mrs. Solomon pretended to smack him, but at the last minute her hand was more like a pat. "All these mythical recipes. I have yet to see proof."

"Turn me loose in *cocina* Solomon and I will prove it to you. But first I need to go to New Mexico for provisions."

"A likely excuse." Then she asked me, "Juniper, want a cupcake?"

I took three. Joseph said, "*Chica!* That means I only get two cupcakes. Glory makes you cupcakes all the time. Have mercy on the cupcake-deprived."

"If you're such a good cook, you can make your own," I said, eating one, and saving the other two for later.

Mrs. Solomon said, "Yeah, chef. I'm sure you have a superior recipe. Here's the keys to my kitchen. Show us your stuff."

In a story, that's called *double entendre*, when a thing can have two meanings at the same time.

The hours went by so fast.

On the beach to the right of the elephant seals, the dogs ran up and down the sand, barking. I threw the tennis ball for Dodge while Mrs. Solomon and Joseph sat on a blanket pretending they weren't dying to kiss. I wondered what it felt like, falling in love. Cadillac herded Edsel for a while, then the little dog turned on him and chased him all the way back to the car. I laughed so hard my stomach cramped.

Joseph said, "That dog needs a new name."

"What's wrong with Edsel?" Mrs. Solomon said.

"Look at him," Joseph said. "Since I started taking him outside, he's *varonil*, manly. It's insulting to call him *chatarra*."

"What's that mean?" she asked, and he said, "A car that's scrap iron, a beater," and then they both started laughing so I walked to the water to watch Cadillac and Dodge rush at the crashing waves, barking as if they thought that would make the waves stop.

I stayed there long enough that Mrs. Solomon and Joseph could kiss.

Later, he had the mammal book and began pelting us with facts. "An elephant seal can outrun a human, though they don't run, they more or less 'locomote' along with their flippers."

"Locomote?" Mrs. Solomon said. "Like a train?"

"I don't know. They have thirty spiky teeth and four sharp canines. They eat small sharks and octopus and skates, hundreds of pounds of fish a day. In the late 1890s, they were hunted to near extinction, but today, they're doing fine and occupying some prime real estate, aren't they?"

One of the bulls flopped across the sand up to the fence, flung his proboscis upward, and brayed. Not only did it sound horrible, but the smell made me gag. Joseph said, "He's protecting his harem. They dive over five thousand feet deep and can hold their breath underwater for two hours. They depend on their whiskers the way cats do—"

"Enough facts," Glory said, pulling the book out of Joseph's hands and running down the sand with it, him limping after her. "You're under arrest for grand theft library!" he said.

I got a chill that made me shudder.

Pretty soon, Joseph would be hundreds of miles away forever. Mrs. Solomon would be back on the ranch, training a new dog. Cadillac would go back to sleeping in his kennel instead of by my bed. At that moment I realized that I loved Joseph like a dad, and at the same time I realized that now he belonged to Mrs. Solomon in a way I never would.

No matter how well you rub a dog down with a towel, plenty of water is still left in his fur to shake all over you. When you drive home in a car stinking of damp dog, even with your face wind-burned, and when you're so hungry you could eat two whole hamburgers without bothering to take off the pickles, when the best teacher you ever had starts singing along in Spanish with the radio even though he has a terrible singing voice, all those things together is the moment you know you have a family.

Every moment after is realizing it will be taken away.

Chapter 12

T HE MEETING IS all set," Ms. Proctor said when she called on Monday.

"But what if I want to live here?"

"I know you do, kiddo."

The whole thing was so unfair I wanted to break every one of those rose-patterned plates in the cupboard. I took a cereal bowl and threw it across the room, but it ricocheted off the couch and only chipped on the edge. I'd have to take a hammer to it like I did with the first one and I didn't have the energy.

"He left me behind like clothes for the thrift store."

"I know."

"He locked me out of our apartment. I embarrassed myself in front of the apartment manager saying my key didn't work. I had nowhere to go to. I stayed up all night in the freaking park."

I expected Ms. Proctor to zero in on that since one of her life goals was to make me talk about what had happened between the day my dad left and the day I got busted for shoplifting, but she let it slide. Probably now that my dad was here, Ms. Proctor thought she could forget about it because pretty soon I wouldn't be her problem anymore.

"Believe me, the family court judge will take all that into consideration," she said. "Meet with him, Juniper. Things will go better if you agree to this. The judge will see that you're cooperating like a mature adult and take your wishes into account."

"As if. Where and when?"

"Tuesday afternoon at three P.M. Lois's office. I'll be there. We'll meet him together."

"What about Mrs. Solomon? Can I bring her with me? Can I bring Mr. Vigil, too? If I have to do this, I want them with me."

"Sweetie, you can't bring them into the meeting."

"Why not? They take good care of me! Why I can't bring along the two people who have treated me like a real person and show my dad what parents are supposed to be like?"

"Because he's your biological father, Juniper."

"Sperm donor."

"Don't talk like that. He raised you for almost fourteen years. He's sorry. He wants to get to know you again. According to the law, he's responsible for you for the next four years."

"The law sucks. He should be in jail."

"Honey . . ."

Every argument I could think of died in my mouth. *The law* was like some Kevlar shield that not even the truth could penetrate. Family court, appointed lawyers, guardian *ad litem* or however you pronounced the word, they added up to more power than anything I had to say. I ground my molars together until they hurt. "Are you going to talk to him before Tuesday?"

"I can," Ms. Proctor said. "Is there a message you want me to pass along?"

"Yeah. Tell him he stopped being my father the day he moved out. Tell him that I came home from school ready to do my homework and make his dinner. Oh, and be sure to tell him that I begged food behind the chowder shack on Fisherman's Wharf and that I shoplifted Tampax from grocery stores."

"Juniper, let me talk to Glory."

"Can't. She went to see Joseph. They're ———." I used the F-word out loud, only the second time in my life I'd said it. I hadn't used it the night Casey didn't come home, or the afternoon my mom would not wake up from her nap, or when the landlord of the apartment looked at me like I was most pathetic person on earth. The only other time I said it was while I was getting my tattoo, because it hurt that much. "I have to go now," I told Ms. Proctor. "I have chores."

That wasn't a total lie because later in the day I did have things to do, just not right at this moment. This moment was not governed by the court or owned by my dad, it was mine. First I went into Mrs. Solomon's closet, stuffed newspaper in the toes of Mr. Solomon's boots, then hid them in my room. I gave Edsel a cookie, but watching him wag his tail so happily made me cry, so I ran outdoors and up the hillside to the top of the ridge so I could look down on the farm that had been my home from Thanksgiving Day until now. I spent the day memorizing every inch of it, from the red chicken coop to the leather bridles and western saddles on the saddletrees in the barn to the damn oak tree that should have done something other than sit there. And the butterflies. I had to go into the greenhouse to see them one last time because pretty soon butterflies will be extinct, I think, what with air pollution and chemicals in the water and all that. Cadillac followed, nudging my ankles. I turned and yelled at him, "Stop it! Go away!"

But he kept on following me. "Go home!" I screamed, but he only lay down about five feet away while I cried like a baby and pounded the ground with my fists. "I hate you! You stupid, asshole dog! You couldn't even take care of my sister! Get out of here! Go!"

I threw a rock, then another, and that did it. Cadillac slunk back toward the farm and finally I was alone until the court made me pack up my clothes and go live with a dad who wasn't all that great to begin with.

That night, when I heard Glory go to bed, I held a glass to the wall and tried to listen in on her conversation with Joseph. They talked every night, mostly about me. But tonight Mrs. Solomon was whispering, and what I caught was "missing you" and "can't wait until tomorrow," and I don't know, it made me sad and angry, more of a loser than ever.

They stopped talking after only ten minutes. I waited a half hour, then got up from bed and put on Mr. Solomon's boots. I took his *Man from Snowy River* raincoat, the two leftover cupcakes, a gallon of water in a plastic bottle, a windup, solar-powered flashlight, and earlier today, because I'd picked the lock on Mr. Solomon's workshop and found the six Percocet still in the bottle inside his tackle box, I took them, too, and just like that they became part of my plan. I left behind all the money I'd saved for the bank account I wanted to open. Where would I spend it? I left the last book Joseph gave me to read, *Ishi in Two Worlds,* because Ishi was dead so what use was he? I went out the front door so I didn't have to see the horses or the baby goats or the dogs or the oak tree and I started walking. I could hear Cadillac barking from his kennel. I put my fingers in my ears.

I knew where I was going. The minute we drove by it on the way to the elephant seals, I made up my mind. The house-size boulder marked my sister's last known whereabouts. What kind of word was *whereabouts* anyway? Joseph wasn't there to make me look it up. A few feet from the highway was a clearing where a car could pull over if it was careful, but after that it was a steep incline of dirt and scrub, a drop of a hundred feet to the rocky streambed that ran dry most of the year.

The first Christmas after Casey disappeared, my mom and I drove there to leave a wreath we'd made of pine branches and dried berries and apples. We sat on the side of the road and I said, *The animals will appreciate the food,* and my mom said, *It will be gone before the week ends,* and that day was the first one I remember thinking I bet she took too many of her relaxing pills, because she drove so slow and kept veering across the road, and I wished like anything I had a driver's license so I could have driven us safely home, but I was eleven not sixteen.

The trees rustle at night like they're secretly talking, too, and don't want anyone to hear. Branches above me crunched and I thought of the animals Mrs. Solomon says come out after dark. Bears, bobcats, javelina, mountain lions. Any one of them could kill you. I wished I could call them out, just get this over and done with. Be with my mom and Casey. Casey is dead. Over fourteen hundred days now. Four years of the California sun beating down, four years of pounding rain. Either way she is a skeleton.

The moon is exiting its crescent phase. If you want good luck, you're supposed to look at the moon over your right shoulder, but not your left, Joseph's grandmother told him. Ishi lived by the moon. Before electricity or running water or clocks or compasses. The moon controls tides. If you act crazy, people call you a lun-a-tic. White Arabian horses are "moon-colored." The pre-Columbians used the moon for telling time, planting crops, everything. Those clever pre-Columbians invented the sundial, so I guess they deserve a place in the history book.

"Everything I love gets taken away," my mother told a *People* magazine reporter a month after Casey disappeared.

I stood in the doorway while the camera crew spread black cables as thick as snakes throughout our house. I tripped over them trying to get from the bedroom to the kitchen. They used our bathroom. I'd go to take my shower and strangers had wiped their hands on my towels. They set up two cameras for interviews, one film, and the other still. Mom cried and made pleas to whoever had taken Casey to *please bring her home alive* and my dad stopped going to work and sat there on the couch not saying anything. After the *People* article ran, lots of crazy people called the 800 number and my dad got really mad. The second month Casey was gone, Mom stopped begging and told reporters, *We know Casey is with her Maker,* though in real life we didn't go to church. She said, *Please let someone know where her body is. No questions asked. We just want to bury our baby.*

If anyone asked, I could have told them about Casey's secret boyfriends. How she sometimes sneaked out of the house at night to meet them. To go riding in their cars, "to get a Coke," she said. Casey was so pretty that high school seniors asked her out on dates, and because she wasn't allowed to date yet, they took her cruising.

That afternoon, it was my fault we got grounded and sent to the room we shared, all because of a powder blue cashmere with silver buttons down the front, each one decorated with a bird flying. Casey wore it once a week. Her blond hair and the pale blue cashmere made her look sixteen at least. I took it out of the dirty-clothes hamper and put it on. If I rolled the cuffs up, it fit. I buttoned my coat up over it and wore it to school. Spilled purple tempera paint on it in art class. Washed it out immediately but there was a stain. At home, I washed it in hot water and added bleach because the television commercials said it unleashed stain eaters, which was what I needed. I put it in the dryer after. Tried to stretch it out when it shrank. The white splotch was right on the front. I couldn't hide it. The bleach took the silver birds off the buttons. I put it in Casey's drawer and waited for her to find it.

"You idiot!" she screamed at me. "You're useless and you're ugly and I wish I was an only child!"

That brought Mom out of the kitchen into our room and she said we were grounded. "But I have to go to the library," Casey said. Casey with all her A grades.

"Too bad," Mom said. "You'll both sit here until you apologize to each other."

At first we did homework. Every time I sneaked a look at Casey, she stuck her tongue out. At four P.M., Casey called, "Mom!"

She stood in the doorway, drying her hands with a dish towel. "Now what?"

"I need to take the dog for his walk. The lady made me promise I'd walk him every day."

The phone rang, and on her way to answer it, Mom said, "You be back in thirty minutes or you're grounded all weekend."

Casey gave me the finger, fetched the dog, and they walked out the front door. I watched from the window until she turned the corner and was out of sight.

————————

One day this psychic knocked on the door and Mom wanted to talk to her but Dad said, *You should be ashamed of yourself, preying on heartbroken people,* and told her to leave. I grabbed my allowance and climbed out my window and ran to catch up with her. She had a bicycle, not a car. Please, I said, this is all the money I have. Tell me what you know. She took it and said, *Casey is close by. Look for the color blue and you'll find her.*

I am an idiot because at first I believed her. I ran into the street when I saw a blue metallic balloon someone let go of so I could follow it and I almost got hit by a car. Then I spotted the blue BEST BUY sign from the school bus window and got off at the next stop so I could go inside because maybe she would be there, and then I couldn't find my way home. A bruise on the arm I gave this kid at school. A jaybird. Blueberries on cereal. Some old lady's dress. The sky didn't have a right to be that blue if it couldn't tell me anything. The kid I hit said, *Did you know that inside your veins your blood is blue until it hits the air? Yeah, someone cuts your vein, it turns red and leaks out and then you die just like your sister.*

I held my breath and looked in the mirror until everything went black at the edges, but I never found my sister.

The free food stopped coming and all the time my mom forgot to make dinner. Pretty soon no one called the toll-free phone number to report leads. When my dad called the police, they put him on hold. Mom went to the doctor and got pills to take for her nerves and pills to get some sleep because night was the hardest time, and sometimes she and my dad argued until the sun came up and they didn't even care if I went to school or not.

Because I am a sister, I saved two of everything: the missing-person flyers, school pictures, friendship bracelets, the *People* magazine article I don't appear in, and the newspaper articles from

Jolon to Portland, Oregon, and the letter from John Walsh with his signature in bright blue fountain-pen ink. *Blue.* At night I spread the papers across my sister's bed and it was almost like she was there.

I should have told my parents about the high school boys, but they were always arguing. I didn't know their names but I could have described some of their cars. After a while it seemed like if I told them about the cars, they would hate me as much as they hated each other. I thought they'd give me up for adoption.

What a dope I was.

When two hours passed, I ate the first cupcake and took the first pill. When it stayed down, I took another one. Then the next cupcake and the next pill, the one after that, and pretty soon the bottle was empty so I threw it on the side of the road because how could I get in trouble for littering way out here and so what if I did because pretty soon I wouldn't be around to punish. By the time I got to the jumping-off place behind the boulder and stood there on the cliff's edge, looking down, I couldn't believe how easy it was to take that step off into nothing. Why hadn't I thought of it sooner?

Here I come, Case, I said, and that first step felt so good, it felt like I was a silver bird, flying.

Chapter 13

GLORY

Glory assumed Juniper was sleeping late, skipping chores, and who could blame her? Today she had to face the father who left her, relive all the loss that defined her family, and soon she'd have to go with him, wherever he wanted. Glory poured a mug of coffee, took it outside, and began tending to the animals. That Caddy was in his kennel seemed odd, but maybe Juniper wanted to be alone. She let him out and he ran into the house before she'd filled his bowl with kibble. She really hoped Juniper's father would let her take the dog.

Dodge's empty kennel bothered her. She needed to fill it, but if she took the trip Joseph wanted her to, she should wait. Every day the same notion cycled through her mind: What if there's a last-chance dog at the shelter and I don't get there soon enough? This afternoon, she'd go to the shelter. She could live without seeing New Mexico, and she didn't need a boyfriend.

JOSEPH

Joseph let himself into the Solomon house around nine. Cadillac ran past him out the front door, almost knocking Dodge down. He and Dodge walked into the kitchen.

"Hey," Glory said from the kitchen table.

He couldn't help it. Every time he looked at her, he wanted to take her to bed. "Good morning. Thought any more about our trip?"

"Joseph, I haven't even got dressed yet. The only thing I'm thinking about is how long it's going to take for caffeine to hit my bloodstream."

"Where's Juniper?"

"Sleeping in."

He looked at his watch. "This late?"

"You're right. Guess I better wake her. Pour yourself some coffee."

Glory's footsteps padded down the hall and he heard a gentle tapping then the door to Juniper's bedroom creak open. An old house with old-house noises, familiar to the point of being alive, was hard to leave. She wouldn't come with him.

"Joseph!" Glory called.

He set the coffeepot down and went to her. "What's wrong?"

"Juniper's bed hasn't been slept in." Glory opened the dresser drawer. "Thank goodness. Her clothes are here. For a minute there I thought she'd run away."

"So where is she?" He opened the closet. On the floor, dirty clothes waited in the laundry basket. "Maybe she went for a ride on the spotted horse."

"Piper?" Glory shook her head no. "He scares her. She's never gone out alone."

"I hate to break it to you, but she has. I've seen her in the oak grove riding the spotted horse."

"Why didn't you tell me?"

"It was Christmas Eve. I knew you'd get mad at her and things were hard enough already."

"You should have told me."

"I agree, but right now we'd better focus on this instead. Maybe she took a sleeping bag into the barn. She can't get enough of those baby goats."

Glory shook her head no. "I was out there a little bit ago. I fed the animals. I think I would have noticed if a horse was missing or she was sleeping in a stall."

"Can't hurt to look again." Out back they counted twice: two horses, two dogs, four goats, and the same number of hens as every day. The truck and old tractor were parked where they were yesterday. Dan's old bike was still propped up against the wall in the barn. When Joseph tried the door on Dan's workshop door, it opened. "I thought you kept this locked."

"Oh, no." Glory went instantly for the green tackle box. "The Percocet's missing. How did she know it was in here?"

"Teenagers have radar when it comes to alcohol and pills."

They headed to the back door and were cut off by Dodge, who started barking as if he'd never seen Joseph before. His tail was up and quivering like a scorpion. He growled and showed teeth.

"Stop that," Glory said. "What's the matter with you? You remember Joseph."

Joseph reached out a hand, and the dog snapped. He backed up to give the dog space and said, "Where's Juniper, Dodge?" The dog raced to the front door and started barking. "Out front?"

"She couldn't go far on foot," Glory said.

Joseph didn't want to tell her just how far some kids could go in eight hours, especially if they hitchhiked. They called themselves hoarse, walked around the property, and ended up in the chapel.

Glory stood in the aisle, shaking. "This is my fault, Joseph.

I told her she had to give her father a chance. Why didn't I fight harder for her?"

"You did what you had to according to the law. Let's call the police."

"Really? You don't think she'll show up when she's hungry? One of our foster boys was like that. He never stayed away longer than four hours."

"I have experience with runaways, too. Most change their minds and come back, but getting the cops involved and not needing them is a lot better than blaming yourself later for not calling them."

Glory's face crumpled. She sat down on the front-row bench and looked up at him. "How can this be happening, Joseph?"

"Glory, she's not Casey."

"But—"

"But nothing." They headed toward the house. "Make sandwiches, Glory. Lots of them."

"Why?"

"Because searchers get hungry, and we're going to get everyone we know to call everyone they know to help us look. Use the cell phone to call Lorna. Ask her to bring over a couple cases of soda and bottled water. I'll use your landline to call the cops."

"I was on the Albuquerque police force for two years, and eighteen in the crime lab," Joseph repeated for the fifth time in an hour. The police, sheriff's office, and S&R were trying to sort out who was in charge, and he wished they'd share information instead of asking him the same questions. "Can we just get on with things already? We're wasting time."

Glory looked like a robot, standing there at the counter making baloney-and-cheese sandwiches with the boxes of food Lorna had brought over. Lorna stood beside her, wrapping them in waxed paper and tucking apples and chips into lunch sacks. Every once in a while Lorna rubbed the small of Glory's back. She was still dressed in her blue plaid pajamas.

Joseph wondered if this was his fault, for leaving. He could stay a little longer. Come to that, why couldn't he stay forever? He had nothing to get back to. He should have told Juniper that. Or was it that Juniper had somehow determined that he and Glory were sleeping together and considered that enough of a betrayal to take off? Add that to the father showing up, and it might have done it. Having so many people milling around and none of them actively searching made him nuts. When he was shed of the questions, he went to look for Glory and found her looking out the kitchen window at the oak tree. He put his arm around her. "I have an idea," he said. "Want to hear it?"

Her cheeks were wet with tears. "So long as it doesn't end in tragedy."

"Juniper's a teenager. A dreamer."

"So?"

"So her destination doesn't need to make logical sense. We need to think like her, approach things in her mind-set. Then we can make a list of places to look for her."

"But what if someone took her? Do they call Amber Alerts on fourteen-year-olds?"

"Of course they do. They already have. Just listen to me a second. What if Juniper thinks there's absolutely no possibility she can stay with you?"

"Joseph, we already know that's what she thinks."

"Okay, so where would she go to hide? Some place she felt safe when she was on the street. Where did they bust her shop-lifting?"

"That's all the way in Pacific Grove. She can't have gotten there in twelve hours, could she?"

"Move over," Lorna said, carrying another box of food in her arms. Bags of potato chips peeked out from the top. "Gotta send those men out with fuel."

Joseph caught her eye and tried to smile but it was no use for either of them. He turned back to Glory. "Any place she thinks of as her dream destination? Somewhere to visit someday? I'm just thinking out loud here."

"Stonehenge." Glory rubbed her eyes. "Big Sur? She told me she wanted to camp by the redwoods. We talked about someday driving to Disneyland. Sometimes she talks about the house she grew up in, but it was torn down years ago. She loves the library, but it's across the freeway. And she told me the day we spent at the beach was the best day of her life. Maybe the beach?"

"What about places she hates? The group home, Caroline's office, that therapist?"

"Joseph! Driving G18 the other day. It just hit me. We drove right past the place where Casey disappeared."

"I'll be right back." Joseph walked into the crowd of volun-teer searchers to find the one in charge. "Can I see the topo map for a second?" Joseph pointed to the spot and said, "Try here."

In the kitchen, pouring Glory another cup of coffee, Lorna said, "When my sisters and I were teenagers, we fought all the time about things being fair. You know, who got a new pair of shoes or a bigger scoop of ice cream. We still play that game. Sisters. You can't live with them, and then they're gone and all you want is to share a room again and talk all night. She's missing

Casey. I think we've underestimated how broken Juniper is. What do you think, Joseph?"

"I think it's possible Juniper believes the only option to set things right is to let what happened to her sister happen to her."

Glory put her hands over her face. "That's a horrible thought, Joseph. How can you even say that to me?"

"Because if Juniper thinks there's no other way to avoid her father than to disappear, that's what she'll do. It's her decision, when all these other decisions are being made for her. She took the Percocet. She left the dog behind. Her clothes, her books are all here, waiting for your next foster. That right there is my biggest concern. People considering suicide leave their most valuable possessions behind."

Glory sat down at the table. Lorna put her hands on her shoulders and rubbed. Joseph said, "If you start crying, it will only make things worse. Save the tears for later, when we have our happy ending."

"What if we don't get one?"

He couldn't answer her question without breaking her heart, so he said, "Come on, we'll take the Land Cruiser. It has four-wheel drive. Grab some of her clothing and put Cadillac on leash. Bring some warm clothes. Her riding gloves, do you have them?"

"They're in the barn inside her jacket, unless she took it."

"We'll get them and take them with us."

Glory seemed to notice for the first time that she was wearing flannel pajamas. "I have to change clothes."

"Let me come with you, honey," Lorna said, and the two of them walked down the hallway.

Joseph watched the Big Sur coastline screen saver on Glory's computer while he paced. Juniper had begged him to show her his photos of the redwoods, but he told her no, not until the portfolio was complete. Edsel jumped at his knees, wanting attention. "I promise that later we'll go pee on trees," he said, and waked out back to get Juniper's jacket. He whistled for Cadillac, called his name, whistled again, but the only dog in the yard was Dodge. "Load up," Joseph said, and Dodge jumped up by himself into the Land Cruiser. Joseph went into the barn, but couldn't find the jacket. Glory, dressed in jeans and boots and a turtleneck sweater, went in the barn and came out carrying a jacket. "Hers?"

She nodded. "Gloves, too. Where's Caddy?"

Joseph started the car. Glory latched the gate behind her just in time for two detectives to block their way. "I thought he was with you. He wasn't in the barn."

"What do you mean?"

"I mean I couldn't find him."

Then it hit Joseph, like a punch in the stomach. This morning, when he came in the front door, Cadillac went out. He was already looking for Juniper. Joseph looked at his watch and tried to calculate how far the dog might've got.

A policeman came to Joseph's window and tapped on the glass. "Best thing you folks can do is stay put."

Joseph didn't want to go through the interview again, but he didn't want to lose this lead. "The dog's missing. I may have accidentally let him out. We're just going to look for him," he said, his hands gripping the steering wheel.

"Black-and-white dog?"

"Yes, that's him. Where did you see him?"

"Yes," Glory said. "Please, tell us which direction he went. Hurry."

The cop pointed toward the left fork of the county road. "When I was on my way here, I damn near hit the thing."

"Thank you." Glory hung out the window calling, "Cadillac! Juniper!"

Joseph drove down the driveway, veering across the lane to pass the cars that had amassed from two to—he counted—twenty in two hours. How could he ever make up for this? "Glory, I'm so sorry I let the dog out."

"What's done is done."

"We'll find him."

"I know." Her words didn't sound convincing. "If only that man had stayed gone four more years, she would be out in the world living her life instead of running away from it."

"It's better he comes now."

"How? He made her run away from the one place where's she's felt safe. Maybe even made her want to kill herself." Glory took out her cell phone. "I'm calling Caroline. Juniper's father should know she's missing, and that it's his fault."

Joseph kept his eyes on the road, looking from side to side for the dog as they drove. He had that same bad feeling he had the day he and Rico were at the warehouse. A feeling he would sell his soul to erase because he knew it would haunt him forever.

Ten minutes after Joseph had been wheeled into the OR, in that ridiculously short time, Rico had bled out. Not the biceps wound, no, but the glancing rib nick that looked fine on the X-ray. The bullet had apparently bruised his spleen. Just as Rico wouldn't have taken a pain pill if his life depended on it, he would lend a hand to anyone who needed one. This was the worst part to Joseph, that his friend died standing in front of the hospital soda machine helping the vendor load up a case of Diet Dr Pepper. In lifting, his bruised spleen had torn. A four-inch organ weighing around five ounces. People survived without them all the time. When Rico's spleen tore, he bled out in seconds. "He didn't even have time to pop the top on the free soda the guy gave him," someone said. "The damnedest thing. They said he was dead before he hit the floor."

A quarter mile before the boulder marking Casey's trail, Glory screamed, "Stop the car!"

Joseph slammed on the brakes and Dodge scrabbled for purchase. "What is it?"

"A prescription bottle. There, by the side of the road."

Glory was out of the car in a heartbeat. Joseph figured it was a random piece of trash until Glory ran ahead to the S&R van. Joseph pulled over, put the car in park, grabbed Juniper's jacket, and got Dodge out of the cargo area and snapped on his leash. "Find your brother, you can have steak for dinner every night from now on."

Glory came back to where he was standing. "Joseph. It's mine, and it's empty. Maybe she didn't take them. Maybe she did, and then changed her mind."

"Let's hope."

She reached out for Dodge's leash. "I'll walk a few feet into the woods." She pursed her lips, but no sound came out. "Will you whistle, please? If Cadillac hears you, he might come back."

She hustled off at a pace Joseph couldn't hope to match. "Please, God," he said between whistles. "Please."

Watching the two Monterey County S&R climbers unload equipment, he thought he might be sick. The level one rescuers were dressed in identical forest-ranger-green clothing that reminded him of the academy training rookies who often jogged by the lab, stoic and determined. The S&R crew had the same kind of expressions. Forget what it feels like right now, he told himself. We're in it for the long haul. They set ropes and pulleys and shouldered backpacks filled with bandages, water, and Mylar blankets, their walkie-talkies clipped to the packs and within easy reach. The civilian volunteers waiting to be called reminded Joseph of the plastic army men he played with when he was a kid, particularly the one in the kneeling pose always ready, never called upon.

A half hour passed as S&R lowered their first climber down the side of the hill across from where Glory had found the amber Percocet bottle. They came back up, empty, just before Glory returned to the road with Dodge. "How many Percocet pills equal an overdose?" she asked Joseph.

"Toxicity in opiates varies."

"The cops and the sheriff are fighting over who gets to keep the pill bottle for evidence. Any news from the climbers?"

"They've cleared this area," Joseph said. "They're moving the ground search up one quarter of a mile."

"Cadillac," she said, just that one word.

"I know." Joseph put his arm around her. Just as with Rico, he knew this was a burden he'd shoulder forever. They walked on.

"Tell me how many pills it would take, Joseph. There were six in the bottle, ten milligrams each."

He blew out a breath. "Sixty milligrams is considered toxic."

Glory let out a cry. "Why didn't I just get rid of it when she stole it the first time?"

"Glory, we don't know for certain that she took all the pills. She could've changed her mind, stuck a finger down her throat. A million other possibilities."

"Don't you lie to me, Joseph Vigil," Glory said, pointing at his chest. "What happens with an overdose? If I'm responsible for her last moments on earth, I have to know what happens."

Overhead, the sun beat down and Joseph could see it was burning her bare neck. "It would be peaceful. She'd just go to sleep." He didn't tell her it was the amount of acetaminophen that worried him. The risk of bradycardia, permanent liver damage. Things were so much more dangerous than he would let on, because that was the kindest thing to do. He'd learned that, at least, when he was a cop.

By the boulder, the searchers began setting up their equipment again. How did they do it so quickly? he wondered. All of them working together.

"I can't just stand here, I have to move." Glory walked across the road toward the S&R van, pulling herself under the yellow tape so she could get as close to the edge as possible. Joseph stood there and let her go.

This time, when S&R pulled their first climber back up, he let out a woo-hoo, and everything changed. As soon as he was on level ground, he reached around his backpack and held up a Red Wing boot. "Size ten. Newspaper stuffed in the toe."

Joseph put his hand on Glory's shoulder. "See? Now they'll head down as a team."

The sight of the aluminum stretcher made Glory's knees buckle. She sat down hard, right there in the road. One by one, the climbers disappeared from sight. A volunteer came over and handed them bottles of water. "It's only a matter of time now, ma'am. We're bringing your little girl home."

Glory said, "Joseph? Tell me. Could that kind of fall be fatal?"

"How about you let me hear that speech you're going to give her father?" Joseph said.

Oh, the *arrogancia* in him. Joseph told Glory that judges not only allowed victims to address their perpetrators at trials, they allowed loved ones to speak, too, so she might possibily meet Juniper's father face-to-face. Tell him what she felt. Glory said, " 'Explain to me how losing one daughter led to abandoning another. There are ways to get help. I would sell everything I own to keep Juniper with me. You weren't here to listen to her crying herself to sleep. You haven't seen her tenderness with baby goats. Do you have any idea how much courage it took for her to love Cadillac? You should be the one gone over this cliff, not her.' How's that?"

Joseph said, "I think you should add a couple of cuss words. In Spanish."

Following a small avalanche of rubble and dirt that briefly clouded the view, they heard one climber holler, and as in one of those relay games, his words were repeated by the person above him, and so on, sending up the news.

A cop turned to them and said, "Unconscious, but breathing. Notify EMS they're sending up the stretcher."

JUNIPER

Are you sure you want this? the tattoo artist asked me. *You can't rub it off, you know.*

More than I've ever wanted anything in my life, I said.

I don't work for free.

I left. I returned with five DVDs, all good movies. Is this enough?

That's a start, he said. *But I need something else.*

Like what? I said.

He unbuttoned my shirt and then I knew. I took off my clothes. I told myself this is what happened to Casey and I owed it to her because of the sweater and the fight and I said, Will this be enough? and he nodded.

My sister looked so pretty in blue. Then, like the finish on the buttons, she disappeared. Flew away. Make it look real, I said when he drilled the ink into my skin. I want it right there on my neck, so everyone can see it.

JOSEPH

Before Juniper went into surgery to put her fractured ankle back together, she said, "Cadillac, don't forget to feed Cadillac."

On the drive home from the hospital, Glory told Joseph, "Turn onto G18. We have to find the dog."

"Glory, it's dark out. We'll look again in the morning."

She bit her cuticles and went silent.

Arriving home, she walked in the front door only to head out the back door. Cadillac wasn't there either.

"Let me feed the animals," Joseph said, but not quickly enough. Dodge ran to the empty kennels and started barking. "Glory, go indoors and have some whiskey. You're spooking the horses."

Two days later, Caddy was still missing. Both days, in the morning before visiting hours at the hospital, Glory rode Cricket into the forest as far as she could go. Joseph walked topside, carrying a walkie-talkie borrowed from Lorna. They covered five long, punishing miles, and no sight of the dog. S&R was long gone, their job completed. People said, it was only a dog, after all.

GLORY

The Narcan took care of the oxycodone, but the acetaminophen level was still a concern. Once the general anesthetic from the ankle surgery cleared Juniper's system, Glory knew there was no putting things off. She stashed Edsel in her purse and drove to the hospital, hoping she could keep up her run of good luck of not running into Juniper's father. He wasn't there. Alone in the room with Juniper, Glory shut the door and brought out Edsel. "I couldn't fit Cadillac in my purse," she said, faking a laugh.

Juniper burst into tears. "He's dead, isn't he?"

"He's lost."

"It's my fault." Juniper began to sob, reminding Glory of their first night together, Thanksgiving and pirates and her headache and the unlikely reunion that eventually led them through all kinds of strife only to arrive at this terrible moment of pain and loss that seemed as if it would never end.

"He could still come back. But if he doesn't, know that he had a good life with you, Juniper. The best months of his life."

After the tears, Juniper was stony. She wouldn't eat the vanilla pudding Glory brought, wouldn't take a sip of her Diet Vanilla Coke, and the red-velvet cupcakes sat there on her hospital tray turning stale.

"Try to nap," Glory said. "I'll be right back."

She stepped into the hall, found a family lounge, and called Caroline. "Where's her father? I thought he was so anxious to see her. She needs him right now."

Caroline huffed into the phone, "I don't know how to tell her."

"Tell her what?"

"Apparently this whole debacle of her missing spread all over the news scared him off. He called Lois to cancel, and that's the last we've heard from him. I don't know. Maybe it was too much exposure. Like a replay of Casey."

"That's ridiculous!"

Caroline sighed. "You know, Glo, I think I'll retire this year. Sit on my porch and watch the weeds grow."

"Don't you dare. What would happen to kids like Juniper without you? Go take a rest and I'll talk to you tomorrow."

Glory called her mother next. "What do I do, Mom? The dog, her father, her ankle; she's in bad shape and I don't know what to do."

"Mothers are only human," Ave said. "You turn it over to God and then you just wing it."

In the hospital cafeteria, Glory ordered coffee. While she waited for it to cool, she nodded off. When she woke, she was leaning her head on her hand, and her entire arm had gone to pins and needles. Dan, she thought. I have to go to him. He needs me. But by the time she reached the elevator, she remembered it was Juniper who waited for her, not Dan, and Glory stopped still because she couldn't walk into that poor girl's room without some kind of plan.

Desperate, she called Halle, who remarkably wasn't having a drinks party at the moment. "I need your help," Glory said, then unloaded on her sister as she hadn't since childhood: Glory sleeping with Joseph, Juniper's father letting her down yet again, the lost dog, the lack of sleep, Joseph's invitation to New Mexico, pending wedding events she'd taken deposits on, the animals that depended on her to provide meals and exercise and attention—and Caddy. It all came back to Cadillac, the black-and-white border collie who'd finally found his human only to lose his life. "Everything's such a mess. You were right, Halle. Tell me what to do."

Halle was silent a minute, then said, "So you can't bring the dog back. It's tragic, but you can find her another dog. You're so good at that it makes me green with jealousy. What am I good at? Shopping? Making drinks? Traveling to other countries and shopping there so I can try new drinks? Well, let me tell you, Glory. I plan to make you the best drink ever made the second I arrive, and I'm leaving right now so not another word out of you. I'm not sure I can feed those *farm* animals of yours, so we'll have to hire someone, one of your former fosters? I'll collect eggs, but I must have a fresh pair of latex gloves every time. As soon as Juniper is ready to travel, I'll bring her to Santa Rosa, and you are getting on that airplane and flying into your future. We'll be fine without you. I'll teach her to play bunco and hopefully do something with her god-awful hair."

That night, after Glory called the Paso Robles hospital supply and rented both a bed and a wheelchair, she remembered the plein air painters scheduled for the day after tomorrow. She retrieved their paperwork from her binder and called the contact number. "I'm sorry to call you on short notice," she said, "but I was wondering if there was any chance we could switch your group to the following weekend? My daughter's coming home from the hospital tomorrow and things are stressful because her dog's lost and . . ."

The excuse sounded pathetic even to her ears, and she wasn't surprised when her suggestion was rejected outright. The president of the painting society, who was also a lawyer, was more than happy to point out the lack of cancellation clause in her agreement form. "This contract of yours is a joke," he said. "You really should hire an attorney to create one for you."

What was that supposed to mean? Did he expect her to ask him to do it? Glory would rather pass a kidney stone than give this man one dollar. "Then I guess I'll see you folks this weekend."

She walked into her kitchen, stood in the center of things, and shut her eyes. Behind her was the sink with the rough spot around the drain; washing three generations' worth of dishes eroded enamel over cast iron. To the left of the sink was the four-burner cooktop that was fifty years old but still worked. To the right, her double ovens had baked countless meals, and the dishwasher to the left of that was on its last legs. Her kitchen was her compass, her true north. In here, she knew who she was and what needed to be done, so she put aside thinking about the dog and how difficult the next few days would be and did what she did best, which was lose herself in a menu that began with local-greens salad and traveled to chicken Kiev and came to an end with a fondant artist's-palette cake and a sculpting-chocolate paintbrush.

Juniper begged to be wheeled outside so she could sit on the porch all day, waiting for the impossible, Cadillac's return. Halle kept her company while Glory handed out gourmet box lunches to the painters. Each had a single-serving bottle of California chardonnay from a new winery that she hoped would give the attorney/painter a headache from drinking in the sun.

Some of these painters had real talent, apparent in every brush-stroke. The layers of paint, a sense of color, and the attention to detail were right there. Glory looked at their renderings of the oak tree and could tell they saw the history in it, but somehow, not its soul. The other painters seemed to have professional outfits and equipment—smocks and visors and field easels made of beautiful hardwoods. Glory searched each canvas, looking for the one painter who'd managed to capture the oak tree, but so far, no one had. Maybe no one could. Maybe it was only there to frustrate photographers and evade painters and to inspire pirate weddings. Joseph walked among the group taking pictures, being friendly and outgoing. When he and Glory passed each other, he whispered, "Your tree's outfoxed every last one of them," and Glory smiled because Joseph made her know that while losing Cadillac would always hurt, they would make it through these difficult days and come out on the other side. That there was another side to aim for.

While the painters finished up their salad greens and moved on to the chicken Kiev, the roar of motorcycles cut into the air, and Glory wondered if someone was lost, or a biker gang wanted to throw a weenie-roast wedding in her chapel. Why not? Money was money. She walked around the property to the front porch to see what was happening.

Lorna Candelaria walked up the driveway dressed in chaps, boots, and the pink cowboy hat that was her signature style. In one hand she held a paper lunch sack, and in the other she held by the collar a burr-infested, seen-better-days, emaciated border collie. "Glory!" she called. "Get a load of what me and my posse found."

The lump that rose in Glory's throat prevented any reply, but she heard yelling, then she saw Juniper launch herself out of the wheelchair and hop on one leg to her beloved, who dropped and belly-crawled up to meet her like the first—no, this was the *third*—time they met. Glory heard the click of a camera and knew that Joseph Vigil was right behind her. He didn't stop to ask questions or argue over wages; he recognized a photo opportunity and seized it. Glory thought, Oh, Dan. This must be what you meant by faith.

A few of the bikers were openly crying when Juniper reached her friend. Between choking sobs, Glory asked, "Where on earth did you find him? I thought we'd covered every inch."

"A mile or so past the Cueva Pintada, the Painted Cave, give or take. I had no idea there was another cave just beyond it, much smaller. In fact, I think we might be the first people to step inside it in a hundred and some years."

Glory reached out to hug her friend. "Thank you, Lorna."

"You're welcome, honey. But don't get slaphappy just yet."

"Why not?"

"We found your pooch next to a pile of bones. Took me a whole package of lunch meat to wrestle this one away from him."

Glory knew they were all thinking the same thing: Casey.

JOSEPH

"May I see it?" Joseph asked. He unrolled the bag until the earth-colored bone was exposed. It had wisdom teeth and molars, too old for Casey. "Were the other bones also human?"

Before the cops got involved, Joseph got in the Land Cruiser and drove to Santa Cruz, located the university's anthropology department, and knocked on the department chair's door. No one answered, but the door was unlocked, so he went inside. The man's desk was a jumble of files and books, papers everywhere: This was higher education? He found a course catalog and checked the man's teaching schedule. He asked directions from a student and walked to the lecture hall where the professor was teaching. He waited by the door for the man to finish, gather his files, load up his briefcase, and amble toward the exit.

"Professor, it's Joseph Vigil, again. I'm here about the bones I left you yesterday. Have you had a chance to look at them?"

"I was planning to call you this afternoon," the professor said, and Joseph thought, *mierda*, manure, you forgot the second you were done looking at them, but stood his ground. "Very interesting, your jawbone."

"What did you find out?"

"It's obviously a female jaw, since the lines run in a curve from the earlobe to the chin—"

"Yes, I know," Joseph said impatiently. "Were you able to determine its age?"

"The late 1890s is my guess. I'd place her age at twenty to thirty-five when she died; hard to pin that down without more of the skeleton. The other bones were from a female toddler, no more than two years of age. If you want to whittle out any more info than that, you're going to have to go to Stanford. Their equipment puts ours to shame. State university budgets, you know."

They walked to his office, and Joseph was impressed that he found the bones without tearing the messy office apart.

"Intriguing," he said as he handed them over. "Found in a place that could have remained undisturbed forever, but for a girl running away and her dog going after her, and those motorcyclists keeping at things, eh?"

The thought of his own role in Cadillac's disappearance still took Joseph's breath away. If not for Lorna—well, he tried not to think about it.

"So where will the bones go? We'd be happy to give them a home."

"That's something you and the Jolon Indians will have to work out," Joseph said.

JUNIPER

For as long as there have been boulders big enough to perch on and sunshine to warm the rocks, people have been lolling around asking each other questions about the meaning of life, which so far no one has the answer to. If you want to know the meaning of something, you need more than reference books. You need imagination and you have to be willing to experiment and take risks. Without alternative ways of thinking you can only go so far in the world. For example, take stories passed down from long ago when there were no books, just oral history. Also, music, poetry, and even jokes can tell you something. You can't just go by facts. Facts are not even the half of it.

In *The Folklore of Eternity*, Comparative Lit 101, Tuesdays and Thursdays, eight A.M. to noon, I read a story about when Plato was a baby. When he slept in his rush basket or papoose or whatever passed for cribs back then, bees supposedly landed on his lips as if they were the sweetest flowers on earth. Stinging bees, but they never stung him. Were the bees giving him sweetness or taking it from him? Science says bees land where they do for one of three purposes: to load up on pollen, get a drink, or they've arrived home and want to protect their queen and make honeycombs.

But the design of the bee shows that flight is impossible.

GLORY

Glory and Joseph changed planes in Phoenix on their way to Albuquerque, and Glory had second thoughts, third thoughts, and so on.

"I'm going to call home, to make sure everything's going all right," she said as they walked from one gate to the other, passing gift shops selling tabloid newspapers and sewing kits and neck pillows for absurdly inflated prices.

"They're fine," he said. "I have a better idea. Pay attention to me. I'll buy you a Grande latte. Or would you rather have Venti? Maybe colossal?"

"Do they have small?" She laughed.

"*Bueno*. Laugh more. You'll need your sense of humor to survive the Vigils. Our parties go on all night."

Glory looked out the plate-glass windows at the jets, amazed at the number of people traveling when it wasn't even a national holiday—just traveling.

They sat down in the waiting area of the gate for their flight. She could tell Joseph's back was hurting him and she rubbed his shoulder. He leaned in closer. "That feels good," he said.

"You're welcome."

"Before I get your coffee, I've been wondering about something."

"What?"

"You've got half a dozen weddings under your belt now, all different kinds. If you were to get married again—theoretically—what kind of ceremony would you choose? Traditional? Civil ceremony? Take your time."

"I don't need to take my time."

"Well, don't keep me in suspense. What kind?"

She smiled. "Without a doubt, pirate."

EPILOGUE

THE WORST THING to happen in 2004 was not my father not showing up, it was the Boxing Day earthquake off the west coast of Sumatra, Indonesia.

An earthquake is a rupture. Plates shift where they are not whole. This one measured 9.1 to 9.3, lasted ten minutes, and was so strong that it made planet Earth vibrate, triggering earthquakes as far away as Alaska. The good part was that plain old regular people opened their pockets and donated more than $7 billion in aid.

Something else good that happened in 2004 was the discovery of *Homo floresiensis*, "the Hobbit," a complete female skeleton standing three foot and three inches tall, found on the Indonesian island of Flores. In the swampy environment her bones did not ossify, so anthropologists could only take a brief look. They learned she was thirty years old at the time of her death, and that for eighteen thousand years she lay there alongside pygmy elephants and miniature Komodo dragons, tiny versions of the species we think of today as huge.

That same year, the world's rarest bird, the Hawaiian honeycreeper, went extinct. Dr. Alan Lieberman, who devoted his life to its study, said, "I held [the last known *po'ouli*] when it was alive and when it was dead. If there's a more fitting example of extinction, it's impossible to imagine."

But nature is unpredictable. Fourteen years after being declared extinct, the Large Blue butterfly (*Phengaris arion*) showed up in the garden of a group of Englishwomen attending a tea at Mrs. Hortense Childs's home in Suffolk, England. She said, "I just turned round and there it was!"

In 2004, the skeleton of a female toddler was found in a previously unknown cave in the wilderness area between Jolon, California, and the coast of the Pacific Ocean. The nearest source of freshwater was two miles away. A dog can survive a long time without food, but death by dehydration can occur in twenty-four hours. Because I ran away rather than face my father, my dog, Caddy, found a woman's jawbone and the skeleton of a child.

On the Internet, you can find just about anybody, if you want to.

In Anthropology 106, you learn that bones tell a story. Wisdom teeth mark the transition from teenager to adult. Ossification, which occurs in eight hundred parts of the skeleton, backs up that fact. But if you have only a jawbone to go on, there are limited provable facts, and everything else is a guess.

Finding human bones stirs things up. People who've lost a loved one hope the bones will end the wondering and the waiting. In some cultures, bones are sacred remains, deserving of dignity, burial, and prayer. In others, bones are meant to be cut in half and studied. They are all stories waiting to be told.

To law enforcement, bones are evidence.

In 2004, the University of California, Santa Cruz, department of anthropology requested the exhumation of Mrs. Alice Halloran's grave on the Fort Hunter Liggett military base. They wanted a DNA sample from her skeleton to see if it matched the jawbone.

After months of newspaper stories and name-calling, Lorna Candelaria, proprietor of the Butterfly Creek General Store (which is no longer for sale), and who can trace her ancestors back to before the mission era, accused the university of desecration. "Bury that child next to Mrs. Halloran and be done with it," she was quoted as saying. "It took a hundred and six years for them to be reunited. Who are we to keep a mother and daughter apart?"

After my ankle surgery, I returned "home" with Mrs. Solomon. My father never came to see me.

"Never let the future disturb you," said Marcus Aurelius in the second century. "You will meet it, if you have to, with the same weapons of reason which today arm you against the present."

Three years have passed, and now I'm in college at the University of New Mexico in Albuquerque, studying—you guessed it—forensic anthropology. I hope it doesn't take a hundred years to find Casey's bones. The odds are not in my favor, but here's my best guess: Someday someone will cut a trail into wilderness, fall down a cliff into a ravine (like me), discover a hidden cave, or dig up land to prepare it for a building's foundation, and they will find my sister. I might not be alive by then. If you look at the timeline of events in 1898, when Alice and Clara Halloran disappeared, it's clear that for every mistake a human makes, a hundred good things happen. Maybe even a thousand. My adoptive father, nature photographer Joseph Vigil, calls that the Theory of Greater Abundance, which is the story of how we met at a wedding for pirates. He misjudged a staged sword fight for the real thing, his cop instinct kicked in, and that was the first time he laid eyes on my mother and me. A day that started with his camera ended with a pirate-ship cake. He tells the story whenever he gets the chance, because he says he's never stopped appreciating the collision of events that caused our paths to cross and become a family.

People make mistakes. They want immediate answers to life's many mysteries. If you wait a few generations, you learn bigger truths than you would have if you found answers right away.

My name is Juniper Tree McGuire Solomon Vigil.

My sister's full name was Acacia Tree McGuire, but everyone called her Casey.

My mother, who was in too much pain to stay on earth, and may she rest in peace, loved trees so much that she gave us names to make us put down roots, stand up to the weather, and hold fast, like Solomon's Oak. Then she blew away like a leaf in the wind, uncovering the rest of my life.

That's how it will be for my sister. The earth will fall away and her white bones will feel the sun upon them, and rise up.

I just know it.

ACKNOWLEDGMENTS

Grateful acknowledgment to Debra Utacia Krol for the use of her mother's, Mary Bishop Larson's, traditional Jolon Indian story "The Headless Lady of Jolon." Mrs. Larson is one of the documented few to have actually seen Mrs. Halloran's ghost.

Robert Latham and Karen Broughton generously helped me with pirate-wedding research and gifted me with the DVD of their inspirational ceremony. Varieties of the pirate-wedding vows appear all over the Internet, on such sites as favoriteideas.com, talk likeapirate.com, blackravenadventures.com, thebeenews.com, fan taseaweddings.com.

Bashō's (1644–94) poem "The Oak Tree" has been translated by many and can be found in anthologies, and all over the Internet. This is my humble interpretation.

Many thanks to Judi Hendricks for the use of two sentences from her wonderful novel _The Laws of Harmony_.

Thank you to Jeffrey Eugenides for my borrowing of his dog's name, Edsel.

Thank you to Laura C. Martin for her wonderful books on the folklore of trees, flowers, and animals. They have inspired me throughout my writing days and continue to be a source I turn to often.

Gracious thanks and love to my agent and dear friend, Deborah Schneider, for her steadfast belief in me, and in this book. Also to her entire office staff, especially Cathy Gleason, who pretty much always knows the answer to every question I ask.

I am thankful and grateful beyond words to Nancy Miller at Bloomsbury USA and Helen Garnons-Williams at Bloomsbury UK for their enthusiasm regarding this book. Also to my copy editor, Steve Boldt, production editor, Laura Phillips, and the sales force for supporting this book.

Thank you also to Dorothy Massey at Collected Works, who is always generous and supportive, and who owns the finest indie bookshop in Santa Fe.

When a writer utters the words "This book could not have been written without the support and encouragement of so many people," what she really means is to acknowledge and truly appreciate the people who put up with her inattentiveness, glum outlook, and whining. A few of my biggest supporters and best friends include Sherry Simpson, Earlene Fowler, Judi Hendricks, Rich Chiappone, David Stevenson, Anne Caston, Kathleen Tarr, Jodi Picoult, Jennifer Olds-Huffman; and my son, Jack, and his wife, Olivia Barrick; my sisters, Lee and C.J.; my brothers, John and Jim; and my mother, Mary, who told me wonderful stories all my life. Without you, I wouldn't ever finish anything.

Dogs (Verbena, Cricket, Henry, Piper, and Rufus) make even the hardest parts of life bearable, and often entertaining.

My husband, Stewart Allison, cheers me on when I'm down, makes me laugh when I'm overly serious, and has loved me all these years. You have so many times over earned your gold crown in heaven that it is blindingly bright with gems. Thank you for believing me to be a keeper.

READING GROUP GUIDE

These discussion questions are designed to enhance your group's conversation about *Solomon's Oak*, the story of three wounded strangers who help each other see the world in a new light.

For discussion

1. *Solomon's Oak* opens with the story of Alice Halloran, the woman who lost her child and her life in 1898. How does the legend of Alice's ghost set the scene for the novel to come? How does Alice's tragedy relate to the losses that Glory, Juniper, and Joseph have also endured?

2. Solomon's Oak Wedding Chapel specializes in untraditional ceremonies. Why is Glory open to hosting all kinds of weddings? How does the pirate wedding at the beginning of the novel spark other unconventional relationships for Glory?

3. Glory's specialty is "last-chance dogs"—training and nurturing abandoned pets (11). What strategies does Glory use to rehabilitate these last-chance dogs? Which of her dogs shows the most progress over the course of the novel? Why is Glory drawn to last-chance dogs—and to last-chance kids, like Juniper and other foster children?

4. Discuss what "closet time" means to Glory (10). Why does she go to the closet when grief overwhelms her? How does Juniper react to Glory's closet time?

5. Discuss the first impression that Juniper makes on Glory. What "sharp edges" does Glory sense in Juniper when they first meet (49)? How does Juniper eventually change those first impressions? How does Juniper surprise Glory, and how does she disappoint her? What characteristics does Joseph glimpse in Juniper that Glory cannot see?

6. Consider the complicated relationship Glory has with her sister Halle. Why is there so much conflict between the sisters? How does Glory misjudge Halle? How does Halle express her jealousy of Glory? How does Halle make up for so many years of conflict at the end of *Solomon's Oak*?

7. The "gospel according to Caroline," says the social worker who brings Glory and Juniper together, is "a pair of unhappy people working together toward whatever kind of life there is after so much sorrow" (85). How do Glory and Juniper eventually build a shared life upon their separate sorrows? Why did Dan secretly make Caroline promise to find Glory the perfect foster child? How is Juniper a perfect match for Glory?

8. Two people live on in Joseph's memories: his grandmother Penny, and his friend from the police force, Rico. How does Joseph balance these two sets of memories: his happy childhood discoveries with his grandmother, and his flashbacks to the shooting that killed Rico? How does Joseph grieve for Penny and for Rico, and how does he honor their memories?

9. What does Solomon's Oak mean to Glory, Joseph, and Juniper? What artistic, financial, and symbolic possibilities does the oak tree offer each of

them? How does the tree inspire each person who comes to see it? Why is the oak so difficult to capture artistically, whether on canvas or on film?

10. Discuss the unique bond between Juniper and Joseph. How does Joseph gradually help Juniper find confidence in men? How does education bring this unlikely pair closer? How does Joseph help Juniper see the world differently?

11. As Joseph talks to Glory at Lorna's Christmas party, "It occurred to him that after separating himself from his own family, here was the person he wanted to tell his story to, but the place was too crowded, and besides, it was Christmas" (216). What is it about Glory that attracts Joseph and makes him want to tell her about his past? How is the Christmas party a turning point for Joseph and Glory's budding relationship?

12. For Glory, "Her kitchen was her compass, her true north" (362). How does Glory find comfort in the kitchen? How does cooking bring Glory closer to both Juniper and Joseph?

13. Joseph tells Glory, "Sometimes you meet people and you just know you've crossed paths for a reason" (255). How does fate bring Joseph, Glory, and Juniper together? Why does their crossing of paths feel like destiny to Joseph and Juniper? Why does Glory have trouble believing in fate?

14. Discuss the meaning of family in Solomon's Oak. Which biological families fall apart in the novel? What nonbiological bonds are forged, and how? How do the characters of Solomon's Oak manage to redefine what family, marriage, and child-rearing mean?

15. Solomon's Oak takes place in 2003 and 2004. Why might Mapson have chosen to set the novel in these years, rather than in the present day? What connections does Juniper, now an anthropology student, draw

between the big events of 2004—earthquakes, extinctions, and bone discoveries—and her personal experiences of that year?

16. In an essay on photography, Juniper writes, "It's about accepting that the picture you end up with will never be the picture you were trying to take" (286). How does this lesson of photography apply to life? What unexpected situations have Juniper, Glory, and Joseph found themselves in by the end of the novel, and how have they come to accept their new lives?

17. Spotting Juniper reading a novel, Glory thinks, "there was hope for any kid that read fiction. A willingness to lose one's self in a story was the first step to learning compassion, to appreciating other cultures, to realizing what possibilities the world held for people who kept at life despite the odds" (76). What can a reader learn from *Solomon's Oak*? What possibilities of compassion, cultural appreciation, and personal endurance can be found within this novel?

Suggested reading

Jo-Ann Mapson, *Bad Girl Creek*, *Hank & Chloe*, and *The Owl & Moon Café*; Kristin Hannah, *Winter Garden*; Jodi Picoult, *House Rules*; Judith Ryan Hendricks, *The Laws of Harmony*; Erica Bauermeister, *The School of Essential Ingredients*; Sara Gruen, *Water for Elephants*; Alice Hoffman, *Skylight Confessions*; Barbara Kingsolver, *Prodigal Summer*; Margaret Hawkins, *A Year of Cats and Dogs*; Kennedy Foster, *All Roads Lead Me Back to You*.

Jo-Ann Mapson is the author of nine previous novels, including the beloved *Hank & Chloe*, *Blue Rodeo* (also a CBS TV movie), and the *Los Angeles Times* bestsellers *The Wilder Sisters* and *Bad Girl Creek*, a book club favorite. She lives in Santa Fe, New Mexico, with her husband and their five dogs. Visit her Web site at www.joannmapson.com.